THE BAHAMAS INCIDENT

THE BAHAMAS INCIDENT

James Frew

Kingston Publishers Limited

The original version of this novel was published as *In the Wake of the Leopard* by Paradise Publications (Editech Press, Miami), 1990
©1990 by James Frew

Previously published as *The Bahamas Incident*
©1997 by James Frew
10 9 8 7 6 5 4 3 2 1

Published by Kingston Publishers Limited
LOJ Complex, Building #10, 7 Norman Road
CSO Kingston, Jamaica.

ISBN 976-625-136-3

Cover illustration by Keith Frew
Typeset by Janet Campbell

To Howard and Joyce, of course.

THE BAHAMAS INCIDENT

Prologue

THE SCHOONER LAY DEAD on the unmoving sea with her sails hanging listlessly from the spars. Her wheelhouse had been ransacked, the chart drawers drawn and tumbled at random. The old man had scrutinized them one by one, but the chart he sought was not at hand. The ship's safe had been emptied, the combination forced from the captain when he was herded forward with the crew. Neatly stacked peso notes had been swept aside, wallets and personal papers examined briefly and abandoned to the litter on the floor. It wasn't money he was after; the wads of currency attested to that. Nor was it the cargo in the forward hold.

The old man searched the lower salon very carefully, examining closets and drawers beneath the bunks. His stocky companion emptied the youngsters' duffle bags and compared tags with the ship's manifest. The name they sought was not among them, nor was it listed with the Colombian crew. They'd gone forward then, the old man with a brush cut waddling splay-footed as if he were accustomed to the sea. They'd peered into the engine room from the bullet-riddled hatchway, played a torch on the ancient diesel, recoiled from the dank humidity, then proceeded to the cook's cabin where the slender, dark-haired girl had barricaded herself.

The cabin had been riddled by an AK-47 from the siding yacht. The portholes were shattered, but the girl was alive when they forced the door with a bar. The old man questioned her with a knife at her throat, methodically, with no remorse... the saber scar pulsing his forehead when they held her to the table. My God, how she screamed, but there was no one to help her. The teenagers and the crew were hostages under heavy guard. The old man knew exactly who she was, but a stray bullet had creased her heart and she died in mortal agony with the answer undisclosed. The boy he sought lay unconscious in the forward hold, an unwitting victim of the gunfire that raked the *Leopard* when she was intercepted east of Turks-Caicos.

The bow gave mute witness to the massacre that followed the takeover. Mangled bodies lay grotesquely by the bloodied jib. The old man had tortured the Colombian crew with his razor sharp knife; slit the captain's throat when he raised his crucifix and pleaded, "Ees no chart, Senor! Ees de boy who con my wheel for fix. He de boss man. I not know de name you ask!" The captain's blurred vision encompassed the stainless steel teeth, the saber scar pulsating on the old man's forehead, before his body convulsed. The blessed shadow of death finally overcame the relentless mid-afternoon sun.

But the nightmare's end was not in sight. The old man turned his malevolent attention to the terrified youngsters huddled by the aft salon.

Vitch ist Herr Vynn? ["Which one is Vynn?"] he rasped in guttural English, menacing the group with his ugly Luger. He pointed to a youth wearing a headband and cut-off jeans.

"Ist you?"

The teenager dropped to his knees and hoarsed a denial.

"No, sir! We don't know who you mean!"

"The Wynn boy was aboard when you sailed from Barranquilla," an angry voice shouted from the yacht. The boarding lines grew taut with the swell as the schooner wallowed, her mainsail swinging unattended and momentarily shadowing the speaker. He was a tall, starkly handsome opposite to the sadistic old man. Fortyish, deeply tanned, his jet black hair graying at the temples, he was casually dressed in polo shirt and spotless white slacks. He leaned from the bridge, as if counting faces for high tea. "Speak up or you'll join the captain!"

"Henry MacDonald, sir! We're on vacation from college and we ran out of money. They offered us a ride to Mayaguana! " The tall man scowled, a mean twist deforming his mouth.

"With a cargo of illicit drugs? Do you take me for a fool?"

"No, sir! He said he'd drop us at Abraham's Bay, but the wind gave out and the engine wouldn't start. He didn't say where they were going from Mayaguana," he added. "We're not involved, mister. We just want to go home!"

The tall man's eyes narrowed. He spoke briefly in German to the old man, then turned to a rumpled pair observing from the stern of the immaculate yacht. They were very old, round at the belly like vintage Mercedeses. The conversation was again in German; they compared notes. Then the tall man bellowed from the bridge.

"You there… step aside!" He pointed to a young girl in pigtails. Her eyes widened… she crossed herself and moved gingerly alongside the wheelhouse. "Tell me, young lady, which is Wynn? I want an immediate answer!" Her jaw dropped, she stared at her companions and shook her head.

"We don't know him, sir. Do you mean Liz's boyfriend?" The tall man displayed his teeth.

"Aha! Now we get somewhere. Which is he?" A crewman appeared from the radar room, saluted sharply and pointed to the south. The tall man frowned, spun about and hurried from the bridge. *Suchen Sie ihn and bringen Sie ihn an Bord !* ["Look for him and bring him on board"] he shouted. *Ein Flugzeug setzt gerade zu*

enier Direktlandung an… wir duerfen auf keinen Fall gesehen werden!
["A plane is approaching… make sure nobody sees us."] The oldster nodded, pressing his Luger to the teenager's back.

"Vitch ist Vynn…? No nonsense, I shoot you dead!"

"My God… they're after Chug!" MacDonald gasped. The old
man turned his icy blue eyes upon the petrified kid.

"Ya! Wo ist?" The kid pointed to the engine room.

"He was fixin' the diesel when you laid it on… sir!" The stocky
man was quick to react. He ran to the hatch and levered the heavy
AK-47, raised the barrel when the tall man shouted from the bridge.

Ablegen und sofort an Bord! ["Stop and back on board!"] The old
man stared, disbelieving.

*Der Junge ist irgendwo hier unten, Kurt! Wir werden ihn gleich
haben.* ["The boy is somewhere under here, Kurt! Should have him
soon."]

*Ach, egal… wir kommen zurueck! Los, mach schon Klaus! Das
Flugzeug ist hoechstens 30 km entfernt.* ["All the same… we come
back. Hurry, Klaus! The plane is only 30 km away."] The old man
scowled his displeasure.

Wir haben Zeugen, Kurt! ["We have witnesses, Kurt!"] The tall
man nodded.

Du weisst was Du zu tun hast! ["You know what to do!"] The
Luger barked, the girl slumped to the deck clutching her stomach.
MacDonald was next; he convulsed upright with blood spurting
from his mouth, then tumbled beside her. The remaining three
begged for mercy, but they were ruthlessly cut down by the thundering AK-47 while the old man cast off the lines. The attackers
dropped immediately to the waiting launch, which was davited
aboard as the yacht gained headway and sped to the northwest.

The boy had no recollection of that terrible hour. All was quiet when he regained consciousness. By the time he stumbled to the engine room and climbed the ladder, the yacht was a dot on the horizon. He crawled on his knees along the bloodied deck where, to his horror, he realized he was the only survivor.

Miles to the south a lone pilot was fighting the tropical depression in an ancient amphibian. The black clouds were creased with lightning; he had no radar, his batteries were down and he was avoiding the cells with a flashlight beamed to the panel.

Thirtyish, tall and lanky, tanned by the sun, with a mop of unruly blond hair. He had dressed to offset the humidity in khaki shorts, a scivvy shirt and oil-stained sneakers. A veteran of Desert Storm, he was a combat pilot of many missions, but the Goose was a task. She was old and weary and leaked from the heavy rain. It had been a bright, sunny day when he lifted off from San Juan. He had been warned of a tropical storm brewing east of Hispaniola, but had decided to barrel it through by dead reckoning, with his radios reduced to a whimper. A lesser pilot would have waited it out, a wiser pilot would have gone roundabout, but Slater vas neither. Another day would have him at odds with his client in Nassau.

He'd graduated from the Air Force Academy. Now he bore the scars of war and a medical discharge had ended his military career. A construction engineer by later profession, he was past due in Nassau with a set of plans tucked behind the seat. Variously described as a vintage airplane buff, a lover of intelligent women and sailing ships, Slater was a nervy type of uncertain means, a soft touch with dogs and old friends. A loner of sorts, he was driven by curiosity and an awareness of the vagaries of this magnificent world.

It was love at first sight when the decrepit Goose came up for auction at Isle Grande, but he'd gambled and capped the high bid. The Grumann was just barely ferryable. Signed off for a one-way trip to Ft. Lauderdale via Nassau, she'd still require an annual inspection for certification. From there in, the cost of restoration would be monumental... she'd be stripped and repainted, need updated avionics, new engines. It would take a capital investment to make her right, but what the hell—he'd sell his Porsche and mortgage his cottage. Somehow he'd manage.

It was his inherent curiosity that caused him to circle when he emerged from the storm and sighted the schooner dead in the water. It was obvious that something was wrong aboard the tall-masted ship. She was riding high, but her sails were undone and there was no indication of a crew, no flag of distress. Was she abandoned? A floundering derelict in the path of an angry storm?

Slater descended for visual approach to Providenciales, miles off course, over the trackless sea. If his ADF had been operational, he would have tracked the beacon at Grand Turks and the massacre would have proceeded without his knowing.

It was the yacht's sophisticated radar that hastened their departure, the sound of his engines that drove the bewildered kid again into hiding. Had they returned to finish their bloody business top side the schooner?

This is a tale of a rebellious boy, an emerald brooch, a beautiful actress seeking her identity, a pompous British secret agent, and five tons of Nazi gold. But let Slater relate the story—he was, after all, witness to the disaster!

One

WHEN I FIRST SIGHTED the schooner, her sails were like flakes of gold dancing on the horizon. They caught and reflected the late afternoon sun in the blue between the layered clouds. Then I lost them in the vaporous tissue that rose again and enveloped the cockpit windows. She would be a tall ship (judging from the enormous expanse she displayed) and a large one at that, judging from the twenty miles that lay between us. I checked the compass bearing and impulsively nudged the rudder a few degrees to bring her up on the Goose's nose when we broke free of the overcast. Dead reckoning would have Grand Turk off our left wing in a few minutes; a half hour should have us on the airstrip at Providenciales.

The altimeter unwound through 3500 feet and breaks in the cloud cover became more frequent. The ocean appeared through the patchy fluff beneath us. I eased the throttles back a notch, loosened my shoulder harness and leaned forward to assess the damage done by the storm. The cockpit was a shambles. The co-pilot's chair was pooled with rain water, leaking windows had shorted the instrument panel, gyros had toppled, radios were dead. I'd flown the last hundred miles with a flashlight torching the panel for a bearing. My legs ached from fighting the rudder controls, my hands were clammy, my T-shirt reeked of nervous sweat. The last two hours had been a nightmare.

Flight Service had positioned the center of the depression 200 miles east of the Lesser Antilles, with a heavy squall line ranging from the northern coast of Hispaniola. North-bound flights (like myself) were advised to exercise extreme caution and anticipate moderate-to-heavy turbulence below 32,000 feet. The Goose amphibian had never seen the high side of 10,000 feet in all of her thirty-five years until I blundered into an embedded buildup an hour out of San Juan. We rode the violent updraft until we were spewed, nearly inverted, from the chimney at 13,000 feet; then came the backside drop. She came out of it popping rivets a few hundred feet off the water, and we reached a mutual understanding. She was old and decrepit, she had no radar, and her avionics were from an earlier time, but she was tough and forgiving. If I were to mind the lightning and deviate a few points to round the cells, she'd shoulder the lashing rain and get us into Providenciales.

The sunlight quickened and cast a halo around the Goose's stubby bow; the clouds thinned and fell away. The sea beneath and around us was a shimmering expanse of quick-silver. I shielded my eyes against the glare. The dark green outline of Grand Turk's eastern shore snaked the horizon off our left wing tip, the black dots beyond would be South Caicos and Middle Caicos. North Caicos and Providenciales ranged sixty miles further west, but they were beyond my line of vision. I leveled off at 1500 feet and turned in my seat to view the fast-approaching schooner.

She was a beauty. The sun bathed her sails with a golden opalescence contrasting with the pale blue sky. She lay a few degrees to the right of our flight path, framed full length by the windshield, a perfect replica of a Winslow Homer painting. Her low-lying hull was sleek and long. She'd be a Halifax type, a two-master, gaff-rigged and fully drawn. Her top sails were furled at the mast steps, she bore a single jib from her bowsprit and her jenny sail had been partially lowered and draped across the foredeck. I'd apparently come upon her while her pilot was bringing her about in the near dead calm, to seek a freshing reach further to the east.

Banking to the east brought the schooner across the Goose's nose, then a sharp left turn gave me a view of her length from the cockpit window. I will forever remember that moment; the ironic twist of fate that brought me there, the braiding of totally unrelated circumstances that caught and held me hopelessly interwoven in the bloody saga that unfolded before my eyes.

The feeling of flirting with a darkened street came upon me when the sun slipped behind a distant cloud and laid a florid path across the water. Was someone tapping my shoulder, urging me not to follow? I shivered and continued the turn, then reached up and revved the props to reduce air-speed. The Goose bucked and her engines wheezed. I wrapped my right arm around the control column, edging the side window open with my elbow. Suddenly, as if that moment had been deliberately chosen, the sun broke into the clear and illuminated the schooner with stark reality. Her masts, her sails, her rigging loomed before the open window and my arm convulsed the wheel.

Her main sails hung lifelessly from their gaffs, like burial shrouds on the gallows. My eyes travelled the drooping, unattended sheet lines to where they trailed the water, to the single jib luffing mindlessly from the bowsprit, to the jenny sail collapsed across the foredeck, and to a dark crimson stain glistening on its folds. The foredeck faded before I could recenter my attention, the stern passing quickly behind our wing float. I looked back, realizing from the absurd angle of the rudder that she was drifting aimlessly with the northerly current, lacking a helmsman, apparently abandoned.

We made a skidding turn and I looked down to appraise the deck for a show of hands along her rails. There was none. I checked again before she passed behind us. The skiff, deviated from her

3

stern, was in place; there was no movement within the wheelhouse aft nor in the forward salon. An engine hatchway midship gaped its innards. The dozen or so fuel drums arranged before it seemed securely fastened, but the door to the cook's house lay at a contorted angle and appeared to have been torn from its hinges. A life raft atop the galley had been overturned against the portside rail, as if a recent attempt had been made to take it to the water.

Our left engine sneezed and began to cough. I leveled off, hit the auxiliary pumps, and leveled the fuel selector to "both." The engine responded and steadied. The aux tanks were dry. A quick glance verified the left main in the red and the right main shading eighty gallons. I'd absent-mindedly allowed one to siphon into the other. I climbed to five hundred feet, giving the situation behind us some thought.

The roar of our twin Pratt-Whitneys should have rattled her timbers as we passed, but no one appeared. She obviously was adrift, abandoned by her crew. But why? Where had they gone, and how? I made a wary turn from the south and reached for the binoculars to study the floundering derelict and the sea behind her.

Her freeboard rose high in the water, so she wasn't sinking. There was no indication of fire in her holds. I puzzled for a moment, thinking of the legendary *Marie Celeste* drifting crewless off the Azores, the cargo of alcohol beneath her decks. Was the schooner hauling explosives, dynamite? Had they found nitro seeping below in a state of volatile decay? I cradled the control column between my knees and focused the glasses on the placid ocean around her. It held nothing. No bobbing heads or low-lying rafts. No debris. Not a blemish marred its surface for miles around, aside from the wake of a single dorsal fin seeking the shadow of the schooner's fat underbelly.

The Goose took quarter flaps gently. I eased back the throttles until we had fifty feet beneath us, then upped them to hold a miserly seventy knots. The schooner lay a half mile directly ahead, silhouetted against the sun. I banked to bring her stern to bear and to scan the starboard rail. Her name plate was important if I were to identify her when I reached Providenciales. I had yet to see her shadowed side. The stern rose rapidly until it bannered the windscreen from beneath the skiff. *Sea Leopard,* Halifax, NS., came up in crisp gold letters. Then my eyes encountered the bloody scene along her rail.

Bodies, mangled bodies, were propped against the wheel-house like broken dolls. Five, six, seven perhaps. I passed too quickly to tell. Cut-offs, scivvy shirts, blonde hair in braids. Young men and girls, mouths agape, contorted, lifeless, oozing blood to the glistening deck.

I pawed at the throttles and banked the bowsprit. Visions of Desert Storm blurred my senses. My hands convulsed on the wheel; I almost lost the lumbering Goose. The bodies had been lacerated from close range; the wheelhouse splintered by gunfire, its windows shattered, the standing rigging shredded, the cook's house raked.

Had they been strafed by a Cuban MIG, pirated by a fast moving boat? Had they been methodically slaughtered by a demented crew member? The blood-stained jenny sail… were there others beneath it? I banked to the south, leveled off at 500 feet and considered my options. The radios were useless—night would fall before I could raise a helping hand. Might there be survivors desperately in need? A murderer glowering from inside?

The schooner was parallel at a quarter mile and I studied the low-lying hull with my binoculars. The inflated raft had been cut away and lowered to the railing; an attempt had been made to escape the derelict. Had it been before, or after, the massacre occurred? And why the raft? If the murderer were aboard, he would have conned the helm until he had a landfall to consider. I puzzled over the open engine hatch, then refocused the glasses. Had I seen a head peering from the hatchway, or was I imagining things?

A wide turn to the east allowed me a view of the wheelhouse once again, my arm anchored around the wheel and binoculars steadied on the window slide. The corpses, their hands strangely clasped, were positioned as if they had been dragged from where they'd fallen. A bloody trail led from mid-deck; could several bodies have been recently carried? Had they been placed in the shadow of the wheelhouse to protect them from the sun? Would a callous mind be so disposed? I edged rudder; as the goose roared past the starboard railing, something caught my eye.

A Jacob's ladder hung from the starboard scupper; a heavy line trailed from a cleat. A second glance confirmed the angle from which they'd been razed. The ladder had been lowered to accommodate a boarding party, a line cast to a boat while it eased alongside. The kids had been *deliberately* shot while they watched from the railing!

I fire-walled the throttles and climbed into the west; I'd seen enough. The schooner had apparently been hailed while they were raising sail, the kids gunned as they scattered, the cook's house searched, the engine room raised to take the odd man out. For what? Was she a pot ship short for the tab? Had they copped out with a Colombian connection? A powerboat of considerable heft had apparently tracked them from miles apart... within the past few hours. Had the boarders heard my engines droning above the overcast, then aborted what they were about?

I gave the raft heavy thought as I continued to climb, given pause by the bodies propped against the wheelhouse; their funeral stance. Was there someone back there still alive, someone I'd inadvertently frightened when I peeled off to circle from the south?

Someone who mistook the Goose for an earlier interception? Had the schooner been scouted from the air?

I leveled off into the northwest on a bearing to Providenciales. Grand Turk curled 20 miles off the left wing, the Caicos Islands a like distance off our bow. There were no ships in view, no yachts or Out Island freighters to hail. I looked back from my shoulder. The schooner's jib had caught a breath and brought her bow around; then it luffed and she fell off once again. She was trying, and I was reluctant to leave her. The sun was reddening; night would soon fall. By morning the northerly current would have her on Mayaguana's toothy rocks or broaching in the deep Atlantic. Further south the sloping clouds rose heavily until they bulged the stratosphere—black, angry, neonized by lightning. I shuddered. A westerly shift of the high level winds could have its cyclonic edge shredding the schooner in a matter of hours. What then? And the unlucky bastard who might still be aboard her… what of him?

I toggled the battery and drew a faint burst of static from the overhead speaker. The mike button, however, was not responsive. The generators had come up and the batteries were gaining, but the radios were soggy and unresponsive. A call from the ground station at Providenciales would bring in a Coast Guard helicopter from Miami, but it would be late morning before they arrived. It was unlikely they'd have a cutter patrolling the straits beneath a tropical depression nearing hurricane force. I reached for the throttles and raised the flaps, still seeking an alternative answer.

The Pratt-Whitneys throated their pleasure. We picked up cruise speed, I checked the fuel gauges against my watch. We'd burned a half hour since emerging from the overcast. Our wheels would hit the strip in 20 minutes and we would be refueled by five.

Locating a constable and a few knowledgeable hands from the basin could take us on to seven. We'd have to reach her before dusk if we were going to land beside her. It was chancy. Far above, Delta's afternoon flight penciled a long white contrail across the sky. If we could only talk! I replaced the useless mike on its hook and rechecked the fuel gauges, counting numbers.

Far ahead, a dark speck moved slowly across the mirrored sea I reached for the binoculars. A lone rooster tail spumed the waters north of Middle Caicos, hell bent for Providenciales. From her speed, I judged her to be a Hatteras homing from a day with the marlin. She was fast, she was rangey, and she'd have a radio, possibly radar.

Shielding my eyes against the sun, I re-examined the cockpit for means of communication. A half-assed idea came to mind. If I tossed a message down and convinced them to turn around, they could backtrack the schooner before sunset, circle her at least, and call out her position on the marine band—perhaps hold her in tow until sunrise. She might even take her into Grand Turk if the weather was a factor.

I computed an azimuth heading from the compass and scrawled an SOS on the backside of a clearance form, with the distance out and a brief summary of the catastrophic scene. Then I reached underseat for my life vest and popped a CO_2 cartridge into its folds, inserted the message in a pocket and readied the vest by the window.

The stern came up slowly on the Goose's nose. She was parting the sea with tremendous thrust and frothing a 30-knot path behind her. The stern broadened as we gained, I became aware of her length. She was no fisherman's fancy. She was a transoceanic yacht, abnormally powered. When I had a mile between us, I eased back the throttles and dropped down to 500 feet to blip the engines when I had her abeam.

She was low and mean. Her long-pointed prow skimmed above her curl like a thrown stiletto. She had fins for stacks, her hull was green, the topside polished mahogany. She would measure 150 feet or more. As we closed, I banked to follow, studying her wake for a moment… the path from which she'd turned. My eyes narrowed. I dropped the vest to my lap and looked back.

Her wake would be long lost to a choppy sea, but the sea was flat and revealing. The thin, milky line that stretched behind her told me where they'd been when I sighted the derelict. I checked the compass against the note I'd intended to drop—compared their 30 knots with the 30 miles behind us. *We had been following identical courses!*

At 1000 feet I was committed to cross their bow (a turnout would only excite their attention), and their attention was already drawn. A crewman raced from the bridge as I leveled off, a second man dropped to the fore deck. I gritted my teeth; the thundering Goose made an easy target if I paced their knots and exposed our soft underbelly. When something long and mean appeared aft of the anchor winch, I kicked hard left rudder and plunged the wheel.

My head stroked the cockpit ceiling as the Goose made a skidding turn to the east. The yacht's spume spattered the windscreen as I hauled back inches above the sea. As the starboard wing tip whipped the awning extending from the fantail, I had a fleeting impression of two startled faces… a tall, black-haired man with white at the temples, and a broad-shouldered oldster with a brush cut of many years duration.

The Goose laid flat across the water until they were well astern, then we climbed to the south and looked back at 1500 feet. The yacht hadn't deviated a degree; it was headed directly for Providenciales. Were they what they seemed? I gave the question serious thought while I steadied my quivering knees. Had I reacted

9

impulsively? Had the crew simply scattered for shelter when the cantankerous Goose appeared suddenly out of the blue? Their wake… was it circumstantial? Had they exercised a turn long before I came upon them?

I circled the yoke with my arm and thumbed the binocular adjustment, profiling the yacht for a moment against the descending sun. Its fore deck seemed relatively clear, aside from a shroud of canvas I might have mistaken for a 20mm gun. An unlikely glistening from the top deck suddenly caught my eye. I followed with the glasses until her exhaust fins interrupted my view, then settled heavily in my seat. I calibrated my remaining fuel and nosed the reluctant Goose into the east. I realized what I had to do. The deck beneath the yacht's portside launch was ringed with water. The launch had recently been lowered to the sea!

The churning vessel was far astern when I dropped behind North Caicos' spiny ridge and followed it until the ocean loomed beyond. I remember the gaggle of native children waving from the doorway of a crumbling cottage, a bewildered flock of goats vaulting the bush as we thundered by. The foaming reefs along the eastern shore came up and receded behind us.

The Goose's shadow paced the graying waters. Middle Caicos and South Caicos fell off our starboard wing. Grand Turk came up dull and green in the south. I checked the minute sweep of my watch. Twenty turns had passed since we'd come about. I rolled back the trim tab to gain a few visual feet and leaned forward in the cockpit. Two minutes elapsed, then a patch of reflected sunlight rose upon the horizon. I corrected to bring the reflection to bear and held 130 knots until the sails stretched a panel of the windscreen.

The schooner was drifting sideways with the current, her bow pointing east. A faint breeze rippled the water from the south. Something was missing... her main sails still flapped from the free-swinging gaffs, her boom lines still drooped to the water. There was no movement aboard her, but something wasn't right. I chopped throttles, and advanced the props to add grist to the humid air. We'd approach her stern a few feet off the sea, rattle her sails, and pray for a show of face.

The stern rose rapidly from a diminishing mile. I tensed. My hand intuitively reached out to arm rocket pods from some other place in time and I returned it dumbly to the wheel. Our airspeed fell to 80 knots. I clamped both feet on the rudder controls and fidgeted with the throttles. The stern loomed from the cockpit window. My eyes locked momentarily on her rudder alignment, then followed the length of the hull from the water line to the railing as we thundered by. A hank of rusty chain, a trickle of blood oozing from a scupper, one Jacob ladder, the dangling jenny sail. A missing item? *The jib was gone!*

I powered the quadrant and banked across the schooner's bowsprit, realizing as I looked down that her rudder was no longer ajar, that the jib had been freshly lowered. *And that a grimy red face was centered in the engine room hatchway!*

I tightened the turn and leaned from the window until the slipstream slammed my head against the stop. He dropped from sight, obviously frightened. I leveled off to avoid the mainsails and blipped the engines. There was no response; he was somewhere below.

Mobile, alive, he was in need of immediate help. Might there be others? I reasoned with the sun and my measure of fuel... had I a choice? Was there an alternative? Did I have the guts to set down and hail from a distance, or was I to abandon myself to a lifetime of nightmarish conjecture?

I dropped a wing, thinking back to the time I'd lain wounded in the desert with my parachute furled around me... waiting, wondering if a helicopter would come to cable me out before the Iraqis descended a distant dune. Were the circumstances dissimilar? Had I not been wary, too?

I made my turn to approach from the west with the surface glare behind us. The wind was light, the sea calm, and the old amphibian responded as if she'd known all along. I held a few knots above stalling speed, banked into the middling breeze, picked a rising slope and gently eased her down. The step smacked the sea with a metallic thud. The Goose showered a geyser to the windscreen, nosed down briefly, then bobbed to the surface streaming brine from her bow.

The schooner, 100 feet away, rose and fell heavily with our wash. The boom pitched skyward, dipped and prodded the sea, as if silently acknowledging our presence. I gunned the engines and taxied across the water until the wing tip lay a few yards from her stern. Engines idling to a cough, I shouted from the window. There was no response.

I waited and tried again, bellowing. The water lapped against the Goose's hull as a minute slipped by. A metal pulley clanged a measured heartbeat against a masthead far above, a severed sheet line flirted with the sea. A quick movement swirled the water... a dorsal fin glided to the line, nosed it briefly and turned away. A white-tipped oceanic, a deep water monster, she'd been circling and scenting. She was hungry. *She'd been waiting, too.*

I leaned from the window to gauge the schooner, working the throttles until our bumper pad nudged the rudder, then ducked inside the anchor well and raised the hatch, with a grappling hook in hand. First toss caught the railing and held. I snubbed the line and waited until the Goose drifted astern. When the line came taut and we were clear of the murderous booms, I reached up and cut the engines.

The propellers made a few halting turns and clanked to a stop. An eerie silence prevailed until my ears became accustomed to the sounds around me—the wash against the schooner's hull, creaking skeleton timbers, gurgling bilge, incessant banging of the pulley far overhead. A heavy blanket of humidity descended on the cockpit, and perspiration beaded my brow and dripped from my chin. I opened the co-pilot's window to ease the sweltering heat and leaned back in my seat. The closeness of the huge wooden ship was un nerving, and I dreaded the prospect of climbing her rail, of wit-nessing what lay beyond it. The dead. The survivor would be some-thing else again. I called out once more. There was no reply. The minute sweep on the panel clock made another turn. In an hour the sun would be red-balling the west; the rising moon would be shrouded in the east by the approaching storm. The darkness would be total. A flicker of lightning on the horizon caught my eye. It was too distant to hear, but its message was decisive.

I went forward again to the anchor well and hitched a second line to the bulkhead cleat and hauled in the grappling line until the bumper pad nudged the schooner's rudder shank. The rudder lay at trail, its mossy topside projecting above the water line. He'd apparently lashed the wheel. Wet and slippery it offered no footing, and I looked about for another means of boarding.

The stern towered above the Goose's bow, its sweep beyond my standing reach; grabbing for it was risky. The alternative was to swing on the grappling line and pray for the hook to hold. I scanned the hull forward and saw the shark lying motionless beneath the blood-caked scupper. I shook my head and played out the Goose's tether. When the bow came directly below the railing, I climbed from the cockpit and tested the hook. It slithered a few inches along the railing and held. I balanced myself and wrapped the line around my wrist. A drop of warm liquid dribbled down my back. I gasped and looked up.

The skiff slung far above us had been neatly laced from beneath. A pale blue sky peered through its bullet-ridden underside. I giggled foolishly, realizing why it still hung from its davits. Another drizzle spattered my face, then as the Goose suddenly dipped, I lost my footing and swung.

My feet slashed the water and my leg slammed the rudder. I kneed the shank and went up the line hand-over-hand. The dorsal fin swirled as I dangled over the sea. I looked down at the shark's gaping jaws, her piggish eyes, as she rose to take my free-swinging feet. I grabbed the railing, flipped my body, lodged a foot in the scupper and clung to the high rising stern. The white-tipped oceanic took the rudder shank and shook it viciously. A long wooden splinter caught in her jaws as she tore it away and sounded beneath the hull. I vaulted the railing and lay prone on the deck gasping for breath.

The block clanged mindlessly from the mast while I gathered my strength for what was yet to come. I got to my feet and checked the long sloping deck for a show of face, glanced inside the wheelhouse while I secured the Goose's lines. The wheelhouse appeared empty, there was no movement forward, *but I sensed I was being watched.*

A darkening pool of blood surrounded the bodies propped against the bullet-ridden paneling. Flies were swarming and gaseous noises emanated from the bloated corpses. I walked cautiously to the shattered door and peered inside. The floor was littered with charts and upturned drawers. Day bunks ranging the perimeter had been slashed and ripped from end to end, the ship's safe had been pried from its casing and forced with a bar. The cabin had been thoroughly searched and virtually demolished... radios ripped from their mountings; papers, passports and other personal belongings strewn at random.

A bundle of cash was jostled by my foot. Purses and wallets had been cleared from the safe, but their contents appeared untouched. The boarders were after something more important than jewelry or money. Had a drug deal gone sour? Were they after cocaine?

I stepped inside and examined the wheel. The spokes were slippery to my fingers and the cabin reeked of recent sweat. The wheel had been centered with the rudder and locked in place. I checked the binnacle; the compass guide was set to 310 degrees. The schooner had been north-westerly bound when she was intercepted. Or had the course been reset since I first sighted her? The throttle was at idle, gear handle in neutral, battery switch in the 'on' position, power reading in the green.

An attempt had been made to engage the schooner's engine, which explained the open hatchway. Wheelhouse controls had been set to facilitate a start; the steerage was aligned. She was old. Her engine would be a wide bore diesel of many years, difficult to start. Heating the cylinders with a blow torch was standard procedure if batteries were insufficient to crank compression. Was that the steady hissing I heard from below? Unattended... as if I caught him by surprise?

There were seven bodies ranging the shattered paneling, including a young girl with long, blond hair and faded cut-offs, clutching a crucifix. A redhead with braids done up in bright green yarn, her palms rigid and fixed, looked as if she had been pleading when she was shot. They were in their early 20s, barefoot, shaggy-haired, college types. A broad-rimmed straw hat with *Barranquilla* stitched on its rise, gave indication of where they'd boarded. Given a few bucks, the excitement, a leisurely sail through the Caribbean to off-load a few tons of grass… which, I assumed, lay baled in the forward hold.

The closeness of sudden death was a staggering thing to behold. The brutality! They were so young! I closed the door to the lower salon, bent down and slipped the locking pin in its latch. The salon would connect with the engine room forward, and I wanted no surprises. When I looked up, I saw a head rising slowly from the open hatchway, and I found myself looking directly into a pair of living eyes.

He dropped from sight before I could get to my feet, but I caught a fleeting glimpse of a bare-shouldered kid with a mop of sun-bleached hair and an ugly gash riding his cheek. I shouted from the window and bolted for the open door. My sneaker hit a patch of blood as I rounded the wheelhouse. I went down on my backside, thudded against an ungiving body in a red bikini, and negotiated the hatchway on all fours.

A ladder led down to the dimly lit compartment. I called down, but he wasn't buying.

A flashlight hung from the beam beneath me, its glow illuminating an ancient Caterpillar, surrounded by a gaggle of diesel drums, a spread of wrenches and a half-empty pack of Bud. A sputtering blow torch was positioned by the engine and a blood-stained T-shirt lay nearby. The engine's panel had been splintered, the fuel drums punctured. The compartment had been gunned from above. He'd either been left for dead, or grazed by a bounding slug and hidden himself forward. I reached under the combing for a flashlight and beamed the bulkhead door. It had been assaulted with a bar; the bar lay on the floor. They'd had him cornered. He'd been in the hold.

I traveled the hatch, locked it with a hasp, and ran forward to the cook house. The cargo hold was battened down (there was no exit from there) but there was the possibility of a ladder to the galley or a crawl space leading to the anchor well. There was movement from below when I rounded the hold... bales tumbled as he worked his way through the stifling compartment, cursing when his head thumped the under deck.

The galley door came off its hinges when I kicked aside a length of board and lowered it to the deck. Had the door been ajar when I buzzed the schooner an hour earlier? Bloodied footprints led from the threshold to the starboard railing, the smudge of bare feet where he'd been sick at the rail. He'd recently been there, then replaced the door for reasons I understood when I adjusted my eyes to the interior and stepped inside.

A beautiful, dark-haired girl lay in repose on the galley table; a candle lit to guide her through the twilight zone. Her hands were folded across naked breasts, a golden chain entwined in her fingers. A pillow cushioned her head. Her eyes were mercifully closed, her chin cleansed of the blood that oozed from her lips. He'd brushed her hair and gently arranged her body as best he could. A blood-stained tablecloth covered her mortal wounds; she'd been brutally mutilated, then bled to death on the galley floor!

Tearing my eyes away from the dreadful scene, I glance about the galley, then replaced the door. The poor kid, she was hardly 20 and obviously his girl. Trapped below when the massacre occurred, he had only just found her!

I stumbled aft to a ventilation shaft and called down with feeling. The sweet smell of grass mingled with the stench rising from below, the rank odor of diesel fumes and bilge. I could hear him moving about, agonizing for breath in the oppressive heat, but there was no answer.

A clattering chain spun me about and focused my attention to the bow. The anchors were lashed to the bowsprit, a length of chain snaking from the forward deck disappearing into the anchor well, its bolt-end unattached and unattended. I shook my head; he'd laboured the crawl space, climbed the linkage from the well, and drawn the chain upon himself.

I walked forward and nudged the capsized sail aside, on the off chance he'd managed a finger hold on the grating. I had a brief glimpse of his face as he scurried aft, but I was totally unprepared for the calloused foot that protruded from the blood-stained jenny.

When I lifted the sail, I came upon the working crew, three olive-skinned Hispanics. They'd been herded to the bow and shot while they were on their knees, except for the captain. The splayed corpse in khakis and tire sandals had been disembowled and shot in the mouth with a revolver! The cartridge casing lay at my feet. I pocketed the thing, shaking my fist at the blood-red sun... stunned, sickened by the senseless carnage that greeted every turn. Re-covering them with the sail, I returned to the wheelhouse.

The ruthless slaughter had a definite pattern. The passengers and crew had been interrogated and quickly dispatched; they'd dwelt longer with the captain and the girl. They'd combed the wheelhouse and were on to the kid when I broke from the overcast. They had wanted something they didn't find. Cocaine was a possibility, but it appeared to be something more elusive. Was it a chart? Had they reason to trace the schooner's course to its rendezvous?

The passports lying on the floor had been thumbed for a name, for a face. Was it the kid they were after? Did he have information worth the measure of eleven lives? If they were bent for revenge they would have torched the ship. Did they intend to return? I examined the cartridge in the fading light. The casing, of German manufacture, appeared old, the brass dull and pitted. The .9 mm shell would fit the clip of an ancient Luger. The burr-headed old man strutting the fantail of the fast-moving yacht... was it possible?

A scuffling from the lower salon caught my attention. I placed my foot against the door and leaned back in the chair. The ship's thermometer was reading 94 in the wheelhouse; it would be over 100 in the hell-hole below. I heard his feet trying the stairs, the thud of metal striking the rising. I tensed. We'd reason with the door between us, but I hadn't contemplated an encounter with a gun!

The door pressed against its latch. I could hear his laboured breath. Moving my feet from the door, I reached for a blanket roll and propped it in the chair. He tried the latch with a screwdriver, working the crevice. I stepped aside and waited. The setting sun was hard upon the door, the chair in silhouette. When he slipped the latch I flung open the door.

The suddenness caught him unawares, his reflexes triggering the shotgun as he emerged from the stairway. The shotgun roared before I could knock it aside, the blanket roll exploding a halo of lint and fiber! I clipped him behind the ear when he lurched forward; his eyes rolled, and he collapsed unconscious on the floor. Then I saw what had lain beneath the cushion on the helmsman's chair... a shredded chart, the schooner's plotted bearing projected with a red pencil!

It was after seven when his face muscles twitched and he fingered the lump behind his ear. The sun was a red blob on the horizon, the sea had grayed and shadows were long from the masts. A long, terrible night would soon be upon us. I folded the chart to my pocket and lugged him by his belt to the rail for an airing.

He was a big fellow, but I was leaner; figured I could take him if it came to a scramble. A bullet had ricocheted off his left cheek and laid it open to the bone. He'd stopped the bleeding with a wad of engine grease, but he'd lost a quantity of blood. I stirred him with my foot; he groaned and blinked his eyes. I tossed him the towel from the water cask by the mast and asked him if he could sit up. He eyed me warily and moistened his lips. He was in his early 20s, had a round, freckled face, a pug nose smudged with sun cream and a fierce Viking moustache. His blue-black eyes were shot with fatigue. He had a focusing problem, but managed a few unpleasant words as we had our first dialogue.

"You lousy bastard! Why'd you have to kill her?"

"Take it easy, kid. I had no part in this!"

"You mother fucker, I don't believe you!" He scrambled to his feet and lunged for my leg. I side-stepped him and spread his ass with my shoe. His shoulder struck the wheelhouse, he rolled and lurched to his feet. We parried for a moment, then he reached for his hip pocket and something glittered in his hand. I drop-kicked his belly, the screwdriver clattered to the deck, and he fell forward clutching his groin. I grabbed a fistful of hair and ground his face into the planking, then levered his wrist until he lay still.

"Lemme go! Lemme go!" he moaned.

"No way, you stupid ass! Knock it off or I'll bust your god-damned arm!"

"Fuck you!" he hissed. I added pressure and he screamed, clawing the deck with his fingers. "Lemme go... for Chris-sake!"

"Damnit, kid, I didn't bust your ship! I landed because you needed help! Are you reading me, man?" I palmed his wrist to help him along "Did you hear me? It's about to crack!" He twisted and reached for the screwdriver; I flipped it away.

"You flew over this morning," he gasped. "Brought them here, you bastard. I'll see you in hell 'fore I give in!" I eased off and bellowed in his ear.

"THAT WASN'T ME, do you understand?"

"OK! OK! For Chris-sake... leggo! " I eased his wrist and he turned his head and groaned. His eyes were glazed, his spittle flaked with blood. I released his arm and got to my feet while he rolled on his back and tested his shoulder. I draped the towel over his head and stood back. "Wipe yourself down."

"That's more like it, kid. I'm clearing out of here and I want it straight and level. Who did it? Do you know?" The towel fell from his head; he fingered his stomach and groaned.

"Jesus man, I hurt."

"You'll live. Out with it!" He leveled with my eyes, shook his head and said, "Goddamn! If you don't know, who does? Mind if I sit up?" I shrugged.

"Keep talking!" He propped himself against the wheel, squinted at the sun.

"Was close to 1500 when the wind gave out. I was down in the engine room warming up the fucking Cat when I heard a bull horn blarin'."

"What happened then?"

"I came up the ladder and saw a boat pull alongside. I thought it was the Coast Guard at first, 'cause I heard a lot of jab. I heard them calling out my name, my real name. Them kids only know me as Chug, so I figured I'd better find myself a hole. Who in the hell are you anyway? You with the DEA?" I shook my head.

"I bought the Goose in San Juan and was only passing through."

"Well, like I said, there's a crawl space under the forward hold. I'm going for it when I hear a lot of shootin'. The gang was screaming something awful. I went crazy 'cause I knew Liz was fixing a meal in the galley. You see what they did to her?" His eyes glistened, he bent forward and covered them with his hands. "For Chris-sake, Liz is only twenty. Been my old lady since high school."

"Take it easy, fella. I saw her in the galley." He got to his feet and stumbled to the railing. When he'd finished, he wiped his

mouth with the back of his hand and shook his head apologetical-
ly. I urged him to go on.

"Well, like I was sayin', when I heard all that screamin' I shot
up the ladder. When I got to the top I saw the kids rolling around
somethin' awful. One was crawling toward the hatch with blood
pourin' out of his mouth. Then, all of a sudden, there's orange
flashes comin' from that boat alongside us... and wham! The next
thing I know I'm lying across the Cat thinkin' I'm dead." He fingered the gash above his cheekbone and winced.

"Don't know how long I was out," he continued. "Was bleedin'
pretty bad. It was sorta quiet. I climbed off the engine thinking they
was gone, then I heard some loud talkin' forward. Jesus, man,
someone started screamin' and hollerin'; in Spanish. I know they
got the captain." He swallowed heavily and pointed toward the
bow. "They must have worked him over somethin' terrible, 'cause
it went on for a long time. I hit for the crawl space like an otter
going for water, but I could hear him pleadin' and yellin' 'neath all
that grass. Then all of a sudden it's quiet. When I took a look awhile
back, I saw how they cut him open." He paused for a moment, his
Adam's apple plunging "They musta' got to Liz next 'cause... man,
I can't say it!... I musta' blacked out again. Next thing I know
they're prying on the bulkhead door."

"They worked it over with a bar," I said. He nodded.

"They was callin' out my name. Then all of a sudden it's quiet!
I heard their engines rumblin' and they took off like gangbusters. I
waited a spell before I came out; then I looked around to see if anyone was alive... 'specially Liz. Man, I went bananas when I seed
what they'd done."

The kid's voice trailed off. He looked down and scuffed the
deck with his toes. When he looked up his eyes had filled.

"Man, I was wantin off this friggin' shit hole so bad I could taste it. I seed where they'd shot up the launch. I'm pullin at the raft and all the time I'm shoutin' to Liz... tellin' her we're leavin', and I know she's dead." He paused for a moment and spread his hands on the railing, his shoulder muscles tensed. "All of a sudden I realize I'm freakin' out. I hear that thunder over there and it got me to thinkin', ain't no way I'm going to make it to shore on no god-damned raft with that shark messin' around. If I'm going to get my hands on those bastards gotta hang in with the *Leopard.*"

He leaned forward and spat over the railing. I was about to say something, but he shook his head and pointed to the bodies piled in the lee of the wheelhouse.

"The sun was beatin' down somethin' fierce. I couldn't leave them lying around like dogs on some damn street. When I was finished I went down to the engine room to lean on the Cat. She takes some coachin' with a torch to heat up her compression. Next thing I know, I hear an airplane and you come whistlin' across the bow. Man, I was scared. I thought you was bringin' them back for sure. When you came over awhile ago, I figured I'd had it."

The time interval puzzled me. They would never have heard the Goose leaving eight thousand. Then I remembered the elaborate radar aboard the yacht and things began to tally. I shoved the thought aside. The kid was opening up. I continued to press.

"Did you get a good look before you were hit? Anything you can remember?" He shook his head.

"They was all standin' there tarted up like somethin' out of Gatsby. Don't remember no faces. Sure in hell wasn't the Coast Guard!"

"What about the boat, did it have a green hull?"

"Shit, man! It all happened so goddamned fast. Could have been green. Could have been black for all I know." He stopped suddenly, quizzically searching my face. "Hey, how come you asked?"

"I came across a yacht rounding Caicos awhile back, a big one for this side of the pond... low slung like a Donzi. Ring any bells?" He fingered his moustache and gave it some thought.

"Was longer than the *Leopard*... kept on thinkin' it was the Coast Guard until the last. Mister, you holdin' back?" I shook my head. "What about the plane that came by this morning?"

"Have a good look at the Goose, fella!" He turned to study the Grumann. When he turned back he was shaking his head.

"Man, I got some apologizing to do. Ain't no wonder they split when they did! One that flew by this mornin' was smaller lookin'. Come to think, it was all red and white. Yours is sorta gray... an' peelin' close up. You flew from San Juan in *that?*"

"Take it easy, buddy. That's your fairy godmother floating out there!"

"Sorry, Mister. Looks like the dogs been at it!"

"I'll tell the jokes until you can handle it, OK, kid? Feeling a little giddy?" He smiled weakly and nodded. I walked to the rail, glancing at my watch. The sun had slipped beneath the horizon. "Get your things together. I'm flying you into Provo. If the fuel truck is working late, we'll go on to Nassau. Someone is after your ass, but good."

His eyes narrowed, his thoughts careening from somewhere else.

"Gotcha, man! Knew I'd seen you somewhere! You were at Bootleggers one night in Lauderdale with a good-lookin' English broad. Freddie said you were a hot stick in Desert Storm. We was at the next table, talkin' business. He said to cool it 'cause you might be with the DEA. Your last name's Slater ...Keith Slater. I remember you now."

"Could be, only I'm not with the DEA, and we've no time for reminiscing. This is a heavy scene, kid. Did you forget to pay up in Colombia, or change your rendezvous for a buck?" I pulled the chart from my hip pocket. "Is *this* what they were after? Did you dump a load a while back, and forget to tell them where it was?"

He slamrned a fist on the rail, his eyes livid. I'd hit a raw nerve, but obviously not the answer.

"For Chris-sake, stop callin' me kid! It ain't nothin' like that. The load's all paid for and the spot's been clean since last month!" He puckered his brow and studied his feet. "Come to think, I'm the only one who knew where we was headed for... sides for Liz. The captain didn't know, it was his first trip and I conned the wheel. Them kids was hangin' around Barranquilla lookin' for a ride. The captain was to drop them off at Georgetown and head back south."

"After you dropped the grass?" He nodded.

"Hell, ain't nothing there but a pile of rocks. It's offbeat, man. I kept the chart under the seat so they didn't know where we were... them kids, I mean."

"There's something they want, there's something there, fella. They didn't come by for target practice." His eyes narrowed.

"I seed where they been lookin' around, Slater. And I heard them callin' my name. But like I said, everyone knows me for Chug... and there ain't nothing on that goddammed island worth talking down my nose!"

Convinced, I eased off. He seemed to be a solid type, although he needed a bit of laundering. He'd blundered into something heavier than a load of pot, but obviously didn't know what it was.

I tried to reason with him, told him it would be better to clear the slate with the Coast Guard and let them take it from there. He spread his feet defiantly and shook his head.

"Ain't goin' to leave Liz, Slater. Not going to have her lying up there like that. I know what I gotta do. Jus' help me drop them sails and stand by 'til I start up the fuckin' Cat. Please, man, I'll make it right. The DEA have me tagged. They'd throw me in the slammer.

I know what I gotta do, man! I'm on my knees and beggin'."

In the end I had to agree. If I belted him, I'd never manage to get him aboard the Goose, and he knew it. We talked while we hauled in the sheet lines and lowered the gaffs. He was a savvy kid, stubborn and gutsy. His voyage through the night would be a terrible ordeal. We discussed the implications at length while he blowtorched the Cat's cylinders and worked the throttle until she rattled and caught. The sun had long gone, twilight was fading when we walked aft to pull the Goose in by the stern. We reached an understanding while we stood by the rail. I penciled a note to a friend on the backside of the chart… a friend he'd be needing further up the way.

It was 8:15 by my watch when I signaled and the kid threw a life preserver from the bow. The waters swirled, the dorsal fin moved quickly, and I went down the line from the stern. He waited by the rail until I had a start on the engines. The Pratt-Whitneys coughed and roared. I cast off and jockeyed a swell, fire-walling the quadrant. The schooner's prop was milking a heavy wake when I circled and took bead on Providenciales. And then I remembered… I'd forgotten to ask his name, although Chug seemed fitting.

The Goose juiced her wheels on the strip at Provo a half hour later. We taxied down the darkened runway and turned into the ramp, where our lights caught a sleek Grumman Widgeon parked beyond a line-up of Pipers and Cessnas. She was all white, except for her stripes and *red underbelly.* There wouldn't be another like her for a thousand miles.

I swiveled to a stop alongside the fuel truck, and chopped the Pratt-Whitneys. I located the customs officer at the airport bar. When he dropped me off at the Turtles Inn, I had my first encounter with Elisabeth… and Elisabeth's sponsors.

Mid-July was strictly off season, so I was surprised to learn I'd been given the last available room in the house. The Inn was the largest of the small yachtels sprinkled along the north shore. Of its 24 rooms, only 23 were usable; a young lady had lost her ring in the toilet and they hadn't gotten it undone.

"You can use the shower and the basin," the room clerk informed me, "but if you have to use the bathroom, you'll have to go downstairs to the bar. We've had a movie crew here for the past two weeks and they took up all the spares. The yacht basin's full up, too," he added. "Don't know where they all came from. This time last year they laid off all the help." He was a light-skinned fellow with greenish eyes, quite personable and accommodating. I thought I might have seen him somewhere before, but I didn't inquire.

The Inn was an architectural delight; functionally, something else again. The two-story guest structure jutted the cliff top with cypress-railed balconies and shingled overhangs. The bar and dining room lay beneath the cliff side, joined to the upper segment by a crumbling stone stairway of 100 steps. The exotic view from the balcony included high-rising palms and moon lit bougainvillea fringing the yacht basin and stone patio connecting the lower buildings. The boat slips were filled with tall masts, short masts, Hatterases, Morgans... the place was alive with postcard stuff. Three larger yachts were anchored in the outer harbor; I took particular note of the largest.

I opened the balcony doors wide to the night and turned on the overhead fan. The air was infused with the vibrant smell of the tropics... a blending of sea and dense vegetation, a reassuring scent to a familiar friend.

The room was pleasant enough, with vertically-planked walls and shutter-ventilated windows. A tropical batik matched the width of the king-sized bed; the spread was Haitian, the furniture Dominican.

I opened my overnighter and stripped down. Figured I'd shower and grab a bite to eat before I checked out the yacht. When I loosened my sneakers, a residue of blood stained my fingers, reminding me of the kid, motoring through the night with his cargo of corpses. He'd pass the north coast of Providenciales at midnight, seeing the harbour glow and twinkling lights from the cottages ranging the hills. Life! It would be a terrible night to follow a horrible day. Where would he be at dawn?

I tossed my topsiders in the shower and ran the water, diluted blood swirling the drain. *Was the Widgeon poised for a morning take off?* The open sea with the sun behind him, a search pattern, a widening arc, the schooner's high-riding masts! I scrubbed the sneakers, deep in thought. The kid would have a substantial lead by daybreak and the yacht's radar was limited to the horizon, but from 3500 feet he was easy prey and they'd have him quartered by noon. Was there a way? *A pair of pliers in the Widgeon's engine nacelle, a friendly hand to re-route a wire or two?*

Cowbells jangled on the patio below. A calypso band tuned and began a merengue. Voices rose, a glass tinkled somewhere, there was laughter. I sloshed the pinkish water with my foot, remembering what the old Bard had said. A cherry bomb exploded in the distance; the drummer missed a beat. I slammed the bathroom door and blasted the shower. The kid would be helpless! *I had to give it a try.*

She was standing at the end of the pier when I stepped to the balcony to dry my shoes. Floodlights silhouetted her thin body through a loose-fitting pajama suit. She was tall and leggy, poised, sensually elegant in her soft white silks... a natural blonde with a golden sheen, carefully brushed and gathered with a scarf.

I knotted a towel to my hips and stared at her effortless grace, admiring the sophistication she portrayed in this unlikely part of the world. She stood motionless, her back towards me... as if waiting someone, or contemplating the stars. When a bell chimed from across the harbour, she peered into the darkness, silhouetted momentarily when a beam from the Benetti pathed the pier. Fascinated by her presence, curious when a bobbing light appeared in the distance, I side-stepped the shadows to see what she was about.

Then the bell chimed twice again... close-by... and she strode to the pier's end. Graceful, unhurried... waving when a launch glided from the darkness swathing a wake of glistening foam. A sailor in whites stood erect on the bow... casting a line to a cleat when the launch throttled in reverse. Seemingly adept to the procedure, she secured the bow and walked quickly astern, accepting a line from the steersman. Disenchanted by the unfolding scene, I watched intently while the passengers disembarked... knowing from whence they came.

First off was a tall, thin man who apparently was top dog. Continental, judging from his demeanor... the superficial smile he oozed when he bussed her lovely cheeks. She ignored the second man while he was helped from the launch. Stocky, obviously very old... I recognized the military brush cut I'd observed from the Goose. There were others climbing the ladder, equally old, but my eyes followed the girl's leggy stride, noticing she'd rejected the tall fellow's hand when he led his entourage to the Inn.

The stocky type elected a cadence apart... measured steps, robot-like, stiffly erect, clinging to a habit from his past. The "tag-alongs" were something else... perspiring profusely, arguing amongst themselves, rumpled suits tightly buttoned despite the overwhelming humidity. Their enormous girths bobbed and swayed as their stubby legs reeled to the task. Seventyish, I thought... overweight, over dressed, strangely out of place in the mid-summer tropics.

I had an excellent view of the girl when they passed beneath me. Her deep blue eyes and strong brown eyebrows framed a smiling face when she suddenly looked up. Her smile lingered as they turned away; had she realized I was watching? She seemed amused. The tall man was oblivious, pointing out a path around the noisy bar, frowning when an obstreperous cherry bomb exploded in the patio beyond.

He wore an expensive-looking jersey, Italian slacks and loafers, a thin gold watch; I judged him to be 40. Handsome fellow... lean, aristocratic, definitely European. Then I noticed something else when they paused briefly beneath a lamp light. He had an unnaturally mean turn to his mouth; corners cruelly set, humorless, self-seeking, calculating... and he'd done it to himself. He spoke sharply to bring the stragglers along. When they turned to enter the dining room, I realized they spoke in German.

It was after nine when I'd shaved and unrolled a wrinkled change of clothes from my pack. My sun-bleached hair needed shears and my eyes were shot with fatigue. I could pass for a boat bum who'd missed the plank. I would be at ease at the bar, but was deeply troubled and wanting a closeup view of the group in the dining room—specifically the girl.

I thumbed the directory while I slipped into my sneakers. The net result was a seven-digit number and a resounding squish when I tried my shoes. The phone was dead and the airport was miles away. Island taxis were seldom on the road after dusk. I locked my door and exited to the porchway, considering the numerous vehicles parked in the circular drive. Would the desk clerk have a car?

Would he rise for a twenty if I hired it later on?

"Twenty-four's out of order, mon," he said. "We cut the line when the girl got to whining 'bout her ring in the toilet. You wantin' Howard?" I nodded hopefully. Would he be at home... was he out on a charter? Green Eyes dialed, then pointed out the desk phone.

"Howard gone to bed, but his wife willin' to talk." I asked if I could use the office extension. He shrugged; I produced a fiver and laid it on the desk.

"Ain't nothing private on this island, mon, but I'll take me a beer and wait outside if you insist... you with the DEA?" I shook my head.

"Howard's an old friend and I need a favor." He eyed me curiously and stepped outside. I was certain I'd seen him somewhere before, but Howard's wife came on before I could give it thought.

I talked to her briefly and waited. A flash of headlights turned me about as a jeep ground to a stop by the door. The screen door sprung open and a young man hurried through the lobby to the steps leading below. He was immaculately dressed in a tailored safari suit. His cheeks were rouged and he'd dabbled with mascara.

"At's our movie star," the desk clerk commented from the porch. "Ain't he pretty?"

Howard was half asleep, confused by the unexpected call; bewildered by my presence and late hour request. He groused himself awake when I explained the situation and emphasized my intent... specifically, the means to disable the Widgeon until noon, allowing a few hours lead when I lofted the Goose at dawn. He didn't question my motive... in fact, he seemed genuinely delighted. He proposed a simplistic 'trick' he'd take on all by himself.

"Gives me pleasure, Keith. Wolfgang been treatin' us locals like shit! Flappin' that Widgeon around... spinnin' gravel, ignorin' the tower. Like we're second class citizens. . . know what I mean?"

31

I seized an opening, quizzed him further. Wolfgang apparently was ex-Luftwaffe, the Widgeon leased from a hawker in Miami.

"Wolfgang's a tall, blond fella' . . . like yourself, Keith. 'Cept he keep to himself and ain't much for the sun. Wear dark glasses, like he watchin' suspicious-like. Works for the man who owns the big yacht . . . same man who making the movie here-about. Fella' named Kurt," he added. "Struts around like he have a burr up his ass!" I whistled softly to myself. If the movie was a cover-up, the scenario was making sense!

"They's hard nose, Keith. Movie folk mostly polite, but them fellas board the yacht are hard to believe. Like they ain't got no soul. Now I'm respectin' that pretty girl who come recent," he added. "She have a nice smile, pleasant with us local folk. Can't reason why she take up with the likes of them."

I popped the heavy question. "Do you know if the Widgeon was airborne between two and five?" Howard wasn't sure; he'd returned from a charter at 8:35.

"Can't rightly say, Keith, but I see'd Wolfgang fussin' around that old Grumman when I taxied in. That derelict yours, man . . . the Goose you was speakin' about? Confide with Howard," he added. "You acquire that 'ting legitimate. . . seein' it peelin' paint and salt water?"

He rambled on when I indicated I'd bid the Grumman in SanJuan; asked if it would be available during the on-coming season. "Like I'm needin' an amphibian, Keith. Providin' she pass her annual inspection." I nodded absent-mindedly, my thoughts on Wolfgang's curiosity. Had they identified the Goose when I circled the Benetti? Heeded my heading when I returned to the *Leopard*?

I cradled the phone when Green Eyes returned to his desk. Howard would pick me up at dawn, the kid's safety dependent on the schooner's time elapse. . . provided he passed Provo undetected during the night. A chill coursed my spine when I considered his state of mind, his lonely vigil while he conned the wheel with the wretched corpses shrouded on the forward deck.

"Yinna disturbed," Green Eyes commented as I stared at my bloodied sneakers. I quickened a response, asked if he could put me through to Miami. . . knowing the Coast Guard commanded a brace of cutters in the southern Bahamas. "No way," he said. "Communications upset by the storm off Hispaniola. Cartin' grass," he added. "Seein' you comes late, while customs sippin' rum?" He averted his eyes when I spun about. . . I recognized him then!

"Constable Seymour! Jesus, man. . . what are you doin in Providenciales?" He scanned the lobby, lowered his voice.

"Makin'joke, Mister Slater. I know's your straight. . . figured you'd remember sooner or later. Now I'm askin' if you'll keep close mouth; can we come to an understanding?"

"What's the pitch, man? Are you working with Paul, the CID?"

"Might say I'm on loan to the Commonwealth, Mister Slater, seein' Turks-Caicos is independent. Now listen careful-like, got something to pass on."

"The movie lot?" Green Eyes shrugged.

"I'm tryin' to advise you, Mister Slater. That Wolfgang fella' came through a while back with a no-count nigger from South Caicos. They was talkin' and I was listening, like I don't know from nothin. You understand?"

I tensed. "What did they say?"

They's sayin' that Goose taste of salt and damp from the sea. They was talkin' bad going down the steps. Now I'm telling you this cause you got to watch out for that nigger. He kill two people in Nassau and we ain't hung him yet!" I nodded, familiar with the term commonly used when there was someone the blacks despised unilaterally.

"Do they know I've checked in?"

"No, mon. See'd to that when I fix you wid room without toilet. They cause no problem here, " he added. "But I advise you keep watch of your airy-plane."

I asked if Wolfgang quartered at the Inn. He shook his head.

"No, mon! He keeps with the yacht. Takes off every morning 'round eight. Bout the same time the *Juanita* leave harbor. Says he's lookin' for background scenery and the like. Them movie folk all the time working on the east end of the island. Ain't see'd them much together wid them fellas aboard the yacht." He paused, pursed his lips thoughtfully.

"Telling you this cause it won't do to be askin' around, would raise suspicion. Get the picture, mon?" I wasn't quite sure, but nodded to press him on.

"Main ting. . . don't want you tellin' no one where you seen me last. We come to agreement on dot?" He extended the flat of his hand. I slapped his palm and winked.

Green Eyes clued me briefly as best he could. The movie crew normally arrived at sunset and headed directly to the bar. The Juanita invariably anchored after dark, but the group aboard seldom came ashore. . . aside from alternate nights, when they commanded the private dining room alongside the pier. They were mostly German, their menu pre-arranged with the chef. The groups seldom mixed, although Kurt often had his coffee with the director. The girl was an exception to the format; she usually sat with Kurt at the head of the table until cigars were passed and the group commenced to sing

"Terrible noise," Green Eyes commented. "Old men beatin' on the table wid some kind of marchin' song. Seed the girl up-tight when she come by to go to her room. Her name's Elisabeth. She Austrian, I tink."

He couldn't "rightly recollect" her surname, but obliged me with the registry ledger. I leafed the pages until I came to a date where they'd registered en masse, but Elisabeth's name was not among them. I'd turned to the following pages when suddenly he coughed. I looked up. Green Eyes rolled his eyes toward the stairs and flapped his elbows. I closed the registry and peered from my shoulder. A tall blonde fellow brushed by and swung the door to the extent of its hinges. He was followed by a burly black in dungarees. They obviously were in a hurry, the blonde fellow cursing while they keyed a nondescript van and thundered from the driveway. I watched apprehensively, noticing their lights when they turned west on the highway.

"They's headin' for the airy-port," Green Eyes commented. "Tall man's Wolfgang. . . black fella' same I was tellin' about. Family with Big Red who recent escape from Fox Hill (Nassau)." I re-swung the screen, whistled softly to myself as I followed the stairs to the bar below.

Hemingway would have loved it. The scene in the bar portrayed his decade. Bimini was glossy with fiberglass and radar equips, but Providenciales was frozen in time by its remote inaccessibility. The heavy-timbered beams, drooping nets, fly-chasing fans, posters peeling from the walls, wafting smoke, the din, all served as a backdrop for a cast of characters described in his novels.

They were all there. . . charter boat captains in sweat-stained khakis, tattooed mates, sun-burned clients with gold Rolex's, bearded yachtsmen and skinny sailing types in faded shorts.

The locals were there, too . . a Conch with a broad-rimmed straw and pickled nose, a black man with gleaming teeth cadging a drink from a brittle-haired blonde. A piano clanged in the corner, a drunk weaved to the men's room fumbling with his fly. The barometer had brought them from the sea, the booze brought them a unity.

Sugar, on his knees on the patio with his microphone on the slant, was wailing a mean merengue. The movie folk had collected cowbells from the band and were snake-dancing beneath the flowering bougainvillea. Waiters were high-legging it with their trays precariously perched on their heads. They were all having a ball. . . bony girls in tight, tight jeans, bosomy types with bouncy halters, long-haired guys with spangled chests, a bi-focaled gal waving a liberated blouse. A firecracker fizzed and boomed beneath the cliff-side, an overweight loser bent forward and slapped his thighs.

The action was to my liking and I was reluctant to leave the primal cliffside, the throbbing drums and sensuous hips. I needed the release, but it would have to wait for another night. Sugar ad-libbed a stanza and stabbed me with a one-liner when I reached for the door to the dining room.

"Hey, mister Slater, man, how come you leave so soon again? Ain't seen you since Nassau in Paradise. . . you trackin' that tall blond gal with the pretty blue eyes?" I turned and winked. His mouth was all teeth, his round black face wreathed with enormous vitality. When I opened the door, the best of two worlds faded behind me.

Air conditioning in the dining room muffled the mayhem shaking the windows. The mood was quiet and apart. A narrow-faced couple sat with a backgammon board between them, while a middle-aged foursome engaged in a hand of bridge. A sun-burned pair, nursing their coffee, discussed the approaching storm. Dinner was over, the remaining tables set for breakfast. The lone waiter, tallying his receipts, came slightly undone when I asked for a chair and a glass of wine.

"Can oblige wid the wine, chief, but the kitchen close, lessen you wantin' me to fetch a sandwich from the bar." I pointed to the alcove behind a potted palm. A clatter of dishes indicated dinner was being served.

"Special party, mon. They's have separate arrangement with the chef. They's movie folk," he added. "Come late when there ain't no one around, brings their own steward from the yacht to serve, like they ain't trustin' us wid der talk." He pointed to a white-jacketed kid emerging from the kitchen with a tray. He was barely 20, pale and pimply. I recognized him as the sailor who moored the launch.

I nodded to the narrow-faced pair and took a seat at a window table. The potted palm was to my advantage, but my view of the private dining room was obstructed by a pair of folding doors. I yielded my 20 and whispered to the waiter when he gathered the extra plates. He nodded and eased the doors with his foot so I had an oblong view of the private party within.

I toyed with my glass and studied the masts bobbing in the slips, venturing a side glance when the steward trundled by with a cart of braten. There were two distinct groups; they were conversing in German, but the conversations seemed unrelated. The table close by was given to the movie entourage, including a bespeckled man I assumed was the director. The far table was occupied by the portly gentlemen from the *Juanita*. The black-haired Swiss commanded the end. His face flushed, he appeared upset. The chair to his left was vacant but to his right sat the lovely blue-eyed girl I assumed was Elisabeth.

She was radiant in the soft candlelight. Her hair was drawn back from her forehead and gathered with a scarf behind her long, slender neck. Her strong facial features commanded attention when she conversed with those beside her. A thinly arched nose and high-riding cheeks had been sculpted by the master's hand. Her mouth, the up-turn of her lips, suggested tenderness and sensuality. The thrust of her chin spoke of her inner self, of determination tempered with poise and refinement. Her ancestors had been selective; her features were flawless, the most exquisite creature I'd ever seen. I gripped the table and stared, unminding, wondering why she was there.

This lovely creature seemed strangely out of place with the longjaws feeding from the trough; an off-beat movie was hardly her lot. Her sensuous figure would be full page in the fashion slicks. Was it the overbearing Swiss entrepreneur? Was she betrothed? I glanced at her fingers; she wore no rings. A simplistic watch encircled her wrist. She was gracious and courteous when the Swiss leaned her way, but I had a gut feeling she was inwardly repulsed and playing a delicate game.

Elisabeth looked up suddenly, as if she'd sensed my thoughts. Our eyes locked as the overhead fan parted the palm fronds. I swallowed and squirmed in my chair. She crinkled a smile, brought a finger to her lips and shook her head ever-so-slightly. Then she turned abruptly and pointed to an incoming Hatteras raising wake along the pier. I tensed when I realized what she was about. As conversations stilled and heads turned, her chairside companion appeared interested in my potted palm.

I swiveled to face the window, leaning forward as if I were preoccupied with the Hatteras. The movie cadre glanced briefly and resumed their conversation, but it became increasingly obvious that the Swiss had focused my backside and was fully alert. There were mutterings from across the table, a scuffling of chairs. I was conscious of the oldster turning about, of his guttural voice when he spoke.

Es ist der Pilot. Wolfgang sagte, dass er kommen wuerde! ["It is the pilot. Wolfgang said he would come!"] Wolfgang had passed the word. I was between a rock and a crumbling ledge.

Studying the churning Hatteras, I cast about for options. . . if I exited the table I'd compound their suspicions; if I stayed I risked a volatile confrontation with four angry men. I shot a glance when Elisabeth added voice to the rising din. She was on her feet, attempting to placate the raging Swiss, fronting him when he shook his fist at my lonely palm. She repeated herself in English, as if to benefit my ears. "It is wrong. Let him be; it is not that important!"

There was mention of the *Juanita* and a juicy expletive as he shouldered her aside. The bridge players behind me had come to full attention and the backgammon pair were watching nervously from their board. I made a hasty decision. . . when the waiter sauntered from the kitchen with my bottle of wine and the steward trudged behind him with an overloaded tray, I would remove myself gently and have my bottle in the bar.

The situation came to a head when I got to my feet and eyed the door. The waiter was oblivious to the tension and chose an inopportune moment to pop my cork. The startled steward, bending an ear to the Swiss, spun about and dropped his tray. The reaction was instantaneous, black comedy at its worst.

The actor screamed as if he'd been shot. The director dove for the floor and came full body through the creamy desserts. His entourage dominoed to their hands and knees and the portly Germans rose in unison with their knives and forks. I stared, unbelieving of the ludicrous mess. I was vaguely conscious of the Swiss exploding from his table, of Elisabeth tugging at his arm, but my attention focused on the old man as he came stiffly erect and wheeled around. He had rotten teeth and a livid scar beneath his cheek. His blue-black eyes were hooded with anger, his blazer was undone, and a long-barreled Luger was emerging from his belt.

I found myself facing a moment of truth with nowhere to run. Reacting instinctively, I shoved the ashen waiter aside, grabbed the bottle from his hand and hurled it through the opening. The distance was little more than a couple of yards, and the heavy bottle caught him squarely in the solar plexus. His eyes popped, he emitted a terrible belch and slumped to the floor, clutching his abdomen and howling with pain. I eyed the Luger as it slid across the floor and came to a stop against the spread of chairs. The old man was out of it, but not the steward—I hefted my chair and flung it at his head. He screamed and fell full-length amidst the clutter of broken chinaware. His fingers fluttered briefly and stilled, but a pulse beat from the vena cavae along his neck.

The waiter cowered beside me as I backed away. There was a clatter of chairs, a scuttling of shoes, as the bridge players and backgammon couple fled the room. The waiter twittered nervously as he gave me a wide berth. I spun around when Elisabeth shouted from the alcove. Her face blanched with terror, she was pointing desperately to my right. The Swiss had side-stepped the slippery floor and was advancing crablike from the opening, wielding a fully bladed clasp knife. The scene aboard the *Leopard* flashed vividly to mind as I grabbed a chair. Blinded with fury, I wanting him at my feet.

Help arrived from an unexpected source. . . a shaft of light from the kitchen door, a burly black arm, and a deep resounding voice. "Yinna cause big problem! Now ya bring quiet to my house 'fore I lose me temper!" The chef was addressing the room in general, but he had the Swiss under arm and his attention was given to the fast folding blade.

There was a stunned silence, then a wild scramble as the movie set streamed from the alcove with the whimpering actor clasped between them. I grounded my chair when the chef released the glowering Swiss. There were hushed words as I turned to leave. The Germans had revived the steward with a splash of beer and were helping the winded old man to his feet. An unbelievable 20 minutes had created a bloody nightmare. My jersey was matted with sweat when I thanked the taciturn chef. My legs felt like stalks of wilted celery when I stepped outside and headed for the bar.

It was after eleven when they emerged from the dining room and walked to the pier. I watched from the windowside of the bar and made careful count, wary of being mousetrapped by someone they'd left behind. The steward, hurrying ahead to ready the launch, was holding a napkin to his ear, in obvious pain. The Swiss followed along with Elisabeth at his side. They were in vehement conversation, his face contorted with anger. I was quick to notice they weren't arm-in-arm. The Germans waddled behind like overfed geese primed for paté de foie gras. . . greedy old men with sordid thoughts, their eyes glued to Elisabeth's free-swinging hips.

The old man lingered in the darkness by the dining room door. His blazer buttons reflected the lamplight briefly as he paced fretfully, muttering to himself. I moved along the bar to window advantage when he turned abruptly and pointed to the end of the pier. Wolfgang parted the doors a moment later. I arched my neck, focusing on the shadows. He was munching a slab of bread and gesturing with a can of Heineken. He'd come late and the old man had been waiting. They struck off immediately.

I slumped in my stool, peering through my fingers, but nobody was behind them. Seemingly oblivious to my presence, they passed the window in cadence, like a pair of Deutsche Arbeiterpartei in the summer of '33. The old man had his hands clasped behind his back, his eyes gleamed with delight when the pilot fluttered his arms and pointed to the limpid sea. I shivered instinctively. The motion was not lost, nor was the smear of grease on his hair. I took particular note of his grimy hands when he drained the can and tossed it in a clump of flowering bougainvillea. *He'd tampered with my beloved Goose!*

We'd come full circle. I'd need Howard's eyes when I pre-flighted the Grumman in the morning. A touch of acid on the elevator cables would have me out of control when I lifted off or encountered a patch of weather. It wasn't my game, but it was easily done. I fingered the shell casing in my pocket. The evidence was circumstantial, but the Luger and the ugly knife were quick to appear. They were obviously angered when I thundered by with the Goose—suspicious; was I a witness? The indicators were in the red. I had reason to believe they wanted me dead.

The unholy fivesome boarded the launch under my watchful eye. The pilot was last in. I caught my breath when Elisabeth dipped beside him, exhaling my relief as she cast the lines and waved them off. I was walking a thin wire, wanting desperately to talk with her before the night came to an end. By morning we'd be on to our various ways. There would be little chance to tie up the threads.

It was mainly a matter of heart. Aside from that, she was a gutsy lady. She'd laid it on the line when the long-toothed daddy stalked me with his knife.

When I saw the launch's wake pathing the harbour, I went outside and walked along the seawall. The Hatteras was tied in, its main cabin lit. The skipper poured himself a double from the side stand. I traversed the gangway to the floating pier. Elisabeth was standing at the end of the floating pier, beneath the floodlights. She'd loosened her scarf and fluffed her hair. Seemingly aware of my presence, her stance suggested she'd wait until they'd boarded the *Juanita*.

The immediate pier was in darkness. A dozen or so yachts were tied on either side by their sterns, in the company of yawls, ketches, a Bertram or two. Their lights low, the foursome from the dining room were making beds, shaking their heads when I ambled by. A nondescript ChrisCraft was tied alongside a rugged trawler. Her stern was low in the water, the windscreen plastered with an official document. She'd been seized recently with a cargo of grass.

My attention was drawn to the trawler. Her booms were lashed, she had no nets and her upper structure bristled with electronic gear. The stern plate read *The Walrus—Nassau NP*. A bearded, middle-aged man, wearing a ragged British officer's cap, sat in a canvas chair with his feet perched against the railing. I recognized him from Nassau. His name was Bower, commander, ex-Royal Navy, retired. I stopped short. He had a lucrative business and a beautiful wife. What was he doing in Providenciales with an off-beat trawler? He pointed with his pipe stem before I could ask. When I turned about Elisabeth was almost upon me! Her head bent low to pace her leggy stride.

She had a set, determined look in her eye. My jaw dropped. I stepped aside but she had my measure. She slung an arm under mine and spun me around without altering her gait. I skipped and hopped to match her momentum. Her arm tightened and she dug me with her elbow. Her comment was bluntly put. I replied as quickly as I could.

"Faster, you idiot! They'll be watching from the yacht!"

"Slow down, for Christ sake. . . I'm losing my shoes!"

We came to a halt in the shadow of the Hatteras. She knelt beside me when I bent to retie, tossed her hair aside and frowned.

"You're to put a finger on the bow whilst you start the second. Do you lose them often?"

"I've had this problem since kindergarten," I admitted. She smiled. She had exquisite teeth.

"Come along, we mustn't be seen. There's been trouble enough

43

this evening." I nodded and got to my feet. She had a low, throaty voice, cultured, pleasant and melodious, her English fluent upper class.

She stamped her foot impatiently as I glanced from my shoulder and held her back. Bower had flared his pipe, pointing again with the stem. A searchlight swept the harbor and settled momentarily on the pier. We crouched by the Hatteras while it focused the gangwalk and played along the seawall. Elisabeth had a clean scent of lavender about her. I could have lingered indefinitely, but the wall went to darkness and she darted from my side. I ran after her, pulling her behind a clump of hibiscus as the beam returned to study where we'd been.

"Easy, honey. . . they're playing games!" Her eyes flashed; she was frightened and gasping for breath.

"You shouldn't have followed! They are terribly suspicious."

"Have they something on their mind? I mean, I'm not for guns and knives."

"They're furious! You spoiled their sound track when you flew over the *Juanita!*"

"I spoiled their sound track?" She eyed me curiously. I clung to her wrist as the light faltered and went out. She seemed determined to leave.

"It was you, wasn't it? The pilot said you landed after dark." I pointed to a nearby bench. She shook her head.

"Look, honey, that's a wide open sky. If they told you I spoiled their sound track, they're up to their bibs with braten."

"They said you flew very low. . ."

"That's right. I have an eye for racy yachts."

"And then you turned and flew toward Grand Turks."

"I was curious. . . did they tell you why?" She shook her head, as if she didn't understand.

"They said you didn't land there, that you continued out to sea." My eyes widened; she was pressing.

"Odd, isn't it? So they tracked me on radar; I wonder why?" Her fingers slipped to mine and I instantly became wary.

"I don't know. Wolfgang let slip that your flying boat tasted of salt and that you might be here. I tried to warn you, but Kurt was suspicious. You were so bloody obvious!"

"Kurt? Did the Swiss put you up to this? Is that why you waited?"

She withdrew her hand quickly from mine. I caught her wrist, but she spun and back-handed my cheek. I gripped both her arms then held her against the bush. Our eyes locked.

"You insufferable bastard! Did it not occur to you that I have a mind of my own? Let go of me immediately or I'll scream!"

I tightened my grip. Her face inches from mine, she readied a spit. I shook my head, she decided not. As I released her arms, a tear cascaded down her cheek. When I gathered her to my chest, she tensed, then brought her arms around me.

"I'm so sorry," she murmured after we kissed. "It has been too much stress of late. It's true, I waited. I did want to talk with you. I have ears. I'm not a silly. I'm curious, too. Please, you must believe me."

She looked up with her startling blue eyes. A tree frog chirped nearby, a horn sounded from the outer harbor. Her eyes didn't waver. I winked. Her eyes softened and a smile teased her dimples. I cupped her face in my hands and kissed her again. Her arms came around me. I felt her small hard breasts press against my chest. The tree frog chided and hopped away, the lights hazed in the outer harbor. I held her closely, believing what she had said.

"You called me Elisabeth," she whispered.

"Yes, ma'am. You're the Austrian femme fatale."

She tilted her head and touched a finger to my lips. "And you are the American. You fly a noisy flying boat."

"Keith Slater, construction engineer. Shall we consider ourselves introduced?"

She smiled and closed her eyes. Our tongues met, the stars glittered. She melted in my arms, as if we'd known each other for a thousand years. The freshing breeze flapped an ensign on the yardarm above us and a flash of lightning illuminated the sky to the south. We paid no heed until a motor coughed in the distance and a searchlight probed the pier. Her body tensed; she was instantly alert.

"Is it the launch?" I shook my head and nuzzled her ear.

"Relax. It's a fisherman coming by for a beer." She watched from my shoulder, still unsure.

"I must leave. I have a scene to memorize and the van is to collect us at six."

"May I see you to your room?" She hesitated.

"I would like that very much, but not tonight. Please, you must understand. I'm. . ."

"In a bind?" She nodded.

"It's been a traumatic evening, I had no idea he would become so frightfully irrational. I must be very careful."

"You're scared!" She swallowed and looked away.

"It's terribly involved. You must leave in the morning; they'll kill you if you don't!"

"Figured as much, but I'm worried about you."

"Don't be. I can take care of myself. I'm not exactly alone."

"Commander Bower?" She peered from my shoulder. The fisherman had docked and was ambling along the pier. She squeezed my hand, vastly relieved.

"Shall we let it go at that? I've said too much as it is. You must

46

inspect your flying boat in the morning. I do believe they've been at it!" My heart lightened . . . she was at odds with the game and the commander's presence was partially explained.

"That, was a clean shot, honey. Let's say we have a basic under-standing. What are they after, what's this all about?"

She brought her hands to her face, obviously distressed and wanting to talk. Her fingers, taut with emotion, were devoid of rings, although there was a faint white circle on her index finger where one might have been.

"I'm unable to say. . . you must believe in me. I'm at my wits end. My God, if you want me, you must let matters be!"

I held her closely, hopelessly snared. She cried a little as we walked along the pathway, firmed up when we entered the patio. Sugar had folded for the night, the crowd dispersing to their quar-ters and vans. An off-tune piano tinkled in the bar, the last vestige of a wild tropical night. It was close to twelve.

"We actually have a bloody good screenplay," she ventured. "We have an excellent director and are well along with filming. I came lately when the lead became. . . indisposed." I gave thought to that. Had she taken sick, or covertly displaced?

"And what's with Kurt? I assume he's the daddy with 51 per-cent."

"He's German-Swiss, owns an electronics firm in Berne with offices in Bonn and Essen. He hasn't interfered with the produc-tion, which is sensible. Stays mostly aboard the *Juanita*. . . I under-stand it's equipped with the latest sounding devices." Our eyes locked. I sensed she was probing, but let it ride.

"And the others?" Elisabeth shrugged.

"They are financially involved; keep to themselves."

"The old man with rotten teeth?"

"Klaus?" She stopped abruptly at the base of the stairs. Her face was flushed when she turned about. Her lips moved silently, as if she were deliberating for words.

"Klaus? He. . . was a U-boat commander during the war. He came along to provide technical assistance." She undid our hands and eyed the steps. "The story has to do with a German submarine that came to grief in the tropics at the close of World War II. . . my, you do limp. Will you be all right?" she asked, changing the subject.

"Go on with the story. The sub was loaded with Nazi gold and they were on their way to Uruguay."

"You've read the screenplay?"

"No, but I'm acquainted with the story." She paused mid-step and turned about.

"It's fiction, of course. . ."

"Not necessarily. There's a legend in the islands that had the natives shoveling sand for years."

"For buried gold?"

"What else? An old fisherman was adrift with his sails blown, so it goes. He sighted a submarine off-loading a dinghy in the middle of the night. He had no idea where he was, but he remembered a cresting reef."

"Is he still alive?"

"Hell, no, that was back in '45. He drifted for days until he was picked up by a mail boat. They thought he was off his rocker, but the story survived. You can ask any Conch at the bar."

"Did he describe the U-boat? Did it have a number?" My ears perked—the question was out of context.

"He couldn't read, honey. Why do you ask?" She turned about and continued the steps.

"I was curious. The screenplay was drawn from a novel I read as a child, but Kurt's writers have changed it to include an enchanted island."

"Palm trees and romance?" She nodded from her shoulder.

"Wives and mistresses bound for South America. Fun and games whilst they fix the bloody U-boat. We have a mock-up of the interior in Berne, but the sea scenes are to be filmed from the *Juanita.*"

"The sea scenes?"

"Profile scans, while they inspect the island from the U-boat, close-up views of the crew landing their rubber boats. The screenplay calls for an uninhabited island with a surrounding reef," she added quickly. "We are filming the close-ups on Providenciales. The usual thing. . . palm thatches, clothes discarded until we're on to nothing. Love scenes, sentries scanning the sky, scratchy records from Berlin. . . tension whilst the crew struggle with repairs. It's kishke, but the Germans will flock to the cinema in droves."

I was gasping for breath when we reached the final five. She stopped short of the final rise, as if collecting her thoughts. The lobby lights silhouetted her lovely figure as she refastened her scarf and looked about. I searched the shadows, vaguely conscious of faces staring from the overhanging balconies. I was totally unprepared for what happened next. . . although in retrospect, I realize she had no choice.

She was a step above me and I was eyeball with her filmy blouse when she cringed suddenly, as if I'd oozed from the depths of the sea. Her eyes blazed when I looked up, her lips drawn. My jaw sagged. She brought a hand from behind her and staggered me with a blow that sent me to my knees.

"You insufferable clod!" she shrieked. "Why do you insist on following me? I told you to leave me alone!"

She turned abruptly and flounced the remaining stairs while I nursed my chin. The words she cast behind were not very nice . . . a mixed bag of Austrian expletives and Yiddish vilification that would have a rabbi off the wall. Muffled cheers came from the balconies as she disappeared into her room. I nodded politely and played my cue . . . the hippie with the cast off shoes, the hawk-nosed drunk who instigated a brawl and made indecent proposals to the Austrian Jewess. Word would pass as she knew it would. They'd watched while we climbed the hill.

Green Eyes nodded as I sulked through the lobby, brightened when I winked.

"Yinna caught one, hey? Now, you're not to worry about the lady, mon. She did right, she not to mingle. . . ya understand? That Swiss fella knock her ass if he find who she is."

"What do you mean?"

"She workin' from outside, mon. Now, I'm tellin' you this 'cause we got mutual friend comin' from Nassau, mon." He opened a drawer and pointed to an enormous Colt 45.

"We's holdin' watch. Best get some sleep, that niggah ain't gonna bother you tonight."

It was twelve when I keyed my door. I was exhausted. Been a long day since I'd lifted off from San Juan. I doused the lights, turned up the fan, lowered the shutters and stretched out on the bed. My thoughts were with Elisabeth and the imbroglio I'd stumbled onto when I'd descended from the storm. My mind churned the sequence of the day as I tossed about in fitful sleep. The fan was whispering softly above me when I became aware of a gentle tapping at my door. I stumbled to my feet and peered through the chainlock, the desk chair close at hand.

She was standing there in half light, wrapped in a towel, barefooted, legs bare to the thighs. Her hair hung damply on her shoulders and the fresh scent of lavender swirled about her. Eyes moist and lips trembling, she let me gather her into my arms. We closed the door on the world.

The violence of that tormented day overcame us and heightened our sensitivity, our naked bodies melted together. A mutual sense of frustration and loneliness invaded from the outside world. It could have been any one of a hundred things, but the reasons were lost to us when we sank to the bed. Our mouths hot and seeking, clinging to one another and making love as if we'd waited a thousand years for this very moment.

I stroked every inch of her splendid body until she moaned with pleasure and guided my fingers to the place she wanted them to be; her back arched, her hands grasped my thighs and drew me deep inside her. Our mouths met; we rode the razor edge of an orgasmic trip until we could stand it no longer. She tensed and cried out. . . our orgasm was volcanic.

When the throbbing ceased she cried a little, clinging to me for long minutes while her body relaxed and her toes uncurled. I eased my weight to my elbows and held her as if she were the most important being in my life. And when she fell asleep, I brushed a lock of hair from her forehead and looked down upon her, realizing how beautiful, how naturally lovely and complete she was.

My mind turned to many things that night before I fell asleep. When my eyes became heavy, I was still holding her, remembering lines from a long, old ballad. . . *Just to keep her from the foggy dew.*

Two

LONG JOHN SILVER WAS pulling himself up the side of the Hispanola with a knife in his teeth when gunfire erupted and his parrot flew away. I jolted awake and rolled from bed. A truck backfired, drawing a column of dust from the hill as it sped east on the island's corduroy. I located my watch on the nightstand; six-thirty. A red hibiscus slumbered on Elisabeth's pillow. She'd slipped away while I fended off John Silver in the lee of Treasure Island.

I watched dispiritedly from the door as the convoy of movie vans hurried east and disappeared into a cloud of spiraling dust. The tropical depression, loitering ominously on the horizon, would reduce the sun to blackness when the stratospheric easterlies came about. A land crab rustled the bush below me, reminding me that God blesses his creatures with an instinct to seek higher ground.

I shaved and showered with mixed emotions. She'd be safe if she stayed with the group and sheltered at the Inn, but tempers were flaring aboard the yacht. God help her if they found her out. If I lingered, I'd compound their suspicions. I had no choice but to carry on.

Chug had until noon to do what he had to do, then I would have to report the massacre to the CID in Nassau. I'd need a glib tongue to explain the 20-hour delay. Paul, inherently suspicious, would presume a drug caper and the offbeat Goose was a likely candidate to raise his eyes.

Scanning the yacht while I packed my gear, I spotted exhaust fumes coming from the double stacks, heard the throb of her engines. Wolfgang was loitering by the ladderway with his flight case in hand. They'd be underway when they dropped him off and davited the launch. I gave thought to the *Walrus* while I penciled a hurried note. Bower's presence was partially explained if he'd been consigned to keep an eye on the yacht. But where had he been when I sighted the *Leopard*, or was he on to something else as yet unexplained?

Howard's pickup was dusting the drive when I closed the door behind me. I hurried along to Elisabeth's room with an eye to her lowered bathroom window, figuring I could excise the screen. I stopped short when I passed her door; an inch of yellow pencil protruded from the stop. She'd deliberately left it ajar! I glanced down the open corridor, and, seeing no one, stepped inside.

She was minutes gone. The bathroom mirror, steamed from her shower, a damp towel clinging on the rack. The bedroom had been tidied, her clothes neatly hangered. I looked about. Why had she provoked an intrusion? Then I spotted her passport next to a briefcase on the chairside table. A note, folded inside, was intended for me.

I scanned it briefly and tucked it in my pocket. It was a sweet note, a personal note, "Believe in me, whatever." She included a double set of telephone numbers, but no address. Her hair was shorter when the passport picture was taken, but her smile was the same. She was 28 and her surname was von Wagner. She was born in Vienna, the Austrian passport informed me. . . occupation, actress. All that she seemed. I returned it to the table and placed my message beneath it. She was well traveled, having recently been to London. Her Bahamian entry on the second of July was quickly followed, the same afternoon, by passage through Providenciales immigration.

Howard was leaning on the horn. While I lingered, savoring her warmth and the scent of her perfume, I noticed something out of context, something she'd overlooked when she hurried to her van. The bedspread had been smoothed and pillows thumped but the fold toward the balcony was caught beneath the mattress. It was an insignificant thing, but it niggled my curiosity. Impulsively I stepped over and lifted the edge of the mattress, revealing a pocket-sized, blue steel automatic. My attention focused immediately on a dark blue passport and a manila envelope that lay beside it.

The passport was British and had been issued to Elisabeth Majlath on the 16th of May. Her vital statistics were the same, but the picture vas recent. This time her birthplace was listed as Scarsborough, England. She had a permanent visa to the United States. Did the departure stamp from Heathrow correspond with her Austrian passport?

With heightened curiosity, I undid the manila envelope. It contained a ribbon-banded collection of old letters, a photograph, and a ring knotted with a handkerchief The ring was a collection piece—an immense emerald ring clasped with double eagles—but it was the dog-eared photograph that riveted my attention.

A young man wearing a naval officer's uniform, attired with dress sword, was standing by a straight backed chair, a visored cap in hand. A young girl wearing a wedding gown and jeweled tiara sat beside him. Her face was familiar; she was tall and slender, but her eyes were brown and the resemblance ended there. The back side was scriptured in long hand, *Wien, 10 August 1932.* I flipped it over and studied the man. He had dark brown hair, brush cut Prussian style and closely shaven along the sides. His eyes were humorless, he had a thin line for lips. . . he wore a sabre scar across his left cheek. *Klaus!*

Howard blared his horn and raised my attention to the morning at hand. Numbly I returned the memorabilia to the envelope and redid the fastener. . . Was the son of a bitch her father? I shook my head, denying the possibility, but the young girl was obviously her mother from another day in time. I replaced the items and smoothed the spread, realizing by the damp spot on the floor that she'd knelt beside it when she was fresh from the shower.

Her dual identity? The visa had been expeditiously granted when the passport was issued in the UK.

I squared accounts with the morning clerk and cleared the swinging door. Howard, standing beside his truck, was frowning, but not at his watch. He nodded silently, climbed into the cab and reached over to unlatch the door. As I swung in beside him, he keyed the engine and headed the lane to the corduroy. Something was on his mind.

The morning had blossomed hot and humid and his ebony face was streaked with sweat. Even with the window rolled down, there was little breeze. The dust was hanging behind us, the sky hazed and heavy. When we turned onto the graveled artery, he pointed to the ominous roll on the horizon and shook his head.

"Is that what's bugging you?" I asked.

"No, man! Least not 'til she reach. Miami weather say she stationary this morning. Can't make up her mind which way to go. Ain't worrying about that just yet." He pointed to an adjacent hill. "That's my new house I'm buildin'. Family be all right. Figured I'd fly the Navaho to Florida if the wind fetch thirty knot." He fingered the brush on his upper lip.

"Keith, you smartin' for trouble? See'd that Goose been set in the water recent. . . you flyin' hash?" He turned and eyed me like a father. I smiled and shook my head, appreciating his concern. We'd been friends since I checked him out on twin engines at Fort Lauderdale International.

"I asked you a question, man. Don't give me no innocence!"

"No way! Narcotics impounded her in Aquadilla. I'm taking her into Lauderdale for a refit and point."

He nodded, still apprehensive.

"You ain't answered what I said. How come you chance to set down on the sea? How come the windscreen all caked like that?" I squirmed in my seat. I wasn't ready to level with him yet.

"I saw a flat stretch and glided her in to test the hull. Doesn't leak," I added weakly.

He fingered his shirt pocket and grimaced. He had something on his mind, but we were still words apart.

"Was just wonderin', didn't think you'd break the law. Man, they're running drugs through here sumthin' fierce these days. See them fuelin' up and takin' off from those dirt strips here and thereabout. They's heavy coming up from Jamaica, short for gas. An mos' every night I hear the big ones coming in from Colombia. Usin' the strip at East Caicos when the law's not around, which is most of the time. 'Cept for them DEA fellas from Miami . . They got no swat with the locals."

"You're drifting, man! Got something on your mind. What about last night? Did you have a chance to work the mags?"

"Yea, man. Wolfgang be havin' a fit when he runs up that Widgeon. Ran some foil around the rotors like you said. Didn't mind doin' what you asked, seein' he short with us locals. Ain't going to hurt nothin', is it, Keith?"

I shook my head. "He'll get a reading on his tachometer that will have him off the wall. It'll take him a couple of hours to figure it out and I appreciate what you did. There's a reason for this," I added.

"Figured as much, but how come you ain't tellin' Howard?"

"Something terrible happened off Turks yesterday afternoon, fella! Maybe Wolfgang had a part in it, maybe not, but someone out there needs a breather and I can't chance the *Juanita* if Wolfgang's doing the recon. Keep it to yourself, OK?" He swiveled his head and eyed me from across the cab.

"You're doin' some serious talking, man! Folks been wonderin' why that big yacht been fussin' round. Fellow who got *Walrus* axed me to keep tab when I'm flyin' in and out. Not to let on, only to watch with the glasses. See'd them cruising the shoals south of Plana Cay day before last. They was towin' somethin' behind. . . told him so, but he seem to know. I figured it got to do with the movie they're makin', about some old submarine supposed to gone down in the forties. Now then, you want to hear what else Howard got to say?" He looked up to scan the sky. Howard possessed a mischievous habit; he'd hold the clincher until last.

"Out with it! We're out of turnpike!"

"Well, seein' you axed. Gave this no particular mind until I came onto somethin' last night. Somethin' definitely not right. Good thing you called Howard, man."

He skirted a group of ramshackle stores and slowed for the airport roundabout while I was pondering what he meant. We pulled in opposite his parked Navaho and ground to a stop. I unlatched my door, but he reached over and grabbed my arm. Removing a thin black cylinder from his shirt pocket, he dangled it by a wire attached to its end.

"Put your eyes to this," he said. Then he handed it to me by the wire as if loathe to touch the lethal thing.

It resembled an old fashioned fountain pen. Heavy for its size; a transistorized timer with a cadium energizer was inserted in its end. The minute hand set to zero, the hour hand to one.

"It's a goddamned bomb!" I gasped. Howard nodded grimly.

"Figured it were. That's why I been axin' questions, Keith. Someone want you dead!"

"Where did you find it?"

"Come offen' that pretty Goose out there! Was wired to the starter on the starboard engine."

"Good God!"

"Amen! See'd it was set for an hour after the engine commence turnin'. Ain't no doubt it activated by the electrical system."

I investigated the cylinder with my fingers. The outer casing was plastic, so it would pass an airport screening. . . a hijacker's delight, an assassin's toy. A set screw on the timer suggested it could be independently activated.

"How did you find it?" I questioned numbly. Howard settled in his seat, fingered his moustache. I unscrewed the timer and stuffed the parts in my overnighter.

"Was black outside, and I was needin' the torch when I was workin' the Widgeon," he said. "Didn't take long. I knows them Continental engines," he added. "When I finish, I decide to check the Goose. . . seein' I'm tampering with his', I'm thinkin' maybe he have sumthin' similar in mind." He paused and shook his head. "Now, the door was locked, I see'd he ain't been inside, and the engines was too high to reach. Then I pass the light to the ground and I sees ladder tracks 'neath the starboard nacelle. Knows that ain't right, went and got my own ladder, remembering to smooth out where it been. When I open up the cowling, I see'd that thing wired to the starter—knows that ain't needed!"

"Son of a bitch!" Howard shrugged his shoulders. "You holdin' back, Keith, but if that your mind, I reckon you got reason! Now, best you fuel up and get off if you headin' up to Nassau. Wolfgang usually come by at eight."

He stood by while the fuel truck topped off the Goose. We borrowed the driver's ladder and checked the engines to make certain I hadn't been dealt a wild card. Talked a while more when customs signed my outgoing papers and disappeared in the bar.

"The leadin' lady took sick, sudden-like," Howard commented aside. "The Swiss fella chartered me into Nassau to catch the Lufthansa flight. Man, she was somethin' else. Had to stop in Georgetown and help her to the johnnie.

"She was takin' pills to get herself right, said something about the water. I hustled her through immigration when we landed at Windsor. She caught the flight to Frankfurt.

"Elisabeth came on the same DC-10. She was waitin', all cool like, nice as could be. Rode my right seat all the way down . . . axed all kinds of questions, carried her own map. She not like the others, Keith. Come to know her . . . seein' lipstick on your ear?"

The island taxi arrived in a hail of gravel before I could answer. Howard nudged my arm. "That Wolfgang, Keith! Come early like he knows you're intendin' to split with the Goose. Won't do to be seen with Howard," he added under breath. "See you in Nassau, man . . . let you know what happen when the shit hit the fan!" And with that he ambled nonchalantly to his Navaho. I waited for a moment in the shadow of the customs building, collected my gear and re-boarded the Goose.

The sun was seeking its eight o'clock slant, the breeze indecisive, when I lofted the amphibian from the strip. I had a glimpse of Howard's red shorts, of Wolfgang's yellow shirt when the Goose broad-winged the morning calm and I collected her wheels underbelly. Leveling off at 1500, I turned to the northwest as if setting course for Nassau, until we had 30 miles behind us. Then I gigged the port rudder, banked sharply to the west, and headed directly for a small atoll called North-West Cay—better known as Hogsty Cay by the folks in Providenciales.

Turks and Caicos remained a British Crown Colony after the Bahamas became self-governing and independent in 1973. Their boundary line lay midway through the Caicos Passage, about ten miles north of Providenciales. When I wheeled the Grumman into the west, I was immediately over Bahamian waters and within their territorial jurisdiction.

It looks much the same from above. The shallow banks and intermittent low, gray-green islands stretch a long, 1500 mile arc from the eastern reaches of Hispaniola to the edge of the Gulfstream off Palm Beach. There's a sameness, but it is forever eye catching. The aqua waters over the shoals are startlingly clear, shading turquoise to deep blue as they plunge eastward into the two mile deep Atlantic, or into one of the many tongues of the ocean.

I could almost see beyond the horizon. The sea was flat and expressionless, waiting a breath from the southeasternly trades. The summer buildups over Mayaguana and Acklins were beginning to form and shower, but to the west there wasn't a cloud in the sky. . . the stereotypical calm before the storm.

Forty minutes passed, at a heading of 200 degrees, when a white, donut-shaped atoll rose from the depths of the ocean. I watched it grow until it became a two-mile circle of fuming reefs centering an inner lagoon of placid aqua. A rusting Greek freighter lay with its innards flowing white water on the easterly reefs. A spit of sand and dune rock rose a few feet above the water reach; a crescent stone tower topped the rise. A lighthouse from colonial times was an indication that man had once been present. I eased back the throttles and reached for my binoculars to focus a point beyond. A surge of relief coursed my spine; the *Sea Leopard* lay peacefully at anchor in the lee of the inlet. *The kid had made it!*

A shallow turn began my circle of the atoll, from which the Goose's profile would come to his view. I blipped the engines twice to signal. The schooner came up as I turned to the south, the sails furled and booms secured in their scissor gallows. The bodies were gone from the deck alongside the wheelhouse. A tarpaulin lashed from rail-to-rail at the bow presumably covered them. The deck had been hosed. A drift of smoke came from the engine's exhaust as the caterpillar idled in neutral gear. The schooner was on double anchor a hundred yards from shore, but there was no indication that Chug was aboard.

I steepened the turn to make another run to the north. The saucer-like lagoon came up and passed beneath us. The sandy-bottomed lagoon was approximately a quarter mile in diameter, no more than 40 feet deep at its center. A shallow inlet curved in from the sea between the outlying reefs and the southernmost tip of the tiny cay. A tan colored launch was moored to a hank of bush nearest the inlet. A faint path led from an ancient rain catch to an over-grown foundation midway along the narrow strip of land, then continued amongst the dune rock toward the tower. I banked sharply and looked down.

The catch was tented with a mottled brown camouflage netting. Like the launch, it blended with the terrain and would have been impossible to detect from above, but it wasn't the suddenness of the unveiling that drew my eyes. A fresh grave had been dug nearby in the sand. A black plastic-wrapped shape lay at rest on the bottom of the shallow pit. Chug was kneeling by the open grave, his head in his arms, his back red from long hours in the sun. He was exhausted, barely able to raise his hand to acknowledge the Goose when I thundered by. I wobbled the wings and climbed into the northwest. It was a private matter; my presence undesired.

I leveled off at 4500 feet to scan the horizon behind me. A half hour brought the northwestern tip of Crooked Island to bear, the Crooked Island Passage and endless blue Atlantic. A flashing light marked the passage by night. If Chug raised anchor within the hour, nightfall would have the schooner on the lee side of the island, with the light to guide his helm.

What tack would Wolfgang's reasoning take when he overcame his erratic tachometers? He would most likely fly east to reconnoiter the area where the *Sea Leopard* was intercepted. I pondered the bastard's frustration, envisioning the consternation aboard the *Juanita*, when he called in to report the schooner's absence. As an ex-Luftwaffe type, he'd probably grid the waters between Caicos and Mayaguana, calculate her drift, and methodically probe an arc to the north. . . until he realized the *Leopard* had raised power and slipped away during the night.

Hogsty Cay lay 120 miles northwest of Providenciales. It was doubtful they'd come upon it if they widened the arc to include Acklins and Crooked Island; a time-consuming process. I was counting on the precious hours off the kid's back. He'd have another 80 miles behind him by sunset, but there was an additional factor to consider—the Mira Por Vos Shoals, the coral-studded shallows reaching for his keel.

A 30-mile shoal, it extended westward from Acklins Island. He'd be all right if he held a northerly course until he pointed the flashing light. If he fell asleep or if he forgot to engage the autopilot and grounded, he'd had it. Sunrise would find him hopelessly marooned miles from the coast. Wolfgang would come onto him sooner or later, and the fast moving yacht would find an easy target!

As I passed over the blighted waters, I shuddered. The *Sea Leopard* was heavy and deep of keel; there were coral heads and shoulder-depth clumps of greenish weed, a navigable five-mile passage, then an expanse of gleaming sand rising quickly to shoreline the western coast of Crooked Island. Pittstown came to view beneath the Goose's float, a peaceful hamlet of thatched cottages in a fishing village of little note. . . identified on the chart for the blinking light. A lonely road wound to the north, turned, meandered south along the Atlantic and terminated a few miles beyond the airstrip at Colonel Hill. I focused my binoculars in passing, studying the unkempt strip and rise of pine to the north. Vehicular traffic was almost non-existent. The island was sparsely populated by a few hundred subsistence farmers and fishermen at the most. Closely knit, close-mouthed and deeply religious, the islanders nevertheless were openhearted to a stranger. . . or to a friend of a friend.

I eased down to 2500 feet as we crossed the Crooked Island Passage. The fast-moving gateway for ancient galleons seeking egress to the mid-Atlantic had a troublesome current to navigate in the dead of night. The spiny ridges of Long Island threaded the Goose's starboard wing. As we continued our northwesterly course, Great Exuma rose before us, then passed beneath our keel. The Exuma Cays stretched the horizon like an emerald necklace. It was strung with white running reefs that bordered the deep blue Exuma Sound.

The sky turned brassy as we penetrated the opposing pressure systems lying to the north and south. A glaze of orange shimmered the flats extending west from the tongue of the sea. The open window vented the humidity and cooled my arm as the long minutes passed. The Pratt-Whitneys purred contentedly as they lapped my dwindling fuel. The radios crackled and came to life; Nassau acknowledged an incoming flight from Congo Town, Andros's southern reach.

The old bird stretched her feathers and gave us extra knots with the lightened load. She was eager to lower her wheels and display her plumage at Windsor Field.

As the four-hour flight came to a close, my thoughts returned to Elisabeth. . . her enigmatic presence in Providenciales, the traumatic evening and the beautiful night we had shared. I fingered the note from my pocket and studied the pencilled telephone numbers. The first was the United Kingdom, apparently intended for the future, but the second had seemingly been added as an afterthought. The seven-digit number was vaguely familiar; possibly the British High Commissioner's? Had she had a last minute premonition when she knelt by the bedside? Had she scrawled the numbers before she hurried to the van? Was it a desperate plea for help?

My thoughts veered to the passport I'd discovered beneath her mattress, to her dual identity and the emerald ring she'd worn until recently. The photograph? Of course! The statuesque bride standing by Klaus's side . . . *had she not been wearing the identical ring?*

My attention returned to the panel when the Goose ruffled her wings. We'd entered a patch of cloud and the omini had centered Nassau's VOR. Normans Cay came off our wing a moment later and the low-lying profile of New Providence lay on the horizon. I called in to traffic control as we sped swiftly over the 60 mile shallows. . . the ring! Klaus would recognise it immediately, but he obviously was unaware of Elisabeth's identity!

"Grumann Foxtrot one-nine-six-eight. Point of departure, please!" I hedged. There were other ears and the DEA would suspect an unlikely amphibian.

"Foxtrot eight, departed Provo at 1300 GMT."

"Are you on a flight plan?"

"Negative. The phones were out." There was a pause. I tensed. Kurt would monitor ATC if they checked with Miami.

"Roger, Foxtrot eight. Call into the tower when you're 20 miles out." I exhaled. He'd bought the abbreviation. Fortunately, my incoming papers had been stamped by Turks & Caicos Immigration.

The Bacardi distillery was in sight when the tower maneuvered us behind an incoming Delta 1011. We made a straight-in approach to runway 32, where the Goose landed with a 'Grumph' and I turned her to the taxiway centering the general aviation ramp. Old Bill met us midst a straggly line of twins and singles and pointed to a vacant pair of chocks. I clicked-off with ground control and swiveled to park the ungainly thing. Customs came immediately to grouse her interior when I killed the engines and went backside to lever the door.

Time-worn, ebony-skinned, old Bill was long in body and thin as a willow. He'd been around for long before I could remember. . . since Pan Am opened Oakes Field to Miami, long before Windsor Field became the international terminal. He was a local institution; close-mouthed, a visored cap fixed firmly to his head, a luggage cart invariably at hand; a source of information to those who knew him well.

"Thought that might be you, Cap'n Keith," he allowed, when the Customs officer was satisfied and indicated I was to follow him to Immigration. "Howard say you expected. You fly dat ting from San Juan?"

". . . Howard said I was expected?" He two-fingered his cap and smiled.

"Came by an hour back. He gas up an gone. Had package for the High Commissioner," he said. "Ain't spose to tell no one but you." I stumbled over a chock, picked myself up. The son of a bitch had passed me in the air!

"Did he have anything else to say?"

"No suh, Cap'n Keith. . . 'cept tell you package came while some fella' fussin' wid a Widgeon. You goin' keep that old Goose, maybe lease for charter?"

Shaking my head, I told him I was flying her to Fort Lauderdale for an annual inspection. I plied him with a 20 when we approached the Immigration office alongside the hangar. Bill was long in the tooth, but he was no fool and knew the ramp. I asked him to keep a wary eye on the old bird. (Kurt had the Goose's number and an endless cache of green. He would be hot for my ass when he verified I'd landed with my wings intact.)

The Immigration officer pointed to his phone when I inquired if I might use it. Bahamians are invariably polite and obliging. He casually inspected the roll of plans I carried while I dialed the seven-digit number. When the High Commissioner's office answered, I asked if he was in. The answer was brusque; "The commissioner's in conference. Would you care to call after lunch?" I gave it up for the moment and leafed the directory.

A sweet voice replied when I raised the CID (Criminal Investigation Department). Paul Johnson was out, but would return at two-thirty. I asked for an appointment, said it was important... urgent, in fact. She said to come along. "He's in a bit of temper, Mr. Slater, but he'll be delighted to see you when he's free." I'd been the object of Paul's "delight" in the past, unfortunately, and knowing his temper, I braced myself for the inevitable when he heard what I had to say!

Frustrated by the delays, hot and hungry... wanting a refreshing swim... I thanked immigration for the use of their phone, collected my overnighter, and stepped outside to search for my car.

A blast of stagnant heat greeted me when I located and unlocked my aged Ford. I lowered the windows to give her a breath of air, cleansed the windshield with my sweat-ridden shirt, checked the mat for keys to my house. A plastic pen drooped from the console like a wilted watch in a Dali painting. The wheel was hot to my hands when I keyed the ignition, the air conditioner in silent

repose. Dusty and decrepit from a week in the elements, she nevertheless was mechanically sound. . . rumbled contentedly when I
turned on to JFK and pointed to Love Beach.

There's a pronounced exhilaration when the ocean is viewed
through the high reaching palms. . . the deepest blue one can imag-
ine, shades of turquoise closer in, then the sparkling aqua of shallow waters framed by the cascading surf on the outer reefs.
Groupers flit amongst the coral heads and an occasional hammerhead shark glides in hot pursuit of a hapless ray. All of this, together with a cooling breeze from the north, provided the uplift I needed when I coasted the lane to my cottage by the sea.

Well, it wasn't a cottage in the true sense of the word, more a
cluster of single-storied cyprus buildings quartering a central patio
that fronted a private beach. An entrance loggia leading to the patio
separated the two units facing the driveway. An archway offering a
view of the sea connected the units facing the beach. The kitchen,
pantry and dining room were contained in one, the second housed
a paneled living room and the master bedroom, which I claimed for
myself. The two back cottages provided a brace of guest rooms and
accommodation for my house-man, Frank. All of this I'd built from
pocket over the years.

Frank was a legacy, in a sense. . . a cast-off from Lyford Cay
when he admitted his years. Sixtyish, pensioned, a creature of habit
with nowhere to turn, he applied at my door one day, knowing I
was a friend of the late Sir Harold.

Taciturn and friendly, bossy on occasion, he had a home and
wife in town, multiple grandchildren he blessed with funds for their
schooling, but he apparently preferred the peacefulness of the cottage.
He joined his wife on weekends and they sang together at church. A
splendid cook. . . his peppercorn grouper and apple crumble made a
double whammy when I invited guests for dinner. And always, it

seemed, he wore an immaculate white shirt and black bow tie.

Frank's vintage Pontiac was gone when I braked the lane alongside the patio. My black Labrador, Happy, was onto me before I could unlock the gate. A ferocious animal at first appearance, his tail waxed friendly. He dropped a coconut at my feet, growled when I bent to retrieve it. . . lunged at my wrist, then guided me peacefully to the archway leading to the beach. Wagging when I cast the nut to the sea, he plunged into the frothing surf. All together, it was a game we played. After he retrieved his collection of coconuts, he guarded the house.

I stripped down, tossed my clothes in the washer and enjoyed a long swim with the dog at my heels. Upon returning to the pantry I savaged the frig and dialed the office in Fort Lauderdale, scanned Frank's notes while I downed a cold beer. The receptionist generalized business at hand, checked my appointments, reminding me of a client meeting at Boca Raton.

"Tomorrow at ten," she said. "Mr. O'Brien (my partner) left this morning for New York, but Marie arranged a conference call and he said he'd stand by." Next she leafed through my telephone calls, indicating Marie had followed through during my absence. . . aside for a late coming call from Boston.

"Caller said it was important she speak to you directly," the receptionist commented. "Declined to give her name, said it wasn't business related," she added, acidly. "We referred your Nassau numbers, Keith. Said you were due from San Juan and would call her back." I checked Frank's notes when we signed off.

On the margin he'd scribbled a 617 area number—"9:30 PM lady call from Boston." Crossing this out with a pen, he added: "call this morning 10: 05. Say she come on Delta. Very important. Nice voice. Say she have our address." Friend of a friend, I assumed. We'd wait and see.

I set up a call to Crooked Island with the Nassau operator. The Out Island stations are dialable, but the remote hamlets are inter-connected by a single strand of wire—necessitating an old fash-ioned "ring down" to summon the wanted party to a phone. Villagers along the line would pick up, of course, listening and exchanging gossip until the party was located.

Five minutes passed while I paced the length of the pantry line, then the operator from Crooked Island came on midst the sounds of a pounding generator. "Nottage somewhere in the field," he said. "But wifey say he due home for lunch. . . axed who's callin'?" I gave him my name. "That you, Keithy?" a third party shouted. "Ain't see'd you since Cat Island, mon!"

Nassau silenced the line. Said she'd set up an appointment with Nottage between one thirty and two. I okayed that, said I'd hang in.

Nottage was an old friend from the past, close and trustworthy. We'd endured the fracas at Cat Island together and I'd seen to his retirement means when all was done. Wealthy in terms of farm lands, he'd returned to Crooked Island, built a comfortable house on a cliff overlooking the sea. A pillar of the community, he had friends the length of the island. . . and I needed help to bring the kid to safety when he'd accomplished what he had to do with the *Leopard* and her ghostly crew.

I'd dressed for town and fed the dog when the operator called back. She had Nottage on the line. I explained the circumstances in part, asked if he'd establish a watch for a jib sail approaching the Crooked Island passage. "She'll come late at night. . . no lights, but her masts are long if there's glow from the moon. You're not to board her," I warned. "She's a funeral ship! There's a boy who will come ashore . . . and he'll need your help." There was audible inter-est along the line when I indicated there'd be dollars in the offing. . . a chorus of 'amens' when I said it was all for a good cause.

Hopefully, we'd be in touch in the morning.

The Criminal Investigation Department is located a block up the hill from Shirley Street. It is a two-minute drive under normal conditions, but a bevy of one-horse carriages were pacing the traffic and it was two-forty before I parked the Ford in a visitor's slot outside the garrison-like building

My facade covered a cauldron of emotions when I climbed the stairs to the second floor and knocked on the door to Paul's outer office. He was a punctilious man. My appointment was tentative, but I'd requested his time and I'd been skewered by his smouldering eyes before—uncompromising, exacting, intransigent. I was in something of a sweat.

A secretary ushered me in and offered coffee; the commissioner was expected momentarily. He'd left word I was to wait. I suffered the next half hour making small talk and fiddling with my cup. Birds chirped happily among the branches of an aged poinciana outside the open window while a pair of chuckling taxi drivers slammed dominoes on the lower steps.

When I heard the door open and close in Paul's private office, I realized he'd entered from the corridor. His secretary allowed a moment to pass, then thumbed the intercom. His answer was brusque. She raised an eyebrow and shrugged, pointing to the door of his inner sanctum.

"Commissioner Johnson will see you now," she said. "He's in a frightful mood, Mr. Slater, but you know how he can be."

Forewarned, I tapped the door lightly, entered Paul's cubicle and was greeted with silence. He was slouched at his desk examining a file of dossiers and handwritten notes. . . a recent dispatch, I assumed, noticing the cover bore the British High Commissioner's seal. Paul removed a section without looking up, but I was aware of an eye following mine when I observed the file marked "Confidential. . . Providenciales"!

Paul was a smallish man of medium complexion, physically trim, his close cropped hair flecked with grey. Immaculately dressed in a tan tropical suit, he wore a thin black tie, a golden ring on his wedding finger, a pair of Masonic cufflinks fastened to his sleeves. Close to retirement, he lived by the rules and was known in the Bahamas as an honest cop. . . to his adversaries as "one tough nut." His seeking eyes belied any nonsense, but despite his demeanor he was a logical man. I hoped he'd evidence compassion when I addressed the bottom line.

"Now then, Keith, what's your problem?" he snapped, without looking up. I walked to the window; I knew the routine. Paul tapped his desk top and pointed to an empty chair. I held fast. The chair was placed to his advantage. . . I'd have to shout. He glanced at his watch, set the file aside. An eye came up, he smiled, motioned me to bring the chair to his desk, leaned back clasping his fingers.

"Out with it, boy! You seem a bit peaked. Did you have a comfy night in Providenciales?" I gripped my chair. He checked my arrival, knew where I'd been. Had Green Eyes bent his ear, the DEA? I intended to find out.

"First things first, Paul! How's for an old schooner coming up Turks-Caicos?"

Paul was startled. He snapped forward in his chair, swept the files aside, hammered the intercom. When he'd instructed the secretary to hold his calls, he ransacked the desk for a fresh cassette, gave it up for a pencil and pad.

Regaining his composure, he had the audacity to ask if I'd care for coffee, marked time with his pencil until the secretary responded with a tray. Then, lowering his voice as if the walls had ears, he questioned me at length.

"Let's have it from the beginning, Keithy. Would you describe the schooner's profile. . . was she under power or rigged for sail? Do you remember her coordinates? The time of day, the nearest landfall, was she in international waters or entering the Bahamas?" I answered his questions, in part, holding the kicker until I could determine where his interest lay.

"Gaff rigged, a 'woody' Nova Scotia type with deck houses and a cargo hatch mid-ship. One classic lady, Paul. . . ninety-odd-footer. I was drawn to her immediately when I came up from San Juan. She lay east of Grand Turk on a northwesterly heading." Paul made rapid notes, seemingly pleased with the schooner's description.

"Yesterday, hey? Did you make note of the time? Was she bent with sail or proceeding under power?"

"Fifteen hundred, possibly later. The sun was on a slant when I descended from the overcast, the sea dead calm although there was a squall approaching from the south. Her sails were partly lowered," I added cautiously. "Jenny sail at loose ends as if they intended to come about under power."

"East of Grand Turk at 1500, becalmed you say? Did you observe the vessel's name, gauge her nearest landfall?"

"*Sea Leopard*, Paul. I buzzed her name plate the second time around. She had a skiff davited aft, if that tallies her description. Is she subject to a search. . . been sighted since?"

"Rightly!" he chortled. "We've waited the *Leopard* since she departed Barranquilla, Keithy boy! Tracked her by satellite for the past two weeks, but unfortunately the trough interfered with the Coast Guard's surveillance and we lost her mid-way in the Mona Passage." Paul turned in his chair, pointed to the chart on the wall behind him.

"Now then, if she fetched breeze from a squall, she'd make four or five knots, seven under power." He produced a ruler from his drawer, calculated a 12-hour time elapse in nautical miles, extended a radii from Turks with the rule. "Which would have her westing Mayaguana in Bahamian waters before midnight. That conforms with her voyages in the past. It's her landfall that confounds us, damnit! Always at night between dusk and dawn," he added to himself. "In fact, the Coast Guard dispatched a Falcon to investigate this morning, Keithy, but until you came to my office, we hadn't a clue."

I exhaled a sigh of relief, scanned my watch, reckoned the *Leopard's* northerly time elapse from Hogsty Cay. If she were leeward of Crooked Island by nightfall, undetected, the kid was marginally safe!

Paul had noticed, however. I realized as much when he loosened a puzzled smile, peered into his file. . . a jaundiced eye came up!

"Fifteen hundred, possibly later, hey? And you say you buzzed her name the 'second time around?' Was there something amiss? Did you observe her later? I understand you landed at Provo after dark and departed at the crack of dawn!"

"Are you referring to the schooner or my social life?" I retorted. He slumped in his chair, raised his palm in resignation.

"I'm aware of your inherent curiosity, boy. You've identified the schooner and I thank you for that, but why do you come to me? What is your interest?"

His jaw dropped when I described the state of the schooner's sails, her trailing booms and gaffs at ends. . . all of which drew me to circle and examine the ship with my binoculars.

"She appeared abandoned, Paul! There was no one at her helm, no show of hands when I blipped my engine and circled close-by. Drifting northwest with the current in a flat dead calm, no exhaust from her diesel pipes, no indication of life when I buzzed her railing."

"Were there boats in the vicinity?" Paul interrupted, scribbling furiously with his pencil. "Might they have lightened her cargo, abandoned her off-shore?"

"Negative, Paul. She was heavy at the water line, the hatch battened down with the raft secured atop. There was a trailing wake in the distance, however. Wash from a large yacht heading directly to Providenciales! Does a Benetti ring a bell? Have you given thought to an interception, a coke deal gone sour?"

Paul eyed me curiously. "Not really, boy. The Benetti's chartered to a movie company, licensed to cruise Turks and the Bahamas. We inspected her thoroughly when they appeared for a permit. We're mystified by her comings or goings, but they berth at Provo before nightfall and we've little reason to think they're involved with drugs. Furthermore, Freddie doesn't deal with cocaine. He's much too clever for that, wary of the cartel."

"Freddie?"

"Masterminds his own thing, boy. Deals with cannabis by the ton! His market's north Georgia, the up-coast rednecks. The *Leopard's* his lode ship and they rendezvous somewhere in the Bahamas. Where, and how? We don't know! His method of transfer is a complete mystery and the DEA is off the wall!"

"Now then," he murmured, "I've answered your questions and assume you're prepared for mine! You say you buzzed the schooner's stern plate when you reckoned she was abandoned. So why didn't you notify authorities, or call the Coast Guard to assist with the search?"

I explained the status of the Goose's radios when I attempted to reach Turks—the storm afflicted communication bands when I tried Miami from the Inn.

"Green Eyes can attest to that. Have you talked to him since?" I added, assuming he was the source of Paul's information.

"Green Eyes?"

"Constable Seymour, Paul. Is he assigned to your desk?"

"No, lad. Seymour and Commander Bower are assigned to a Crown inquiry in the Turks and Caicos region, for reasons undisclosed. Although the commander does confide in our CID if he encounters information that appears to be drug related or undetermined. Such as your antics in Providenciales?"

"Mind if I ask a slanted question?" I countered, realizing I'd raised Bower's suspicions. Paul turned wearily in his chair, summoned his secretary to fax the Coast Guard with the information I'd given.

"Tell them the vessel appears to be abandoned, most likely drifting west of Mayaguana. Should they locate the schooner, please advise immediately!"

"Is that all, Mr. Johnson?"

Paul gave it thought. "Stress need of thorough search of wheelhouse for charts and navigational notes. There's a possibility we can determine their intended rendezvous provided they board the vessel before she holes and sinks."

"Charts?" I muttered, picturing the ransacked cabin and tumbled drawers. "The heavily creased chart beneath the helmsman's seat?" Paul turned to face me, aware of my slip of tongue.

"They'd hardly steer by dead reckoning, boy! Now then, your slanted question. . . should I answer obliquely or do you have something to add before we call it a day?"

"You've mentioned the Crown inquiry in Turks-Caicos, Paul, and I suspect it has to do with the Benetti. Why else would they assign a British commander and a ragtag trawler to watchdog the yacht unless they're on to the same damn thing?" I furthered my question, describing the Walrus's unlikely electronic gear, my standoff with Kurt, Seymour's covert help and the commander's fortunate appearance.

"Might there be a link with British Intelligence, like maybe the Swiss is from outer space?"

"Possibly, Keith, although I'd be last to know! Something's amiss in Providenciales. I've had reason to query Seymour, but have since been directed by the High Commissioner to confine our activities to the Bahamas. Strange you should ask," he added. "As of last week we've observed a British frigate cruising easterly off our archipelago. Only this morning I received an inquiry from commander Bower, requesting confidential information from Interpol." Paul paused for a moment, shrugged and pointed to the file on his desk.

"Needless to say, the information is to be relayed by Interpol to the High Commissioner," Paul added. "I find it interesting to note the message was delivered by courier, not by fax or the usual means. This indicates the commander's distrustful of communicating by telephone, me-thinks."

I analyzed what he said, ruling out the *Leopard's* interception by a drug caper gone sour. That would lay the massacre onto the Benetti once and for all. I was baffled, however, by Kurt's motive. What in God's name was he after? Why would they murder innocent kids, savage the wheelhouse and torture the crew? For a lousy chart? Had Chug stumbled onto something, unknowingly, in his checkered past? I gave heavy thought to that, rationalizing my sixth sense, realizing there was more than met the eye when I let the kid go. But how to handle it with Paul? Kurt would have Chug at knife point if he tossed him in the slammer. . . myself as well, when he learned I'd hacked it to Nassau with Goose intact!

"You're curiously silent," Paul observed. "Have you something in mind that caused you to stare at your watch?" I gave it up, dropped the other shoe, my shoulders hunched to fend the onslaught, realizing I'd drawn his patience to the extreme.

"You're not going to like this, Paul, so grab your chair and hear me out! It has to do with the *Leopard* and most likely the Benetti." Paul inserted a proper tape in his machine, punched the record.

"Out with it, boy. I suspected you were covering up!"

I described the scene aboard the schooner when I buzzed her starboard railing—the mangled bodies, blood seeping from her scuppers.

"The *Leopard* was shot to hell, Paul, riddled above her water line from bow to stern. She was a bloody mess, and I mean that literally. I counted a half dozen bodies, mostly kids, and there were more beneath the jenny sail. I haven't witnessed anything like it since Desert Storm!"

Paul leapt from his chair, casting it violently aside. His eyes were saucered white, pupils ablaze with fire, his expression a mixture of anger and disbelief.

"May god forgive you, boy! Why didn't you report this sooner? Have you given leave to your senses, lost your soul to the devil? Matilda! Phone the Commissioner at once! Tell him I have an urgent message and I'll not reason with high tea! Sit down," he thundered. "I'm not through with you yet!"

"Cool it, Paul. I called you as soon as I could, phoned the Commissioner from Immigration, but he was out for lunch." Paul wasn't deterred.

"You could have gone on to George Town—their phones are in order! So you chose to spend the night in Provo, instigated a fracas and rollicked until dawn with the Austrian actress. Is that your style, boy?"

"High Commissioner's on the line," Matilda interrupted from the intercom. Paul coddled his phone, indicated I was to mark time in the outer office.

I slunk through the door, envisioning myself in chains, stared haplessly from the window. A covey of birds chirped from the aged poinciana, oblivious to the whims of man.

The busy line continued red. . . conversation's long winded. . . while I checked my watch, furthering thought to the kid's landfall at Crooked Island. Had he taken to the raft? Was he safe in Nottage's hands?

"Commissioner Johnson can be like this," his secretary offered sympathetically, while she puzzled over the chattering fax machine. "But he has a heart of gold, Mr. Slater, don't you fret!"

Finally the line blinked off and Paul called on the intercom indicating we had a matter to discuss in private.

"I've been instructed to deliver your transcript to Her Majesty's Representative, the High Commissioner," he said, pointing to the revolving cassette. "Furthermore, I've been told to hold my investigation in abeyance, aside for our regional interest, should the *Leopard* be found in Bahamian waters. In which instance, I shall be obliged to hold you as material witness. And God help you when I determine your involvement!"

That said, he addressed my present status, requesting my immediate plans. I told him I had a client's meeting in Fort Lauderdale the next day; that the Goose was in need of an overhaul and I planned to leave early in the morning, returning around four in the afternoon. Paul made note, scanned his watch for the time of day.

"All right, Keith, you're free to go, but I insist you remain on the island overnight, and to anticipate a call from the High Commissioner. He intends to question you independently, depending on a call he's waiting from London at the moment. Now then, a word of caution, boy! You're to keep a close mouth in regards to this matter, confide in no one, aside from myself and the High Commissioner! Do you hear me rightly? " he added, extracting the cassette from his recorder.

Paul nodded to himself, sealed the cassette in an envelope, hammered the intercom, instructing his secretary to hand deliver the item to the High Commissioner.

"Demand a signed receipt," he bellowed, when she appeared in the doorway.

"We've received a fax from the American Coast Guard," she volunteered politely. "They've dispatched a Falcon per your advice. Do you wish to return your comments, Commissioner Johnson?"

"Tell them to search the area minutely!" he snapped. "It's not to do with the Crown's inquiry, not at the moment, that is!"

That said, having expressed his frustrations, Paul turned in his chair to stare reflectively at the chart, commenting to himself, but indicating I should stay put.

"We were so close! We've worked day and night with the Coast Guard and DEA, Customs, the Treasury Department. For once the agencies cooperated with one another, exchanged information with our CID and Defence Department. We felt we were on the verge of cracking an ingenious ring that's been operating from our waters with impunity."

"Freddie's employed electronic devices known only to your military," Paul continued, raising his eyes to determine my reaction. "Our radar station at Andros has twice been dampened by counter-pulsation during the night. A highly sophisticated mobile command station has been detected along your coastal highways, voicing coded instructions, jamming communication bands. Ex-military, like yourself, he moves about freely although he's been indicted twice and presently is under bail. Might you know him?" Paul added, examining his cuff links at length.

"Not until you mentioned him," I answered truthfully, detecting a hint of suspicion in Paul's razor sharp mind. He swiveled in his chair, noticed the phone was blinking unattended. Apparently the High Commissioner. They talked briefly, Paul answering respectfully.

Seemingly bewildered when he anchored the phone, he again turned to me. "I've been officially informed of a delegation arriving from London tomorrow noon," he said. "They will be accompanied by a British admiral and a contingent of Marines together with another party who is authorized to assume the Crown inquiry in the name of the Queen! They intend to question you at length," Paul added. "The High Commissioner insists you be on hand by four o'clock, at your house! Now then, I'm letting you go at my discretion. And if you have no further questions, I have other matters to attend."

I tried a parting shot. . . asked if the dossiers on his desk pertained in part to the Austrian actress, citing Elisabeth's surname from the passport I'd discovered from beneath her bed. Paul's eyes lighted up and he loosed his knowing smile.

"I prefer you direct your question to the Queen's delegation," he replied. "Better still to the portly gentleman who is presumably aware of your past, me-thinks."

It was after four when I broke free of the downtown traffic and made the turn at the British Colonial to head west on Bay Street. Fort Charlotte came up gray on the left, the HMg Island light on my right. A large liner was outbound in the channel.

The sun was in my eyes, but the ocean breeze was cool on my face. The next few miles were a strain. I threaded the horde of mopeds, rental cars and taxis, weaving past joggers and walkers, circled the roundabouts, then ground past the jam-up at Cable Beach. The hustle thinned after Delaporte, where I caught the breeze again. The shore road wound past the coves at Orange Hill. The

reefs were cresting, the tide was low as I entered my drive and coasted downhill to the cottage. My mind was centered on the reef and
a quick dip in the sea.

Frank hadn't returned from the market, but a car was parked in
the driveway alongside the portico gate. I levered the gear handle to
low and reached for the tire iron beside the seat, checking the turn-
around for a quick way out. The lab bounded from the steps and
pawed the Ford's window just as a young lady appeared with his
coconut. They'd obviously become friends.

She was dressed in city clothes and wore a broad-rimmed hat.
Twentyish and freckled, she had large brown eyes and dimpled a
sparkling set of square white teeth. . . lovely smile, outgoing and
natural, as pleasant as her face. I dropped the iron to the floor, grinning sheepishly to myself.

"You're Keith!" she said, thrusting her hand through the window.

"Yep! What a pleasant surprise."

"I'm Pamela Wynn, a friend of Maureen's. She told me I'd find
you here. I called from Boston yesterday. They said you should be
back by noon today and I caught the morning flight. I hope I'm not
presumptuous."

"Not at all! You're a friend of Maureen? How is she? I haven't
heard from her since she sent me a bunny card at Easter."

"She married that nice chap in London several months back.
We're so pleased."

"She's married?"

"Why yes! She met Clive last winter, didn't she tell you?"

My stomach tumbled. I reached to pat the dog "No, not exactly."

Pamela looked up. Her eyes dropped when she saw my expression. "I'm sorry. I don't know what to say," she murmured.

"It's okay. Maureen's a terrific girl. I had my chance but wasn't ready for it yet. You look warm in that hat," I added, changing the subject.

"I'd enjoy a swim," she said. "It would be nice if you'd join me. Would you fetch my suitcase from the car? I intend to stay the night."

"Yes, certainly!" Her eyes warmed, she reached up and touched a warning finger to my lips.

"In the guest room. Maureen said I should insist!"

"She would do that to me?" Pamela nodded and led me to her rental. I unloaded her bag from the boot—a canvas hold-all type, somewhat battered. A snorkle pipe protruded from its middle. "I'm a marine biologist," she said. "I'm doing a research paper at Wood's Hole. I was, until a serious matter came up and I chanced your being here. I brought my mask and flippers along at the last moment, but that isn't the reason for my visit."

"I've been wondering."

"I would think so. May we talk about it later, or do you have plans for the evening?" I shook my head, unlocked the gate.

"I've come to ask you a personal favor," she added. "I called Maureen when I remembered her saying you lived in Nassau. Would you accept my apology for being so impetuous?"

"Delighted. It's not often I find a pretty girl on my steps." She blushed a little. The breeze from the patio lifted her hat and sent it tumbling.

"Don't worry about the hat," she said. "Now, if you'll show me to my room, I'll change and meet you on the beach. . . but first you must fetch water for that poor Labrador. He's dreadfully thirsty, I think."

"If you insist."

"I insist!" she said, extending a tiny hand. I showed her to the guest cottage and explained the workings of the overhead fan and the inner latch.

We met on the beach a half-hour later. She'd slipped into a conservative black bikini, that showed off her femininity. She had a delightful figure that there was no way to disguise. And she was freckled to the tips of her toes. She took to the water easily, swam gracefully. I was a half-dozen strokes behind her when we quartered the reef.

Pamela was no novice. She probed the crevices with her spear, ignoring a moray eel and flushing a pair of crawfish that she hurried along the bottom. When we came upon an old dad grouper, she shook her head, pointing instead to a yearling peering from the grass. I back-watered and waited. When she surfaced, she had him wriggling at spear end.

"Any hammerheads about?" she shouted. I shook my head. "I'll take him back to the beach, then," she called back.

"There's another grouper down there. We have three hands for dinner," I added.

"If it's your roommate, she can have the head!"

"My houseman, Frank!"

"There's enough for the three of us. You shouldn't overfish the reef," she added, backstroking to shore holding the grouper above her.

Pamela had filleted the grouper and squeezed a lemon on the cuts when I came upon her in the kitchen. She wrapped the fillets in paper toweling, placed them alongside the stove and started a pan of water to boil as she searched the cupboards for rice and whatever.

"I see you have a charcoaler outside on the veranda," she said, "but I would prefer to broil them in the oven. Do you have tomatoes and onions to top them? I don't see any vegetables in the fridge!"

"If you take over Frank's kitchen, I'll lose the gent! Hell, it's only five-thirty. Shall we have a drink and watch the sunset? I'm shot."

"I'll have a Pepsi. I'm not much for rum."

"Champagne?"

"Love it!"

I searched the fridge for something special and came up with a bottle of Tattinger. I polished the Sheffield wine bucket with a dish cloth and filled it with ice. She was amused, had the audacity to ask why I hadn't frosted the glasses.

We sat on the garden wall and talked for a while. She'd gone to the University of Miami while I'd been doing my thing in Iraq. Her father was a doctor, a widower, from an old family in Broward. . . the Fort Lauderdale Yacht Club set.

"I have a younger brother and a married sister who lives in Chicago," Pamela said. "She hates it there. Kids brought up in Florida are water babies; away from the ocean they're a miserable lot. We'd go off to Bimini on weekends and come back late on Sunday night. We were a little spoiled, I guess." She tossed a coconut down the beach and giggled when Happy tumbled and spread the surf. "He's a delightful animal, Keith. We had a Lab once, but he got heartworm and we had to put him down.

"Diane takes after Dad," she continued. "She's tall and slender; Mom was Irish and short, like myself. She was a beauty; Dad sort of rolled up when she died. Edwin is somewhat of a mix. He has Dad's physique and Mom's attitude towards life. Dad sent him away to pre-med, but he dropped out his freshman year. Took a job in a boatyard at the Ft. Lauderdale marina. Dad is very upset. . . they haven't talked in months, which brings up the reason for my visit. Are you listening? You're frowning."

I topped her glass. She tousled her hair and gazed at the poodle dog clouds rising on the horizon. She had a lovely face. Lacked Elisabeth's classic features, but she'd be pretty when her time was spent. Her earthy quality underscored a certain beauty that glowed from deep inside her.

"Dad called me from Fort Lauderdale a couple of weeks back, Keith. He usually calls on Sundays, but this was a Thursday and it was after eleven. He's normally in bed by ten," she added, twirling the glass in her fingers. "He was overwrought. I'd never known him in such a state."

"Your sister? Your brother?" She shook her head slowly.

"He'd had a visitor that night. A man came to the door, displayed a badge and asked for Edwin." She hesitated for a moment. I studied the tilt of her nose in the sun, her freckled cheeks. There was something about her that was vaguely familiar.

"Dad's no fool," she added. "He kept the screen door locked and asked to see the man's credentials. They had words. The man asked if it was Edwin's Stingray parked in the garage. Dad told him it had been there for months and that it was none of his business if he hadn't a warrant. The man forced the screen and Dad slammed the door, then called 911. When the patrol car came, the man was gone."

"Was he from the Sheriff's office?"

"Definitely not! The police checked on their computer. Edwin's name didn't come up, but they knew of him," she added. "When he was younger he'd hang out at the corner of Las Olas and Atlantic with his gang from junior high. They smoked pot in school, skipped class and hitchhiked to the rock concerts up state. They were mindless. The cops knew them by name and would tell them to take off for home when it was late. They seldom took them in."

I nodded an understanding, asked her to continue.

"Well, Dad tried to reach Edwin in the morning, called the boat yard; they hadn't seen my brother for weeks, but came up with his address in Pompano Beach. He'd been living with a girl he knew from high school. . . a drop-out from college, a rather nice person who comes from good family, but mixed up like my brother. You know the type. . . live for the moment, think they can have it all on a platter. . . like the Corvette Chug bought when they sold the brooch for a pittance!"

"Chug?"

Pamela nodded. "He was diving with Liz in the Out Islands when she discovered a beautiful emerald brooch by a reef. She wore it when they came by Dad's house at Easter, then tired of it and sold it to Taylor's in Palm Beach."

My hand tensed, snapping my glass at the stem. The sun seemingly cartwheeled the horizon. . . poodle dog clouds. . . sails of orange. The grisly scene in the schooner's cookhouse careened before my eyes. The girl's hands folded across her breasts, the smile of death on her chalk white face.

"Chug is your brother and Liz his girl friend?" Damnit to hell, I muttered to myself, picturing the devastated kid kneeling at her grave.

"Good heavens, look what you've done." Pamela retorted, pointing to the crimson spreading over my fingers.

I collected the glass and applied a napkin to my hand, averting my eyes to the quieting sea. Pamela puzzled over my reaction, but I shrugged it off, repeating my question when she determined my injury was minor.

"Yes, Keith. He hates to be called Edwin! Chug's nickname came about when he was chugging beer to Cardinal Puff with friends at the beach one night. They've called him Chug ever since! You seem disturbed," she added. "Have I upset your equilibrium?"

She had, but I down-graded my response. "I'm tired from a long trip, honey. You mentioned a brooch. Is there a possibility they came on to something else in the vicinity? Did he mention the Out Island by name?"

"I never thought to ask, Keith. They were sun tanned and happy, returned from a long trip. Do you know my brother? Might you have seen him recently?"

Fortunately the sound of screeching brakes intervened and Pamela bounced to her feet, pointing to the driveway. "Good Heavens, what terrible noise!"

"Frank's Pontiac, honey! When his brakes give out he curbs the stone wall. Hold your ears," I added, and there followed a resounding thud! Happy leapt through the patio, looking for a goody from the store.

I excused myself, ostensibly to help Frank with the groceries, but really to sort out matters in "his" kitchen. He nodded dourly to himself, inspecting the marinated grouper, seemingly pleased with the cuts. "She done all right," he admitted. "Same girl who call . . . stayin' in your room or the cottage by the gate?"

I sorted that one out as well, then returned to the wall by the sea. Pamela was toying with her glass, admiring the sunset while shouldering a towel against the evening breeze.

"You have a nasty scar on your leg," she said. Is that why you limp? Were you injured in Iraq? Maureen said you flew jets. . . that you were a hero of sorts."

Pocketing the change of subject, I said I'd spent six months at Walter Reed. "No big deal. I'm still flying, Pamela. Get on with it, honey. . . a man appeared at your Dad's door and your brother is missing."

"I didn't say he was missing!" she snapped, quizzing me again with her round brown eyes.

"You've implied as much!" She turned to the sea. I topped her glass with the last of the Tattinger.

"It's true," she admitted. "I've come to ask you to help me find him. Dad's worried sick. They've been watching the house, even called in the middle of the night asking for Edwin. Called Dad's office during hospital hours and questioned his receptionist."

"Edwin, by name?"

"Odd, isn't it? Everyone in Lauderdale calls him Chug, even Dad. That's why we think it's someone from outside."

"Did your Dad call the police when he realized the house was being watched?" She drained her glass and placed it next to the bucket.

"He did just that, and the police questioned a couple of men fishing at the end of our bridge. Now, that's legal. . . anyone can fish off the bridge, but Dad's a fisherman. . . there are no fish on the dead end of a canal."

"Did he describe them?"

She nodded. "Black trousers, sleazy shirts. . . city types with dark curly hair and dirty fingernails. They alternate, drive rental cars and there's always one there. . . day and night."

"Spooky!"

"You said it. Dad bought himself a pit bull; they don't come near the house anymore."

"Did he check Chug's apartment?"

"He didn't have to. He called Mr. Stone at the DEA office in Miami. They'd already searched the apartment; no one had been there for weeks. Liz's VW was found at the airport and they were going to call her family, but Stone didn't want to worry them. Chug wasn't wanted," she added. "They only intended to question him about Freddie."

"Freddie?"

"You're pulling your ear!"

"I know, one of these days I'll pull it off. Tell me a little more about Freddie."

"I've known him since I was a kid. We finished at the university together. He majored in business. He's a redhead, too, brighter than hell. He's made a lot of money. No one seems to know how, but word gets around. He's been indicted twice—once in New England and lately in Broward but they had to let him go for lack of evidence."

"Have you been in touch?"

"That's the other reason I'm here, Keith. He called me at Wood's Hole yesterday morning. He was upset. . . knew I'd been phoning his friends and they'd given him my numbers. He didn't make a todo about that, but he asked me if I'd heard from Chug lately and I hit the fan! Told him Edwin had been missing for weeks and that Dad's house was being watched. Do you know what he said next, Keith? I was absolutely flabbergasted!"

"What?"

"He owned up. He came clean! He said he'd bought an old schooner in Nova Scotia last summer; that they'd been loading pot off-shore from Colombia; that he'd sent Chug along to payroll the crew; that they'd talked every day. . . something like a single . ."

"Sideband."

"That's right! He said they'd lost touch all of a sudden. You know more about this than you're saying, I think."

"I've heard of Freddie."

Pamela got to her feet. "I mentioned your name, Keith. I told him I'd been in touch with a girlfriend who knew you had a plane; that I'd made up my mind to search on my own!"

"You're coming on pretty strong, little thing." She put her hands on her hips.

"I might be small, but I'm aggressive," she said.

"I'll buy that!"

"Do you know what he said next?"

"Obviously not."

"He said that you'd worked with the DEA in the past and told me not to trust you. Said he'd charter a plane and check for himself. He was nervous, Keith, stuttering. Told me not to worry. That did it!" she exclaimed.

"OK! I'm going to Fort Lauderdale in the morning. I'd like to check a few things out, but I'll be back by four. Can you hold your water until then?"

Her shoulders slumped and she toyed the rim of the bucket with her fingers. "I was hoping we could start in the morning. I've got a check in my purse for $10,000," she said, fighting her tears.

"I don't want your money, honey. Let me do it my way."

"Don't you always?"

"I make a good friend. Just hang in."

"I'm sorry. It's my nature to be pushy. Maureen said you had a big heart."

"Does your Dad know you're here?"

She shook her head. "It would only upset him. He's beside himself, he hasn't slept well. I told him I'd inquire around and call him on the weekend."

I showed Pamela the ways of the house. . . the stereo and my tape collection, the security gates we locked at night. . . then introduced her to Frank. He was polite, but somewhat aloof.

She handled him nicely, all dimples and curiosity inquiring about the herbs growing in the shade of the house, about the photos of his grandchildren he displayed from his wallet. They were side-by-side, slicing vegetables, when I left them in the kitchen to tend my lacerated thumb. Heard them discussing the pros and cons of sour oranges and limes.

Aside from a wrong number, there were no further calls when we dined on the patio by candle light. The High Commissioner apparently was waiting the London delegation, but I was wary of

Paul. There was the possibility that he'd change his mind and cancel my morning flight. He'd probably screened his suspicions with the DEA.

As for Pamela, there was little I could say until I had word from Nottage. Divulging what I knew would send her off the wall. These were the things I had to consider as we quietly dined.

She was a brave sort. I was taken with her impish personality and her appealing femininity when she appeared in a slinky cotton gown. Five-feet-two, firm-breasted with wide sprung hips, she obviously was aware of my interest when I rolled my eyes to the whispering palms. She had established her presence as a girl who'd attained maturity, rather than the preppy student I'd assumed she was.

We discussed marine biology. . . the curious linkage of crawfish off Bimini when they migrated for miles in a singular line. . . together with the thesis she was writing to complete her master's at the university. Never once did she mention Chug, although I realized he weighed heavily on her mind. When the dinner wine and the ordeal of her early morning flight exacted its toll, she excused herself for the night.

Three

PAMELA WAS FAST ASLEEP when I walked quietly past her window at dawn. I tiptoed across the patio to the kitchen with Happy at my heels. Frank had coffee bubbling on the stove and bacon sizzling in the frying pan. The radio was turned low when he handed me a steaming cup laced with Carnation. We sat at the kitchen table and talked while we listened to the morning news.

"That hurricane been actin' strange-like," Frank commented. "Six o'clock advisory say she centered over the Mona Passage driftin' west. They reporting thirty-five knot winds over northeastern Cuba. Ain't reach force jus' yet. Lots of rain messin' up their sugar cane," he added. I nodded; tuning the seven o'clock newscast from WINZ, Miami.

The southern Bahamas, Turks and Caicos, and the Florida keys had been alerted to a hurricane watch. A northerly turn was anticipated during the next 48 hours. The high pressure ridge over Bermuda had abated, and the low-pressure had begun a circulatory movement. The newscaster then gave a rundown on international events, a stateside summary, then the Dade and Broward issues. There was no mention of the *Sea Leopard*. We listened briefly to the traffic report, to the usual jam-up on I-95. I switched off the set when the commercial intervened.

"I'm expecting a call from Crooked Island when the operator comes on at nine, Frank. Fellow by the name of Nottage will be calling. He's to give you a message. You might know him. . . young man about your age."

Frank grinned. "You mean that old rascal who used to caretake the club at Cutlass Bay? Man, I've known him since 1940. You pullin' my leg?"

"Tell him I'll be off the island until four this afternoon, but that I'll get back to him before the operator shuts down at five. Take down what he has to say, but keep the message in your pocket. Mum's the word with the girl. OK?" He tightened his bow tie, sided his chair to stir the bacon.

"Was plannin' to go into town, Mr. Keith. We gots some goings on at the church this evening."

"Can you hold off until four? I have to get on to Fort Lauderdale. It's important to me, Frank." He shuffled his feet and scratched an ear.

"If n' you say so, must be important."

"There's something else, Frank. If I receive an overseas call, try to get the number. Tell them I'm in Lauderdale for the weekend if they ask." He turned to me and shook his head.

"Ain't much for spoofin' if n' you going to be here like you said."

"I'll be here, but I want to draw someone off for a while."

"You plannin' to lone it up with that nice little gal?"

"No way, but it would be a good idea to keep the gate locked, and if a stranger comes to the door don't let him in."

"You want your eggs over or scrambled, Mr. Keith?"

"Scrambled. Let her sleep as long as you can. Don't play 'drop the pan' if she's late for breakfast. OK?"

"I'm hearing you right. She could be late for breakfast, and I'm to lock he gate. What if she decide to take off to town?"

"Let her go. Don't try to stop her. I don't want to arouse her suspicion, but keep a close eye on her if she goes down to the beach.

Let the dog tag along. Don't hold him in." Frank set the table word-lessly and handed me my plate. Refilled his cup and sat down across from me, befuddled and concerned.

"You in some kind of trouble?" he asked. "Ain't seen you in such a state since Miss Maureen went back to England. That little girl. . . was noticin' last night she mos' upset 'bout something When we was washin' the dishes she was cryin' a little. Didn't say nothin'. . . was meanin' to make mention this morning."

I toyed with my fork for a moment. He lowered his eyes; he meant well and God knows I depended on him. I told him a little of the story then. . . that her brother had disappeared, that I'd seen him, but I didn't want her to know until I knew he was okay. I told him there were other parties involved and that Pamela might be in danger if they knew she was in Nassau. I left certain things unsaid, but Frank was canny enough to grasp the situation. When I got up to leave, he said he'd go along if she drove into town; also, that he'd stay the night if need be. I felt a little better then.

Time was shading eight o'clock when I parked the Ford in the airport lot and walked to the ramp to scout the Texaco truck. I made use of the ladder when the attendant was filling the wing cells; checked the Pratt Whitneys very carefully. Bill came by when the driver was retrieving the petrol line, lingering until we'd settled accounts and the truck had driven on.

"Mister Paul came by yesterday, 'bout an hour after you left for town," he said. "Thought you'd want to know, Cap'n Keith. He didn't axe me anthin', but he was mos' interested in the Goose. He let himself in with somethin' from his key chain, then borrowed a step from Customs and went inside the cabin. I seed him in the cockpit. Was lookin' over your charts. Was servicin' a Cherokee when he left."

"Anyone else been looking around?" He touched his cap and

nodded.

"Lear 24 came up from the south, near about three. They was in for fuel. . . I knows the pilots. They fly charter for Greff. Young fellows wid them, I don't know. Express particular interest in your Goose. He friendly enough. . . axe who it belong an' I give mention of your name."

"Was he younger than myself?" Bill shadowed his eyes and peered at my face.

"Near a'bout. . . but I knows you to be older." He cracked a smile. "My, time do fly. Member you as a young Lootenant wearin' Air Force wings, came in wid your daddy in one o' dem F-4 jets. What happened to that nice man? Ain't see'd him 'round for a spell."

"He retired from the Air Force a few years back. Lives in Greece," I said.

"Sure 'nuff?. . . Now 'bout that young fellow you axe. He 'bout head shorter than you, Cap'n Keith. Weared a beard. . . sorta red-like. Face all cover wid sun spots. . . weared a cap like mine. 'Mos polite. They gone back to Fort Lauderdale, heard tell."

I thanked Bill for the information. His description tallied with Paul's. Freddie had kept his word, apparently hadn't turned up the schooner. Most likely searched Turk-Caicos and missed it by a country mile! I walked to Immigration, then on to file my clearance. Deep in thought when I realized Bill was hopping along beside me.

"Ain't finish yet!" he said. I stopped short.

"Night watchman say a Gulfstream 11 came in, near 'bout midnight, Cap'n Keith. They taxi up next by the Goose and shut down their lights. . . watchman knows that ain't right. He call Customs wid that CB ting. Officer come runnin' from the terminal." A shot of adrenaline stroked my spine. I had him by the arm before I realized what I'd done.

"Sorry, Bill." He touched his cap and continued.

"They was three men who came down from the cabin. . . they was all dressed up in city suits. One of them fat-like, watchman say they have 'mos terrible words with Customs man. . . somethin' like 'none of his damn business why they is there!' " He shook his head solemnly. "Now you know, Cap'n Keith, you ain't to talk to no Bahamian that way. Customs say they mus' state their business. They come to further disagreement. Little fellow display a hand gun an' wave it in his face."

"Good God! What happened then?"

"Customs officer mighty scared. . . call back to the watchman to raise the police. Fat man try to calm the little fellow. . . they have words 'mongst themselves. All dark like. Ain't much to see. Pilots sittin' up there in the cockpit all the time, like they don't know what goin' on. Next ting that happen, they climb the stair and close up the door. Pilot taxi out and take off."

"Where did they come from?"

"Don't rightly know, Cap'n Keith. Now I knows them fellows in the tower. I axe them this morning after I talk to the watchman. They say Paul tol' them to keep close mouth." He shrugged his shoulders. "Ain't posed to say nothin', 'cept you an' me has an understandin'."

I reviewed the fast turning events on the climb out from Windsor Field. Andros slipped by, the Berry Islands fell behind the Goose's starboard wing. A heavy stretch of seagrass marked the halfway point to Bimini. I sipped from my coffee and gave thought to the tumultuous 48 hours since I'd sighted the *Leopard* lying helplessly on the sea. Money seemed no object to the impudent Swiss; he'd gone to considerable length to remove me from the scene and check my arrival. Had he assumed, correctly, I'd harbored the kid when I returned to the *Leopard?* Was the brooch the key to a desperate search with international implications? Was Elisabeth involved, for personal reasons, on to the self-same-thing?

The ADF homed 396 and turned half circle when Bimini fell behind us. The Goose throated her pleasure as we crossed the rolling Gulf Stream and raised the tower at Fort Lauderdale. She was distressed and weary, wanting her cosmetics and a fresh view of life. I let her down easy on a long approach, spun her wheels on runway 27 and turned her about on the taxi way. There was the usual gaggle of private aircraft at Immigration. I waited my turn with the engines stilled, endured a close hand inspection when I presented the Goose's documentation, then taxied to Hellman's ramp for a long overdue overhaul, a paint job, and a brand new set of avionics.

The Goose was a beautiful creature despite her peelings, vintage '45, a collector's item, but she was completely overshadowed by an ancient PBY when I spun her around and coughed the Pratt-Whitneys to a halt. I was reluctant to leave her when Hellman strode from his hangar; we'd had it hot and heavy since San Juan. It was like taking an old friend to the hospital and abandoning her there. There was solace, however. The PBY Catalina was freshly painted, her engines brightly chromed. She evidently was new from the shop. They were only a few years apart, so she would have someone to rub wings with while I went about my business and checked the circumstances that had Pamela at odds.

Hellman was an ex-Air Force type in Texas boots, an A and E mechanic, a friend of sorts. We rounded the Goose and discussed things to be done. He'd give her a fresh annual and top her engines before he prettied her up. I told him the cockpit windows leaked like a sieve and that her avionics were a decade apart, but that I might need her before he completed the annual. . . to hold off, aside from her radios and a walk-around inspection.

He tallied his list and said he'd run a quick total. . . that he'd need a deposit, but he'd get on to the Goose at once. It would take a few minutes to calculate the tab he said, but he'd have a line man run me to Greff's to collect my Porsche, if I cared to wait. I agreed, patted the old girl's rivets, and wandered over to the ancient PBY to mark time.

She had an air stair astern, an innovation that eliminated the necessity of climbing her massive hull. Her engines were the original 1200 HP, three bladed stance. She'd be hard put to make 90 knots, but she'd be long for range. She had a few additional things about her I'd never seen on a civilian conversion, and she'd been considerably updated. A rear-sensing radar scan was mounted behind her vertical stabilizer, a forward seeking scan positioned above her nose pad. A down scope too? Naturally I was curious.

"I'd trade you for the Goose, but she's not mine to offer," a voice announced quietly from behind me. An emaciated man stood beside me wearing loose-fitting khakis. He appeared to be seventy, with flowing white hair flattened under a sun-bleached flight cap with gold Navy wings attached. Tall once, he had since withered. His face, drawn and wrinkled, was centered with red-tinged eyes. He reeked of booze and spearmint gum.

"I'm Andy," he said, offering his hand. "I belong to the PBY and she belongs to a wealthy Brazilian with a yen to explore the Amazon. I'm taking her down a few days from now, when the trough lifts. Couldn't help notice the way you handled the Goose. Ain't too many pilots around who can squire a tail dragger anymore. Ex-service, hey?" I nodded.

"I flew Corsairs with the Navy until I was killed," he volunteered matter-of-factly. "Later on I flew with the Marines for a spell."

"You were killed?"

"Oh, yes. Caught a direct hit over the China Sea. Next thing I know, I'm flying a PBY rescue mission north of Okinawa. Time slipped for a moment, but we managed somehow. Never flown a PBY until then."

"You managed somehow?"

"Bet your life! Had an A-20 crew sitting there beside me. They'd caught one over Formosa. . . never had a chance. We compared seniority to see who would fly first pilot, but seeing I was already in the left hand seat they decided to let me fly it."

"You compared seniority? Tell me, wasn't the base CO a little upset when the PBY landed with a mixed bag of dead pilots?"

"Oh, yes, seeing we'd never met before, but things being as they were—there was a shortage even then—he put us on the roster. We flew with his unit until the end of the war."

"The PBY?"

"Odd you should ask. Yes, we flew that same PBY. Didn't have a serial number, you know. . . was brand spanking new." He chuckled to himself, grabbing my arm to lead me elsewhere. "You should have seen the expression on the old man's face when we landed on Okinawa that day. He pulled up alongside the cockpit in his jeep and asked us where we're from. Well, we had to tell him we didn't know. Now, that didn't seem to bother him so much as the fact that we weren't wearing any clothes. . . all those Marine pilots gagging it up. You know how they are."

"I suspect it was a bit unusual, but then boys will be boys." He nodded.

"Well, the old man sent the sergeant for flight suits and invited us to his tent for a drink. He was somewhat of a card, come to find out later; a 300 mission man, 12 Zeros and a couple of Bettys. Unfortunately, his four-star found reason to ground him. Seems as though he'd taken to flying with his bottle."

"I can understand. Tell me, what's happened to the rest of the crew?"

"Nice that you should ask. Well, we have our reunion every summer at Spring Lake, Minnesota. Call ourselves the Flying Dutchmen. . . fellows on Okinawa came up with that one. Billeted us in a special tent near the officers' club bar. So far, none of us have re-died."

The old card was rambling on, reminiscing his reunion, when Hellman intervened, motioning from his office. I excused myself and followed him in.

"Jake will drive you over to Greff's, Keith. Would you mind signing the work order? I'll have her out of the shop by tomorrow afternoon, but you'll have to allow two weeks before I can sign off an annual. Plus a couple of weeks in the shop for paint."

"Sounds okay! For Christ sake, that old geezer out there. . . Is he off his nut?"

Hellman smiled and sat down at his desk. "No one really knows. He showed up with the Catalina about six months back. . . claims it belongs to a South American. Disappears every month or so, flies it all by himself strictly against FAA regulations. Takes off at night when no one's around, comes back a few days later. Pays cash for gas and maintenance. Who in hell am I to ask as long as he pays his bills?"

"Narcotics? Customs?"

"They've been all over the bird and haven't found a damned seed! They've had him in a couple of times for questioning, but he comes out clean. Got one helluva war record. Saved over a hundred lives in the Korean War."

"FIying PBY's?" Hellman nodded.

"Comes up with that WWII story every time someone noses around. Did you notice how he led you away?"

"I noticed he chews gum and wears a flask on his hip." Hellman shrugged his shoulders. He was an old war bird himself.

I set up a twin Cessna rental at Greff's when I picked up my Porsche. The girl said it would be fueled and ready by 1400. She'd make out the immigration forms for entry into the Bahamas; I could sign later. I rolled down the Porsche's windows and idled her engine to bring up the oil, then swung down Federal Highway to Oakland Park and checked with my office.

We finished the client meeting on time. I rounded up a set of plans for the St. Maarten job and took them along to do my homework, then skipped an invitation to lunch with the fellows. Remembering the call I'd placed with Nottage, I had Marie put me on to Nassau. Frank picked up the first ring

"Nottage call like you said, Mista Keith. Gots some important news, I think." He went off the line for a moment. I heard the dog barking. "Scuse me, suh, someone at the door. . . big man in a white suit."

"A big man in a white suit? Don't let him in!"

"Yes suh! " I stared from the window. . . traffic was heavy on the boulevard, the pavement shimmering with heat.

"Son of a bitch!"

"Yes, Mista Keith. Shall I tell him you'd be back by four?"

"Don't let him talk to Pamela!"

"She down swimmin' off the beach."

"Okay, okay. . . what did Nottage say?"

"Say have guest for breakfast!" I exhaled my relief. . . the kid had made it! I bent over impulsively and bussed Marie.

"It's about time," she beamed.

"Mista Keith, did you hear me? That man's kept bangin' on the gate. But now I seed he's drove away."

On to one final call, I scanned the Palm Beach directory until I found a listing for Taylor's Jewelers-Appraisers. A young man's voice answered the ring, inquiring politely. "Is there something I can interest you in?"

"Is Taylor about?" I asked. His response was negative. Put off, I inquired of an emerald brooch. Shall we start with ten carats?" I could hear the sudden inhalation of his breath.

"Do you realize the price? You are talking upwards to a hundred thousand," he responded sweetly. "Perhaps you'd better speak to Mr. Taylor," he replied. Taylor came on the line a moment later.

"Keith, good Lord, I haven't heard from you in years! What can I do for you?"

I came directly to the point. He seemed deep in thought, finally responding, "I remember the kid and the piece; I remember very well, Keith. He told me his girlfriend found the brooch lodged in a reef when they were diving in the Bahamas. Hell, I've known Doctor Wynn for years. . . I didn't have to check out his son and I knew the piece wasn't hot when I examined it with my glass. The silver was corroded; it had definitely been in salt water, but the emerald was in beautiful shape. I told him it wasn't a Spanish piece, that I thought it might date around 1870. The girl was sort of torn. She rather liked it, but they wanted to buy a car and needed the cash. I offered them 10 thousand, and damned if they didn't take it. I'd have gone to 25. I re-sold it to a dealer in New York for a bundle. Do you know what the piece brought when he put it up for auction at Christie's? A half-million pounds! Someone recognized it for a Johnnes Brasso original. Word got around it had once been part of the Habsburg collection."

"Go on," I begged.

"An agent bought it for someone unknown. . . possibly an Arab," Taylor continued. "They're the only ones who have the bread these days. He was close-mouthed about the sale. He wouldn't talk to the press; took possession and disappeared. They found him the next day with a bullet in his head. A maid discovered him in his room in one of London's plush hotels."

"That's a pretty heavy story."

"More than that, Keith. He'd bought other pieces at the auction. They were found in his valise, undisturbed. When the police compared notes with Christie's, everything checked out except for the brooch. It was gone. Someone had evidently waited until he'd checked the valise from the hotel vault that morning. He had a first-class ticket to Jeddah and a letter of authorization from one of the princes. The information was officially suppressed, but I was told about it later."

"Any clues?"

Taylor's voice was edgy. "A single shot behind the ear, Keith, 22 caliber, very professional. Unfortunately for me, the brooch had a pedigree. We keep a record of every purchase we make in the jewelry trade. Interpol visited me first. I knew the brooch had been sold at the auction, but I wasn't aware a murder had occurred. I showed them the file They copied the Wynn boy's name and address. I described the piece, its condition. I told them I was sincere in my belief that the boy had found it in the Bahamas. They probed me for the location, but I told them that was all I knew."

"You said. . . Interpol visited you first! " Taylor lowered his voice and continued. "The kid's *hot*, Keith, and Robert, my employee has long ears. What's more, I've discovered he's gone through my files. The key was missing from my drawer one morning when I arrived for an early appointment. I found it an hour later in the drawer. I said nothing. I would have let him go, except he's good with the ladies. Last week he showed up with a brand new Eldorado . . . said it was a gift from his boyfriend."

"Bribe?"

"Exactly. I checked with the dealer. He'd paid for it himself with cash. I'm letting him go at the end of the week and changing the locks, but I think the damage is already done. There have been no further inquiries since the second visitor stopped by. . . that is, until you called."

"Was the second caller European?"

"Said he was an insurance agent for the royal family. Had all the credentials, but he was too damned affluent, too well-dressed. Furthermore, he didn't have a copy of the pedigree when I asked. Now, in this business, agents invariably announce their presence quietly and we discuss matters in private. Not so in this instance; he was incensed when I put him off. We had words in the showroom. I switched to French when I noticed Robert was listening. He spoke with a Swiss accent."

"Tall, tanned, black hair combed back, gray at the temples?"

"He's all yours, man! I called the FBI. They checked their computer and said there was no such name on record. He was gone when I came out of my office. I saw him once after that. He was driving down Worth Avenue in a black rental when I was closing up the next afternoon. I haven't seen him since.

"I did a little checking when I was in New York last week, Keith. The piece had been made up by Johnnes Brasso for a cousin of Franz Joseph—Baroness Elisabeth Majlath, a Habsburg. The family collection has been missing since the Nazis overran Austria at the beginning of World War II."

I was running late, but I wanted to check the doctor's street before going on to the airport. There was a noticeable absence of shoppers about when I drove down Las Olas. The seasonal stores had their windows shuttered The storm was centered six hundred miles to the south, but the old timers weren't taking any chances.

I continued east on the boulevard and made a left turn to round the median at Venetian Island. The towering royal palms were listless and unmoving, traffic sparse. I crossed over and humped the bridge leading to the island. I made note of a yellow Chevelle parked alongside on the grass as I glided down the backside. The owner was seated on a folding stool atop the retaining wall at the junction of the canal. He held an unlikely casting rod; the line sagged unattended amongst the floating debris. There he was, ringlets of curls, rinky dink shirt, black trousers and a Gucci belt. His suit jacket lay carefully folded alongside the stool; his face flushed from the heat, he'd topped himself off with a broad-rimmed straw, but otherwise the description jibed with old Bill's. His eyes followed me down the street when I passed.

I drove by the Wynn home very slowly. The doctor recently had installed an iron gate at the entrance; the paint was new black, the latch secured with a huge padlock. A sun-chalked 85 Ford was parked in the driveway. . . the housekeeper's, I guessed. The three-car garage was open and empty, aside from Chug's red Stingray gathering dust. The doctor would be at the office or making his hospital rounds. I turned about at the cul de sac and idled by the house again to backtrack the bridge, then rolled the window halfway and locked the door from the inside. The "fisherman" was next on my list.

He was standing by the left side of the street, his jacket slung over his right arm. He motioned for me to stop. I braked the Porsche, geared down to first, riding the clutch. He came up quickly. I had a blurred impression of his jacket falling away and a

'Saturday night special' pressing my temple. I raised my hand to make it go away, but it stayed.

"OK, Edwin, slide over. I'm driving!" he said. His beady eyes were uncompromising. He had a long-time broken nose, pockmarked cheeks and a nasty curl to his mouth. I noticed a Cartier watch on his wrist when he roughed my ear with the barrel and tried the door.

I lowered my head and pointed to the bridge. His eyes wavered for a split second. I ground-up the window and released the clutch. The Porsche spun rubber and shot forward. I dragged him to the bridge with his wrist wedged in the window, then slammed the brakes. The momentum flung him at arm's length and the sudden stop hurled him screaming across the bonnet. The .32 fell to my lap and clattered to the floor. I cut the ignition and swung the door. His wrist slipped from the window and he slumped to the pavement. I grabbed a handful of greasy hair and belted him one behind the ear to keep him quiet. He collapsed face down on the macadam. He'd have a broken wrist to remember me by. My shoulders caved; that was a close one.

I dragged him by his belt to the canal and checked the traffic whizzing down Las Olas before I bent down to examine his wallet.

Angel Gasperillo, brown hair, brown eyes, 5'8", 185. Born December 24, 1949. Address 6030 Crescent Avenue, Queens, NY., his license said. I thumbed the cards. American Express, Avis, Long Shoreman's Union. . . New Jersey Chapter. Vice president of a garbage collecting company in the Bronx; his mother would be proud. She probably had lofty aspirations for her child, born as he was on Christmas Eve. The wallet was loaded with C notes. An Eastern ticket indicated he'd flown first class from Newark. I returned the wallet to Angel's hip pocket. A horn was sounding from the bridge.

The driver was a fluffed, blue-haired type, driving a matching Seville. She was patient and smiled sweetly when I fired up the Porsche and backed from the bridge to let her pass. I tossed the snub nose special into the canal and tooled down Las Olas. My legs were shaking when I braked for the light before Atlantic.

A customs service Citation jet was ingesting fuel from Greff's AV truck when I pulled into the ramp to unload the Porsche and sign the papers for the 310 I'd rented.

They'd borrowed heavily from the Air Force to outguess the druggies. The jet's nose appendage was loaded with an array of infra-red sensors and look-down radar that would credit the F14's I'd flown. She was a long range spotter, just returned from a surveillance mission over the lower Bahamas, according to the linemen.

The pilots were wolfing sandwiches in the lounge when I entered. We had a nodding acquaintanceship, but they averted their eyes and conversation dropped to a whisper when I walked by. They gathered around the girl at the desk after I had filled my clearance with flight control and collected a raft. I caught the action in the reflection of the swinging glass door as I left. The word was out! Slater's name had been added to the watch list. The 310 would be tracked, narcotics had been alerted. Paul had communicated with the DEA before the High Commissioner intervened.

Ground Control verified my suspicions when they slowtimed my clearance before handing me over to the tower. A Delta heavy rolled into position and took off while I waited, then a Carnival 727 took over the number two slot. I finally was cleared when they'd climbed through five thousand. I throttled the twin Cessna down the runway, folded her gear, and picked up the Bimini VOR, realizing my routing would flash the ATC computer and trigger customs' hotline if I didn't land at Nassau within the hour. I knew the procedure; the faster Citation would take off immediately and scan the Cessna's exhaust with their space-age sensors if I deviated to the south. They'd call ahead and a long range Coast Guard 130 would pick up the track and monitor my flight path. The Air Force would scramble a pair of F-16's from Homestead if I penetrated the ADIZ. They'd circle at an altitude and watch. It was my ultimate destination they'd be wanting; the caution flags were up. I'd have until morning to reason matters further.

We topped the sultry lemon haze at 5500 feet and leveled off to pick up cruise speed. The 310 was light and fast, sensitive to the controls. She was indicating 175 knots when I coupled the auto-pilot. I called in to ATC and reported our time. Then I sat back in the seat to relax.

The outside air was choppy at altitude, listless; the sea flat and brassy. The warm air mass had moved up from the south, but the fishing flotilla was out in force, bobbing about with their outriggers extended, a scattering of white ships tracing wake across the Gulf Stream. A hulking super tanker in ballast moved quickly against the current beneath us; beyond our left wing, a rusty freighter plodded slowly northward. I wasn't above noticing the red-striped cutter closing rapidly from astern, nor the pair of foaming cigarettes circling warily nearby. Their maneuvering would draw flies. I turned in my seat to scan the northern reach. A broad-beamed Hatteras with a 20-mile lead was racing for the horizon. I watched her until she was lost in the haze. Then Bimini came up and fell behind us. I channeled Nassau's VOR and cycled my thoughts to other matters.

Bill walked me in after we'd tied down the Cessna; he had a bit of information. The redhead had come through around noon, he said, with a prop job he'd chartered out of Miami. I gave Freddie a few more points. He hadn't given up, but it seemed the sortie had been fruitless.

"He appear mos' upset, Cap'n Keith. Sat on the ground all time they was refuelin' wid his head ben low."

I nodded. Freddie's conscience would be giving him acute indigestion, but he was savvy enough to diversify his charters and keep out of sight. He was a hot number. He knew he would be tailed. I thanked Bill and asked if anything else had happened since morning. Any private jets? He came up with an unrelated tidbit, insofar as he was concerned, but it was a bouncer.

"One of them Royal Air Force VC-10's landed after you was gone, Cap'n Keith. British High Commissioner's limousine drove right out on the ramp to meet it. Mistah Paul and the high commissioner was sittin' in the back seat wid their air conditioner on." I stopped short. He adjusted his cap to shade the sun and scratched his ear.

"That mean sumpthin', Cap'n Keith? You lookin' mos peeculiar."

"Bill, did you notice who got off? Were there passengers aboard?"

"They was tree, maybe four, besides the crew. Cause me to wonderin'. Cost plenty the Queen's money to bring that big plane all the way from London. They were dress military like. . . 'cept for one fat man wearin' a white suit. He were puffin' a cigar mos' the time. VC-10 refuel and depart. You wantin' gas, Cap'n Keith?"

I mumbled something in the affirmative and filched my pocket for the green. Bill's description tallied with Frank's. It would take something very special to drag the old buzzard out of retirement, and I was apparently high on his list for questioning

The temperature was edging ninety and I swung on to JFK and made the turn to the shore road to pick up the breeze. My mind was in a turmoil; there was no point in deluding myself. Someone had blown the whistle after Paul laid me out. Someone, aside from Kurt, figured I'd come across the kid. I drummed the wheel while I coasted the drive. It had to be Dan. He'd pieced it together from inside information. . . Bower, Howard, possibly Elisabeth?

Frank's Pontiac was gone from the drive but Pamela's remained in its original parking spot. I rounded the house with my bounding dog to shag a few coconuts to the sea. The Pontiac rattled the lane a half-hour later while we were having a leisurely swim and I was pondering a dialogue with Pamela. It would be unfair to hold back and not tell her, but how could I go about it without divulging the nasty interlude that preceded Chug's re-appearance?

She was standing on the veranda dressed in all white with a spray of yellow hibiscus clutched in her hands, her skirt billowing softly in the light breeze, a peasant blouse hanging loosely from her shoulders. She wore an enormous hat with a trailing scarf—a vision by Renoir of a young girl by the seashore, under a hazy blue sky.

I stood waist-deep in the shallows for a moment, remembering Maureen. . . tall and bronzed from the sun, her long dark hair braided in a pony tail. And Judith, with her enigmatic smile, her thin willowy body wrapped in a towel to her chin. Where was *she* now? I looked down to my reflection in the rippling water. What a fool I was! Did I expect them to come through the turnstiles forever?

"We have grouper from the market," Pamela called from the veranda. "We're marinating it for the broiler if you'll be so kind to set the fire. Frank decided to let me in his kitchen. . . after I visited his church and made a donation. He's such a dear."

"That was your day?"
"No, not exactly. I stopped in to have a talk with Commissioner

Johnson. You're friends, I assume. He said you'd been by for a chat yesterday afternoon." I sat down on the wall beside her and stretched my legs to the sun.

"You asked him to help locate your brother?"

"I certainly did! I told him Chug had been missing for several months, and that he might possibly be somewhere in the Bahamas. I didn't mention the DEA or the men who'd been watching our house."

"Did you mention the schooner?"

"Only that we've heard he was aboard a large sailing boat, that I was deeply concerned and determined to check it out."

"Did you mention Freddie?"

"Certainly not! I gave him Edwin's description and he made notes; his tape recorder wasn't working," she added. "He asked me where I was staying. I told him your cottage, and that you had agreed to help." She turned to me then, her freckled face lined from worry, but she managed a smile. "That was presumptuous of me, of course. I hope you have," she added quickly.

"We'll discuss it later. Pamela, did Paul seem to be holding anything back? Did he give any indication that the schooner had been sighted? Did he mention the *Sea Leopard*. . . ?"

I caught myself mid-sentence. She raised her head slowly.

"What a curious thing for you to say," she murmured. "Until this very moment I wasn't aware of the schooner's name. You've been lying to me, Keith. You know more than you're telling! You scare me. You have no reason to withhold information. . . unless. . . something dreadful has happened!" I studied my big toe. Her fingernails bit my wrist. Her Irish was up; I laid it on the line.

"Chug's all right, Pam, safe for the moment. That's all I can tell you. Would you let go of my wrist?"

"Oh, my God!"

"He's OK, honey, but he has a small problem."

"Thank heavens. . . Is Liz with him, are they together?" I averted my eyes, but she wasn't noticing. She was on her feet and staring at the sea.

"They are a lovely pair," she murmured. "They've been together since high school. . . if Daddy hadn't been such an ass!" She turned about, her eyes had filled with tears.

"Where are they, Keith? Can we go to them now? Do we have to wait until morning?" I nodded.

"I'm expecting company, Pam, serious business. Your brother's into a spot of trouble. Better he stays put until we sort matters out." She blinked, her freckles coming to force.

"Is he going to jail?"

"Negative, honey! But if I take you to him now we'll have the law on our back. Just take it easy and don't lose your temper. There'll be questions, so for God's sake forget what I said. Dan's a pro, he'll turn you inside out if he thinks he's on to something hot."

"Dan?"

"The Queen's best! He flew in mid-day. . . something heavy has happened or is about to happen," I corrected.

"You're evasive!" I nodded.

"You'll have to accept my word, Pam. Chug hasn't the vaguest idea of what it's all about. He just happened to stumble on to something that has the baddies and the authorities hot for his ass."

"Drugs?" I shook my head.

"Minutely so. . . something else but I'm not sure what it is. Why are you staring at me?"

"You're lying! You lied about the schooner. . . you knew right along Something dreadful has happened. I can see it in your eyes!"

"Deceptive, perhaps, but I have a good reason. I made your brother a promise . . . he's in good hands, in good health. I'll take you to him as soon as I can, but you'll have to button your lip or you'll have his head on a stick!" She sat on the wall and cried a little.

"Paul said you were covering up."

"Paul has a forked tongue, honey. Did he have anything else to say?"

"He said if you tried to leave the island, he'd impound your plane."

"Do you see what I mean? Are we going to be friends?" She nodded and clasped my hand.

I gave thought to Dan's presence while I showered and changed. He'd obviously had a hand in things from the very beginning and had flown from London to intervene with Paul. Green Eyes' remarks tallied with his velvet touch; he was a master puppeteer.

The covert apparatus in Providenciales had apparently been deployed before the Juanita arrived on the scene. Suddenly the reason for Elisabeth's late arrival was made vividly clear. She'd evidently been coached for the eventuality by British Intelligence, waiting her cue when the leading lady became suspiciously ill. Interpol would have identified Kurt with the missing brooch; her personal reasons were apparent, but why risk her neck? And why had a legendary M-7 agent been drawn from retirement for a handful of jewelry? The answer eluded me.

Twilight had faded to a faint glow in the west and sparks from the charcoaler were tracing the veranda when I stepped outside. Four o'clock was long gone and Dan hadn't rattled the gate. He undoubtedly compared notes with Paul, but I was certain he hadn't clued him to the brooch nor, for that matter, confided with the DEA. The kid was up for grabs, but Dan was wily. He'd manipulate the situation to his best advantage. I had Pamela and her high strung emotions to consider. He'd be on to her immediately if he sensed a lead.

She was seated on the wall with the last of my Taittinger beside her and a pair of goblets hanging loosely from her fingers. The transformation was unbelievable. She wore a low-cut cotton Batik, her hair accented by a red Hibiscus. Her face was aglow and she'd freshened her lips with a touch of lip gloss . . . she was absolutely stunning. I'd anticipated a square-toothed smile and a dowdy frock from the depths of my overnighter.

"It's a glorious evening, Keith . . . I'm so happy inside. Why are you staring?" I averted my eyes and sat down beside her. She was crackling clean and her boobs were at odds with the thin Batik.

"You, are something else. I had you pegged for high buttoned shoes!" She blushed and edged away.

"I'm a prissy Irish-Catholic and you're not to coax me to bed. . . besides, the celebration's for Chug!" she added sweetly. I shrugged and topped her glass. Frank smiled from the charcoaler. I studied the evening stars.

"Grouper?" She nodded.

"Fresh from the sea and marinated with sour orange. You may kiss me on the cheek if you'll control yourself."

"The table's set for three. Have you invited a priest to keep us apart?" She promptly emptied her glass in my lap and thumbed her nose.

"That will cool you off, you lecherous clod! Sir Daniel called when you were playing in the shower."

"Sir Daniel?"

She nodded. "You're surprised! I thought you knew him well."

"I do, but I didn't realize he'd conned the Queen's list!"

"Would you care for a napkin?"

"No, thanks, I'll sit this one out."

"He was most polite. We had a nice chat."

"My God, be careful. He'll nimble your fingers and pick your brain. Did you mention Chug?" She shook her head.

"I'm not that stupid, but I'll keep to my room if you insist." I reached for her hand. She came willingly and sat down beside me, a tear streaking her freckles. "I'm sorry, Keith. It was an impetuous thing to do. I'm worried and confused by all this."

"Hang in and bite your lip, honey. He's gruff, but he carries a soft heart. I met him a few years ago when he was working another case, another story. He was top dog with British Intelligence when he retired and I suspect he was recalled when the investigation centered in the islands.

"Chug's wanted for questioning and it has nothing to do with drugs or the DEA. . . it's the brooch, Pam. The brooch was part of the Habsburg collection that disappeared in WWII and they are desperate to know where he found it."

"Oh, my God, no wonder they've been haunting Daddy's house!"

I shook my head. "That's not Dan's style. Unfortunately, a gaggle of neo-Nazis picked up the lead and they've been fanning the streets from Fort Lauderdale to Barranquilla ever since."

"Paul mentioned none of this. . ."

"He doesn't know," I added quickly. "He realizes something's up, but he hasn't a clue to what it's all about. There are underlying factors, plus the status quo of the Turks and Caicos Islands. I was in his office when the High Commissioner cooled his hand. He was furious. . . he was juiced for a bust when the Crown pulled the rug."

"The *Leopard*?"

I nodded. "Loaded with grass! The DEA had it as far as the Windward Passage when they lost it in the storm. Paul's a hardnose, Pam. . . stubborn. I figured as much when I hustled Chug off to Nottage."

We sat down to dinner at the patio table when Frank forked the fillets to our plates and indicated he'd wait no longer. Dan had yet to make his appearance, but I assumed he'd been delayed and was probably enroute. It was highly unlikely he'd let the evening go by and risk my slipping away in the morning. I made a go at table talk, but Pamela's euphoria was on the down slope and she was deeply immersed in her own thoughts. I'd said too much; she was obviously worried.

It was past nine when I checked my watch. We were on to coffee and Frank was itching to clear the table when we heard Happy barking in the distance. He had a special bark for investigative matters so I wasn't that concerned, but when he throated a pained yelp and came to sudden silence, I tensed and rose from my chair.

"Land crab?" Pamela volunteered.

"Could be; he'll never learn."

"I thought I heard a car in the driveway a moment ago."

"It's probably Dan. I'll unlock the patio gate and take a look!"

"Don't! Please, Keith. I have a creepy feeling that something's not right. Someone's out there! He surely wouldn't have kicked the dog."

I reached down and patted her hand. A pan clattered to the kitchen floor. . . she spun in her chair and clamped her fingers on my wrist.

"Take it easy, honey! It's Frank's way of telling us he wants to go to bed. I'll check the gate and ask him to collect the plates. Unwind a little; if it's Dan we'll see his lights."

The candle dimmed from a surge of air as I rounded the chair. A chill rippled my spine; something was amiss. We'd drawn the seaward doors. An unlikely hiss erupted behind me and then Pamela lurched forward with her hand on her shoulder.

"Ouch! You have some king-size mosquitoes here!" Her arm dropped to her side and she slumped in her chair.

I reached out to brace her and felt something barb my wrist. I looked down to see a needled dart imbedded to the bone. I tore the thing away and spun about; a long-barreled hand gun pointed from beyond the candlelight. I lunged forward, lost my legs and sprawled face down on the patio floor. I lay still for a moment, my right arm numb to the shoulder. I tried my left, managed my knees and reached for the chair. Pamela lay across the table with her arm dangling by her side, a dart lodged in her shoulder. I realized she'd taken its full impact. The candle fuzzed and swirled about. I bowed to the stone and collapsed on my face, my ears ringing, my vision blurred, my mind uncomprehending the nightmare that had come upon us.

An immense white cloud seemed to gather and tower over our antagonist. An arm rose and descended. The dark blob dissolved with a sickening thud. There was a brief silence, then the sound of scuffling shoes. I rolled and turned my head; a blurred shape was silhouetted in the kitchenway. . . then my eyes ceased to focus. I moved my hand to locate the chair and felt a hand tighten on my belt.

My next recollection was cold and wet. . . I was rolling about with the surf, attempting to swim with limbs that couldn't move. A cresting wave struck my head; I groaned and came backside in the sea gagging for air, fighting for my life. The next wave overcame me. I opened my eyes for a final look and witnessed the bright yellow light that had been sent to guide me. I mumbled the prayer I'd been taught as a child.

"Thought you'd had it, hey?" A thunderous voice resounded from the fleecy clouds. An enormous white suit materialized from the shadows. The jowled, aged face that looked down upon me was crowned with a glaze of thinning hair. A pair of close-set blue eyes stared unsympathetically, lips curled mischievously. . . an arm rose and I was unceremoniously doused with a bucket of water from the kitchen sink.

"Where's Pam, is she all right?" He pointed with the bucket. I rolled my head on the carpet. She was stretched on the living room sofa. He'd pillowed her head and arranged the lamp to shadow her face, but turned it full onto mine.

"She'll sleep it off in a few hours, my boy, as will your houseman and shaggy retriever. Now you know how the lion feels when he's pinged in the bush."

"Dart gun!"

A miniaturized version, cleverly adapted to bring one in with a minimum of force. I retrieved it and discharged it into your adversary's backside. There was an accomplice in their car, but I do believe we have a fatality."

"You didn't?"

"Oh, but I did, Keithy. He started a fuss."

I got to my elbows and collapsed on my stomach.

"They were after Pam," I groaned. He raised his eyebrows and smiled.

"Is that a fact? My, my, I do believe they had you in mind as well. We'll have our little tête-à-tête when I question her later, hey?"

I made it to my knees. A white shoe, stretched out to try me, sent me rolling onto my side.

"Leave her be, you bastard! She's worried about her brother. . . she's in no condition!"

He took time out to fumble in his vest pocket and light a panatela. "Now, now, is that any way to address your liberator? You and I are old friends. I'm sure we can come to an agreement when you come to your senses. You're lucky you dislodged the dart when you did. The drug loosens one's tongue, you know." A powerful hand reached down and grabbed my belt and I was unceremoniously deposited in a chair.

"Collect yourself, Keith, while I attend to the chap on your patio floor." He crossed to the doorway, looking back briefly when Pamela moaned and fluttered her eyes. I reached over and wiggled my fingers. She blinked, but was unable to work her tongue.

"She will be able to hear you, but she'll have lost the use of her limbs for an hour or so," he called over his shoulder. "My, my, what do we have here?"

Pamela mustered a smile when I asked her not to fight it, to sleep if she could. She nodded weakly and closed her eyes. The room made a sickening swirl as I got to my feet and staggered to the doorway. Dan was seated on a patio chair with an unconscious sack of flesh at his feet.

He'd rolled him on his back and loosened his tie, unbuttoned his jacket and removed a .22 automatic from a shoulder holster. The gun and a lizard skin wallet lay on a handkerchief he'd spread nearby. The fellow would be in his mid-40s, heavyset, with receding hair. He wore a dark gray business suit. Urinated on himself when the double shot of curare loosened his kidneys. He was one sorry-looking son-of-a-bitch.

"Ballistics will be most interested," Dan muttered, looking up. "It's not often a weapon is found in possession with fingerprints enjoined. I suspect we have a hit man in tow, laddie. My, my, what else do we have?"

He rippled a sheaf of Swiss francs and hundred dollar bills in an envelope he'd spotted in the gentleman's pocket, pencilled a notation and added it to the pile.

"It would seem a staggering sum has been advanced to secure your apprehension, my boy." He looked down at the sodden character and shook his head. "I'm afraid we'll have to fly the pair to the other side and turn them over to the FBI. I promised Paul we wouldn't clutter his bivouac with needless garbage. How's it going, Keith? Can you manage the wheel?"

"You mean, am I able to drive?"

"Precisely!" I studied the candle on the patio table for a moment, focusing my eyes until it came to one.

"I think I can make it."

"Splendid. Now step outside and gather up the handkerchief. Knot it neatly and follow me up the lane with your sedan. I'll need your headlamps to show the way. Their automobile is parked on the crest by the carriageway."

The man easily weighed 200 pounds, but Dan had him by another fifty. He had lugged him by the belt halfway up the lane when I caught up with them. A blue Colt with rental plates was parked facing out. The Lab lay alongside a fender. I stopped and beamed the headlamps on the scene. He whimpered when I removed the dart from his neck, then licked my hand. I stroked his ears and peered inside the Colt. The driver was slumped over the wheel, his eyes open. A drool of blood oozed from his mouth.

"Jesus, Dan!" He plopped his burden on the gravel and pointed to an automatic lying near the door.

"Never stop to reason when confronted with one of these," he said. He nudged the thing with his foot. "Pick it up with a twig through the trigger guard and wrap it with the handkerchief. A basic .22 is a lethal thing close up," he continued. "It utilizes all of its power with a minimum of muzzle blast. When the bullet enters one's skull it bounces around like a rubber ball. Be fleet of foot if you have no counter. Fortunately, I chose the alternative."

I bent down and did as I was told. "Now then, if you'll assist me, we'll redeploy the gentlemen. I'll take the back seat, you drive. Are you all right, son?" I nodded numbly and opened the door to the Colt. We deposited the unconscious man on the seat. The driver had run his string, however. Dan's Webley had torn his chest apart. I took one look at the bloody mess and gagged.

"We'll need towels and a sheet to wrap this lad for shipment, Keithy. Best you take a breather. Look in on the others while you're about it." I collected Happy and coasted the Ford down the lane with the creature's head in my lap. My wrist hurt like hell; I was numb to the shoulder and my tongue felt like a cotton ball, but I managed the automatic shift with my elbow and was reasonably on course when I navigated the turnabout and braked to a stop by the patio door.

After easing the dog onto his pad in the kitchen, I sidestepped the litter to check on Frank. He was stretched on his bed with his head underarm, his eyes glazed, completely befuddled. I explained what had happened, adding that I'd be back within the hour. Then I turned on his fan, left a glass of water on the bedstand and went on to the living room to investigate my guest.

Pam opened her eyes. She was able to move her legs and make it to her bedroom with an underarm assist. I propped her up on the bed with a bevy of pillows. She murmured questions when I knelt by her side and raised a tumbler to her lips. I filled her in as best I could, making no mention of the scene on the hill. She managed a faint smile when I bent down and kissed her. I turned down her bed lamp, locked her door from the inside and closed it behind me.

We slipped the dead man onto a sheet and rolled him like a mummy to the right side of the tiny Colt. I sponged his bloody residue from the seat, spread a fresh towel, and climbed inside to fire the ignition. Dan expanded his girth in the back with the semi-conscious mobster sacked against the window. I waited for a passing car, then turned on the headlights and headed east to pick up the cut to JFK.

"Avis isn't going to like this, Dan. There's blood on the seat and a bullet hole in the door."

"Best to leave it in the lot and return with a taxi."

"Is that how you managed? Or did Paul drop you off?" He waited until I'd swerved to avoid an oncoming vehicle before he answered.

"Chap from Customs telephoned the CID. He recognized one of the gentlemen when he was reporting for evening shift. You can thank your devious stars I hastened by, my boy. I sent my driver ahead to detain their charter on the off chance you might be on it!"

"Would it be impolite to ask who sent them? I'm a little confused!"

"Need I answer your question, boy? Do you think I'm so naive? You know bloody well who sent them, and you jolly well know the reason why! Turn left," he ordered. I turned off JFK and shot down the airport road.

"Turn left again and stop at the security gate. Your driving makes me nervous."

"The guard will head for the bush when he sees what we have!"

"I'll handle the situation!" he growled.

We stopped with a spiral of gravel. The guard paled and reached for his phone. Dan panned his identification wallet.

"Fellow's seriously burned!" he shouted from across the seat. "We're flying him to Lauderdale for medication." The guard bought the act and passed us through.

I drove the Colt across the ramp and stopped when he pointed to a Gulfstream II. Dan huffed from his seat and had a word with a pair of uniformed constables standing guard beneath the wing. They hoisted the corpse to the cabin floor, returned for his buddy and handcuffed him to the seat. He stunk to high heaven; he was barely conscious, his eyes rolling from side to side and a drool of saliva coursed his multiple chins.

"Where are the pilots?" I asked when it was done.

"They'll be along. They are being questioned at the moment. Now then, boy, I shall stay over in Miami until morning. You are to remain on the island. Do I make myself clear?" He studied me while he lit another cigar.

"I think it best we set a time," he added. "Shall we say lunch at your cottage? I understand your houseman is an excellent cook and I have reason to believe we have matters of mutual interest to discuss."

"Like what? A mixed-up kid? A handful of emeralds? You'll have to come up with something better than that, you old fart. Tell you what I'll do. I'll book luncheon at the Pizza Shack and we'll cut cards for the check. OK?" I reached for the door handle. He clamped a hand on my shoulder and spun me around, his jowls trembling, his face the color of strawberry Jello. His balled-up fist told me to angle my head.

Wagging a finger, I said "You do and you'll regret it." I wrenched my arm away. "Take it easy, Dan!" Our eyes locked for a moment. He clamped his jaw on the Panatela and shook his head. With drooping eyes and sagging shoulders, a very tired old man suddenly stood before me.

"Very well, Keithy. There was a time, but I'm afraid you've advantaged my years. Listen carefully, lad. You have until noon tomorrow to reach a decision. You've become deeply involved in this imbroglio, as we've come to understand, even if not by choice. You do possess certain information—a key, so to speak. The Wynn boy unwittingly stumbled upon it and we believe you may have probed a little further." He paused for a moment to flick an ash.

"Have you reasoned what it is that draws men to madness. . . to murder their kind, to seek out and torture for the want of it? To exact blood and flesh for one's ultimate gain, to serve up one's own soul for the devil's delight? Virgil had a word for it, Keithy, 'the accurst craving for gold'."

"Gold?"

"Exactly, boy. Five tons, 120,000 troy ounces filched from the coffers of central Europe during World War II!"

"Jesus Christ!"

"He wouldn't smile upon us, boy. I leave you with your conscience until tomorrow noon!"

Four

I PUNCHED OFF THE alarm at six, rolled out of bed and stumbled to the veranda to catch the mood of the morning. A mare's tail of cirrus feathered the troposphere, the upper air in motion. The sea, flat and silvery, shaded total darkness to the west, yellowing with the sky to the east. A long-billed kingfisher called intermittently.

An early charter droned north from Windsor Field and disappeared in the early dawn as I studied the sky. The 310 would be watched. . . but there was another way! I returned to the bedroom and leafed through my pad for a home number. Sonny was usually up and gone by seven and when I cradled the phone I had the means. The remaining question was how! Paul would have alerted the security gate and the Ford was known to guards. As I studied the depths of my closet, I wondered if they would anticipate a battered Pontiac and a pair of nondescript Conchs from Spanish Wells.

Forsworn was my morning shave. After I showered, I attended my wound with iodine, then dabbed my sideburns until they took on an auburn hue. My wrist shot pain the length of my arm when I reached into the closet for a pair of jeans and a couple of sun-beat shirts. I raised a broad-rimmed straw from the upper shelf, collected a sun visor and a fishing pole from the hallway locker, and ventured forth to wake up my guest.

Pam didn't respond at first and the door was locked. I rattled the screen and whistled Dixie. She groaned and dislodged a glass from the bedside table, came awake when it rolled across the floor. The door handle turned a moment later; she stood before me in the buff rubbing her eyes.

"I hurt," she said. "Make it go away." She turned her back and fingered the angry blotch on her shoulder. "Aches. . . my mouth tastes like the Boston Mall."

"There's aspirin in the kitchen. Slip into these while I check it out." She took the bundle from my hand, unrolled the jeans and held them to her thigh.

"Aside from the hips, I think they're a little long."

"Roll them. . . the baggier the better."

"What am I to do with the shirt?"

"Wear it and bob your hair. They'll be watching for a feisty red-head with a healthy set of boobs." She blushed and slammed the door before I could hand her the visored cap.

I located Frank in his bathroom angling the mirror. A fresh shirt lay on the dresser together with the aspirin. He was puzzling the gash in his chest and mumbling to himself. The dart apparently had caught him full center when he was washing the pots and pans.

"Man, that ting hit bone! Seed where he cut the screen, Mistuh Keith. They must come round backside when you and that little girl was havin' coffee. Seen she all right, sleepin' peaceful like when I came by her door this morning."

"Sorry, fella', how's the head?"

"Head comin' fine, but feets wrong side. What you doin' dress like that? Man, you get better clothes in your closet."

"I need your help, Frank. I'm flying Pamela to Crooked Island and there's a police car parked at the top of the lane. They'll be watching at the airport, too, but I think we can pull it off."

"Now I'm seein' watch you say. . . they ain't spect no rusty Pontiac?" I nodded.

"If you don't mind, I'll be back by one if we pull it off. Leave the kitchen door unlocked; the fat man will be along for lunch and I'll come backside if I'm running late."

"Same man who make tings right?"

"Same man, but he's not to know we've split for Crooked Island. Fetch up something super, Frank. He has an appetite as big as his waist."

"Reckon I owe him some favor."

"Strawberries and Dover cream. . . you know what I mean."

"I'm agree, you leave dot to me."

Pamela was showering when I dropped off the aspirin and an Aloe leaf to salve her wound. I called in to hurry her along, then went immediately to the beach to console my suffering dog. I found him curled in the sand beside his cache of nuts with his nose between his paws. His feelings were hurt and his tail wouldn't wag. He had a king-size lump in the folds of his neck, but his soulful eyes were disproportionate to the pain. Labradors are like that. . . they have the heart of a child.

I flapped his ears and rolled a coconut along the beach, hoping to reestablish his masculinity. His tail went up and he staggered to his feet to give chase when I rolled another to the surf. I was pressed for time. . . I had a four hour flight and the odds of the morning to contend with. . . but animals are important, too. He was hard on my heels and barking for more when I rounded the cottage and glanced at my watch. It was 6: 25. Frank had maneuvered the Pontiac to cloak the portico and was anxiously waiting our guest.

She was a ten-year-old on vacation when she came down the steps. . . more boy than girl. . . a fishing pole on her shoulder and my diving watch dangling from her wrist. The denim shirt reached her knees and the rolled-up jeans were at odds with her ankles, secured at the waist with a twist of twine. She'd pinned her hair beneath the visor and had a pair of out-sized sun glasses perched on her nose. I would have passed her on the street if it weren't for her spread of freckles and square-cut teeth.

"I'm scared," she said. I retrieved her overnighter and pointed to the floor of the Pontiac.

"Don't worry. . . they won't be watching for Huckleberry Finn."

"Frank said there was a police car at the top of the lane."

"Make yourself thin; he'll cover us with a blanket."

"Will you promise to behave?"

"If you'll button your shirt."

"Have we time for coffee? My head's a bag of nails."

"I'll fill the thermos. Anything else?" She shook her head. She was frightened, but she realized we were pressed for time.

We managed to squeeze ourselves between the commodious seats of the vintage Pontiac. Frank tucked us in and accommodated the Lab in the front when he pawed the door. It was a ticklish situation at best; if he caused a commotion we'd have the constables on their feet when we hit the rise.

Frank idled down the deserted highway, passed the airport's outer boundary, then swerved into the service road. A DC-10 charter was parked at the main terminal, its lights aglow. The forward door opened while we circled the parking lot to see if we were followed. A motorized ramp moved slowly into position. A white-capped customs officer mounted the stairs, his attention centered on the new arrival.

"Police car parked by the security gate," Frank allowed.

"Play it cool. You're doing all right."

I pulled the straw hat down on my head until my ears were extended, rolled my under lip over my upper lip and hunched my shoulders. Frank ventured a startled glance and slowed the Pontiac to a crawl. A khaki-uniformed lieutenant in a red-banded hat waved us to a stop and tagged the windshield with his swagger stick.

"What bring you here before the sun rise, man?" he called in to Frank.

"Folks goin' to Elutra, suh. I oblige them with a ride. They come to wait for Sonny."

The lieutenant bent down to look inside the car. I smiled and stared blankly at his Sam Brown belt. His eyes narrowed as he peered into the back seat. The Lab growled.

"That your daddy up front?" he asked. Pamela frowned and nodded her head. The officer straightened. He looked me over and stroked his chin.

"Daddy ain't much for talk," Frank offered. "Sumptin' to do wid genetics, heared tell."

I rolled my eyes, puffed my cheeks and leaned my head from the window. Pamela giggled. The lieutenant stepped quickly aside.

"Pass on," he grunted. "Have a nice time in Elutra, chile," he said politely to Pam. He briefly glanced at me and turned away.

The sun was casting morning shadows when we unloaded Pamela's luggage. The general aviation ramp was unattended, but the day shift was due at seven and I was in a hurry to be off before they arrived. I signed a check for Frank and had a calming word with the dog. We watched until they were safely past the gate, then I turned my attention to a Cessna 182 parked on the far end of the ramp.

"What a terrible thing to do, Keith. The officer thought you were going to spit."

"I was afraid he'd hold us at the gate." She unloaded her auburn hair and stamped her foot.

"I refuse to fly with a man who has dog ears and slobbers!" I slammed the straw to the ground and pointed to my 310 parked mid-way down the ramp. A constable was sprawled on a cot beneath the wing. He appeared to be asleep, but a heady conversation would raise his head.

"Quiet, Goddammit! Sonny's plane is at the end of the line. Unlock the doors and mind your manners. The key's under the nose wheel," I added.

"Good heavens! Are we to fly to Crooked Island in that?" I puffed my cheeks and rolled my eyes. She arched eyebrows and darted ahead. When she was safely past the constable, I retrieved the straw and plodded zombie-like across the ramp.

The 182 was in excellent condition despite its years. Sonny used it for business trips and was savvy to the conditions. At altitude, with loss of power, it could be glided to a stretch of beach. The open sea was another matter, but the islands were closely linked and we'd follow a circuitous route. I stowed Pamela's luggage on the back seat where he'd buckled the raft; drained the sumps and checked the oil while she untied the lines. It was seven o'clock when I completed my pre-flight and pointed to the right seat. She was at loss for words when I flipped the battery switch and turned the prop.

I raised ground control and requested the active runway as we taxied out. The operator was busy with the DC-10 turnabout to Frankfurt and vectored us without questioning the nature of our flight. I checked the mags and called in to the tower when we were aligned with the run-up ramp: we had a tight minute when I told them we were on a local flight and would file a clearance if we extended our plans. I fidgeted with the controls and looked back. A Bahamasair prop jet was hard behind us with its beacon flashing. There was spurious action on the private ramp. It was 7:08 when they let us go.

I picked up a 120 degree heading and climbed until we topped the haze at 3500. New Providence disappeared behind us. The shallow banks lay green below us, the sun blazing orange in the east. I lowered the visor and turned to Pamela.

"Time for coffee, honey. How do you feel?"

"Shaky! I hope you know where we're going. I don't see anything but water." I pointed to a string of black dots on the horizon.

"The Exuma Cays. Normans Cay is off the right. The dark blue water is Exuma Sound. It's going to be a long haul, Pamela. I've throttled back to save fuel. The tanks will be rattling before I get back to Nassau." She nodded thoughtfully, dimpled, and put her hand beside mine on the wheel.

"It's been a bummer, hasn't it? I appreciate what you've done, despite my carrying on. I don't understand you though. Why are you so evasive?"

"That's the southern shore of Eleuthera off to our left, Pamela. Cat Island will be coming up in a half hour." She squeezed my hand and looked away.

"You kissed me last night," she said. I leaned over and cradled her chin. Our lips lingered for a moment, then the overhead speaker blasted and I fumbled for the mike.

"Cessna Foxtrot Bravo, do you intend to file?" Nassau repeated. I thumbed the button and gave the operator our numbers, told him we were on a round robin to San Salvador and would return to Nassau by 1300. Pamela questioned me at once.

"I thought we were going to Crooked Island?"

"We are, honey, but I don't want *them* to know." She blinked and sipped coffee from her thermos.

"Cessna Foxtrot Bravo, repeat pilot's name and number of souls aboard." I held the microphone at arm's length and mumbled my mother's maiden handle. He called out once more. I clicked the button and turned down the volume.

"That will hold him for a while. He'll think we've outranged our signal. There's no ground station at San Salvador, but they'll call the commissioner by telephone if I'm not back by one."

Pamela pointed to the sky, to the blackness in the south, as we climbed above the rising haze.

"I was hoping you hadn't noticed," I said.

"I studied meteorology, Keith. The mare's tail is leading to the northwest and your altimeter was reading 29.7 inches before you reset it."

"You've got the picture, honey. Nottage built himself a house on high ground. You'll be OK if the weather gets heavy." She refilled my cup and tightened the cap on the thermos.

"Do you plan to leave us indefinitely?"

"That's Cat Island under the port wing, Pam. Hawksnest Creek is at the toe of the boot, Columbus Point at the heel. Columbus was supposed to have landed there, but the House of Assembly changed things around in 1910 when they voted to change Watlings Island to San Salvador." She crossed her eyes and put a finger to my nose. "It's called San Salvador or Catt Island on all the old charts," I added. "Catt was a Spanish sea captain."

"It's called a masterful change of subject, Keith. Do they have similar plans for Crooked Island?"

"I was afraid you'd ask."

"You're pulling your ear. . . you're holding back."

"You're not going to like what I have to say."

"You'll have to tell me sooner or later, particularly after what happened last night."

I watched Conception Island pass through the propeller blades, then nudged right rudder to pick up Long Island. As I glanced at my watch, she stamped her foot on the rudder pedal and the Cessna skidded.

I sponged the coffee from her lap and told her what Dan had said the night before. I added the information from Taylor, the history of the brooch and the Habsburg emeralds, the murder in London and the assumption someone had pinched the brooch to identify it with the original collection.

"My God, Keith, no wonder they've been after Chug! Would he know about the gold?" I shook my head.

"I'm sure he doesn't, Pam. There is more to the story, but I'd rather it came from him. He's been through a bundle of hell lately. You'll have to grab yourself when you see him." She paled and bit her lip, crumpling the plastic cup in her hand.

"It's Liz, isn't it?"

She's dead, Pam."

"Oh, my God."

"Chug's in rough shape, honey. He didn't take to it lightly. He's confused, scared, in no condition to be interrogated by the police, or Dan, at the moment."

She pressed her face against the window panel, knotting her fingers in her hair. I reached out and brought her head to my chest. She sobbed, gasping for breath.

"That poor kid," she murmured, "and Liz! My God, what are we going to tell her family?"

"That's a toughie, honey."

She blotted her tears with tissue as I told her about the gaggle of neo-Nazis that had taken over Providenciales, of the unlikely movie and mysterious yacht, but refrained from divulging what I'd seen when I circled the *Leopard* that terrible afternoon.

I made no mention of Elisabeth or underlying reasons for my continued involvement. She didn't push, but I believed she sensed

I had more at stake than the motley cache of gold. I told her I hoped to make a deal with Dan to get her brother off the hook. At the moment Chug held the key, a bargaining position. . . a tenuous position, with the goons and authorities hot for his ass.

We had the southern tip of Long Island underwing at 0830, then an open stretch of sea. . . the Crooked Island Passage, where Chug was to have abandoned the *Leopard.* I dropped down to 1500 feet when I had the rotating beacon in sight and picked up the coast of Crooked Island at 0855. The haze had lifted and the sun was brightening, but the dark mass of clouds I'd encountered from San Juan hung ominously to the south. We followed the beach at 500 feet until we sighted the rise of Colonel Hill, then I banked to the east to come about when I had Nottage's bright blue cottage on our starboard wing.

"Are you sure?" Pamela questioned.

"It's his favorite color, honey. No one else would dare."

"It's a pretty house. . . is it new?" I nodded.

"He's done himself proud! Hang in, we're going to spackle the roof."

I leveled with the cliff top and throated the engine. We wing-tipped the eave, swerved to avoid a string of laundry and banked to look back. A red pick-up was parked alongside the house. Mrs. Nottage was framed in the doorway and a half-dozen goats were hell bent for the bush.

"It's him!" Pamela screamed. "It's Chug! He looks so brown and healthy!" Two figures had emerged from a patch of banana trees and Nottage was waving his cap.

I circled over the ocean to keep our noise level below the cliff and made visual note of the approach to the airstrip at Colonel Hill. The cottage would be an excellent marker for a night-time leg to the west; a lone road paralleled the coast between the strip and the eroded cliffs and the habitation was widely dispersed. The strip had been swathed from a cut of pines and was accessed by a mile-long lane from the road.

"Perfect!"

"You're talking to yourself?"

"Sorry, I was on to something else."

"I'll wet my drawers if you don't land immediately!"

I dropped to quarter flaps when we crossed the cliffs and followed the airport lane at 300 feet to minimize our profile from the coast. When we had the strip beneath us I banked sharply to the south and looked down. There were no planes on the ground; the tiny airport was deserted aside from an abandoned vehicle parked in the weeds. I made a 180 degree approach a moment later, touched down and turned off on the taxi way.

"My God, it's desolate," Pamela murmured.

"It's the Out Islands, honey. Bahamasair comes twice a week; if there's no activity they buzz the field and go on!"

"Do they have a ground facility? I'm in somewhat of a twit!"

I gunned the Skylane to the ramp and cut the engine. She was out the door and running before I could fan the switch.

The ground facility consisted of a small, one-story building with a lofted gravity tank to service its needs. A portable fire extinguisher and a four-step metal ramp indicated the bi-weekly flights from Nassau. A rusty Ford LTD was parked alongside the building, its right front tire flat and its windows caked with salt. There was no one about. The next commercial flight was scheduled for the following Thursday.

I opened my door to catch the breeze. The morning sun was arcing over the pines and the sultry air invited my shirt to cling to my back. The temperature, now in the 80s, would be sweltering by mid-day. I eyed the thermos and slipped to the ground to relieve myself in the bush. Pamela emerged from the ladies' room when I was zipping my fly. She'd removed her visor, brushed her hair and was down-right pretty in my oversized shirt.

"Cheat!"

"It was your idea to bring the coffee."

"I hear a car. Do you suppose it's Mr. Nottage?"

"Has to be. There were no vehicles on the road when we were on the approach. There's a small village about five miles down the coast, a couple of trucks. . . that's about it."

"Heavens! It's so provincial."

"Gets to you after a few days. The natives subsist on fish and vegetables, drink a little rum and breathe the air from the sea. The pace is slow, but they live a bit longer than we."

"How did you ever meet Mr. Nottage? Did you know he was here when Chug. . ." She blinked and stared at the trail of dust rising from the trees; she was on the verge of tears.

"It's a long story, honey. Not for now." She grabbed my arm as the red pick-up darted from the lane and careened across the ramp.

"Is it the police?" I ran for the wing tip to wave them off. The truck made a half circle and slowed with its tires curling smoke.

"It's Nottage. . . he can't shift gears!" I shouted, waving my straw and pointing to the runway. If he totalled the Cessna, we'd had it.

The old man struggled with the wheel and came to a screeching halt mid-way across the ramp. The engines humped and clanked as he abandoned the clutch, his black face loosened an enormous grin as he spilled from the cab and came running to my side. I closed my eyes momentarily, but the truck drifted forward and stalled.

"Lordy. . . we's so happy to see you, suh!" He gripped my shoulders and searched my face with his rheumy eyes. "You ain't change one bit. How come it I, who comin' to years?"

This old man had been a faithful friend. He'd aged somewhat; his close-cropped hair was sprinkled with white and his leathery features were drawn, but he was remarkably unbent for the years he admitted. . . muscular, flat-bellied from his time in the field. A splice of rope sufficed to belt his trousers. He wore a bright red shirt knotted at the waist and a faded commodore's cap with braided visor, a special gift from a Christmas past.

"Who dat?" he whispered, peering from my shoulder. I winked and walked him to the truck. Chug, leaning from the window, was scrubbed and fresh. The gash on his cheek was scabbed and the swelling had subsided. He was wearing one of Nottage's shirts and a pair of dark glasses. I pointed over my shoulder.

"Got yourself a visitor, fella'. . . your sister's standing over there."

The kid exploded through the door, tumbling to the ground. Pamela ran screaming from the shadow. They met in a swirl of arms mid-way under the wing.

I'd witnessed tender scenes before, but never one so ecstatic. Their compassion made the past few days worthwhile. My eyes blurred and I turned away. It was their moment. I hustled Nottage to the shed, to have a quiet chat.

"My, she tiny ting," he said. "I see likeness now. . . boy talk mos' about *she*, last couple day." He rubbed a knuckle in his eye and stared at his calloused feet. "Boy shapin' up. Man, he were a mess when I pick him up at Pitts Town. Folks there feel deeply when he came on the beach. They bathe him, make him drink ganja tea."

"Did they pass word down the island?"

"No suh! Tell them, he Nottage chile. . . come from big problem. They know I strong deacon with Rasta connection. . . 'mos

137

fear I Obeah eye." He shook his head and turned a pebble with his toe.

"Boy hard put to sleep couple night. Raise screamin' when de moon was bright. . . he, I have long walk on the beach. Tell I 'bout dat terrible ting. What plan now, Mista Keith. . . reckon to bring responsible party to judgement hill?"

They were walking arm-in-arm in the shadow of the Casuarinas. I turned to the old man and told him part of the story. About the emeralds and the brooch that Liz had come upon. He nodded thoughtfully, raised his eyes when I told him what I had in mind.

"Mus' first seek confidence wid de boy," he said. "He, I talk plenty. . . never once mention dat emerald ting. He mainly want justice for dat girl he bury."

It was nine-thirty; I had an appointment to keep and a light tank of fuel to worry. I climbed to my feet and walked over to the Casuarinas to join the pair.

We sat in the shade and discussed matters, talked about Hogsty Cay, the brooch and the state of the weather. We weighed the odds of locating the gold, the ways and means. The kid was one-minded at first. I couldn't much blame him. It was blood, not gold, he was wanting. When I explained the circumstances and told him I intended to bargain a package, his interest turned and he volunteered to come along if I returned with the Goose.

"It's an even swap if they guarantee to take Freddie off the hook," he cautioned.

"First things first, kid. You're wanted by the Bahamian police and Freddie's hanging loose until the DEA knocks on his door. If he cooperates, Brisbane has enough swat to clear the record, but I can't promise a thing until we come to an understanding."

"Sounds like a shotgun marriage," Pamela added ruefully. "Why don't they arrest the murderers before they get away?"

"Brisbane's an M-7 agent, honey. He can sidestep the Bahamian police, but he'd need Chug's statement to press charges with the Turks-Caicos authorities, and Kurt's no fool. You had a taste of what he can do last night. If Dan hadn't come along, we'd be hanging by our toes on his bloody yacht."

"Keith's right, Sis. . ."

"Hogsty Cay is the last place they'd expect to find us. If we find the gold we'd have a chance to suck him in and bust his ass."

"Meaning?"

"A fast trip with the Goose, providing Dan covers us from Providenciales. If the weather holds we can make it in tomorrow night and dive the reef at dawn."

"I'm concerned for my brother, you mercenary pip. If Chug goes, I go. I want that fully understood!"

"Why don't you sit this one out? You've had your lumps."

"Because I intend to keep you honest! Your past reputation is at odds with my Irish-Catholic mind."

"I can't promise a bed of roses."

"I can handle myself, thank you very much. Just call my Dad and tell him Edwin's all right." I shrugged. She was determined, but I'd rather she'd hassle it with her brother.

Chug joined me by the wing after I'd had a quiet word with Nottage and was checking my fuel. His face was drawn and he was fidgeting with his scar. I sensed he had something on his mind and was wanting to talk. He waited until Pamela was aboard the truck, then he drew me aside and unloaded a bummer.

I studied his face for a moment and asked him to repeat what he'd said. His eyes were level, his voice steady, when he repeated his stunning announcement. He'd done what was probably for the best under the circumstances. The harsh publicity that would befall the next of kin if the *Leopard* was found abandoned was intolerable.

He'd reached a decent decision without reacting from raw emotion or a sense of fear. And I realized something else. . .I was witness to the transition that occurs when an adolescent reaches maturity. In Chug's instance, it hadn't come easily.

She was standing by the cockpit window when I latched the door; frowning, questioning me with her eyes. I winked and gathered her under my arm; she tidied my collar and said she was sorry. When I gunned the Skylane from the strip she stood apart from the others; waving, touching her lips. . . a tiny thing in rolled-up jeans and my loose-hanging shirt. I wobbled the wings to acknowledge her when I passed by. . . she was a lovable little cuss. She'd reached out and warmed my heart.

I banked over the tree tops and fanned the cliff tops to the north until Crooked Island faded behind me. At 1500 feet I turned to the northwest. The ADF had us 10 degrees off course; I was cutting it close with my remaining fuel, but I wanted to probe the passage while I had a few minutes to myself.

The outgoing current would have piled the schooner on the island's northern reefs if her autopilot had yielded before she glided into the two-mile deep. She'd be drifting with the flotsam eddying the rocks if she'd turned her helm before she went under. But there were no masts slanting the reefs, no dismembered planks afloat. He'd said her bowsprit was knifing the swells when he went over the side, that the sea valves had already flooded the forward compartments. He reasoned she would plummet to the bottom while he was swimming to shore.

I was mid-passage when I looked down and saw her ghost. Her tall masts were trailing their lines fifty feet below the surface. The jenny sail billowed from the bowsprit with the current as if a following wind was contending. My hand tightened on the wheel. I banked to get a better view, shuddering at the sight of the apparition suspended in the depths. The *Leopard* had reset her sails.

She was moving slowly with the current into the deep Atlantic; it was as if she'd found a helmsman to guide her. Her mainsail had broken free, her hull canted for a long reach, like an iceberg beneath the sea. I choked and felt for her soul; how long would it be before the bales of grass ruptured and bubbled the air trapped in her holds? Days? Weeks? Chug had battened her hatches with the bodies coffined inside her hull, but she was reluctant to take them down. I saluted the floundering derelict, dipped a wing to her stubborn soul and leveled off to track my heading.

The return flight was without incident; we had a head wind at 6500 feet, but the Skylane was light and I flew directly across the Exuma Sound to shave the time. We had 40 minutes of fuel in the tanks and Normans Cay behind us at 12:35. I throttled back to set up a descent and cancelled with Nassau radio when I drew a bead on the island. There was a long pause before they acknowledged. . . I assumed they were busy with other traffic, but raised an eyebrow when I called into the tower with the south coast under wing at 1500 feet. They had been awaiting my arrival. I was vectored number two behind a Delta 1011 on final; a close-in Aztec was forced to go around. I touched down at 12:50 and turned off the runway with mixed emotions; my point of departure normally would be questioned, but I was greeted with a stony silence. My suspicions heightened when I taxied to the ramp and parked by Sonny's chocks. The Cessna 310 was tethered where I'd left it the day before, but the constable and his cot had been conspicuously withdrawn.

Bill was off-loading a Cherokee Six when I signaled the AV truck to top the tanks. I wasn't wanting to embarrass the old man if Paul was standing by to take me to the pokey. I tied down and signed for the gas, anticipating a tap on the shoulder any moment.

The ramp was oddly deserted and I began to wonder. When the truck pulled away I clung to the shadow of the wing for a moment to consider my immediate alternatives. I had no intention of attempting the security gate. I'd planned to cross to the domestic terminal and raise a taxi, but the ramp was temporarily blocked by an outgoing DC-8 and Bill was advancing with his cart piled with luggage. A tense situation resolved itself a moment later when he wide-berthed the Skylane with the bewildered passengers following behind him. My suspicions tallied with his expression when they passed me; he glanced briefly at my broad-rimmed straw, then closed his eyes as if I'd arrived from outer space.

The police car was gone when we pulled off at the head of my lane. I'd anticipated as much from the play at the ramp. I paid off the cabbie and jogged the driveway until I had an unobstructed view of the cottage. A black Rolls Royce was parked alongside my Ford. A consular Union Jack fluttered from its fender and a white uniformed constable was asleep at the wheel. My castle had been blessed with his company. Sir Daniel had augmented the guest list and they'd accepted his invitation for lunch.

Happy met me at the kitchen door. I paused for a moment to waggle his ears and followed him to the pantry where his attention centered on a Norwegian salmon gracing a Wedgewood platter. Frank turned quickly when he sensed my presence. He was wearing an apron reserved for special guests, but he seemed disturbed and was muttering to himself.

"Dan?" I whispered. He nodded.

"Came by near 12:30. Told him you was fishin', like you said."

"Is that his car in the drive?"

"No, suh. Came four gentlemen while ago. Act like he was expectin' when they rang the gate."

"Have any idea who they are?"

"No, suh. They's dress fancy-like, mos' polite. Ain't paid much heed since I fix them drinks. Mistah Brisbane brought this fish along, an I been curin' it like he said." I eyed the capers and spread of Norwegian bread. Dan had honed his appetite when he overnighted in Miami.

"I'll have to change. . . is there anything in the dryer?"

"What you was wearin' last night. Little girl all right?"

"She's with her brother. Has the fat man been asking?" He shook his head.

"Ain't said much, been busy cuttin' blossoms. Has that table on the patio set like sumpthin' I ain't seen befo. Bes' you hasten, Mistah Keith. Come to remember, his face mighty red when he seed they ain't no clothes in the little gal's closet."

I had a quick shave in Frank's shower and switched clothes from the line, retrieved my sneakers from the dryer and joined him in the pantry when a long forgotten buzzer gave vent to my impatient guest. He'd arranged service for six on the dolly tray. . . strawberries and Dover cream, eggs Florentine with English muffins and the last of my favorite champagne. . . a demijohn of Taittinger iced in a Sheffield bucket with six long-stemmed glasses I'd hidden away. He'd squeezed oranges from the market and supplemented the tray.

"Done it like you say, Mistah Keith. Fat man brought heavy cream when he came." He paused and peered from his shoulder.

Dan's white suit was silhouetted in the entrance way. He seemed mildly surprised, but not unfriendly. "Cut them myself," he chortled. He displayed a hand of Hibiscus as he appraised me with his close-set eyes. "Come now, Keithy, I"ll introduce you to your guests." He smiled benignly and waddled to the parlor; if I'd had a choice I'd have kicked his bloody ass.

"Admiral Cavendish, your host, Keith Slater," he announced a moment later. I stared at the Admiral's ribbon and acknowledged his hand. He was close to 70, tall and gaunt. Towered inches above me when he got to his feet.

"Pleasure," he gruffed. "Sir Daniel's made mention of you often in the past." He hocked a swig of Scotch from his glass and turned to a smallish man standing beside him.

"Lord Barclay, our host, Major Slater. Lord Barclay is under-secretary to the Ministry of Foreign Affairs," he added. The per-spiring Englishman was dressed to the nines in a pin-striped suit, but he was affable and not unpleasant when he turned to the thin-faced man standing beside him.

"Major Slater, Chester Thompson. Mr. Thompson hastened from Washington when this matter came full force. He's been authorized by the State Department to familiarize you with the file." Thompson studied me with an easy grin. He was fortyish, could have been an Ivy League professor, but instead was hard and lean, fully at ease in a seersucker suit. I assumed he'd been loaned by Central Intelligence, but kept a tight lip when he winked and introduced the diminutive man by his side.

"And Doctor Schmidt, Keith. The doctor represents the Austrian government. He joined our group in London at Sir Daniel's request. It's the doctor's first visit to the tropics," he added briefly and removed his glasses to dab his brow with a mono-grammed handkerchief. He grasped my arm while we walked to the table; he was well mannered, articulate and immediately down to business. I was totally unprepared for what he had to say.

"We have hopes to bring an end to this unfortunate affair," he said. "I am to understand you have knowledge to where the bullion is hidden." I sat him down and turned to quiz the beaming Sir Daniel.

"Later, Doctor," he purred. "Now then, gentlemen, loosen your ties and enjoy your lunch. I've been advised that the young lady has altered her plans for the morning." He peered over his shoulder and clapped his hands. Frank strode from the pantry with a tray of glasses and the decanter of juice. He returned to the pantry for the champagne, setting the bucket beside Dan's chair.

"Mos' pleased ifin' you open the bottle," he whispered. " 'Fraid I spray the guests." Dan glowered, worked the cork and tasted the vintage.

"Ah, what an exquisite bouquet! Gentlemen, taste of it before you add the orange."

"I'd appreciate a finger of whiskey," the admiral growled. I nodded and excused myself to the pantry. When I returned they were toasting the Queen.

"To the President!" Dan offered, turning to Thompson. Thompson acknowledged and toasted the Chancellor of Austria. I sipped quietly while the admiral toasted the Falkland Islanders and glared at his empty glass.

And on it went; when the magnum was finished they were into my box of cigars. The Englishmen talked old school and politics, while Thompson conversed in German with the Austrian. I was the forgotten host until Frank served coffee with the last of my VSOP. Then Thompson edged me aside and we sat by the parlor window for a little chat.

"I had a conversation with General O'Brien yesterday morning, Keith. He's strong for you, kid." I salvaged my cup. The nervy bastard had checked my credibility with my old CO.

"He's into this?" He shook his head.

"We were closeted briefly with the Security Council when the

British Ambassador requested logistical assistance. Your name surfaced with Sir Daniel's report and he suggested we sound you out."

I'd been wondering why my Air Force reserve status had been dusted from the shelf.

"Give, Thompson, give! Let's get on with it before the old folks get juiced." He twirled the cognac in his glass for a moment. He was a hardened professional—intelligent and factual. I was an ex-Air Force type with sand in my shoes, a total unknown. Obviously not his choice, but I'd have to do.

"Have you heard of the Gehlen files?"

"No."

"Then listen carefully and I'll fill you in from the beginning. The matter was referred for me to decide, Slater. I'm taking a flyer on the basis of your record. . . with Sir Daniel's approval," he added. "I caution you not to repeat what I have to say. Do we understand one another?"

"OK, OK!"

"General Gehlen was a German intelligence officer who headed the branch that covered the Russian front during World War II. He was never a member of the Nazi party. He was highly respected in the military circles and headed Bonn's Intelligence Service until 1968, when he retired. He died several years ago."

"I remember him. He was written up in the *Times.*"

"The Germans are chronic record keepers, as you know. Their military knew the end was near and gathered certain classified documents during the Berlin holocaust to keep them from the Russians. The V-2 program was one such instance," he added.

"The documents were dispersed amongst the chosen few, photographed, then destroyed. General Gehlen made copies of his own records and hid them in 50 steel chests, pending the surrender. He turned them over to Western intelligence at the end of WWII. A few of the lesser documents and microfilms, unfortunately, were consigned to the trash bin. The U-831's manifest was among them. The U-831 was one of the last Nazi subs to leave Germany before the Allies overran the north coast. She was bound for Argentina."

"With a cargo of bullion and Nazis in civvies."

"Exactly! The Allies had no way of knowing what she carried. Her radio signals were intercepted in the North Sea. She was depth-bombed, an oil slick appeared, and she was marked as a kill. The facts of the matter came to light years later when the microfilms were found in an obscure West German bookshop by an undergraduate student from Vienna." He paused to sip his cognac before continuing.

"The student, not realizing what he had, made a joke of it. He had an enlargement made and posted it on the wall of his room. One of his friends had the sense to notify the police. The student was questioned briefly and released, but the copy was seized. The next morning he was found dead in his room; he'd been tortured and shot. The negative had disappeared, of course."

"Sounds familiar."

He eyed me from his glass and smiled. "You talked with Taylor! You know about the brooch and the nasty business in London. You were observed at the airport this morning," he added. "That limp is a dead give-away, fella"

"I give up. Let's get smashed."

"We'll get to that later, let me finish the story," he countered. "The manifest listed five tons of bullion together with a collection of Habsburg jewelry that had ben stashed in Switzerland by the Nazis during the war. The Austrians identified the pieces from the manifest and immediately contacted British Intelligence. Needless to say, they filed claim to the gold," he added. "The British checked their files and turned to the Pentagon. My department was brought into the case several months later."

"The Pentagon?" I stammered. Thompson nodded.

"Long forgotten tapes, Keith, filed away in vaults. The Navy Department recorded radio transcripts from Nazi submarines during the war. They'd broken the code and used them for interception. We replayed the tapes and ran them through a computer. The U-831's sound pattern was established from an earlier transmission. Her history was consolidated into a single tape and re-run chronologically—an interesting story in itself," he added.

"A bloody balls up!" the admiral bellowed. I spun about. Brisbane was drawing on his cigar. The admiral hocked and peered into his glass.

"The tape disappeared, Keithy," Dan explained, "together with a yeoman from the Navy Department. His automobile was found in a parking lot at Atlantic City."

"We have a copy," Thompson exhorted. Dan shrugged his shoulders. The admiral excused himself and lunged to the kitchen. Dan settled his girth in a nearby chair. He seemed drowsy, but his eyes were intent, urged Thompson to get on with the story.

"It was determined that the sub reversed her call letters after the kill was reported. No one was the wiser in 1945. It was assumed an oddball submersible had surfaced in the mid-Atlantic. Her daily reports were duly recorded, but a side note on the tape called attention to the fact that some of her transmissions were unintelligible, that she was utilizing an abstract number code they hadn't broken."

"The code requires a duplicate set of journals," Dan added, "one ashore, one aboard. The one ashore apparently was held by someone in high trust. It was, undoubtedly, destroyed when the bunkers were blown." Thompson nodded and continued.

"Nineteen days later, the naval station at Key West picked up a radio transmission from the submarine and homed it, using a converging vector from Miami. Two PBY's were dispatched immediately. The PBY's returned to base eight hours later and reported 'no contact'. Two hours elapsed, then the sub broke silence and twice repeated her position, or what was assumed to be her 'position' by the battled cryptologist." He paused to extract a cigarette from his pack and light up.

"It was night fall by then. Standby crews were alerted, but it was after dawn when the PBY's reconnoitered the suspect area. One of the crews detected an under-surface shadow and dropped a depth bomb. There were no further transmissions. The Navy Department believes her plates were ruptured when she was depth-bombed in the North Sea; that she managed to survive until she reached the Bahamian Archipelago; that she went down during the night with all hands on board."

"End of story?" Thompson nodded.

"Until the brooch was found. Until the uncanny circumstances surrounding the manifest intervened. . . as if the dead were calling for an honorable burial."

I excused myself and went to the kitchen to pay Frank and let him off for the afternoon. Schmidt was sound asleep in his chair, his hands clasped on his vest, a contented smile on his face. The Lord was shouting into the telephone when I entered the pantry. The connection was 'asinine', he bellowed. The Admiral was stretched on Frank's bed, deep in a rolling snore, with my bottle of Scotch nearby. I figured he'd been sent along to upbraid the locals, I let him be.

I wrote Frank a check and thanked him for what he'd done. His Pontiac was hammering the lane when I rejoined Dan and Thompson in the parlor. They'd spread a chart on the coffee table; a roll of photo copies lay nearby. Thompson waited until I'd settled in a chair. His briefing was military, short clipped and to the point.

"The entire area has been examined by satellite," he explained, referring to the chart. "A Navy Orion worked the grid electronically; known wrecks have been relocated and circled." He pointed to a marker southeast of Turks. "This one was previously undetected. We believe it's the U-831; she lies at 12,540 feet. We have no way of knowing, of course. A probe with a deep water submersible was considered until the brooch came to light. We now believe the captain jettisoned his cargo when he realized she was sinking. . . somewhere within this triangle." He outlined the area of Somana and Plana Cays east of Acklins.

"This is the area the PBY's searched that morning," Thompson stated. I raised my head and stared at the water barge inbound from Andros. They'd be watching my eyes. . . the search pattern had missed Hogsty Cay by a country mile.

Dan drew on his cigar. Thompson shook his head and re-rolled the photocopies. "It was worth a try," he muttered to the old man. Dan blew a halo to the overhead fan.

"Keithy boy, we've been friends for a long time. Be reasonable, lad. This is an international matter with far-reaching implications. The bullion may lie within the Turks-Caicos waters, which technically are under the jurisdiction of the Crown. . . or it may have been cached on one of the Bahamian Out Islands. In either instance, if we were to bring in an array of recovery equipment, their interest would immediately be aroused and they'd lay claim to the lot."

"Come off it, Dan. Things are out of hand at Providenciales. The word's out, time's running short and people are getting killed."

His face reddened. He flung his cigar through the open window. "Exactly," he thundered. "How long do you intend to hold this matter on your conscience, boy?"

"Until we come to terms, you old fart! You've got your own conscience to grind. You've got an old wooden trawler with a makeshift crew watching the store, a greenhorn constable and frightened young lady shooting dice with a gang of pros." I hesitated for a moment and tossed one in his lap. "How long will it be before they catch on to Elisabeth and cut her throat. . . *answer me that?*"

His eyes expanded like a great white owl on a barn yard fence, his jowls colored blooded crimson. He exploded a spray of spittle and climbed to his feet. Schmidt snorted and came awake.

"Quiet down!" Thompson snapped. "Get yourself a drink, Dan. Keith's on to something. Let me sound him in private before the doctor finds his glasses."

Dan thumbed his vest for a fresh cigar, lit up and flung the match to the floor. Muttered something beneath his breath as he stomped to the pantry. Thompson rolled the charts under his arm, handed the doctor his glasses and pointed to the veranda.

"You shouldn't have done that," he cautioned. "The old man realizes the situation is out of hand."

"It was the only way I could pry it out of him, Thompson. She needs help and she needs it fast."

"They're planning to go down in the morning; an official visit with the admiral's ribbons and six Royal Marines."

"That's nice. The natives will spread roses and dance the merengue while Sir Daniel and the Governor are having tea."

"The marines will be wearing civvies, asshole. They'll pair in eight-hour shifts while the delegation tours the facilities. It's the best he can do short of calling in the police," he added.

I shook my head in disbelief. "You mean he intends to sit on his paddy until Kurt comes up with the loot?"

"If you have a better idea, lay it on the line. I came to talk business. I'm not interested in your caustic remarks."

I studied him for a moment and was greeted with an icy blue

stare. "Are you familiar with the situation at Provo, aside from what you've told me?"

"I've read Borer's report; it's inconclusive."

"Then you realize what we're up against?"

He nodded. "A miniature task force in the land of Oz."

"Exactly. He's set up the movie as a blind while he operates off shore. They're methodically gridding the area west of Mayaguana while the *Walrus* is making change. If the weather holds, they'll be onto it in the next 48 hours. . . with or without Chug's assistance."

I hesitated for a moment. I was past the point of no return.

"I'm scared, Thompson, really scared. Kurt's suspicious of Elisabeth and it's my own damn fault. If Dan tips the lid, he'll muscle her aboard the yacht. . . if he finds the gold, she's dead!" He fanned a light and stared at the sea. The water barge from Andros was off Kelly Island and turning into Arawak Cay. A young couple strolled the beach hand-in-hand, it was a glorious day for them.

"A glimmer of motivation, hey? The old man thought you were involved with the drug scene before he read Bower's report.

"Figured as much, but the CID's not convinced. I stashed Chug in orbit for a double-barreled reason. Paul's hot for his ass and Kurt wants the gold. They cut up the kid's old lady like you wouldn't believe, fella. I was aboard the *Leopard*, Thompson. Circled back when I realized the *Juanita* was responsible. You'd toss your cookies if you'd seen what they did."

He paled and stubbed the cigarette on his shoe. "Sorry, I didn't know about that, Keith. I read your statement, but there was no mention of you going aboard."

"I was afraid Paul would toss Chug in the slammer before I had a chance to sort it out; jails are easy to spring and the Swiss is a clever man. If you're not convinced, sit back and relax. I'll be back in a minute." I looked in on the drowsing Austrian and went to my bedroom, returning moments later to toss the bomb in Thompson's lap. He recoiled immediately and went over the wall.

"It's defused, asshole! It was wired to my engine while I was in Providenciales."

"You're spreading leaves, Slater; we're back to point one. What's your pitch?"

I retrieved the cylinder and motioned him to sit down. He eyed me warily as he logged the wall. If nothing else, I'd salvaged my self-respect.

"You hit the nail on the head, fella; the old shell game. If the *Walrus* can draw him off for 24 hours, I believe we can deliver."

"What are the terms?"

"To get the kid off the hook and hang the bastards."

"He's willing to cooperate?"

"With that understanding."

"Elisabeth?"

"I want an ironclad promise she'll be covered, or I'm going down there tonight and take her out. The kids are safe for the moment; the gold isn't worth the price of a trash bin if you cut me short."

"I'll have a talk with Dan. What's your plan?"

"You'll tell me yours and I'll tell you mine."

He grinned and tossed his cigarette to the wind. "Sparse and inconclusive, until now. The old man's had you in mind since yesterday afternoon, smartass! The entire operation is grossly undermanned and ill-equipped at the local level. He needs your expertise, but he's hard put to say it himself. The Navy proposed sending a brace of helicopters with gravitometers months ago. They outlined a plan to grid the lower islands and would have provided scuba teams to investigate any positive readings. The British would have none of it. They sent the Walrus instead, informing the State

Department they intended to low profile the matter to avoid a confrontation with the Bahamians." He paused to eyeball a passing bikini.

"Eyes front, Thompson, she's married."

"You checked her out?" I nodded.

"She comes by every day at three," Thompson smiled.

"The story of my life. I latched on to one in Berlin and learned she was KGB!"

"The Bahamas are members of the British Commonwealth, but their territory is sovereign and our Navy would have to be invited," I explained.

"Exactly! The *Walrus*, on the other hand, is ostensibly on a survey trip to mark the shoals for shipping. Bower has a gravitometer aboard, but it's a tedious process at best and the *Juanita* is better equipped. The Swiss-German group has been under surveillance for some time," he added. "M-7 was tipped off by Bonn when Klaus was identified with a neo-Nazi cell bank-rolled from Zurich. . . the Hoffman cadre, a gang of brainless terrorists with their fucking minds zeroed on the Fourth Reich."

"You're wandering," I said.

"I know, but I want you to realize you haven't taken them on by yourself. That's why I checked you out with General O'Brien. Gold has no soul, Keith, it just buys! It brought Hitler to power and made a handful of industrialists powerfully rich. Kurt's an industrialist. . . all it takes is a tiny mouse with a loud squeak and the masses have a lion. More to the point, the British had an operative aboard the yacht when it was chartered. He reported twice, then was found floating face down in the Straits of Gibraltar."

"Why didn't they impound the yacht when they arrived at Providenciales?"

"The Swiss is within his legal rights; he knows damn well the

Crown isn't going to ring the publicity bell. It's a Mexican standoff. The yacht's fully documented and you can well believe there's no evidence aboard to collaborate your story."

"I figured it all by myself."

"So I understand; one more item while we're calling spades."

"I'm all ears."

"Stateside, this operation is a hush job from the Security Council on down. Treasury, the Coast Guard, Customs and DEA *have been deliberately left out of it*. . . do you read me?"

"Are we on the same wavelength or did you toss that one in for kicks?"

"I had it in the back of my mind when I checked Freddie's record with the DEA. It takes two to tango, old buddy, and he has the apparatus to pull it off."

"He's running scared . . . it'll take a little persuasion."

Thompson nodded. "I have a copy of his indictment and I'm prepared to bust his arm. The Defense Department will screen the action if we clue them to the bottom line."

"You mean a one-shot run through the ADIZ with five tons of gold?"

"Affirmative! An offshore run to Jacksonville. The DEA's dependent on the radar screen for track. If the military looks the other way, we could wrap this up in the next 48 hours. We're not above a bit of subterfuge if it will hurry things along."

"Why Jax? Miami's closer."

"The Navy Base. . . Cecil Field. It's extremely important to avoid the media. If the DEA moves in for a bust, State would go up the wall."

"They're bound to track us by other means."

"But they can't force you down! We'll be counting on your expertise, Slater. Sir Daniel tells me you hiked a cache of diamonds out of the Kalahari with the South African Air Force hot on your ass."

I stared at the sea; the bastard had turned every stone. He crumpled his empty cigarette pack and tossed it in the sand, where the Lab promptly retrieved it.

"First things first, Thompson. The kid agreed to swap information and you've upped the ante. Does the guarantee hold if we come up with a pile of rocks?"

"Absolutely. If you locate the bullion, it's a plus. If you take it out covertly, the Crown has authorized a double reward."

"OK! I'm sure he'll agree, but for my part I want Elisabeth on hand when we make the run. . . regardless of what we find."

"I understand your concern, Keith. Frankly, I wasn't aware of the situation at Provo until you spread the cards. It's not my bag, but I'll do everything I can to help. The girl should have been covered from the outset." He searched his pockets for a cigarette and changed the subject. "If we've reached a basic understanding, I think it's time we bring in the old man."

We furthered the discussion in the pantry while the Austrian drowsed in his chair. Lord Barclay voiced his approval after they'd finished my cognac and were into the gin. I washed glasses and chipped ice from the frig while they discussed communications and protocol. I renewed my respect for Dan's flexibility when he suggested they utilize an RAF Hercules as a command post, rather than the overbearing VC*10.

"It's too ostentatious," he growled. "The local folk would anticipate the Queen. Better we explain our presence as an evacuation team, in view of the pending storm."

Thompson was long gone when the Rolls pulled away at five. I led Dan to Pamela's room and put him to bed, looked in on the Admiral, eased the bottle from his hand. Then I dialed Howard's number in Providenciales.

It was on to six and fortunately he picked up on the second ring. Muffling my voice with a napkin, I mimicked Hellman's Texas drawl, indicating there was an open slot for the Navaho in the paint shop, should it be available in Fort Lauderdale by tomorrow at noon. A four o'clock charter to the Bahamas would be available if he chose to borrow a plane from the ramp.

There was a pause while Howard cycled his thoughts. He knew Hellman, of course, but not well. Moreover, he'd be surprised by the unsolicited call. I was dependent on his comments in Provo regarding the Goose's need of cosmetics, wherein I'd mentioned Hellman's shop. Secondly, I'd tossed in the charter to arouse his interest, realizing Kurt would monitor Provo's long distance calls.

Howard rose to the occasion, as I thought he might, knowing he'd never let a charter slip by. Cautiously, as if aware of the double play, he responded. "Come to think that Navaho needin' paint for the season, man! An I sure do thank you for keepin' me in mind. Now you say there's a charter wantin' Howard, like maybe it pay for all of that?" I tickled his ear with a key to the past. Said there was a group wanting to scout for marlin at Cutlass Bay (Cat Island). . . indicating a three-day charter and promising his Navaho from the shop on return. Howard picked it up immediately.

"Gotcha, man! Now you tell them folks Howard will fetch in around one. . . an we'll be needin' an eight seater, if'n your referin' to the one on your ramp." I signed off before he elaborated further, realizing he'd read me loud and clear.

That done, having established an experienced hand to ride my right hand seat, I rounded the house to inspect my snoring guests. . . keyed the Ford and drove into Nassau for a change of scene. Bone tired, verging on pre-mission jitters, I turned off from Shirley Street and stopped at the Poop Deck for a quieting beer.

Unlike Provo, the bistro was orderly. Beset with tourists and a gaggle of locals at the bar, you could eavesdrop on a mixed bag of conversations regarding the storm and events in the past. I eyed the swanky yachts, the long-stemmed gals strolling the docks in their preppy shorts and flat-breasted overshirts. Watched a woody Trumpy cast its lines, presumably heading for the safety of Broward Marine. My thoughts returned to Elisabeth. . . of the robust night we'd shared in Providenciales and then to the downer of her well-being, if Kurt flushed her card before Dan arrived with the Royal Marines.

It was after seven when I traversed Bay Street. Traffic came to a halt at the corner of Queen, waiting for a funeral procession to pass. They were all in step with the big, bass drums; women dressed in black with their Bibles in hand, pallbearers trundling the coffin on a pair of rickety wheels, Masons with their tassled caps, wide-eyed kids in their Sunday best. There was a feeling of tranquility when they were gone to the hill, an acceptance of things that had to be. Would I be so honored when my time came to pass? Would I be re- membered as the man who walked a lonely road as he sought for himself?

A hatchback Mustang rumbled behind me when I passed Delaport Point on my return to the cottage. I'd slowed to enjoy the sunset, accelerating to allow an open stretch of road when they fish-tailed and leaned on their horn. They hugged the Ford until an oncoming taxi passed, then roared by and narrowly missed a tag-along mini-bus. I came across them again at Traveller's Rest. They'd apparently stopped for a six-pack and were gabbing with the girlies on the long veranda. Gone from my thoughts when they shot past me again at Gambier Village. A bottle spun from the window as they rounded a curve and disappeared. Curiously, I came on to their brake lights at the head of my lane. I swerved, as if intending to pass, but they laid rubber and were gone when I geared to make my turn.

I collected by watchhound at the gate, locked the house from the inside and turned on the ground lights. A reoccurence of the previous night was unlikely, but I needed the sense of security.

The admiral was asleep when I checked his room. When I looked in on Dan, he was tented beneath a sheet, snoring peacefully. His shoulder holster lay on the bedside table with a bottle of aspirin.

It was after nine when I stretched out on my bed with Happy on the floor beside me. I stared at Judith's portrait as I turned out the light, remembering the wonderous weeks we'd shared in the Kalahari; the epic night at the Balaika when we'd made love in the tub and nearly drowned. I closed my eyes when I thought of the note she'd penned before she disappeared, of my agonizing when I realized how stupid I was to let her go.

My dreams were interwoven with past and present; Dan's glowering face when we crossed paths in Nairobi years before; Elisabeth standing on the pier at Providenciales, her willowly stance, her elusive smile. I was fending off Kurt's knife when the phone shrilled from the bedside table. It took me a moment to place Green Eyes's voice. The ragged transmission was brought on by meteorological interference, or a roundabout connection.

"She gone on that yacht this morning," he blurted. "Now they's havin' dinner downstairs an she ain't among them. I check her room, Keith. Her clothes is all there, like she weren't plannin' to spend the night somewhere." I got to my elbows when his signal faded. "Figured I best call when I seed the *Walrus* gone from the dock. She keen for you, man. She axe. . ." We were abruptly cut off. I shook the phone but it was completely dead.

I sat up in the bed, fully awake. The patio lanterns were casting shadows from the potted palms; there was movement that was at odds with the spurious breeze. I blinked to clear my eyes and lowered my feet to the floor when Happy growled and rose to his haunches. I tensed as he crouched to spring. A machete glinted in the half-light as it probed my bedroom door, piercing the screen as I slipped from the bed. As I groped for the dart gun, a dusky arm reached in to try the latch. I palmed the gun and aimed from the bed.

When the screen door flew open, the Lab barked and lunged at the intruder, who wheeled and raised his blade. I pinged him in the stomach as the machete descended, the dog's momentum deflected his arm and razor-sharp steel clanged to the floor. I dove for his legs and slammed him down, belting him behind the ear when he reached for the machete. He was unconscious when I climbed to my feet, pulling Happy from his wrist. I had a brief moment to consider what we had when a shot echoed from Pamelas room and I realized there were more.

A black teenager lay screaming by the door with blood spurting from a shattered knee. Dan was standing in the doorway with smoke curling from his Webley, pointing to a bullet hole in the screen. He was wearing an enormous pair of boxer shorts that fell just short of his ankles. Gestured with the Webley when he saw me standing outside with the snarling dog at my heel.

"Fetch a tourniquet, Keithy. The fellow is hemorrhaging. Best call an ambulance and notify the police." He bent down to retrieve a sawed-off shotgun that lay by the step. "Take this along; I'm not sure what we have," he added. I reached for the gun and spun about when the mayhem exploded in the kitchen.

It began with a gruff command and ended with a piercing scream. Dishes fell, a door slammed, glasses were swept from their shelves in the pantry way. The admiral emerged, holding a mean-looking kid by the neck, his feet dancing above the patio floor, his arms swinging wildly for the admiral's belly.

"Let me down or I teach you a lesson," the kid shrieked. "I cut you up, man. I fix you good! You ain't show no respect!" The admiral stopped short when he saw Dan standing in the door and the unhappy thug groaning on the floor.

"Two of them, hey! Found this monkey standing by my bed with a knife in his hand." He held the screaming youngster at arm's length and soccer-kicked his ass. The kid skidded across the patio, got to his knees and reached for his hip; Dan placed a shot by his leg whereupon a car spun gravel in the driveway and the kid gave it up, bursting into tears.

Running toward the entrance way, I triggered the shotgun. The Mustang's taillights exploded in a haze of crimson glass. The driver sideswiped a palm, swerved across the grass and fantailed the lane. I waited until his tires screeched onto the highway, then I went to the pantry to locate a flashlight and pliers. They'd cut the telephone line where it was stapled to the eave, entering the house by forcing the kitchen door.

An ambulance arrived within minutes of the police. They'd stopped briefly to radio for a follow-up when they came upon an accident at Orange Hill; a Mustang belly up on the road with the decapitated driver spreading blood from the windshield.

Paul appeared while they were applying the tourniquet to the teenager on the patio. He was sympathetic, but not displeased. They were wanted for a brutal hold-up at the Royal Bank on the 16th of July. The belligerent kid was a three-time loser — breaking and entering, assault with a deadly weapon and attempted rape.

"We'll put him away until he comes of age," Paul commented when they led him away. "This man you disabled is a Turks Islander, Keith. They call him Big Red. He was serving 20 years for second-degree murder when he escaped from Fox Hill. We understand he's been seen in Providenciales of late. Best you exercise caution, boy! He have family, one bad lot of niggers, if you know what I mean."

Five

THE TOWER CAME UP with the answer to Big Red's appearance when I filed to Fort Lauderdale early in the morning The night shift landed a Widgeon at nine o'clock the previous evening. The pilot had cleared with immigration and refueled. He'd taken off again at 0100 and filed IFR to Providenciales. The pilot's name was Wolfgang von Wilhelms. There were no passengers listed upon his arrival, nor on his manifest when he filed his return.

When I was airborne, I banked the 310 sharply and scanned Coral Harbour road to where it paralleled the runway in the south. It was an isolated area, difficult to patrol, a known rendezvous for ganja runners from Jamaica. The Mustang possibly waited alongside the road until the Widgeon landed, then turned about. . . a short pause, an exchange of lights? The security fence was an easy lift. Red could have made it to the road while Wolfgang requested taxi instructions from ground control. I picked up the Bimini homer on the ADF as I climbed to the west. It had been close; I'd be sweating it out in Providenciales if my guests hadn't been so handy.

The storm's center was 50 miles south of Santo Domingo, according to the eight o'clock weather report. The force winds were reading 100 knots; forward movement had stalled, but was expected to intensify once it passed over the mountains of central Hispaniola. It would either veer to the north and strike Turks-

Caicos, or continue west and hit the north coast of Cuba. Gale warnings raised in the Turks-Caicos group cautioned inter-island freighters to remain in port.

My thoughts turned to Elisabeth and my deferred conversation with Dan. I'd exacted his promise, if the *Juanita* was at anchor when he arrived, but it was a slender chance at best.

It was nine fifteen when I cleared customs and taxied to Greff's to sign off the 310. Hellman agreed to have the Goose ready at 1400 when I phoned to tell him Howard was expected at one and intended to leave his Navaho in the shop. He was busy with an incoming call and asked me to call back. I had second thoughts when I tooled the Porsche and drove to the Dive Shop on 17th Street. Hellman hadn't listened and Howard would be at odds when the Texan was confronted with his requisition for paint.

It was ten thirty when I parked at my office. Marie was onto a hissy fit, but I waved her off and went upstairs to have coffee with the boys and utilize the telephone without interference. When I emerged from the drafting room she was tapping her foot and waiting at the bottom of the stairs.

"Where in the hell have you been?" she snapped. "A couple of meatheads came by yesterday morning. . . one of them with his arm in a sling. He wasn't very nice. Wanted to know when you were expected. I told them you were on your way to St. Maarten and locked myself in the john. Playing around with the Mafia, lover boy? Building yourself a catacomb?"

"Anyone else?" She smoothed her skirt and nodded.

"A pair of straights from the DEA. One of them flashed a badge. Same questions."

"I made a side trip to the Out Islands and blew a tire."

"That's a likely story; you've been carousing with the broads and left me to watch the fort."

"Has my partner been in?"

She shook her head. "Same damned thing. He took off for New York and saddled me with his kids. If I was in my right mind I'd quit," she added.

"Come off it, honey. A little excitement is the spice of life."

"Don't put me off, you boudoir acrobat! I've his wife hammering for checks while I watch her brood of chicks, then you have the gall to sneak in with your fly undone." She brushed her hair and freshened her lipstick. "I run this operation and I'm not about to quit, but you worry me, Keith. Why don't you call it off before someone clips your golden locks?" I kissed her and parted the door. I had a one o'clock appointment and was running late.

Freddie was waiting at a dockside table when I inquired at the bar. He apparently was a regular at the popular bistro on the Intracoastal. He had an extension phone at his disposal and the attention of the teenage waitresses, but his conversation was given to a pair of hot shots who had tied in with a gleaming cigarette. Dismissed them curtly when I approached the table. He was a smallish fellow in his thirties, brown-eyed with a thatch of red hair. Wore a short clipped beard, a navy jersey, white slacks and an immaculate pair of topsiders.

If Pamela hadn't clued me, I would have assumed he was a corporate type on a holiday jaunt. He'd actually made it in commodities while his contemporaries were finishing college; parlayed a fortune in oil leases while they were nine to five with IBM. He had a luxurious pad in Boca Raton and a custom Hatteras. An avid fisherman, he followed the tournaments from Walkers Cay to Newport in season. A low-key fraternizer, he'd mingled freely in high society and contributed generously to their charities. . . until he was indicted for financing a load of grass into a Rhode Island estuary and was abruptly dropped from the invitation lists.

Streetwise, he was top dog. His organization was the envy of every druggie from Maine to Barranquilla. His vans and boats were equipped with space-age electronics, his airlift with counter radar he'd covertly diverted from military. The scourge of the DEA; when they fingered a bust, his fleet would be 300 miles up coast. There had been a slip-up in Rhode Island; the Boy Scouts has discovered his cache of grass on a Sunday outing and helped themselves before the scoutmaster summoned the police.

Freddie was understandably nervous when I introduced myself and pulled up a chair. He had a million dollar tag on his collar and my urgent call had him doubly upset. He'd obviously checked me out, seen me around and realized I wasn't a patsy for the DEA. I ordered a beer and told him I had a message from Crooked Island . . . I wanted to string him along, get a glimpse into his mind before Thompson arrived to lay it on the line. He squirmed in his chair and eyed the departing cigarette.

"Get to the point, Slater. I'm a very busy man."

"It has to do with a two-masted schooner, Freddie. Got a message from one of the crew." He paled, reached for his cigarettes, visibly shaken, managed to light up on the second try.

"What are you after, Slater? If it's money, I'm fresh out of bucks!"

"I'm not after money, shithead! Chug needs immediate help and I want to know how far you'll go." His eyes darted to my face.

"Chug?" I nodded.

"Is he all right?"

"Not exactly."

"Spades, Slater. I'm not a little boy."

"Then grab yourself, fella. You're not going to sleep tonight! Liz is dead and your crew is under water." Freddie balled his fists. I shooed the waitress away when she rushed to his side.

"Is he sick, mister?"

"Not yet, honey. He's giving it thought."

"Jesus, man, what happened?" he mumbled. I waited until the waitress returned to the bar and put it to him gently.

It was to have been the *Leopard's* last trip. He'd planned to quit and hack it straight, but he'd laid out two million bail to spring his boys from the Rhode Island jail and was short on cash. He was one sorry fellow, close to tears, when Thompson came along. We had a heart-to-heart talk for the better part of an hour before we reached an understanding. It was close to three when I pulled onto Hellman's ramp to unload my gear. The Goose was on the line and Howard had arrived. The stage was set.

"We gave the old bird an annual, caulked the windows and topped her off like you said," Hellmann explained during our walk around. The Goose wasn't very pretty. Her hull was blotched with anti-corrosive, her windows streaked, but she seemed relieved to be out of the emergency ward.

"I'll have the windshield washed, Keith. Jake's gone for his ladder." He glanced at the gear I'd lugged from the Porsche. "You picked one hell of a day to go skinny dippin', fella. Crawfish are out of season. . . watcha' got in mind?"

"Keep it under your hat. We're going to roll the casino at Paradise Island."

"Like it's none of my damn business?" I nodded.

"Now, Keith, you know I ain't much for telling tales, but the DEA was nosing around when we towed the old girl from the shop and stored the seats."

"She's clean!"

"I know, but they were asking questions when they gandered that new single side-band. Like, why's Slater springing for long-range radio when she's peeling paint?" He pointed to Andy's PBY at the far end of the ramp. "Same questions. They wanted me to plant a beeper in the tail. . . told them to blow it out their ass. Incidentally, old buddy, Howard rolled in this morning with his Navaho for a paint job. Is he good for the dollar or are you mailing me flowers?" He squinted at the sun for a moment. He was from another generation and lost with his thoughts.

"Don't worry it, Hellman. I'll guarantee the tab."

"I'm an old turkey buzzard from Texas," he mused, "but I'm willin' to learn. That Navaho was clean as a whistle when we opened it up, best-kept machine I've ever seen." He shrugged and turned on his heel. "Loaned him my Caddy when he was wanting a ride to town. Said to tell you he'd be back at three thirty."

Howard was reluctant when we gandered a chart and I explained what was on my mind. His charter license was on the line if there was conflict with the DEA or Bahamian police. Thompson pulled alongside in a nondescript Ford while we were discussing the pros and cons. Displaying his State Department identification, he explained the urgency of the matter to Howard's satisfaction.

Hellman lurked about, peering from his hangar. Undoubtedly there were other eyes when we off-loaded the Ford and secured its contents to the cabin floor. An unexplained delay when I filed for Cape Eleuthera with Air Traffic Control. The vintage Goose was as obvious as the Goodyear blimp over Ft. Lauderdale Beach when we lifted off at 4:45 and droned to the east. Howard eyed me reproachfully when ATC acknowledged our take-off time and I immediately switched frequencies to the Coast Guard's channel. . . assuming ATC had relayed the information, which they had, acknowledging

"Roger, Miami, we're scrambling a Falcon at 1800 EDT."

Howard flew the stretch to Cape Eleuthera, getting the feel of the cranky amphibian while I explained her whims and tricks. He'd flown Beech 18's and was familiar with the 450hp Pratt-Whitneys, but the overhead throttles were a twist until he adjusted to the quadrant and synchronized the gauges. We simulated a water landing when we passed the Gulfstream and were on to the flats; climbed to 3500 to exercise a series of turns until I was satisfied he could handle the old girl on his own.

He'd completed a 360 over Andros and leveled off to regain our heading when a shadow flitted by from somewhere above us. I tensed and swiveled in my seat. Howard grimaced and pointed to his window. We had the DEA on our starboard wing a moment later—a brand new Cessna Eagle with two beaming faces. I dipped the Goose's wing to warn them off and triggered the mike to ask what they were about. I'd anticipated a radar track from altitude, reasoned with our chances in the dark. . . but a clinging vigilante?

"Just keeping you honest, Slater," they called when I cycled l21.9.

"Get lost. You're wasting gas."

"Take us to your leader and we'll call it quits."

"We're going for a transatlantic. Howard needs the practice."

"Come off it, Keith! Do we have to tag you all night?"

"It's a long way to Tipperary, sludge head."

"Twenty-five thousand will buy a lot of paint, lover boy."

"Heavens to Betsy! Do we look that bad?" He muttered something aside. I turned down the volume. His voice was a blast.

"You know damn well what we're after, Slater. It has two masts and a raggedy-ass kid with 60 tons of grass. Do yourself a favor; it's worth 25 G's in hundred dollar bills."

"Are you asking me to rat on a friend?"

"I'm telling you, dammit! We'll have your Goose on a stick if you're planning to fly it out!" We encountered a patch of weather before I could answer. Howard drilled the squall dead center hoping to lose them in the rain, but the pilot apparently was an ex-military-type and rode our wing in close formation until we broke into the clear.

"Last chance, hot stick! Twenty-five thousand in hundred dollar bills."

"Come off it, fellas! You're making me nervous," a voice called from somewhere apart. I clicked off and glanced at my watch. We were two hours out and had the curl of Eleuthera on the horizon; in an hour we would be onto the night.

They banked to the north when we commenced our descent to the Cape. I was somewhat relieved, anxious to avoid a continued harangue in the air. The Goose had long-range tanks, but the Eagle was pressing the point of no return. They'd evidently been dispatched on the off-chance we'd make a deal; more likely to divert our attention while they relayed our position to the high-flying jet that was to be off at 1800.

"They's havin' to turn back," Howard ventured. "Ain't no AV at the Cape, closest being Nassau or Georgetown."

I played a hunch and set up the Coast Guard frequency. We were greeted with a burst of static and unintelligible voices. We were too low to intercept an over-the-horizon signal communication. "Are you thinking what I'm thinking?"

Howard nodded. "They're circling and talking to the Falcon, man. He must got off late or we be hearin' his talk if he's over the Cape."

I gave the situation heavy thought while Howard three-pointed the goose and taxied to customs. He was pleased with his no sweat landing in the unforgiving amphibian, tossing me an easy grin, but I was on to other things. I was puzzled by the Eagle's casual circling from a distance; the given opportunity to ram-rod the throttles and scat for the hills, wary of being mouse-trapped when we touched down at Crooked Island. Hellman's voice echoed in my mind when we stepped from the Goose and walked to the terminal. The ramp was deserted; a lone car sat in the lot and customs was about to call it a day.

"Do you know that fellow?" I asked Howard when we were short of the door. He peered inside and turned about.

"Commissioner Moss. He's on the phone."

"The telephone or unicom?"

"Can't rightly tell, " Howard replied. I handed him my passport and arrival forms.

"Tell him we're going on to Cat Island and hang in while I check the aft compartment," I added, remembering Hellman's comments at the ramp. Howard paused for a moment, then nodded as he stepped inside.

I located the beeper behind the aft bulkhead, strapped with adhesive with its antenna full play. I was familiar with the working of the Air Force emergency locater, had a facsimile strapped to my parachute when I ejected over Iraq. And knowing Hellman as I did, I realized it wasn't included in his bag of tricks. The device probably was installed by the DEA while he was preoccupied or home for dinner.

Here was an opportunity to misdirect the circling Cessna, I thought, disengaging the transmitter from the bulkhead. With the Commissioner's car sitting adjacent to the arrival building, I re-fastened the transmitter inside the rear bumper, extending the antenna full length.

"Commissioner was talkin' to Paul Johnson," Howard confided as we taxied to take-off. "Hush up when I came in, but seed the CID numbers where he was writing on the wall. Been conversin' with that Cessna likewise, Keith. Unicom light was blinkin' when he was signin' our Trans-Air. Reasoned he was waitin' to pick up, seein' he was hurryin' us to depart."

We ruminated further while I checked the mags and exercised the props, delaying our take-off until the Commissioner closed shop and walked to his car. The sun was low ebb when I nodded to Howard and fire-walled the quadrant. I upped the volume on the Coast Guard band and followed the macadam to Bannerman Town. We came onto the commissioner's car about five miles out. He'd switched on his lights and was idling center of the road.

"He be wonderin' what he has, come morning," Howard observed. I banked and looked back. The Eagle's homing needle would indicate the beeper was in motion, but they were nowhere in sight.

We hugged the sea when Eleuthera was behind us. The Goose's mottled gray blended with the swells, making us difficult to visually track in the dwindling light. The Coast Guard Falcon was radar-equipped for offshore surveillance. . . its down scan had a radius of 50 miles. There were mitigating factors, however. The Goose was an easy target over water, but its slow-flying characteristics were adaptable to the rugged beaches and Howard was islandwise with the terrain. If we wing-tipped the shoreline while we worked our way south, we had a distinct advantage. A pulsing radar search would echo the land mass, but a paralleling target would be difficult to follow. An infra-red scan was another matter. We'd light up the screen like a poppy field in Flanders if an electronic-laden EC-2 joined the fracas.

". . . Falcon over Nassau VOR at one niner thousand, Eagle Two!" I snapped upright in my seat. Howard tensed and stared at the overhead speaker.

"Røger, Falcon, we're circling Bannerman Town. We think the bastard set down on the highway."

". . . Do you have visual?"

"Negative. It's getting dark, but we have the beeper loud and clear!"

". . He's waiting you out, Eagle. How do you stand for fuel?"

"Beggerman's choice. . . stand by, stand by! Goddammit to hell, *we've been homing a fucking car!*"

"Eagle Two, Coast Guard Falcon. Do you read?"

"Shit!"

". . . What say?"

"Slater pulled the chain! The car's parked in front of a lousy bar." There was a long pause while the information was absorbed. The Falcon apparently was in contact with Miami control. Little San Salvador passed beneath our portside wing; the dark outline of Cat Island appeared on the Goose's nose. We activated the panel lights to monitor the altimeter, our eyes glued to the windscreen.

"They's a 400-foot hill at the Bight," Howard cautioned. "If you plannin' to go backside, I'm suggestin' we pick up 90 degrees."

"Easy does it, Eagle Two. Gladstone advises continue visual to Cutlass Bay. We'll be overhead at 0100 GMT."

"I'm gonna turn in my fucking wings," the Eagle's pilot muttered.

". . . do you have sufficient fuel to check the Bight and Hawks Nest Creek?"

"Roger, Falcon. We have enough if we RON at Cutlass Bay. That bastard musta hooked it to the car when we were jabbering with CID."

"OK, OK, do what you can. Advise, monitor Gladstone Control on channel 12. We have a three-way with the police planes at Georgetown and Acklins Island."

I eyed the single side-band and dialed the illegal chip Thompson had thoughtfully provided from his covert bag of tricks. We had a bead on the DEA's private channel when we skimmed the beach and came on to the low riding hills. The Eagle was miles behind us, but it was after eight and we were teasing the Falcon's down scan if we remained over the open sea.

I turned down the panel lights to adjust to the terrain. When a cottage flashed by, Howard squirmed in his seat. "God Almighty, Keith!"

"Close your eyes. . . we're going to spread some leaves!"

We topped the central ridge and dropped immediately to take advantage of the radar-reflecting hills. We banked sharply to the south when we'd passed the island's eastern reach. I hedgehopped the beach at 50 feet while my co-pilot called the shots from his open window. Twilight was fading in the west, but total darkness enveloped the Atlantic side. We had only the surf to follow.

"They's buzzin' the Bight. . . I can see their lights!"

Howard called when we were midway to Columbus Point. I dropped to 20 feet; the Pratt-Whitneys' exhaust flames would be a dead giveaway if they overflew the ridge.

"Bight airstrip negative," the Eagle called in a moment later. "We'll buzz Hawk's Nest and Cutlass Bay before we call it a night."

"Roger, Eagle. Falcon over Little San Salvador and working 160 degrees." They were closing their scissors on the 85 mile island and hoping to catch somewhere in between.

We had Columbus Point in the salty haze at 8:15. From there

on we were faced with a 20-mile stretch of open water until we rounded the cliffs of Long Island. I climbed to 100 feet to ease the sweat and take stock.

The Eagle would be circling the boot tip to the west while we were coming off the heel. The Eagle was hopelessly out of it, but the Falcon was pulsing behind us, like a headlight beaming on a darkened road. We only had a few precious minutes before they ticked our feathers.

I glanced at Howard and pointed to the compass as the chalky face of Columbus Point fled our starboard wing. He nodded and spread the chart on his knee and turned up the map light to call out bearings. I laid the Goose on the deck and gave her full rein. Long minutes passed as the open Atlantic fled beneath our keel. We bent an ear to the overhead speaker and listened while the frustrated Eagle announced they'd spend the night at Cutlass Bay.

A fisherman's lantern was bobbing the outer reef when Conception Island passed to the east at 8:25. We had the north tip of Long Island in sight when the Falcon called in to Gladstone Control. Howard shook his head when the call was returned. . . there apparently was a flurry of confusion. I turned up the volume to sweat them out while they determined our credibility. The Falcon had picked up a northbound blip 20 miles west of Hawks Nest Creek and was circling at nine thousand feet.

". . . We're tracking a heading of 300 degrees, Miami. They're 30 miles west of the Bight and moving fast."

". . . Roger, Falcon. Is the Eagle in the air?"

" . . Negative. They landed at Cutlass Bay."

" . . Stand by. We're trying to raise an EC-2!"

"Man, we come to a piece of luck," Howard commented. "That gotta be some pothead sneakin' up from Jamaica with a load of ganja!"

" . . Gladstone Control, Falcon with an urgent! We have a fringe target five miles south of Stella Maris." I tensed the wheel. Howard shrugged and opened his window when I opted for the cliffs. We were tucked away at 50 feet when the Falcon called in to report he'd lost our blip.

" . . . It has to be Slater, Gladstone. Number two is pegging 220 knots at 1500!"

" . . Hold his fix. Navy advises shortage of equipment. We're requesting assistance from Homestead Air Force Base."

We barreled the coast to the south while their attention was divided. Eight-forty rolled by as Long Island slipped away to the west. I climbed to 500 feet when we calculated we were over the Crooked Island Passage. We were flying the gauges in total darkness when Gladstone admitted they had a problem.

" . . Coast Guard Falcon, Gladstone Control. Homestead advises their F-16's grounded for technical reasons. What is your present position?"

" . . We're over Cat Island at nine thousand, Gladstone. Target maintaining 300 degrees. . . We're going to lose him if we continue to circle."

" . . Primary target?"

" . . We had a piece of one before it went off the screen. If it's Slater he's pulled every trick he learned in Desert Storm. . . he just up and disappeared like a chicken on Saturday night."

"Roger, Falcon. Primary target's latitude and longitude?"

"Latitude 23 north, longitude 75 projected if he's maintaining 130 knots. That would put them in the vicinity of Diamond Roads if they're skimming the cliffs."

" . . OK, Falcon. We are alerting police planes at Acklins and Georgetown to check the strips from Crooked Island south."

" . . And if he hits for the drink?"

" . . You said it, I didn't. Gladstone advises track secondary target to the coast. We think it's no-flight plan from Montego Bay." We pulled up to 1000 feet to get a bearing on the Crooked Island beacon. Thompson had performed. The military were sitting on their hands, but I hadn't counted on Paul's tenacity.

"Them fellows ain't goin to fly after dark, Keith. Aero-Commanders got problems, man." I shrugged. I respected his judgment but I wasn't that sure. Paul was aching for a bust and he could pull the top pilots from Bahamasair. We set up their channel to guard against the possibility, then continued to monitor Gladstone on the single-side band set.

"My eyes are weary, Howard. Am I seeing things or do we have the light?" He pressed his head to the windscreen. "You got it, man. She lyin' dead ahead. Got some cloud. . . cain't see it now."

"OK! I'm turning five degrees east. Let me know when it's off the wing." He bent to his window. The windscreen was hazed with salt and playing tricks.

"She's off to the right, Keith. It's clear up ahead. Musta passed through some scud."

"All right! Count ten and watch for a signal from the cliffs. You'll have a two-plus-two if the strip's clear; if she flashes red we're to pick them up five miles down the road."

"God almighty, Keith. Howard's not keen for roadside. . . got it, man? Someone wavin' a torch and it ain't comin' up red like you say." I made a wide 270 over the sea and crossed the cliffs to follow the lane I'd reconnoitered the previous morning.

We buzzed the strip with our landing lights to make certain there were no surprises. Nottage blinked his lights when we thundered by and made a 180 for a low approach. I dropped the gear and chopped the throttles as the Goose slipped over the pines and settled heavily on her wheels. Nottage's truck drew alongside as we braked midway and swiveled about.

I idled the Pratt-Whitneys while Howard dropped the door and took them aboard with their gear. The Falcon's signal faded, but the police plane from Georgetown was loud and clear. They'd buzzed the strip at Diamond Roads and were homing the Pitts Town light . . . in touch with an Aero-Commander, proceeding north from Acklins Island.

I sensed a presence slip into the seat beside me, a hand reach for mine. . . then a glimmer of white teeth and shining eyes. When I felt her lips brush my cheek, I reached up and turned down the jab-bering avionics; we had 15 minutes before they could converge on Colonel Hill. What the hell!

The police planes were closing in when we lifted off at 9: 25. Nottage's taillights gleamed briefly from the lane, swerved onto the coastal road and disappeared as we banked sharply to the south. I treetopped the narrow island until the inky terrain glinted of sea.

We had 20 miles behind us when they circled the strip and called in a negative to Paul. Their signal faded as we proceeded south and turned to the heading Howard had calibrated. We had a glimpse of the stars through the thinning clouds; we were over a desolate stretch of shoals and squalid mangrove, the dank, unin-habited curl of Acklins Island. Then we were over the open sea again, the gateway to Hogsty Cay.

"Reckon 30 miles," Howard ventured nervously as he studied the rolling swells. "Best climb to 2500; they ain't goin' to fuss with us now, Keith." I advanced the throttles and exercised my clammy hands. The air was fairly stable in scattered rain, but the glimmer of lightning on the horizon was an ominous reminder of the hurri-cane's shift to the west. "Man, that ting jus' waitin' to tear us apart," he added, as if he'd sensed my thoughts. "Spit of sand ain't fittin' for God's creatures if she come rollin' in from the sout."

I leveled off at 2500 and throttled back to minimum cruise. The cockpit air was pungent with our sweat, the volatile odor of high octane gas and the acrid heat of the radios. We continued to monitor the frequencies on the off-chance a secondary Falcon had been dispatched. I enhanced the panel display and switched the NAV set to standby. We were into the critical portion of our nocturnal odyssey; a blind approach to the tiny atoll with a vintage amphibian, an uncertain splashdown in the dead of night over a treacherous span of reefs. . . the uncertainty of the kid's technical ability and a vague promise that a full-time alcoholic had accomplished it on his own in the past with a creaky PBY.

The accelerating tension and the glow from the Pratt-Whitneys' exhaust brought back memories. Howard's black face reminded me of my F-15 wing man over Iraq, the blue fire of our F-15's as we angled across the desert to shield the B-52's over Kuwait. The tenseness, the loneliness we'd felt, the wondering of why we were there. My thoughts changed channels, focusing on the Swiss, the whereabouts of the *Juanita* and Green Eyes' aborted call. Was Elisabeth aboard? Was she still alive? How close we were to Providenciales?

" . . High time!" Howard said. I nodded and gripped the wheel.

"Time to con the helm, fellas," I called to the pair huddled in the rear. Chug came forward to the jump seat, Pamela peering over his shoulder as he buckled in. She had the clean scent of sop about her, a certain freshness that negated our long hours at the controls.

"Where are we?" she had the audacity to ask. I pointed to Howard's chart.

About here . . . if we raise the radio beacon we have it made." She stared into the blackness and closed her eyes.

"OK, set up 111.42 on the omni and count one to ten on l20 1," Chug commanded. "Your voice will activate the beacon. It switches off automatically after 60 seconds," he added. Howard set the frequencies, triggered the mike and began to count. The omni needle lazed.

"Shit! I hope them fuckin' batteries ain't dead!"

"Mind your language, Edwin!" He shrugged and leaned forward in his seat. Howard enunciated from the count of five . . . the needle responded and began to rise.

"That's it!" Chug shouted. The needle swung five degrees west and steadied. I banked the Goose and came back on the throttles.

"Best allow for drift . . . she slidin' off," Howard cautioned. I nodded and made the correction. Sixty seconds elapsed, then the needle wavered and fell full circle.

"OK! Now give another count on 120 1," the kid interjected. "The strobe underwater light will switch on for three minutes."

Howard waited until we'd passed through 1500 feet; at 1400 he thumbed the mike and began another count. Chug fingered his scar. Thirty seconds passed. Pamela tensed up and gripped my arm. A thin silver thread suddenly appeared in the blackness ahead. I dropped quarter flaps and chopped the throttles, heavy-footing the rudder to offset the crosswind. We were on a high approach over the eastern perimeter of the lagoon.

I marveled Freddie's ingenuity as I rolled back the trim. The underwater lights bisected the lagoon neatly through its center, illuminating the shallow bottom like an interstate highway caught beneath a tide. I cast an eye on the cresting reef as we glided across its outer reach; added a touch of power to cushion our flare and hauled back until the yoke was in my lap. The Goose's keel rumbled across the basin as she settled on her step. She nosed down briefly as I cancelled the Pratt-Whitneys, showered spray from her bow and bobbed gently to the surface on her outer floats.

"Keep moving!" Chug shouted. "Nose her up on the beach

before the lights go out. There ain't no rock by the water, Keith!"

I blipped on the landing lights to make doubly sure, jockeyed the throttles to maneuver with the tail swinging breeze. The strobes blinked out as we caught the soft rise of sand. Howard dipped into the anchor well and raised the hatch when we grounded on the shallow beach. I idled the engines until he was over the side with the bow line in hand, waited until his crimson shorts disappeared behind a stand of bush . . . until the line was taut and he waved from shore, then I cut the Pratt-Whitneys and doused the beam.

A moment of silence followed the props clanking to a stop, the pinging of hot metal from the overhead nacelles; the soft lap of water against the Goose's keel and the sound of distant surf cushioned the rawness of our surroundings. A lonely wind swept the tiny island and played with our inner thoughts. I methodically locked the controls and unbuckled to steady my knees as Chug rose from his seat and went silently aft to tether the Goose's stern. A long, tedious flight had come to an end. A wide-eyed redhead clung to my arm when Chug swung the door and went over the side.

"He's close to tears," Pamela murmured. "Is she buried close by?" I dimmed panel, cut the battery switch and pointed from the window.

"There's an inlet about 200 yards down the beach, honey. He swam ashore with the raft when he anchored the *Leopard.* Liz is buried on the high land in that clump of bush."

We broiled a Grouper over a low burning fire that evening. It was a night to remember. . . the stars blinked intermittently through the fast-moving clouds, the moon ventured on its lonely path from the east, the surf boomed in the distance on the surrounding reefs. I was reminded of my campfire days as a little boy, of things too soon forgotten, of shining faces gathered by a fire, of ghost stories told by our elders, of anxious faces when a barn owl hooted from a nearby tree.

We talked of many things as one does on the eve of danger. We nipped from a bottle and sipped our coffee, pondering the tons of gold lying somewhere beneath the turbulent lagoon; analyzed the captain's strategy when he unburdened his sinking submarine. We touched lightly upon the brooch, its proximity to the outgoing current when Liz came upon it, then fell to silence when Chug rose quietly and disappeared into the darkness.

"He's gone to be wid his gal," Howard whispered. I nodded, shook my head when Pamela climbed to her feet.

"Let him be, little sister."

"My God. . . he's all mixed up!"

"It's bigger than the three of us, honey. It's better to leave him alone."

"You shouldn't have mentioned the brooch!"

"Had to come," Howard observed. "Rest your pretty feet, boy's of age. Be all right when he cry's his eyes." She acknowledged the well-meaning islander with a buss on his cheek. . . she had a new friend.

We were comfortable enough in the lee of the ancient tower. The ancient rocks shielded us from the wind and an occasional spatter of rain. We spread our sleeping bags hand-to-hand, made our toilet by Coleman light and doused the fire. Our thoughts were on the morning as we conversed quietly for long minutes until Howard drowsed and blessed sleep sanded our eyes. An endless, tormented dream had me half awake when Chug lunged from the darkness and fell heavily upon his pad.

Six

ELISABETH BECKONED FROM THE greenish depths as I drifted dreamlike across the limpid lagoon. She teased me with her enigmatic smile, flashed the emerald ring for me to see and motioned that I should follow. Down and down I went, parting the stringy weeds with my hands as I descended into the half light. Her golden hair streamed behind her, her long white gown trailed from my fingers as she darted elusively amongst the coal heads. . . seemingly beyond my reach. We glided over a tumble of tombstones, the graveyard of an ancient wreck, coming upon the hulk of a U-boat submerged on the edge of a black abyss.

Elisabeth tossed her hair aside and pointed, bubbled words I failed to understand. Was it there, inside the rusted submarine? She shook her head. Buried in the sandy shallows? She shrugged and pointed to the strobe lights blazing from the grass behind me. A long, dark shadow passed quickly overhead. . . the coppery sheen of a racing keel, the whirl of powerful propellers shedding a glow of opalescence. I cried out to warn her, swam desperately to reach her, but my legs were strangely caught and my arms were wooden sticks. I gasped for air and shouted again and again, watching helplessly as she tumbled end-over-end in the spinning spume. Her gown came apart in her hands and drifted away; her naked body, her splendid thighs, passed before me in the eerie light. I tore at my bindings and managed to grasp her fingers, but she slipped away and floated lifelessly to the surface. And then suddenly she was gone.

A change of wind stirred me awake. My legs were caught in the sleeping bag and my arms were spreading sand. I lay still for a moment to clear my mind; was it real or a dream? Was the object in my fingers her emerald ring? I rolled on my back and brought a pebble to my eyes, rose to my elbows and tossed it aside. A land crab raised a pincher and scurried to the bush as I blinked to focus in the early dawn. Pamela was sleeping quietly beside me and Howard was snoring from beneath his haversack. I stumbled to my feet in a cold sweat. . . was it a psychic nightmare that gripped my heart? Had a ghastly premonition reached out and grabbed me in the black of night?

The morning star was a diamond in the north as I looked about. Dawn was casting light in the east and illuminating the tower with a grayish-rose sheen. A squawking gull whirled overhead, then dipped into the lagoon for his breakfast. I side-stepped Chug, toed the empty bottle aside and traced a faint path to the sandy beach. The gale had abated during the night. The lagoon quick-silvered quietly in the early light, but the lead winds had come full about and the lull was only temporary. The pressure system to the north had opened the gate to the gigantic storm in the south; by mid-day we'd be in its claws. It was a matter of diminishing time.

I stripped to the buff and plunged into the lagoon, swimming along the beach until I came upon the anxious Goose. She'd floated free when the tide was high and weather-vaned with the shifting wind. I'd come none too soon; she'd dragged her anchors with the outgoing current and tautened her bowlines to a nylon frazzle. I consoled the old girl with a pat on the nose, cast off the danfords and led her gently along the beach. She needed a place to rest, a sanctuary from probing eyes.

Following the shore in semi-darkness, we shortly came to a

sheltered cove where the launch was moored beneath camouflage netting. I paused for a moment to judge the drooping net, to determine if it would accommodate the Goose's wings and high riding props. A cable had been stretched to span the cove with a pair of oars positioned to adjust its height. The netting had been laced to the cable and carried to higher ground where it blended with the surrounding rock.

The launch was tied to a makeshift dock inside the cavernous interior. I snubbed the bowlines and jiggled the oars until I had sufficient height to clear the props. Then I tugged and pleaded with the feisty amphibian until she reluctantly glided inside, coming to a stop with her tail snared on the overhead cable. She would go no further; the rudder was too much for the sagging net and the oars were short for length. I eased her back a bit and spread the anchors from her stern, tied her securely alongside the launch and arranged a brace of bumpers. Then I reached inside the cabin for a mask and waded into the lagoon.

The sun had raised its brow in the east and feathered the lagoon with streaks of yellow. The camouflage netting blended perfectly with the morning shadows; the mottled rudder was not that obtrusive, but the opening I'd devised was black and too sharply defined. I waded in and dropped the oars, the netting settled quickly and closed the gap. The jutting tail would pass unobserved for a casual fly-by or a boat offshore. A buzz job was another matter, however; Wolfgang possessed a practiced eye.

It was 0600 when I retraced the shallows to where we'd grounded in the dead of night. I adjusted the mask and explored the down slope until I came upon a strobe light pinioned in the grassy weed. The dream was vivid in mind as I followed the sequence into deeper water. The strobe line stretched the underwater plateau dead center and terminated on the opposite rise. The cable would be easy to follow . . . a base line to guide us while we searched the saucerlike lagoon. I shot to the surface when I was beyond my depth, cleared the brine from my eyes and treaded water to scan the circumference of the tiny atoll.

The outgoing tide was streaking for a break in the reefs to the east. I'd check with Chug, but I assumed the brooch had drifted along the sandy bottom until it was caught amongst the coral heads (the current would have carried it there). I studied the tower on the northern rise, the crumbled ruins of the lightkeeper's cottage and the concrete cistern below the ridge where Freddie cached his grass . . . near where Chug had buried Liz. The atoll was mostly dune rock underlying a thin layer of sand. The submarine's crew was pressed for time; they would have had to blast if the gold was hidden ashore. It was highly unlikely they had, so the answer lay somewhere within the lagoon.

I turned about in the water and traced the ridge to where it dipped and formed the sheltered cove. A tidal creek led to the off-shore shoals where Chug had anchored the *Leopard* when I thundered by with the Goose. The creek was navigable at high tide (when they fetched the launch to offload their grass) but the sub would have been forced to idle beyond the shoals and con a time-consuming approach with a rubber dinghy in the black of night. The crescent-shaped island terminated at the creek, then continued full circle as a cresting reef until it rejoined the rise to the north. The German captain could have motored in close to the reef; there would have been a hundred fathoms beneath his keel. Maybe . . .

A giant ray leapt from the lagoon and thudded the surface when I was shoulder-deep in the shallows. I waded quickly to shore when a dorsal fin cleft the water behind me and disappeared in the murky depths; a hammerhead shark had juiced him from the bottom and rolled to take him in. The waters swirled in a widening circle as I watched from the beach; the ray broke free and shot for the outer reef with the shark hard behind him. I shielded my eyes from the sun as they maneuvered the tidal channel to the east. The enormous manta whipped his tail to fend the predator, zigzagged through the break and rocketed into the deep Atlantic. The frustrated hammerhead returned a moment later to forage on lesser prey.

I nodded to myself; the ray had sought a quick way out and the fractured reef was his natural choice. He was a deep water, surface-dwelling creature. He would have entered the lagoon when the tide was high; the eastern reach was the obvious approach. The fisherman's description tallied! The U-boat would have lain close in to the cresting reef, probed the break with a search light, then dispatched a raft through the flooded channel.

Liz had found the brooch in the immediate proximity . . . if it had drifted from the center of the lagoon, it most likely would have become lodged in the strands of grass. I toed a spur of weed aside and calculated a 400-yard radius from the center of the atoll to the eastern rise. Time was short and our means were limited to a half-dozen tanks of air. If my theory was on target, it would make sense to float our raft across the lagoon and explore the eastern slope inward from the channel.

I pondered the captain's strategy as I walked along the shore to collect my clothes. He was desperate; the sub was taking water from its ruptured plates. He had five tons of unnecessary ballast to offload in total darkness. A rubber dinghy had limited capacity and would be hard put to manage more than a few bars at a time. They would have had to transport men and equipment to frog the bottom and bury it in the sand, fighting the surge while they paddled the unwieldy thing. The immense effort involved seemed at odds with the span of time. It was highly unlikely they'd dropped the ingots at random and buried them where they lay. Surely they would have concentrated the lot and marked their charts for future retrieval. A half-ass inspiration came to mind when I considered the means at the captain's disposal. Was it possible? The low-lying reefs would be awash at high tide; could he have calculated their depth during the twilight hours, then projected the proper time?

"My goodness, Mr. Slater!" I spun about with my shorts at half mast. Pamela rolled her eyes and smiled. "My, my. . . the good Lord has rewarded you. Come, let me lead you to the garden of Eden."

I blushed and tugged at my zipper. She handed me a mug of coffee and shielded her eyes to the sun. She was decked out in a bikini and a floppy hat. She was a cute little trick, all freckles and lips. She came beside me and pouted for a kiss; it would have been an idyllic morning for casual snorkeling or misbehaving. Our conversation quickly turned to other subjects as we followed the path to the tower. The reality of what we were about was upon us and the wind was tightening from the south.

We scrambled a carton of eggs over the Coleman stove, drew diagrams in the sand and sipped our coffee as we plotted the course of the morning. I explained my theory and referred to the satellite scan Thompson had sent along. The photograph had been magnified to focus the sea mount in detail; opposing tidal channels were clearly defined, as was the rapid drop-off to the east.

Howard was quick to agree. "That sub havin' to lay in from the northeast, man. South coast too shallow. . . you see what happen to that rusty freighter!"

"The gravitometers have a range of twenty feet," I added. "If we dive in pairs we can swath an 80-foot path along the strobe line and float a pair of markers."

"And what, may I ask, is a gravitometer?"

"Sorry, Pamela. I thought you knew."

"I'm a marine biologist but I have an open mind."

"You've heard of a magnetometer?"

"Of course! They detect cannons. . . and wrecks, I suppose. Is that what they've been towing behind the bloody yacht?"

"A magnetometer detects iron or steel. I believe they've been searching for sunken chests; a base metal is non-magnetic and is measured by its specific gravity. You have to be literally on top of it to know it's there."

She raised her mug to acknowledge. "Your enlightened pupil regards you with awe, smartass. And how did you come upon a pair of gravitometers?" Howard activated the portable radio before I could answer. A blast of static erupted from the set. Chug raised a bloodshot eye from his blanket and shuddered. We handed him a cup and bent an ear to the seven o'clock newscast while he stumbled into the bush to retch.

Tropical storm *Christina* was straddling Haiti with torrential rains and winds exceeding 80 knots. Turks Radio advised, "The eye is expected to pass over Port-au-Paix by 1700 GMT. The storm is expected to intensify when it reaches open water. Hurricane force winds of 110 knots are anticipated over an 80-mile radius if it continues its northwesterly shift. Gale force winds are reported from Great Inagua and Eastern Cuba." The announcer advised the residents of Great Inagua to exercise extreme caution and seek higher ground; shipping interests were advised to remain in port.

"That ting lying due south," Howard muttered. "Family all right, but I'm commencin' to worry for myself." He got to his feet and studied the sky. "Wind shiftin' to the west, Keith. Reckon she pass?"

The odds favored a near miss, but if it hooked to the north we'd have to lift off when it accelerated over the open sea. Gale force winds were manageable if the anchors held and we could maneuver with the engines. Above 35 knots, it would be nip and tuck. A snapped line would have us on the rocks with a shattered wing and no way out. A full-blown hurricane would bring green water over the atoll and spume its highest rise. The crumbled tower gave evidence of the grinder that reduced it to a pile of rubble in the distant past. The upshot was to get on with the business at hand, take advantage of the lull and work the bottom from its deepest point while we had the uncertain sun on our backs.

The kid identified the location of Freddie's covert electronics while we smoothed our campsite with a hank of palmetto and stored our gear. Communication with Florida was a must if we fingered the bullion. The Goose's long-range radio was suspect at sea level, her short-span antenna ineffective from where she was moored in the cove.

Providenciales lay 95 miles to the east; our VHF was limited to the line of sight, roughly 30 miles. . . 60 miles if we were airborne at 5000 feet. Ridiculous as it seemed, we were dependent on establishing contact with the mainland, then a roundabout relay to Dan's Hercules 130 at Providenciales.

"We spiked the side-band antenna for Vero Beach," Chug explained. "Freddie has a standby van parked near the Driftwood Inn with a mobile relay to Daytona and Jax. Andy flies off coast until he's east of St. Augustine. If he has a problem, they vector him to Beaufort," he added. "We have a homer 20 miles up river when he can't make it into Lake Wales."

I studied his bloodshot eyes for a moment; the information he'd passed would have the DEA chewing their nails. "And the side-band's in the well?"

"Half-way down the ladder, Keith. Don't let on to Sis. . . it's sorta scary inside."

I was tempted to give it a whirl, but decided to put it off until we had reason to contact the outside world. The *Juanita* would undoubtedly monitor the signal if a transmission erupted from the obscure atoll . . . home the bearing if we dallied with the key. We gave measure to the speedy yacht while we unloaded our equipment from the Goose and inflated the raft. We'd have a three-hour lead if they detected our presence, but how were we to know?

"Best we stand by on the VHF" the Turks Islander suggested. "Wolfgang spot that raft he raise plenty hell." I grimaced at the thought of the marauding Widgeon.

"I'm afraid for the batteries, fella. We'll need the juice to turn the Pratt-Whitneys."

"Was meanin' that VHF that steered us in."

"There's a jack in the tower," Chug said. "It's underneath a brick where the steps run out."

"Man, you got this laid back like Miami International. How come you been wastin' years haulin' grass. . . causin' all this trouble for kinfolk when you could put your good sense to better tings?" It was the kid's turn to wince, but he had little support.

Pamela maintained her silence when we decided to alternate turns at the watch tower; volunteered the mirror from her overnighter when we discussed the means of signaling the raft. She changed to a wet vest in the Goose and tossed a belt weight to her brother while I uncapped the containers from Thompson's package. I passed the gravitometers to the pair when they'd strapped on the tanks and blown their masks for a test run in the shallows.

The rapier-like equipment was Navy type, lightweight, designed specifically for underwater use. An illuminated gauge was molded to the handle and charged with a cadmium cell. A nylon line attached to the handle snapped onto their belts. The Navy had provided a sonar shark-repeller, but they decided against it in favor of a leg knife, should it become necessary to deflate the raft.

"OK! Activate the thumb switch. . . the green line indicates your power reading." I waited until they'd adjusted their masks, until they had an arm over the raft.

I towed my charges on a line until we'd centered the lagoon. The sun was hot to my back when they flipped and went under; a quickening wind ruffled the surface of the water but the bottom was crystal clear. Chug loosened a flag buoy when they located the strobe line. They fanned out until they were about 20 feet apart and frogged to the east over the grassy expanse. I motored slowly toward the inlet to guide them along with the raft. The going was slow when they encountered the high-standing weeds, tedious as they circled about to prod the clinging mass. They were experienced divers; they knew their way around the gaping eels and burning coral, but it was a laborious undertaking at best, time-consuming with the limited hours at hand. When they came to the rising sand, they glided effortlessly across the bottom, wielding their sensors as they probed the outer shelf. It was after eight; they were on to the last of their air when the raft swirled with the tide and I realized we'd penetrated its inner channel. Chug was scissoring in eight feet of water, Pamela off to his right, the soft sheen of her bubbles tracking her slender legs. They'd cut a 40-foot swath from the center of the lagoon but there was no indication of gold.

We'd been drawn to the inlet by compulsion. . . the proximity of the brooch Liz discovered imbedded in a strand of coral. It was time to empty our brains and give way to logic.

The brooch obviously had drifted with the outgoing current, perhaps caught with the floating weed, but the current was erratic; it could have come from within the perimeter of the eastern half. I reviewed my theory of the early morning. . . the captain's strategy as they lay off coast, the means at his disposal with the sun on its downturn to the west. The tower ruins would be in stark silhouette on the far side of the atoll. If he maneuvered the submarine near the cresting reef, with the tower as a reference sight, they could have positioned their bow torpedo tubes on a direct line with the center of the lagoon and waited until the evening tide was over the reefs. The compressed air from the launching tubes would provide sufficient trajectory to carry the torpedos across, the guidance motors pre-set to zero.

"I've an academic question!" I called out to Chug. He unslung his tank and waded until he was short of the raft.

His eyes were red from salt; he was in something of a daze. "Got a fucking hangover. . . whatya' got in mind?"

"The strobes. How did you line them up?"

He fingered his scar and gave it thought. ". . . Freddie set up a transit in the tower and guided us across; we strung the wire from the launch," he added.

"Did he have a reference point to the east? A fix, I mean."

"Jesus, Keith. . . I wasn't watchin'!" He turned slowly in the water and shaded his eyes. "Seems like it was over there, was low tide and the surf was boomin' somethin' awful." I pivoted on my haunches. . . *He was pointing directly to the cresting reef!*

Pamela scrambled to her knees while I studied the marker buoy and calculated the strobe alignment with the raft. I was conscious of her pawing the sand like my shaggy woofer in pursuit of a crab, the gravitometer glinting by her side, but my attention was given to the angle we'd tracked from the center line of the lagoon.

"If I'm right, we're a hundred yards off course!"

"I'll trade my share for a can of Heineken," Chug muttered. I handed him a water flask from the raft.

"I have a wildass hunch it's somewhere along the strobe line, fella! Grab your tanks. I'll team up with Pam while you sleep it off."

"Got something!" Pamela shouted. The kid gagged and dropped

the flask. I spun on my knees; she was on her feet, running.

"It's all slimy and crawly, but the gravitometer says it's gold!" She waded waist-deep with a mossy chain dangling from her fingers. . . her eyes flashing with excitement, her teeth chattering from the damp cold of her vest. I drew the anchor and tossed it to the bar; she pulled on the line until the raft was bobbing by her side.

"There's more," she said, unclenching her fist. "It broke from the chain while I was digging it out." I rubbed the crucifix on my shorts to bring it to luster. It was about three inches long, heavily worked with ornamentation, solid gold. I turned it in my hand.

"It's very old; it's inscribed in Latin."

"Would it be from the Habsburg collection?"

"I don't think so. Francis Joseph's jewelery was turn-of-the-century. The Thompson brothers found some coins a few years back," I added. "They figured a Spanish man of war broke up on the outer reef."

"Oh, well, finders keepers. I'll wear it to. . . is there something wrong? You're blinking your eyes!" I raised my hand to make it go away, the blinding light wavered and climbed my leg. When it reflected my watch I realized what it was.

"It's Howard!" Chug hoarsed. "He's flashin' a mirror and wavin' Sis's hat." We swiveled to scan the horizon. Howard had the sense to wait until our eyes returned to the tower.

"Two blips!"

"A ship?"

"Grab your tanks!"

The trolling motor was hard put to manage the overloaded raft. The quarter-mile crossing seemed endless, an exercise in anxiety with the *Juanita* looming in our minds. The under-powered inflatable plowed against the wind, flailing with paddle when the unwieldy thing threatened to broach. I scooped the flag from our marker buoy when we were midway to the cove, cautioned them to stow their reflective masks when the reefs were astern and we were exposed to view from the sea. The kid peeled off with the line and swam ashore when we were in the lee of the sheltering knoll. The lightened raft shot across the shallows, swerved heavily as he tautened the bow, coming to an amicable understanding when we glided beneath the camouflage netting and thudded against the launch.

"My God!" Pamela gasped. "Are we going to be shelled?" I retrieved the chain and helped her to the launch. She scrambled to the pier and eyed me from the shadows.

"Take it easy, Sis!"

"I didn't ask you! I want an honest opinion from our silent partner." I peered from the netting; the horizon was clear to the east, but a steady *boom boom* resounding from the water indicated a vessel approaching from the south. "I hear it! Are you going to sit there and smirk while they storm the beach?" She confronted me when I slipped from the raft and waded to the pier.

"We panicked, honey. That's an old Cat diesel working its way north. The *Juanita* would be pounding 40 knots!"

"I don't understand."

"A mail boat coming up from Inagua." Howard played it cool. "If they spotted us in the lagoon, they'd wonder what they had."

The tension eased from her eyes; she lowered her head and stared at her feet. I ruffled her hair and pointed to the Goose. "We'll need a fresh pair of tanks, Pam. I think we're onto it, but we'll have to wait until she's over the hill."

"They'd call back on the marine radio, Sis. I sweated a couple when we was guarding the weed."

She spun on her heel. "I can be certain of that, you illiterate ass!" He popped a beer and smiled. It was love or hate. I tried for a change of venue.

"Hole up and sleep it off, kid. If it's a mail boat we'll take time out and clean up our act. . . Freddie's radios for one, how long has it been since the batteries were checked?"

"Two or three months; didn't look the last time around." He blinked and averted his eyes. . . tilted the beer and wiped his mouth with the back of his hand. "You could pop the Honda if they're down, Keith. Takes 'bout an hour. Them strobes were fadin' come to think."

"OK, I'll check them out. If the gold is where I think it is, we'll need outside help and we'll need it fast. . . think you can handle it, kid?"

"You're asking the impossible!"

"Take it easy, Sis! There ain't going to be no divin' until she pass!"

"Don't you dare speak Bahamian to me!"

"Come off it, Pam! I want Chug on the tower when we're ready to dive; he's acquainted with the radios and knows the procedure."

"Meaning he's to contact the underworld if we come up with the bricks?"

"In a roundabout way, honey. Don't worry it. . . the lever's with the man in the big white suit."

"I'd feel safer with Howard on the hill."

"And I'd feel a hell of a lot safer if he babysits the Goose!"

She questioned me with her eyes for a moment, then turned to busy herself with the tanks. She'd thought it through; if the *Juanita* appeared on the horizon we'd be playing for keeps. She was a gutsy lady, all sharp tongue and emotional; but she pulled her weight under pressure and I was happy to have her on my wing.

Howard met me at the base of the tower and confirmed my suspicions. The mail boat from Inagua was two miles off coast and heading for Acklins with a pair of fishing smacks in tow. He handed me his binoculars and yawned, a picture of composure beneath Pamela's floppy hat.

" 'Fraid they'd see you, man. . . figure you was druggies or ship-wrecked Haitians. Feared they'd call Paul and raise interest at Providenciales." I focused on the freighter; she was a large, double-decked trawler. "Mos' time they stops by Mayaguana, but they's fleeing the storm."

I lowered to the buoy, raised them slowly on a direct line and focused again. Howard crouched by my side when I pointed to the cresting reef.

"What you have in mind, Keith? Seeing you came up with nut-tin' but a piece of string."

"If you were lying over there in a leaking sub with five tons of gold and a dozen torpedoes, what would you do?"

He grinned and reached for the binoculars. "Man, Howard have similar thought while you was foolin' with that raft. Channel ain't fit for navigatin' more than a few bars at a time, an' that sub's havin' to stand a mile off shore. Captain be scratchin' ass! Come night, reef be wash with tide an' he got all them torpedo weightin' him down. Now, you know what we do when we lose an engine, Keith. Out the door goes all the trash, 'cept them poor souls strapped to their seats!"

"To put it gently."

"Bothersome thought?"

"The warheads. They don't come out like flashlight batteries."

"Yeah man, but you forgettin' what you tell us last night. This ting planned long time back. . . *supposin' they ain't loaded with explosives from the start?*" I could have wept. He'd hit it on the nose.

"*Thats it!* The torpedoes weren't mentioned in the Gehlen file. He wouldn't have known they were sealed with gold and the top dogs would have kept it from the crew!"

"Ain't acquainted with what you speak, but when Howard come to extra cash, he don't let on to his wife."

The mail boat passed as we watched impatiently from the bush; as it proceeded north and crowned the horizon, a drift of smoke caught with the following breeze until she dropped beyond the curvature and disappeared. Howard monitored the 10 o'clock news while I climbed the tower to investigate the jack and trace the lead to where it was creviced in the stone. Precious time had been lost, but the passing had served a warning. It was important to realize we had radio communication if the *Juanita* was next in line.

"Turks say she over open water, Keith, fetchin' 80 knots!"

"Prediction?"

"Ain't say. Satellite picture comin' up at noon." I nodded numbly to myself; that, too. "Can you pick up Miami?"

"No, man, nothin' but static and music from Havana."

The wire led directly to a pile of rock at the base of the steps. I tried the earphones again, but Howard was probably right. . . the batteries conked out when we triggered the strobes.

"OK, we'll have to pull the generator. The kid said it's on a ledge near the top of the well."

He switched off the portable to join me when I jumped to the ground and peeled away the rocks that disguised the trap door. The ancient well was within the circumference of the tower and predated the cistern by 200 years. The tower's foundation was constructed of ballast stone, from a time when piracy was a fact of life. The upper part joined with bricks and mortar when it reverted to a maritime light.

"Man, this some spooky place," Howard commented when we pitched the rocks aside and located a layer of planking. "Ain't no wonder folks shy from fishin' hereabouts."

"An old watch tower?"

"Ghost keep watch, from what I hear'd my daddy say."

The boards were weathered, as if they'd been collected from the beach. They were fitted side by side, but not connected. Howard jumped back when I pulled one away. A fetid odor rose from beneath. I probed the opening with my flash and looked down. An aluminum extension ladder angled the darkness, its legs resting on a pile of slimy debris. . . the beam wavered as it circled the hand-hewn rock and came full stop.

"There's your ghost!" I gasped. He peered from my shoulder and blanched.

"Man, oh man! That ting come from long ago."

The skeleton was in a sitting position with the skull dangling between its legs. Layer upon layer of crab carcasses covering its feet, the residue of creatures who had fallen over the years. His clothing had rotted away, but a cap hung by its band on a stick by his hand . . . a makeshift crutch of sorts.

The corroded emblem on the cap was vaguely familiar. "It's a Reichsadler Swastika. . . he was a German officer!"

"Meanin' he come from that sub?"

"He was either abandoned or fell. . . his right leg's splintered above the knee."

"Man, what a way to go. There ain't no way he could climb that wall."

"It's a nasty, all right. It happened 50 years ago and it links the sub with the brooch. I think we're on target."

"Reckon they pull out in one big hurry, leavin' a man to die like dot."

"If the PBY's came over at dawn they'd have no choice. We can moralize, but it was wartime." I added, "He would have gone with the sub in either event." I pocketed the flash to pull the remaining boards aside, took a deep breath and toed the ladder.

The equipment was arranged side-by-side on a metal shelf seated on a ledge about four feet below the opening. The ledge would have been used as a cooler for edibles in colonial times, judging from the pottery shreds and broken glass. The shelf held a series of zinc chloride batteries. A portable Honda generator, with a coiled cable leading to the breaker panel, was stored alongside.

It would take a full-time genius a week to wire it all together. I recognized the omini transmitter and relay system as a highly classified package that had been developed since Vietnam. . . the single side-band in particular. The scrambler attached to the transmitter would render the sender's voice an unintelligible pattern if it were intercepted by the DEA or the *Juanita!*

"What you have?" Howard called down.

"A raytheon single side-band, for one thing. It's phased to a scrambler; the de-coding analyzer is in Freddie's van. They reply on an open frequency with a numerical code," I added. "Chug memorized the numbers; that's why we need him up top."

"Man, he can have this place. What's with the VHF?"

I looked over the short-range set; it seemed OK. It was limited to a pair of transistors for transmitting, but the receiver was capable of multiple channels, including the DEA's private line. . . and the military's off-limits chips.

"I'm getting a downer on the batteries! The strobes must have juiced them last night. I turned the tiny speaker to max and cycled the channels; I was greeted with a faint voice on 121.9, a burst of static. "Hit the earphones. . . I'm picking up something I don't like!"

He climbed the tower while I bent my ear to the receiver. There was an audible click when Howard plugged a headset to the jack, a startled voice when he called down.

"Gotta be the Widgeon, Keith. I hears engines and they's talkin' German. . . mus' be communicatin' with the yacht!" I strained, caught a word or two, but the battery was low ebb.

"Hang in while I try the Honda!" I hoisted the tiny generator to the top of the well and rolled from the parapet with the battery cable underarm. The Honda started on the first pull, coughed and stopped. I opened the needle valve and tried it again. The generator came alive and rattled at my feet. . . I throttled it down and raced for the tower. Howard handed me the headset when I topped the stairs.

"It Wolfgang, Keith. . . man, he somewhere close by!" My NATO German was hard-pressed, but the surging power clarified his transmission.

"He's circling Little Inagua at 500 meters. Kurt's on the horn, but I can't make him out. . . hold it, Wolfgang's calling back." I pressed the earphones, his signal was loud and clear.

"Da ist ein PBY auf dem Rollfeld von Inagua, Kaeptn. Warum weiss der liebe Kuckuck. Es gibt absolut keinen Grund dafuer, se wie der Wind steht!"

"He re-fueled at Great Inagua and saw the PBY parked on the ramp."

"He know that PBY?"

"I don't think so, but he can't figure why it's there with the winds the way they are." I passed the earphones, picking up Kurt's faint reply. The *Juanita* apparently was miles to the east.

"Ob es Slater ist?"

"Nein! Der Pilot ist ein alter Kerl mit weissem Haar, und das PBY traegt die Aufschrift 'Navy'?" I grinned. Andy had doctored the Catalina with Navy insignia from WWII. . . Father time, with snow white hair and his apparition from the past.

"Sind Sie ahnsinnig?" [Are you out of your mind?] Wolfgang was hesitant to reply.

"Ich bin mir da nicht so sicher, in jedem Fall bin ich total durcheinander!" I nodded. He was totally confused.

"Na schoen! Fliegen Sie weiter nach Norden—Laengengrad 73—

und bleiben Sie im westlichen Spielraum. Wir fliegen nach Providenciales zurueck, da haben wir auch ein Problem." [The Widgeon was to continue its search along longitude 73, then turn about and parallel a grid to the west.]

"The *Juanita's* inbound to Provo," I explained. "Something's up. Let's pray it isn't Dan." Or Elisabeth, my inner voice added.

"Coffee, my luvs?" We spun on our heels. Pamela was standing at the base of the tower with a steaming pot. She'd skirted the open well, unknowing, but she looked down when she rested the pot on the wall. The result was pedictable—her screams pierced the sky as she flung herself from the well.

"My God. . . it's all rotty and green!" she shrieked. I leapt to the ground and led her away, explaining the history of the thing . . . the officer had apparently stumbled into the well at twilight. . . macabre proof of the U-831's presence. "What a sordid way to put it, Keith. He was in agony . . . he starved to death!"

"He would have gone down with the sub, regardless!"

"He'd have had company at least!" I changed the subject. It was impossible to accommodate her rationale. But then again, maybe she was right.

"Old bones aside. . . we have a problem, honey. We picked off a conversation between Kurt and his pilot. It's going to be dicey from here on in, like lunch on the run."

"Wolfgang?"

"Right! Bad news. He's flying a north-south search pattern from Acklins to the Inaguas and working his way west at 20 miles a cut. He's loaded with petrol and will be on to us in a couple of hours, give or take."

"Oh, my God!"

"Now, don't get rattled! He's searching for a raft, I think. . . mainly Chug. . . wreckage, anything he could cling to. They've cased the islands for the *Leopard*, but they haven't given up on the kid."

"Can't we just leave?"

"No, honey, we've gone too far! We have to keep a close watch from the tower and snag the buoy if he buzzes the atoll."

"If? Do you think I'm an idiot? You know he will. . . and he'll discover the Goose. Be reasonable, Keith!" I signaled Howard for help.

"Camouflage good for a fly-by, Pam. He be lookin' for tracks, like Keithy say."

"Phooey! I can see it from here! And what of the bloody yacht? Am I to make sandwiches and invite them to high tea?" She simmered down, sipped from her gritty cup while we explained that the worst Wolfgang could do would be to relay our position. The yacht was inbound to Providenciales, for whatever reason; to that we didn't allude. "They've been working the islands with a magnetometer, Pam. Wolfgang's job is second gun, scouting from the air. If they weren't so methodical, they would have dragged the atoll a week ago."

"And Liz would be alive!"

"I know, honey. . . fate has curious ways. Have you thought of what might have happened if they'd discovered the kids at Hogsty Cay?"

She nodded glumly. "I'm frightened, Keith. I don't know if I can handle it. I'll be looking over my shoulder in 40 feet of water."

"I know you can. . . are you ready to dive?"

"If you insist."

"Okay, we'll take it from the beach, side-by-side, but you'd better wake up your brother," I added. "We'll need his expertise on the hill."

She smiled and turned to follow the path, toes turned in like a child on her way to school. Such a pretty little thing, all coppery hair and stubborn soul.

"Man, you ain't tol' her how Wolfgang can mess us up. All he gotta do is drop a couple of flares, an' that Goose one big puff!"

"Do you tell everything to your wife?"

He grinned. "How come you got ready answer, Keith? Is cause you reside wid yourself?"

Howard monitored the tower earphones while I took a reading on the batteries and switched on the side-band. I waited until I had five illuminated dots on the digital display. . . three came up, then four. When I had five, I triggered the mike. We were on the air!

"Red Fox . . . this is Angels Four, how do you read?" The scrambler activated automatically; the analyser in Freddie's van would voice the message in proper sequence a fraction of a second later. I pressed my ear to the speaker. . . a crackle of static from the storm, then two blips followed by a long sounding dash and two more blips in rapid succession.

"Got our two-plus-two" Howard shouted. "We's in contact, man!"

"OK! Relay our position to all parties and advise White Cloud to hold tight!" I glanced at my watch. . . it was 10:35. "Anticipate update within the hour, situation yellow. Advise." Reply was instantaneous; four blips widely spaced. I switched the set to standby and climbed the ladder. Seven blips indicate a problem. The stage was set for go! All we had to do was to come up with the GOLD.

Howard wiped sweat from his brow and pondered the ruffled lagoon. "Best get on with it, Keith. . . seein' your mind set an' we got a couple hour. Must be important, bringin' that fella down from Washington. . . an' that ol' man with them six marines." He reached for my hand and collected my gear. He had more to say.

"Send up that boy for close talk with Howard. Wantin' to know he have clear head for them radios, seein' he been strokin' the beer, mournin' for that gal. . . like you been worryin' for Elisabeth, man. God bless!"

We aligned ourselves with the tower and adjusted our masks. The buoy seemed so far away, the outer reefs a thin line of white from where we stood waist-deep in the shallows. We synchronized our watches, electing to pair until we located the strobes. We'd surface at 10 minute intervals to check the tower, signalling if we had a read from our gravitometers. We had an hour of air (snorkels if we overstayed), a clutch of markers strapped to our belts, and with our tanks and flippers looked like creatures from outer space.

"Ready?"

Pamela flashed her square, toothy smile. "If we spike a torpedo, will we. . .? Heavens, I just remembered what Edwin said when we were staying with Mr. Nottage!"

"Give."

"He hit something when they were setting the lights. They thought it was a cannon and fixed the light to the side. They were in a hurry. . . Freddie was offshore in his Hatteras, complaining about the bugs. It was a year ago August, I think."

"Where?"

"He didn't say, except that the tide was low and they were free diving without a tank."

"It's a lead, honey. . . let's go!"

She lowered her mask and frogged the sandy decline. I followed at a distance, paralleling from a half dozen yards to keep her in view. She was a graceful diver, gliding elflike across the bottom with her gravitometer pointing the way. We checked our bearing when we encountered the first strobe, surfacing to signal the tower. A flashing mirror immediately waved us on.

"OK . . . follow your compass; I'll be off to the right." She sliced the water while I took a bead on the buoy and followed her under. We kept visual contact by the sheen of our bubbles, then lost sight of each other when we entered a towering stand of weeds. I had no indication of a reading, so I tracked the cable from light to light. I sighted Pamela when our 10 minutes were drawn. She'd worked ahead of me, hovering impatiently by a strobe. . . pointing to the next in line, then to the surface. When I frogged alongside, I nodded to goon. We fanned the strobe line to the east, swathing a parallel path until we sighted the bobbing buoy and realized we were midcenter with the lagoon. We then rose to the surface and raised our masks.

"Negative." She clung to the buoy and rubbed her eyes.

"I'm pooped."

"Hang in, they have to be close by!" We checked our air, closed our secondary valves to the minimum and waited for a flash from the tower.

I had a fleeting view of her flippers as we angled down to 40 feet. We separated again, thrusting the gravitometers before us as we tracked to the east. A strobe passed to my left; I corrected with my compass and went on to the next. Eight minutes were gone when the needle moved ever so slightly. I fanned the rapier for a reading and frogged slowly to the east. The indicator made a rapid turn and fluttered against its stop. My heart sounded. . . I was onto the torpedo. . . or a massive piece of Spanish gold! I set the marker and circled with the gravitometer. The signal faded as I swung to the north, returned full force when I glided to the south, gyrating when I fanned from left to right. . . the meter had gone wild! I shot to the surface and raised a glove. Pamela emerged a moment later, yards away, waving her arms and shouting from the top of her lungs.

"What do you have?" I clasped my hands overhead. "A basket of gold!"

"Macho luck!" A beam flashed from the tower as she swam alongside. They'd read the action; we were in the clear!

We dove together in a haze of bubbles, arcing to the marker as we pierced the green. An inquisitive grouper stood by while we probed the sand with our knives. . . flitting away when we struck metal and pawed the slit with our gloves. It was definitely a torpedo, a twenty-foot monster of corroded aluminum buried full-length beneath a 50-year residue of sand and debris. The bronze propeller within its circular shield had been cast by a foundry in Essen, in 1944!

We fanned our gravitometers to the next and set another flag. There were six in all, arranged side-by-side at two-meter intervals They'd obviously been gathered by a scuba team and lightly covered with sand. But what of the legendary 12? The instruments showed negative when we searched a widening arc. Our tanks were at quarter when Pamela pointed to her watch. I nodded; she was shivering her face pasty white from the chill. We surfaced and blew masks.

"I can't believe it!" she gasped.

"Hit for shore, honey! We need Chug on the Watts line and a pair of tanks."

"Are you staying to count the money?"

"Buzz off!"

"I'll invite you to our wedding if you'll promise a gold Mercedes."

"Bring the raft; I'll be out by the reef"

"An empty promise; a golden pumpkin for Cinderella!"

"Git!" She grinned and struck for shore, jettisoning her tank when she rounded the buoy. I trod water for a moment; she was so endearing. . . her freckled smile could bring an army to its knees. Why was I so enamored with a dream? I mouthed my air; I had fifteen minutes to squander in the deep.

The gravitometer proved negative when I fanned the following strobes; nothing. The dream flooded my mind when I encountered a maze of coral heads. . . brain coral, long dead, bleached white, strewn like tombstones on a cemetery hill. *Elisabeth's gown swirled before my eyes*. . . a shimmering school of minnows caught by the penetrating sun; *her beckoning fingers*. . . a wisp of weed; was I hallucinating, giddy for lack of air? Then my flipper dislodged a strobe and I realized the water was shallowing, that I was on the easterly rise (I'd wandered a bit while I was immersed in my dream). I looked back and tensed, remembering what the kid had said to Pam. . . the strobe was staked off line! The needle hit the stop when I probed where it should have been!

I inserted a marker and followed the vacillating needle. . . counted four additional readings and flagged the lot. The torpedoes were grouped together like the others. . . at two-meter intervals in 15 feet of water. They'd apparently grazed the cresting reef when their buoyancy valves opened and sent them to the bottom. The sub's initial salvo had fallen short; they'd been abandoned in the lee of the shelf a hundred yards short of the tidal channel. Where was the sixth?

An unlikely mound of sand caught my eye; a curl of purple drew me to where the current was drawn by the tide. Was it possible. . . had a torpedo been deflected by the reefs and settled apart? The needle lunged as I glided along the shelf. I was mesmerized by the tint seeping from the sand, surprised by a spurt of indigo when I pulled a rooted weed. I waited for the water to clear and probed the cavity with my knife. A battered torpedo lay at rest beneath a thin layer of sand; my knife had grazed the ruptured casing and pierced its wound.

Dark blue flannel came apart in my gloves; the lining of a rotting rosewood container hinged with silver and inlaid with mother of pearl! The wood fell away when I filtered through its contents with my gloves. An emerald tiara came to light, then an emerald necklace fastened with gold and a wire of heavy rings. There was more. . . a gold chalice from the twelfth century, a gold crucifix set with diamonds, art nouveau from 1910. The Habsburg collection. . . there was no mistaking the royal eagle embossed on a porcelain plate I scavenged from the sand. I slipped the jewelry into my net bag and set the heavier objects aside to explore the cavity at depth. An insulating bulkhead fled with the current when I probed with the gravitometer. . . the soft glitter of gold!

The bullion had been cast in wafers and holed dead center to fit a central shaft of stainless steel. The shaft was suspended within the head compartment to an X-bar welded to the torpedo's casing, extending aft to a duplicate truss. The casing was torn where it had struck the reef, peeled away and spilled the jewels when the torpedo settled by the shelf. I fingered the disks with my glove, counted twelve when I traced the fracture at length, and there were more behind. They were approximately two inches thick, 20 inches in diameter, 50 pounds each on a penny scale. A quarter ton of solid gold. . . precisely balanced in the warhead compartment to offset its weight in TNT! Mind-boggling!

This torpedo seemed larger than the others. Its elongated nosecone was non-metallic and housed a homing device of sorts. Strange! Space-age technology in World War II? The power source was missing; the rosewood box had been fastened where the battery should have been. Had the captain known when he released the torpedo from the U-831? Possibly not, but he certainly would have wondered why it failed.

And the brooch? Snared by a sprig of weed, it must have caught on the outer reefs. Discovered by a mixed-up teenager who held it aloft while she shrieked with delight; traded for a triviality, setting off a ghastly scenario that would eventually claim her life. . . What a monstrous turn of fate!

My vision blurred while I was attaching the net bag to my belt. I opened my line valve to max. . . was I sipping an empty tank? Then the water vibrated around me as if struck by a bounding ray, pulsating my eardrums. . . was I hallucinating again? I studied my watch, but my eyes refused to focus. I dropped my belt weights as I fought the rapture of oxygen starvation, floating to the surface and tearing at my mask.

I was greeted by the blinding mirror, by pounding engines and fleeing gulls as I trod water gasping for air. I had a fleeting view of the Widgeon as it thundered the lagoon at 50 feet and banked sharply to the west. . . then the mirror flashed repeatedly and arced to the buoy, returning again to dazzle my eyes. The message was bloody clear. . . collect the buoy and take it down! I jettisoned my tank and frogged for the marker, raising my head to watch the Widgeon. Wolfgang made a shallow turn to the south and revved his prop for a second pass, banking again with the sun on his back, dropping as I lunged for the buoy. . . a vulture onto a kill! I made the final yards underwater, grabbed the buoy and forced it down. A fleeting shadow crossed the lagoon, then the surface quickened and I had a watery view of spinning props as the Widgeon whistled overhead and climbed to the north. Had he seen it? I humped the float, reasonably sure he'd targeted the flag from his earlier pass. I hitched the line to reduce its length, knotted it midcenter and shot to the surface.

Wolfgang was rattled! He'd banked sharply and was onto a high climbing chandelle to the west. He was leaning from his window, hanging his props as if he were flying an F-4, forgetting what he had until the ungainly Widgeon buffeted a stall. I frogged immediately for the cove, intent on covering the Goose, watching when the Widgeon dropped heavily and entered a spin. I was on the stand of weed when he recovered and leveled off. . . mouthed my snorkle and submerged when he made a shallow turn to the south from a half-mile. I hovered there for a moment, knowing he'd raise his binoculars; did I blend with the weeds? His engines ruffled the surface briefly, diminished to a drone from beyond the hill when I cleared my mask.

He'd continued south, climbing. . . banking slowly to the east with his props revving high pitch. He'd be calling the *Juanita* from altitude, would circle and bide his time. The atoll was marked for another pass! I discarded the snorkle and swam for the beach, kicked my flippers free when I encountered the slope. . . paced Howard's graphite legs as I splashed from the shallows and raced for the cove. He drew ahead of me, hurdled an outcropping, shouting from his shoulder.

"Move it, man. He comin back!" I pointed to the netting.

"Cut the tie!" A knife appeared in his hand as I rounded the mossy rock. The netting collapsed on the Goose and shrouded the opening from the lagoon. Howard ducked beneath it and disappeared inside.

I faltered for a moment, completely exhausted. My heart was throbbing, my lungs pleading, shooting sparks to the conea as I shielded my eyes from the sun. The Widgeon was low in the south banking to the north, gaining speed as it came about. I stripped off my wet suit and slipped beneath the netting to gather my wits. . . waved Pamela down when she reached from the raft. The camouflage would suffice a casual pass, but Wolfgang was an experienced hand and the Goose's tail stood stark to the sun, a bloody billboard to a practiced eye. He had the means to disable us if he careened an incendiary flare, the means to communicate with Kurt and draw the Juanita in a matter of hours.

Pamela wide-eyed me from her straddle of tanks as I hurried

waist deep to the fuselage door. She stared fretfully at Howard's ashen face as he pawed the overhead panel and raised a crackle of static. She'd had the sense to hold tight, but was frightened by the free-wheeling action, bewildered when I scavenged the compartment for the last of Thompson's gifts. . . confused no end by the dialogue resounding from the Goose.

" . . *Ich habe eine Boje gesuchtet, Kaeptn, aber jetzt ist sie nicht mehr da!*" There was more, but her fiery Irish overcame Wolfgang's irritable voice.

"Heavens! Can't he speak English?" I cautioned her to be quiet, signaled Howard to up the volume while I fielded a heavy parcel from our stores. She was most indignant . . . she'd been ignored.

"What do you plan to do, Bwana, spray him with Off?" I cupped an ear to the Widgeon as I fumbled with the bindings, eyeing her freckled legs.

"Einverstanden! Ich werde das Atoll fotografieren und sofort zurueckkommen!"

"Get under the dock, dammit! He's making another pass!" She dissolved to tears.

"Oh, my God! Is he going to drop a bomb?"

I drew a pair of M-16s from the parcel, then a long-nose rifle with telescopic sight. Pamela cringed.

"Split! If he flares the Goose, we've had it!" She rolled from the raft and cowered beneath the dock. Howard tumbled from the cockpit as I fed an armor-piercing round to the magazine.

"No, man! I ain't one for killin'!"

"Take it easy. . . I'm going for his prop." He dropped beside me, pulling at my arm as I waded aft and thrust the barrel from the netting. I elbowed him aside, aimed as the fast-moving Goose loomed the sights. I had a momentary view of Wolfgang's pasty face, of a camera protruding from his window as he jockeyed the rudder to center the lagoon. I hesitated. . . would he film the atoll and pull out? I squeezed the trigger when I recognized the military hardware beneath his wing. . . the rifle recoiled!

The proptips dissolved in a blur of shredded metal and hazed the nacelle as the engine overcame the decimated blades; the Widgeon careened out of control and skidded sideways across the lagoon. . . yawing violently on its dead wing on a collision course with the Goose. Pamela screamed and Howard dropped to his knees, but the Widgeon was on us before I could react. The rifle cartwheeled from my hand as the amphibian roared overhead and snared the netting with its portside float. Netting ripped from the cables and fled with the float . . . lofting as it was dragged astern, twisting and curling like a banner flaunting Fort Lauderdale beach. I crossed my fingers, but Wolfgang was on the controls. He feathered his useless prop and hammered the starboard engine. . . skimming the rise, banking to avoid the tower. The netting fell away when he leveled off, tumbled end-over-end and splashed amongst the outer reefs. The would be no looking back. . . his mangled float was dangling from its strut and he had all he could do to hold 50 feet.

"Man, oh man, he ain't botherin' wid that radio for a while!" We clung to the naked Goose, completely spent, watching until the amphibian was a speck on the horizon. I retrieved the rifle and tossed it in the launch.

"You nearly killed him . . . you despicable jock!" Pamela's voice dripped with ice.

"I didn't promise a bed of roses!"

"How can you be so callous!"

"I learned the hard way, honey, but that doesn't mean I lost my soul." She stared at her tiny feet, trembling from shock. I waded to her side but she'd have none of me.

"Does that terrible scar on your leg cause you to hate?" I shrugged; she was on to Desert Storm from a passive generation.

"Not really, but it's one hell of a reminder when I see rockets strapped to a wing. Collect your brother," I added brusquely. "We're not out of this yet!" She raised herself to the dock and turned her back, close to tears. I was immediately sorry for cutting her short.

Howard was not oblivious. "She upset, Keith. She ain't encounter nuthin' like this before. Still shakin' from that ting wid Big Red!"

"I know, but we need a breather, fella. Did you contact Florida?"

"Boy did."

"Did they confirm?"

"Spoutin' numbers I ain't rightly understand. Boy say they was intend for the PBY." I exhaled my relief. Andy would be lifting off from Great Inagua and Thompson would be scanning his charts at Cecil Field. Signaling all points!

I pointed to the twisted cable truss as we waded to assess the damage. The Goose's props were miraculously unbent, but the cable was draped across her wing, unyielding when we levered it with an oar. It would take a hacksaw to cut it free. . . and precious minutes.

"There's a blade in my kit. . . I'll go topside and cut it by the nacelle."

"Plan on waitin' for the PBY?"

"No way, we haven't time!"

"Whatcha got in mind? Confide with Howard. . . plannin' on doing what you said?"

"He caught us short, but we'll have to carry on, bite the bullet. . . collect Dan and the marines. If the *Juanita* pounds 40 knots, we'll have time to set the trap and scat for the coast. The kids will be all right," I added. "We'll swing south to see if Andy's on his way, cancel if there's a problem. I'm not going to risk their lives." He waded alongside me as I reached inside the Goose to search my kit. He had more to say.

"Was hoping you'd say that; now I'm offering Howard's advice. I ain't fright for Provo, knowing my family is all right. Kurt's a mean man, you show face he liken to shoot Keith. . . got plenty nasty friend an' Big Red's kin will be axin' about, seein' the Goose be cause for regret. Short it, man! We can refuel at Inagua while them Navy divers are struttin' their stuff. Haul ass, leave it to the Crown to bring arrest."

"I know, but there are too many oars in the pond. The plan was to draw the crew ashore and pin them down while the *Walrus* quartered from the sea. . . mainly to arrest the yacht in Bahamian waters while the locals were four at the bar, away from Turks and Caicos and corrupt politicians."

"Man, that *Walrus* burn like Sunday paper if the *Juanita* turn-head."

"We considered that, but the admiral has a long nose. The HMS Penelope is cruising off Mayaguana with a hotline to Bower's bridge."

"How come you reluctant to tell Howard all of this?" I located the blade and waded aft to straddle the Goose's tail, working my way to the wing. Had I lost a friend?

"We hatched the plot when the admiral was half-mast. I wasn't sure I could trust them until Thompson leveled Freddie and came up with the goodies. Dan's sly; plays games. He promised to sack the bastards if we drew them from Provo to where he could get at them and cause an arrest. That's the deal we made with the kid. . . give or take the gold, but it was left for us to ferry the troops. Do you follow me, man?"

I grappled with the cable while he gave it thought. The blade was meant for softer meat; the cable was composed of braided steel. I'd sawed a half dozen strands when he climbed the wing and offered a hand.

"Plannin' on leaving them here, then?"

"With a 20mm gun from the PBY. . . they'll have grenade launchers and nightscopes for after dark. They're pros, fresh from the Falklands. They're to hole up until Kurt drops anchor and lands a party ashore. . . draw their fire and cut them off while Bower engages the yacht."

He tugged at his moustache. "Fat man knew we be at Hogsty Cay?"

"Not until you called in, but it's damn important he be along when we lock horns with the DEA. You can call it quits while we're still ahead, fella. Ride Andy's right hand seat. It'll be a nasty game from here on in." He was quick to react.

"You putting Howard down?"

"You've got a wife to worry."

"An' you got worry in them blue eyes of yourn! Ain't spoofin' Howard wid all that talk . . . whatcha gonna do if Elisabeth held hostage?" I had no answer for that. He eyed me silently while I fumbled with the saw.

"Best leave that with Howard," he said. "Have talk with that boy an' sister Pam. Be mos' upset when she learn we leavin' for a spell. Been watchin' her eye. . . come from straight-lace family. She not aquainted wid tings come your way of life, dig me, man? She fancy your style, but she belong to some doctor-lawyer type. . . be fetchin' tears while you have mind for Providenciales."

"Stand back!" I shouted. He shielded his face. The cable snapped and whipped from my hands, lashing our knees as the ends curled and slithered from the wing. The Goose wrenched free and bobbed happily on her lines.

"Man, that hurt!" I crawled forward to examine the props while he nursed his bruises, glancing back when the sun reflected from the hill. The Crown's prize witness was treading the path with a foaming beer clutched to his chest, Pamela at his heels. Howard grimaced, shading his eyes when they emerged from the bush. "Fess up with that girl. . . an' I ain't settle for no omission, Keith. Be cause for disrespect!"

He dropped from the wing to drain the sumps while I checked the dipsticks and balanced my thoughts. The kid was savvy; he'd been apprised in part. . . not fully, too many straws in the wind, but he'd realize it was impossible to take them along, suicidal with Kurt on the prowl. He apparently had words with Pam, explained the circumstances, judging from her stance as she wide-eyed the proceedings from the dock. Of Elisabeth he wasn't aware; had his own thoughts to grind. . . the mangled body he'd so recently buried. Revenge. . . the promise I'd exacted from Dan.

Had I been cowardly for avoiding an issue so deep in my heart, knowing I was driven to keep a promise I'd made to myself? Pamela was constrained when I explained the situation at Providenciales, from the beginning. . . mainly my concern for Elisabeth following Seymour's midnight call. She eyed me silently, her jaw jutting when I explained Elisabeth's role in the scheme, the risk she'd taken when Kurt came at me with his grotty knife.

"She infiltrated the cast when the leading lady was dosed with a heavy laxative," I added. "Elisabeth auditioned the part while they were filming in Europe. . . she was on call, but I believe Kurt was suspicious when she arrived before the poor soul made it back to Berlin."

"How dicey . . an honest-to-goodness femme fatale!"

"High stakes, kid! She was walking a slippery plank, and I didn't help matters when I eyeballed his party while they were on to *heil seig.*"

"Couldn't keep your eyes off her, hey?" I ignored the aside; she was sharpening her blade.

"She wouldn't have gone aboard voluntarily, Pam. She's either dead or up for barter. Don't you understand?"

She shrugged to express her interest and proceeded to read me off. "I understand women, you insensate slob. Did it occur to you she might be laughing up her sleeve? Barter. . . you mean she'd trade her body for the emeralds you hid in the Goose? I'm not so blind; she's probably trysting with the Germans if I know her type. You brought us to this godforsaken reef against my better judgement, now you're abandoning us for a slovenly actress with caps on her teeth!"

"Take it easy, Pam."

"I think I'll throw up!"

The ends didn't meet. . . constrained, my ass! She glowered from the pier while we warped the cable from the wing and freed the netting from the props. When Chug joined me by the stern I told him Andy was due momentarily with the PBY, pointed to where I'd located the remaining torpedoes and the cache of emeralds. She bit her nails while we discussed Brisbane's strategy, crossed herself when I suggested they take the rifles to the tower and hold tight until the Catalina was moored in the lagoon.

"Andy knows what to do if the weather kicks up," I added. "He's been glued to the action and will hold as long as he can. We should be back by four, five at the latest."

"And if you aren't?" Pamela shouted.

"Don't play Beau Geste if the *Juanita* shows face. Take what you can and get out!"

She examined me with her liquid green eyes. She was hurt and bewildered, frightened by the unexpected. I wanted to gather her in my arms for a quiet word, to reassure her. . . she was a lovable ball of fire, but she'd have none of me. When we cast off the last of the cable, her eyes softened as they often did when her temper subsided. She stared silently for a moment, motioned me to her side, and looked down to her tiny feet.

"I care about you, you stubborn clown," she murmured. "I know she's all you say, but I worry, Keith. You seem to be seeking something you'll never find. . . don't you know when to quit and be loved for whatever you are?"

They loosened the bowlines and held fast until Howard started the engines and steadied her with the throttles. I cast off the holding anchors from the hatch and climbed into the right seat, prompted by Howard's command performance in the lumbering Goose. He held her to the wind and allowed her to drift until we were midway in the lagoon. I dropped quarter flaps and nodded. He gripped the throttles, advanced them slowly and fire-walled the quadrant. The Goose gathered speed and rose on her step.

"Gig the wheel to break the suction!" I shouted. He porpoised the old bird and brought her up. We had shed our salty residue, climbed to the south, then banked to the east when we sighted the PBY.

The old Catalina was a beautiful thing to see. . . a stately lady who had weathered her years with unblemished pride and humility. She was angled for a long approach to Hogsty Cay, her immense wing slanted to the graying sky, her props spinning a spiral of vapor from the super-saturated air. . . a classic apparition from the 30's. She was hard put to maintain 90 knots, but it didn't much matter when she was a chick. . . DC-2s were headline news when they made it coast-to-coast overnight, Boeing sleepers an oddity when they stopped for morning coffee, at Salt Lake City, in 1939.

They flashed their passing light when we climbed above them and continued to the southeast. Andy lowered his wing floats as we watched, crabbed with the crosswind in the lee of the cresting reef . . . a reassuring sight to the pair watching from the rise. . . a huge black condor coming home to nest with Andy's navy numbers emblazoned on the tail (a last minute inspiration while he was parked at Hellman's shop). They were swathing wake in the center of the lagoon when we climbed through the scud; when we leveled off at 3500 feet, we had the DEA on our starboard wing. . . the Golden Eagle pilots highly confused about which way to swing.

"Man, best ting for them is head straight up!"

"They're turning back for a looksee; they'll be calling in to Miami Control."

"Reckon they tag us to Providenciales?" I nodded. We were in for an interesting afternoon.

The *Juanita* was a smudge on the horizon when we touched down at Providenciales. An eight-foot swell was pounding the island's southern flank; a 30-knot gale had Howard on the ailerons when we taxied in. The harbor was protected by the cliffs and the sea relatively smooth until it was pummeled by the offshore gale. The *Walrus* would be hard-pressed to shoulder the storm, much less tag the speedy yacht, if the Swiss laid wake for Hogsty Cay. It was of prime importance to leap frog the 120-mile passage while the old tub wallowed along behind—equally important to covertly vector the *Penelope* while Kurt was landing his troops.

The objective, of course, was to draw the *Juanita's* fire and raise the Union Jack. . . ultimately to press charges for unlawful use of arms and piracy in Bahamian waters, with Chug in the witness box. The strategy required finite timing and clandestine communication from aloft. If the Penelope advanced prematurely, Kurt's radar would paint her blip; if she laid back, there would be an unholy interval before the frigate could display her guns. The immediate problem was to convince the Swiss that he had it made. . . could show his face to refuel while he gathered his hands from shore . . . take advantage of a gratis hour while Wolfgang paced the docks.

An RAF Hercules 130 was parked by the tower when we swiveled to front the AV truck and stilled the Pratt-Whitneys. A crewman and a threesome in cutoffs were loitering in its lee, making a stab at a game of whist. They acknowledged us with a rosy-cheeked wink when we loosened our belts to lock the controls. I nodded quickly, returning my attention to the ramp. . . Dan had performed—our gunnery team was on hand. The remaining marines would be awaiting a signal from Commodore Bower, provided they'd avoided a rhubarb with the rowdies in Turtles Bar.

A red-striped Coast Guard Falcon was parked alongside, its airstair drawn, intakes battened. I gave it short shrift, my attention riveted on the Widgeon tethered on the far end of the ramp. Wolfgang had been a busy little boy. A pair of ladders enclosed the starboard nacelle and the destroyed float removed. The Juanita's van apparently had towed her in and provided the brawn.

"Here we go," I muttered. "The Coast Guard's found us out. The DEA's on the approach and Wolfgang's scouting for another prop."

". . . Is them kids her Majesty's marines?"

"Queen's best; we take what we get!"

Howard tugged at his moustache and pointed to a ragtag Aztec parked in the grass by a peeling DC-3. "Mos likely he pinch a prop from yon Aztec," he said, "seein' she missin' some blades. . . that no count with the cutlass is kin to Big Red," he added. A light-skinned fellow was lounging beneath the Widgeon's wing with a bush knife

in his belt. "An' that be Red's cousin watchin' from that blue LTD."
I rose from my seat . . . I'd anticipated as much, but the Widgeon
posed a worse threat if they got it together while I assessed the situation at the Inn. A pair of flares would incinerate the PBY if she
were caught flat out in the lagoon.

"Is there a machine shop nearby? He'll need a vise to set the
blades."

"Sims have garage back of hardware store."

"Friends of yours?"

Howard scowled; I'd come up with a negative. "Same kine.
They've been lickin' German ass since movie ting bring the green;
supplyin' them with cocaine an' little boys. . ."

We dropped to the tarmac and locked the door, discussing the
situation while we chocked the wheels and paid off the AV truck
with a pair of hundred dollar bills. The LTD was long gone when
we went to clear with immigration. I stooped to tie my sneakers
when we passed the transport, glanced at the distant Widgeon and
tossed the keys to the rosy-cheeked marine. The Goose was parked
into the wind with the door facing the transport, topped and ready
to go. It would take less than a minute for them to load their gear;
the implication was to cover us if we returned on the run.

The double eagle taxied in while the immigration officer dou-
bled for customs and gave my flight case a casual glance, tried the
strap and passed it through. He watched nervously when the
Cessna parked alongside the Widgeon and disgorged its crew, frit-
tering away time with our arrival forms. He obviously was in tune
to the heightening tension and would rather join the locals in the
adjacent bar.

"Fat man say you call the Turtles, Mistah Slater. RAF sergeant
rang him while back to say you was on the ground; they's watchin'
from the bar," he added. "Wolfgang head for Sims wid a piece offn'

his airyplane. . . ain't much I can do 'cept keep close mouth."

I thanked him with a ten spot and waited until Howard called his wife, averting my eyes when the DEA strolled in and presented their credentials. The bearded one was uptight and steaming from his collar, the lean one gloating with a spread of grubby hands.

"Gotcha, you son of a bitch!"

"Easy, fella. . . Howard's on the phone!" He rolled his eyes and smirked.

"That nigger a friend of yours? Man, just wait until he comes after his bloody Navaho!" It was an unfortunate thing to say. Howard cradled the phone. I rounded the counter and slanted one to his groin. The bearded one was reaching for his flight case but immigration intervened.

"Mind your manners, white trash! I ain't put up wid no trouble while I's tendin' store for the Queen! Now spposn' you accompany me to your airplane while I inspect for contraband. . . seein' how you carryin' mouth full of shit!" He waited until the lean one dragged himself from the floor, then pointed to the door. His eyes were coal black as he glanced from his shoulder, his jaw tautened to his upper lip.

"Best call Seymour ifn' Howard fixin' to carry you to the Turtles. . . tings mix up, like I don't rightly know myself." I nodded and reached for the phone.

Howard was a study in indifference when I apologized for the DEA while I waited for Green Eyes to pick up. "Pay no heed, mon. They's angry 'cause we fade them in Cat Island. Folks talk nonsense when barometer fall. . . somethin' do with atmospheric pressure, accordin' to my daddy."

There was tension in Seymour's voice when he lifted the receiver on the seventh ring. Sugar's drums resounded from the cliffs, muffling laughter and the clank of cow bells from the patio below.

A hurricane party was in progress, but the beat was erratic, tilted, as if an undercurrent of nervousness prevailed.

"Mr. Dan say you go directly to the Leeward Marina," he said. "Problems aplenty, man. . . you ain't spose' come here under no circumstance, he say!"

"Leeward Marina?"

"Thas right! Out east at turn of road; Joyce be expectin'." I counted three and popped the question.

". . . and Elisabeth?"

"Yinna keep low voice, folks passin' through."

"Is she all right?" He put me on hold. I manhandled the phone until he came on again. "For Christ's sake, answer me!" I shouted.

"No need for loud word, mon, yinna do what Seymour say."

"She's. . . OK?"

"Yea, mon. I wouldn't send you to smell the flowers. Now I'm tellin' you to avoid this place. Dan say take her directly to RAF an' be watchful you ain't follow."

"Tell him the *Juanita's* due momentarily."

"Lordy, mon, dot all we needin!" he gasped. A hysterical woman was screaming in broken English from the vicinity of the steps. "Red's cousin collide with young lady," he whispered. An abrupt silence followed; he'd pulled the plug.

I explained matters to Howard when we piled into his truck and spun gravel for his house on the hill. Could we abort Wolfgang's plans short of an outright confrontation with his guard? We questioned the availability of a length of cable and a sober hand to play it off. The stores were tightly shuttered as we rumbled through the village. The hurricane had spared Providenciales, but the locals had made their plans and were gathered in the countless bars. He nodded quietly to himself when we turned his lane, pointing to an out-of-licence van parked in the weeds at the juncture of the road.

"Belong to some dragline workin' the road to Club Med while back. Reckon she have splice of cable an' clamps inside. . . come rightly to a set of keys Howard fix for himself, seein' she abandon," he added. "Now, come to think of a wily boy no one suspect ifn' he crawl backside to that old DC-3. Ain't much for school, but he got brain for hand." He slowed to front his house and applied the brakes.

"The Missus come to the porch, she ask questions. Best you take my truck an' fetch Elisabeth. Hurry along, Keith. . . God bless. I be waitin' by the Goose come three or three thirty."

I sped the pick-up down the ten-mile stretch until Joyce's sign came into view, turned in and rumbled the ruts until I came to a nicely landscaped circular drive.

Her cottage, directly on the water a hundred feet from the circle, sat amid a cluster of white-roofed buildings; a hot complex lay somewhat beyond. The driveway was cluttered with vans and a generator truck. The movie crew was housed there, but there was no show of faces. I assumed they'd taken off to juice up at the Turtles.

Joyce was sound asleep with her hand on her desk and cats underfoot. She came awake immediately when I knocked on the screen door. Putting a finger to her lips, she said "S'cuse a minute while I get my breeches on. It's been bloody hot and I've been waiting since two. Your friend Dan brought a bottle of wine for lunch, the old crutch!"

I waited by the door while she disappeared into her bedroom. She was a good natured redhead with brains and wit, a round freckled face, a little plump and edging 40. She appeared in a pair of faded jeans, knotting a denim shirt around her middle.

"Now then, I see you have Howard's truck," she said. "I'll drive; I know the turns. The cottage is about a half-mile up the coast." She keyed the pick-up and headed down a sandy lane. "I suppose you want to know how we found her?" she shouted. I grabbed the cab top and hung on. She down-shifted and swerved around a clump of bush.

"I heard someone calling from that island across the bay. It was the middle of the night. . . thought one of my cats had been treed, but they were all inside licking their chops. I got up and loaded my shotgun. Hell, you never know what's going to happen next. They steal my gas, even pinched my generator off its pad last month. Can you believe it?" I eyed the tiny island lying across the fast-moving water.

"Finally figured someone was in trouble," she continued. "So I took the dorry across. . . she was bare-assed and all cut up; been in the water for nine hours . . ."

"Is she OK?"

"Dehydrated. . . feverish. She'd been hit over the head and tossed from the bastard's yacht. . . had a hank of scarf wrapped around her tits. Just asked if she could have some water. . . and she's been asking for you. I told her what a cruddy womanizer you are, you can damned well believe."

"Thanks, Auntie Joyce." She smiled and put her hand on mine.

"We're a couple of tropical birds, Keithy love. We weren't counted when they took the census. . . it takes one to know one," she added. "If I were you, I'd hang on to that girl."

She pulled to the front of a screened cypress cottage. An old Negro was seated on the plank steps with a shotgun in his lap. He touched his hat when Joyce swung from the cab.

"She's in the bedroom. You'd better announce yourself or you're liable to get a chair over your head," Joyce said. "We'll wait outside and guard the fort, old chap."

I unlatched the screen, stepped inside and called her name. A voice answered weakly from within. I crossed the porch and tapped on her door. The dream flooded my mind as I stood in the semi-darkness, hesitating for a moment.

"It's alright, Keith. I've been watching from the window," she whispered. I eased the door.

She'd propped herself on a pillow pile by the head of the bed. Her face was drawn, lips bruised and parched. Her long, thin arms were lacerated from shoulder to fingertips. The faded shirt she wore was blood stained where it clung to her back. When I knelt beside her, I noticed her right ankle. . . deeply cut to her instep, but it had been neatly stitched.

Her arms came around me and our mouths met hotly for a long moment. I moved my hand behind her head to draw her closer and felt blood on my fingers. She winced and laid her cheek next to mine.

"I bleed a little where he struck me," she murmured. "The medic was to stitch me up, but he insisted on shaving my head and I'm much too vain for that." I found myself fighting tears. Her massive bruises must hurt like hell. "I'm all right. . . I can walk," she added. "I took a tumble over the reef when I came ashore. It's only a sprain."

"What happened, for God's sake?"

"Stupidity. Kurt called and made an appointment to review a change of dialogue. The *Juanita* was berthed by the pier at the time and I was idiot enough to believe I'd be aboard for only an hour or so, until I heard the engines and realized we were slipping away. I objected, of course, but they said we'd have lunch aboard and return by five."

"And then?"

"Most likely the statuette from his desk. I should have known better, Keith. He apparently followed me when I went below. They'd been drinking heavily at lunch and singing their wretched marching songs. I excused myself and headed to the guest state-room to lie down. The door to his parlor was ajar and the desk drawer unlocked. It was probably wired to an alarm on the bridge." She winced and put a hand to the back of her head.

"He'd apparently been suspicious since the day I arrived. I found a radio transcript from Wien lying face up in the drawer, as if it had been deliberately left for me to see. I heard the door open and everything went black."

"And they tossed you over the side?"

She nodded. "I regained consciousness while I was being dragged along the deck. They didn't hesitate to throw me over; then I heard those terrible propellers. Strange how one's mind functions when the end is near. I let myself sink until I thought my lungs would burst. . . I knew it was my only chance. It was so terribly green at first. . . then it came to be beautifully soothing, as if I'd fallen asleep and was dreaming a part in an opera I'd seen. I was dancing on center stage. . . a spotlight shone from the balcony. . . I raised my voice to sing, then someone shouted from the wings and I realized I was drowning." She shook her head is if she we not quite believing.

"The propeller's wash must have cast me to the surface, Keith. The voice. . . I don't know, but the sun was shining. I knew I was alive and wanting to live. The *Juanita* had drawn some distance away. I floated on my back and managed to keep my mouth above the water. I was sick. . . I vomited and wanted to sleep, to dream that beautiful dream again. Then they were gone and I heard the voice telling me to swim, not to give in."

"Did you know where you were?"

"The sun was setting and I had a sense of direction. I remembered someone pointing to Pine Cay before I went below. I slipped out of my dress and swam until the sun set. It was so terribly black after that. My head throbbed and I was to the point of exhaustion. Suddenly I sensed a presence beside me, a swirling in the water."

"Shark?"

"I thought so at first. I said my prayers and wondered which part of me was to go. . . then I heard it spout!"

"Porpoises!"

"A school's a family, I think. I felt a sudden warmth when I realized I was not alone, that they were trying to help me stay afloat. The stars came out after a while, then I saw a light in the distance. They nudged me several times when I lost direction and made impatient clicking sounds. One rolled at my side until his dorsal fin grazed my arm. . . he towed me through a break in the reefs, Keith. It was an unbelievable experience. God bless those lovely creatures!"

"That's one for the testament!"

"Incredible! Joyce was hard put to believe. They stayed until I had reached the shallows, then disappeared. I cut my foot on a piece of coral when I crawled ashore." She placed her lacerated limb on the floor and grimaced. I put my arm around her waist and helped her to a sitting position. She pointed to her closet.

"Joyce loaned me a pair of jeans. If you can draw them to my legs I think I can manage." A blood-stained scarf came away when I undid the jeans from a hanger.

"And that, too." Elisabeth added. "The brooch is pinned to my scarf, Keith. I found it in Kurt's drawer."

I fingered the heavy emerald for a moment; it was absolutely exquisite. . . the workmanship and intricate design all matched her ring and the pieces I'd drawn from the lagoon earlier in the day. The tragedies that followed in their wake weighed heavy on my mind.

I drew my flight case from the doorway and unbuckled the straps, moving aside my service revolver to lift the necklace from between the charts. . . dangled it for a moment before Elisabeth's eyes, then pressed it into her hand. It was a proud moment, a sense of setting something right. The reward? "Oh, my God, it's mother's necklace!"

"There's more, honey. The tiara, earrings. . . they're locked in the plane; they've been hidden away since 1945."

She held the necklace to her breast, bowing her head. When she looked up she was smiling proudly through her tears, as if the heavens had slanted a pathway of gold into the tiny room. She brought my hand to her lips and closed her eyes.

I sat down beside her and drew her head to my side. She gasped for breath and sobbed convulsively until she was emotionally spent.

"They belonged to my mother, Keith. Klaus abandoned her before the war, but she never told me. I had no way of knowing her past until after she died. I found her photograph and the ring in her suitcase when I was given her clothes." She paused for a moment to finger the necklace, then turned her head to the window.

"My father was a Russian officer, Keith. He found my mother in a concentration camp. They lived together and went into hiding when the Russians withdrew their troops in 1955. They had a small farm in the country and enjoyed a measure of happiness. He was shot by the KGB when I was a little girl. I remember he was a kindly man, tall with a blond moustache. Von Wagner was our pseudo name."

"And Majlath was your mother's maiden name?" She nodded.

"My grandfather was a first cousin to Franz Joseph; my grandmother was a Rothschild. . . a Jewess. The archduke recognized my mother from the photograph when I appeared at his office. He remembered she'd married a Prussian lieutenant, but I was told she'd been given up for dead at the close of the war and he was unable to verify her subsequent years."

"How old were you then?"

"Six. . . she'd passed away in an asylum and I was living with a foster family in Wein. They did what they could, but the Nazis had destroyed the records and the Austrians were loath to establish her identity. You'll never know what it meant to live day-to-day as a bastard orphan, Keith. The humiliation I felt when the state clerk refused to change my surname from Von Wagner to Majlath; the inference, she was the Russian's whore. I was a skinny little girl in pigtails with only a tattered photograph and a ring he insisted had been stolen by the Soviet troops.

"Klaus was identified from the photograph when I was briefed by British Intelligence. I brought it along to be certain there was no mistake. I shared a table with the monster, knowing it was he. . . my God, how I agonized for my mother when they sang their wretched songs."

"It was risky to leave your door unlocked."

"I was desperate, Keith. We had so little time together, but I realized it was best you knew. I sensed your curiosity was driven by something terrible that occurred aboard the yacht. . . a woman's intuition, perhaps. I could see it in your eyes."

"Dan told you what happened?"

"Yes. . . how ghastly! I'm so dreadfully sorry for the boy. Dan photographed the brooch as evidence of the murder in London," she sobbed. "I shall never wear the accursed thing, but it was important for me to know it matched my mother's ring. To that end the finding was a blessing, Keith."

"Proof of the coin?" She smiled proudly from her tears.

"My heritage. I'm an Austrian-Russian Jewess and my name is Elizabeth Majlath."

The horn beeped a high note . . . Joyce had called time. I helped Elisabeth into the jeans and stood by while she tested her balance. We wrapped the necklace with her scarf and walked arm-in-arm to the pick-up; Elisabeth and Joyce exchanged a few womanly words before Joyce turned and motioned to the caretaker to hand me her gun.

"You might need it, Keith. Kurt's meatballs were casing the Turtles this morning when I slipped the note to Seymour. A Mafia type with his arm in a sling was giving me the eye, can you believe?"

"Angel!"

"Hardly! He had the hots for me hub-caps; he's restoring his hearse. His buddy was talking spaghetti with that tight-ass Nazi. What a lovely couple they made. . . gold bangles and stainless steel teeth."

"Klaus?" She nodded.

"If I were you I'd haul ass for the airport, Love. Could be one of me boys has snitched. . . come to think I was missing a head when they returned from lunch." She frowned and pointed to the truck. "I'd better walk back with Roy. . . take the first turn to the right and don't look back. . . I'm something of a twit." She turned her head and blinked her teary eyes when I bussed her cheek.

It was close to three when we turned the highway and headed west. A Club Med van barreled along behind us and passed on an open stretch, but the pike was clear of traffic when it rounded a curve and disappeared. I clung to the left side of the road and alternated the gear box to soften the ruts; slowed to a crawl when a squall spattered the windshield and shrouded the roadway with a veil of rain.

"How did you meet Dan?" I ventured to ease the tension. "Up

to questions. . . or would you rather not? " She wrapped her arms around her legs and leaned back in the seat.

"We met a year ago in London, Keith. It's a long story, if you'd really care to know."

"It's a long ten miles to the airport, honey." There was an awkward silence, the wiper drawing a negative finger across the windshield. I attempted to change the subject, but she shook her head.

"When I finished my schooling I applied for a work permit at the British Embassy. I was weary of Austria. . . I'd had several parts with the state TV and had been offered a role in a series they were screening with BBC; a minor role, but I was to spend six months in England." She hesitated for a moment; I reached for words. "Problems?" She nodded.

"They held my permit in abeyance when they learned I spoke Russian. I was told if I'd work with British Intelligence for six months, they'd give me what I wanted. A year went by. . . I lost the part, of course. I was placed in a sleazy cabaret as a go-go dancer. It was a loathsome job; I could hardly face myself in the mirror each morning." She turned her head and stared at the scrubby palmetto, winced when a tire bounced off a rut.

"East Germans, Russian officers, pimply-faced soldiers. . . I was their whore, if you must know. One night I was badly abused; when I was released from the hospital I was given my permit. Later I worked with BBC and had a few promising cinema parts, but they never let you go, Keith. When my permit expired, I was summoned and told I had a choice."

"Same old game?"

"Yes. . . the under-secretary to the Russian embassy in London. I was to seek his pleasure and report twice a month. I refused. They gave me 60 days to complete my contracts and return to the continent. I became a fashion model in Bonn," she continued. "When my photographs appeared in Stern I was contracted by a film company and enjoyed a degree of success. I had stature for the first time in my life. . . recognition, but my heart was in England. . . English-speaking roles, the countryside where I could unwind and forget my past. When the BBC offered a part in a Regency series, I leapt. As a recognized actress, my permit was promptly reinstated.

"I should have known. I rented an apartment in Chelsea and bought a modest cottage in Yorkshire. . . never once did it occur to me that Klaus might still be alive," she added, "until Dan came by my apartment one rainy afternoon."

"The old bastard! I know his ways."

"A gentleman nevertheless. . . straightforward. . . he knew more about me than I knew myself. He'd researched my dossier and had been in touch with the grand duke and my foster family in Wein. He knew exactly what I wanted—a British passport and a legal change of name."

I shifted to high when we encountered a stretch of newly-laid tar. The squall had spent itself and was rolling to the north, I switched off the wiper.

"Strings?"

"Of course! But when the U-831 matter was explained, when I learned Klaus had been living in Paraguay and had been seen in Switzerland, I accepted the assignment at once."

"I admire your guts; I'd have climbed the fence."

She smiled and reached for my hand. "I doubt that; you've shown tenacity. . . and your feelings, I hope."

"Get on with the story before I pull off in the weeds!"

"I've a lovely cottage in Yorkshire, Keith Slater." I cautioned her to hold tight. We were on a curve and the Turtles had come into view. She winced when we rounded the turn, then cried out sharply and pointed directly ahead.

"There's an automobile blocking the road, Keith. . . My God, they expect us to stop!" I eyed the blue LTD and leaned on the horn.

The vintage Ford straddled the road where it narrowed, a deep ditch on either side. The intent was obvious; they'd been waiting for us to round the bend. I reacted instinctively. . . if we stopped we'd had it. I shouted to Elisabeth, firewalling the accelerator.

"Grab yourself, honey!" She ducked her head and clasped her knees. I aimed for the Ford's protruding trunk and quartered the ditch. A door popped open when we were almost upon them. . . I had a brief glimpse of a gleaming rifle as it swiveled from the door and fired.

The windshield dissolved as the truck hammered the LTD and veered for the ditch. I spun the wheel to the left, the truck tilted and Elisabeth fell to the floor in a shower of broken glass. I wrenched the wheel to the right and blasted the accelerator. . . the truck gained balance and skidded sideways across the road. The unwieldly thing fought me but we averted a spin, caught a piece of pavement.

The Ford, angled across the road, was a mess, its rear end gushing petrol from a ruptured tank. The driver, hot on the wheel, was attempting to turn it around. Our rear window exploded as I gained the straightaway. As I wiped granules of glass from my neck, I lowered my head to the outside mirror. The LTD was crabbing behind us on its broken springs with the rifleman aiming from the open door.

"Are you okay?" I shouted. She reached for my hand and pulled herself to the seat. "Can you manage the wheel?" She slipped beside me and centered the road, tried the accelerator with her mangled foot. I reached for the shotgun and swiveled in my seat. "Okay. . . goose it!"

The truck lunged forward before I could level the gun from the window. I released the safety and steadied my arm on the back of the seat, aimed for their tires and pulled the trigger. The shotgun roared and vaporized their radiator. . . the swerving Ford, smoke curling from its hood, came back to the road again. A bullet ricocheted from inside the cab as I levered the magazine and blasted the LTD from point blank range.

The explosion was totally unexpected. . . raw gasoline perhaps, a spark from the ignition system or the seething heat from a shattered radiator. . . the LTD blossomed orange and exploded in a horrendous ball of fire, careened into the ditch and was flung upside down with its passengers hopelessly engulfed in flames.

"Oh, my God!"

"It couldn't be helped," Elisabeth gasped. I shuddered and closed my eyes on the terrible scene, opened them quickly when the truck made an abrupt turn and jolted me against the door.

"Where the hell are you going?"

"To collect my things, you idiot!" The Turtles' sign flash by as my foot shot for the brakes, stopping short of her bloodied foot.

"The place is a boiling volcano, Goddamnit!" She elbowed my ribs when I reached for the wheel. I was greeted with a pair of steely blue eyes and a granite chin.

"My passports, my ring! Don't you understand?" I reached for the hand brake. "Don't you dare!" I eased off and clung on while she shot between a pair of vans, paralleled a row of decorative shrubbery and came to a clanking stop by the Turtles weathered room section. I slumped in my seat; she'd made her point.

"Now what?"

"My room key!"

"Hold tight while I check the lobby."

"I can manage the back steps. . . just toss me the keys!"

I helped her from the cab and gave it thought. The circular drive was jammed with vehicles; jeeps and vans were parked in the grass, motorcycles chained to the trees. A lone taxi was parked by the entryway, a skinny pony tied to the porch. A hurricane party was in progress beneath the cliff, judging from the din. . . cow bells and drums, Sugar's heavy electronics. I guided her to the railing and waited until she tried the stairs. A plume of oily smoke marked the burning LTD, a siren sounded in the distance.

"How's the foot?" She shrugged and gripped the railing midway.

"Please, darling. It's no good if you help me to my room."

The *Juanita's* horn erupted from the harbor as I skirted the shrubbery and ran to the lobby. I hesitated for a moment when I saw the van parked by the entry, edged the screen door when I determined its windows were up and there was no one standing by. Green Eyes was bent over the PBX. I called out softly; he snapped erect and rolled his eyes.

"Lordy, man!"

"Elisabeth's keys!"

"She here?" I pointed to the outside balcony, he staggered to his feet. "Oh, Lord. . . she break the old man's violations!"

"Quick!" He fumbled the pigeon holes and slid her key across the counter. I darted for the lobby and found her leaning from the upper railing.

"Fifteen minutes. . . take the back way and wait by the truck!" She nodded and bent to retrieve the clattering keys. I waited until she tried the door and hotfooted it back to the lobby. Green Eyes was beside himself; he hammered the PBX and pointed to the lower stairs.

"Yinna come to a big problem, Keith! Old man in the bar wid the admiral an' I ain't raise em since you call. 'Spect trouble, man. Bartender phone disconnect."

"The marines?"

"Blind drunk since lunch, 'cept ones by the airport. They's sleepin on the *Walrus*, ain't no help." He stopped short and craned his neck. A lanky thing, with her hair wrapped in a towel, slipped by and ran for the lower stairs. "She keep two doors from Elisabeth," he whispered. "Hab somethin' on her mind, man!" He closed his eyes when the screen door hit the stop. A local hurried through and followed behind the girl.

"Lordy, that be Sims! Got to do wid that car burnin' down the road. Same car came by when starchass were talkin' wid some kid," he added.

"Starch-ass? You mean Klaus?"

"Call him what you like. Ain't fit for Christian name."

A chill iced my spine. The bases were loaded and the *Juanita* would be nuzzling the pier.

I asked if he had a gun. He opened the cash drawer and pointed to his service .38. We discussed the situation briefly, mainly the urgency of covering the lobby as the imbroglio erupted from below. He was rattled, but he commanded the bottleneck; Dan's taxi was standing by, the driver asleep at the wheel. I pondered the odds of hacking it alone. I was reluctant to leave Elisabeth with Green Eyes, but I couldn't abandon the old horses if they were short for change.

"I'm going below. . . if Klaus comes up the stairs, hit the PBX and tell Elisabeth to hole up in her room!" I pointed to the cab and asked him to grab the keys. He shrugged; he'd give it a try.

"Watch yourself, man. . . Kurt havin' outside help from Miami! Fella wid bad arm mos' likely cause for disconnection."

I gave Angel consideration as I paired the stairs to the lower rise. He was streetwise; could have slipped behind the pair and palmed Dan's Webley while they were shoulder deep in the bar. He'd be out for blood and carried a mean .32 . . . the guile to disarm the old

237

men and prod them to the yacht. Why else would he be there? unless his capo sensed heavy . . . perhaps a coke connection?

Mafia mentality. . . a piece of the action for services rendered and a pair of sugar plums for dessert. I cringed at the thought, knowing Kurt's diabolical mind. With Dan under knuckle, he'd consider Angel redundant and feed the lot to the sharks.

Whatever the motive, I reasoned Angel would hold tight until the *Juanita* cast her lines, then exit the bar from the rear. What to do? A frontal move would be suicidal; the hoods would be watching the patio doors. The alternative. . . circle the enclave and approach the room from the pier. Barehanded, without a gun? Bower was in a position to head them off, but prematurely he'd compromise his cover and I'd risk a merciless bloodbath if I angled for the trawler. I had no illusions. . . Angel would have an unobstructed view. . . he'd react immediately, hose the old men or use them as hostages. No way!

A lesser evil involved a circuitous route through the kitchen and service doors to the bar. The doors, off to the side, were a double flap hustling with trays . . . difficult to see from the rear of the room. With a bit of luck I might solicit help from the chef. He was a fearless giant of a man, contemptuous of Kurt. If we staged a donnybrook the locals would be receptive (they were juiced from high noon), but we'd need a diversion of sorts to block Angel's path to the pier. I leaned from the wall to study Sugar's high-stepping band, appraised the raucous crowd as he teased them with a reggae. He was completely in command, spinning and flashing his ivory teeth. The patio was a sea of waving arms and gyrating hips, susceptible to high jinks. Why not?

I'd attracted an observer while I pondered the mob scene below. The pimply steward, stationed by the lower steps, had recognized my thatch of hair. We had a moment of eye play, a cocky smile when he scanned my empty hands. . . then he darted behind a patch of shrubbery, rounded the patio and raced for the pier. A heavy rumbling echoed from the cliffs as I vaulted the wall to cut him off. . . the unmistakable beat of laboring engines, oily exhaust fumes. . . I stopped short; the kid was long of leg and time was short. Buildings blocked my view, but I realized the *Juanita* was maneuvering to anchor. It would be minutes until they lowered a launch, miserly minutes. . . five or ten at the best, until Kurt came dockside and reacted to developments ashore. Would Angel hold?

I angled for the patio and shouldered the crowd in desperation, hoping to catch Sugar's eye. They were a happy lot, oblivious to the drama unfolding nearby, to the bloody tragedy that could erupt momentarily in the bar. The hurricane party was full force and would go on for hours. They we juiced out of their minds as they whirled to the thundering drums, but they provided a measure of cover as I jostled my way to the low hanging porch.

The kitchen window was directly above me, out of reach and effectively screened. The dining room sliding doors, to my left, were closed, but apparently unlocked. The bar entrance was a long step to my right, to my immediate left when I turned to hug the kitchen wall. . . alive with waiters toting drinks, a dangerous avenue if I collided with a tray. With Angel watching from inside, and Sugar's platform exposed to his line of view, the danger multiplied. A thatched bandstand, wedged against the cliff, was unattainable. I jumped and waved my arms, praying *Sugar raise your eyes!*

He was low on his heels, twirling his microphone, leading the crowd in a wild merengue, his eyes centering on the open sky. I had decided to give it up and chance the kitchen when he scooped a hat from his drummer and arced it neatly to his feet. He winked and pointed to the bar room door and I realized he'd been watching all the while. When a waiter dipped and jammed the straw on my head, I realized they'd been communicating since I vaulted the stairs. . . Afro style, a play of drums, a subtle monologue that only the blacks would understand.

"Be cautious, man!" Sugar whispered from his microphone. "Certain folk been axin' if you seed about." He jumped high and raised the band to a Calypso beat. . . waited until they were full blast, then adlibbed from the schooner *John B.*

"Hoist up the *John B* sail, folks' needin' help. . . now raise your hand!" he shouted to the unknowing crowd. They responded with a roar.

". . . We feel so break up, we wanna go home!" Sugar smiled and dropped his voice. "They's backside de bar man. . . watcha plan to do?" I pointed to myself and the roundabout way to the kitchen. He nodded and raised his mike; the beat was pure percussion.

"Fats have gun to head, marine boys gone to bed . . . now let's hear plenty voice!" he shouted overhead. The response echoed from the cliffs.

". . . We feel so break up, we wanna go home?" He dropped to his knees to whisper an aside. "Chef give plenty arm, but dat boat comin' up behind." I pointed to the crowd and shuffled my feet, pointed again to the dining room doors. He brightened and displayed his magnificent smile.

"All right, folks, let's have some fun! Now, it ain't New Year, but wid rage rakin' sky. . . I say, it time for Junkanoo!" He whirled on his toes and shouted, "What say you?" The response was a thunderous, "Junkanoo!" Sugar splayed his legs and upped the band to a pounding merengue.

"Let's dance. . . let's dance!" He whirled again and lowered his voice. "Give five minute and we come backside wid all behind. . . pay heed to the Rasta bartender," he added. "I talkin' to him now."

He supplemented the beat with a reggae monologue . . . spoke softly to the walls in backstreet Jamaican, the mystifying dialect of the Afro-Caribbean, random phrases with implicit meaning. Foreign to the ears of the stomping mob, but not to the waiters. . . nor the kitchen staff.

"Pay compliment to the chef," Sugar sided, when they answered with a clatter of pans. "Sayin' dey please to play the game. He waitin' for you, man!"

There was tension in the kitchen when I parted the dining room doors, apprehension when a waiter emerged from the bar. The chef eyed him silently, doffed his apron and cut the ranges. "Speak up, boy. . . what Rasta say? Dis man waitin' to hear."

"Say mon wid sling cut phone connection. . . sneak up de ole man's, an' take them gun."

"I knows dot! Where's they go?"

"Back side de bar, mon. . . dey's waitin' for de boat!"

"Is Klaus inside?" The waiter turned to me. "Mon wid steel teeths." I nodded.

"No, mon. . . tink he on the hill."

"God damn!"

"Mon, don' say dot!" I apologized immediately.

"Now, you boys listen to me!" The chef interjected "I wants you to look behind an' comfort dis mon while I make face, understand?" The waiters were quick to agree. . . the chef was six feet three. "Now, I come backside de window. . . an' when I raise head you's to shout, Junkanoo!"

"Praise you, mon!"

He turned to me then. "Now, I show you what I goin' to do." He produced a key to the storeroom closet, unlocked it and pointed inside. The shelves were stacked with noisemakers from Boxing Day; horns, clackers and bells. He pointed to an enormous headdress wrapped in plastic and I realized what he had in mind.

"Reckon it do?"

"Absolutely!" He grinned and cut the bindings.

"Won me first prize last Boxing Day. Come New Year, I busy wid kitchen. . . miss de action," he added remorsefully.

We had a rapid conversation while the waiters stripped the shelves. . . the sequence of things and means of communication, instructions to his boys. They were to disperse the horns to the crowd. . . pass word to Sugar and the Rasta in the bar, flank the bar and watch for trouble. "Tell Sugar sound bugle an' I answer wid sid." He produced a boatswain's whistle from a drawer and tied it to his wrist. "Blows once, I be ready. . . two, I raise head. Come three, dey's come backside an bust de door! Yinna understand?" They nodded and melted away.

"Now den," he added to us, "them gangster ain't seed no mask like dot, cause plenty fright. . . Be quick, mon . . . take heavy bottle and knock them head, seein' you ain't carry no gun." He turned to shoulder the cumbersome thing. I canted the hat to hide my face and pressed the barroom doors.

The room was a blast, a mass of inebriated humanity shouting unilaterally from all sides. There was no rhyme or reason. . . they were in to a world of their own. Locals were soldiering the length of the bar, charter boat captains and clients stood shoulder deep in eddies of four and five. The piano was planted dead center, a blonde floozy from yesteryear atop with her foot flexing a battered bass drum. The piano player was juiced, a flute wheezed out a tune, but somehow they were managing. . . *Rule Britannia, Britannia rules the waves!*

I sidestepped a reeling Conch and worked my way to where a bartender with dreadlocks was drawing suds from a barrel of beer. He raised his eyes when I scouted him with a fiver, scrutinized my face briefly, pointed a bony elbow to the phone cradled at the end of the bar. I was to understand why Green Eyes was at odds. The line was neatly severed, cut at arm's length by a very sharp knife.

"Angel?" He nodded and passed me a bottle of Barbados rum.

"Same smartass holdin' weapon to the ole man's head!" I scanned the room through the boozy haze, following his pointing finger for direction.

Dan was seated by the dockside window with the Admiral. An oaken table had been drawn before them as a buffer to the gaggle at the bar. Dan was slumped in his chair with arms folded across his enormous stomach, eyes fixed to the ceiling, his jowls trembling with indignation. A temper vein pulsed the Admiral's forehead, but he seemingly was preoccupied with his empty glass. . . staring for-lornly at the swirling fan. An unlikely pair in sodden jackets stood directly behind them with their backs to the wall. I recognized Angel immediately. . . Sir Daniel and the legendary Admiral had been sapped by a pair of punks from the Jersey docks.

Angel's attention was focused on Dan and the exit door to his right. His free hand was obscured by an improvised sling, but I had no illusions. Close behind the Admiral stood his beady-eyed part-ner, a hand in his jacket, grotty cigar cornering his jaw. They'd positioned themselves with the window between them to watch the docks *and* the old men.

Clackers and horns reached a crescendo as the rumble of pounding feet echoed from the walls. The euphoric mob trailed Sugar's band and exploded into the halls. Angel turned nervously to the window; he was confused by the horrendous noise, by the rolling drums as the snake dance circled the dining room and explored the dockside doors. His companion shifted the cigar in his teeth and fretted with his jaw. . . he was at odds with the ground swell rippling the room, wary of the wide-eyed locals rising to their toes. While words were exchanged between the jittery pair, I took the moment to make a sidelong approach to Brisbane's table. . . stopped short when the Rasta dug me in the ribs.

"Have caution," he whispered. "Them ole man's readyin' to jump!" I had a glimpse of Dan's lidded eyes, of a pudgy hand reaching for his garter, of the Admiral gathering his feet.

Their unfortunate timing was fraught with desperation. They obviously hadn't seen us and were going for broke. I tensed; we were yards apart. . . an impetuous move would alert the cigar-chomping thug and erase our advantage; if I hesitated, they'd risk their lives and the odds were uneven. The decision was made by my mentor; he dipped low and spun his billystick across the floor. . . pulled me down as it struck Dan's lily white shoe.

The old man's baby blues copped an incredulous stare when I tipped my straw and cautioned him to hold his cool. The catalyst was unexpected, as if a drunken actor had wandered from the wings. The toothless Conch staggered between us and fell headlong into a group at the bar. The donneybrook was instantaneous. . . three-fold. The locals took exception and went after the hapless Conch, Angel whirled to face the mayhem and drew his ugly revolver. It was then or never. . . I stood full height and flipped my hat to the overhead fan, gripped a bottle and shouldered my way to the oaken table. Angel spun about, undecided, his eyes fixed on the spinning straw. The whistle shrilled from the window and his partner bellowed *Jes-us Christ!*

An unearthly silence descended upon the room. I was vaguely aware of Sugar's drums as the locals turned to stare. One-by-one they rose to their toes and shouted, *"Junkanoo!"* An enormous mask was framed by the salt-encrusted glass . . . a bright green creature from outer space with multiple tendrils of paper maché. A gleaming cleaver in a coal black hand rose from its feathered cloak. The crowd roared approval and toasted the monstrous thing. The terrified thug backed away and collided with the Admiral's chair. . . a brawny arm reached out to grasp his belt. I had a blurred impression of a clenched cigar as he sailed across the abyss and came to grief with the upright piano. I reacted before Angel could gather his wits and hurled the bottle at his broken arm. . . *my God, how he screamed!*

His face was wracked with pain and disbelief as he slumped against the door. His arm hung uselessly from the sling, but the .32 was unwavering as he thumbed the safety. "Awright! Who trew the fuckin' bottle?" No one volunteered, of course. The crowd backed away, the Rasta melting to the floor. There was a stark moment of truth . . . instant recognition. Angel's eyes narrowed, an insidious smile creased his lips as he aimed the lethal thing at my heart. I lunged forward, but the shot was never fired . . . a derringer cracked from Brisbane's garter as Sugar breached the door and burst inside with his raucous parade. Angel stiffened and stared blankly at the ceiling, the .32 tumbling from his hand as he pawed his severed jugular vein. A froth of blood cornered his mouth as he was trampled by a hundred feet dancing across the barroom floor.

I shuddered when his mangled body disappeared from view. The floozy screamed and dispatched his partner with the heel of her shoe. The steward, caught by the incoming tide, darted through the malingerers, hellbent for safety as he scurried for the patio. I gave him up momentarily to extract my charges from the volatile mob ... gave thanks to dreadlocks and parted with my remaining cash. "Split it with Sugar and the Chef; it's all I have."

"Don't worry it, mon. . . bless yo' heart, we's got talk for plenty a day."

"Hasten, boy!" Sir Daniel bellowed. They were an incongruous pair, bickering, complaining of the oppressive humidity, leveling accusations. . . mainly at me.

"Salvaged your bloody ass, hey?" he muttered as he bent to

retrieve his Webley from beneath the piano.

"Dry up. . . Klaus is on the loose!"

"And where is Elisabeth?"

"In her room; she forgot her cosmetics!" I added, grabbing his arm to lead him across the deserted patio.

His face reddened. "Counter to my instruction, hey?" A pair of shots echoed from the cliffs before I could reply. The first was muffled, the second a sharp report from the balcony above.

I took the stone steps two at a time, brushed by the Admiral and wrenched the lobby screen. Green Eyes was sprawled face down on the floor with an ugly gash behind his ear. I tried his pulse and lugged him to a chair, ransacked the cash drawer for his gun and sprinted for the upper stairs. The steward collided with me on the turn, sobbing incoherently as he attempted to pass me on the run. His pimples were etched in stark relief to his ashen face as I drop kicked him into the stairwell and called down to Dan.

"Keep me covered, Goddamnit . . . it has to be Klaus!" A clash of gears spun me around as I reached the upper railing, the taxi rooster tailed a muddy spume as the terrified driver cornered a turn and disappeared. "The truck!" I called down to the Admiral. "Grab the truck!"

"Where is it?" he shouted. I pointed as I ran along the balcony to Elisabeth's door.

It was strangely quiet inside. The door had been forced; a pool of blood oozed from beneath it and dribbled on the step. The door moved a few inches and stopped against something soft and yielding. I called in to Elisabeth but there was no answer. I shouldered the door and looked down. A lifeless hand fell to the floor. . . an old hand with dirty nails. I stepped over the body and entered the room.

Klaus was lying on his back staring at the ceiling. A grotesque smile framed his face and a drool of blood seeped from his stainless steel teeth. A massive hole blossomed on his embroidered jacket; he was very dead. The *Juanita* hoarsed three short blasts as I crossed the room; an AK7 rattled from somewhere, but the reasoning was lost to me.

Elisabeth was propped against the balcony door, her blue automatic pointing to the floor. Her eyes were glazed with pain, her shirt blotched with crimson where it pressed her slender waist.

I knelt beside her; her lips moved and the automatic slipped from her fingers. I waved my hand and her eyes followed, focusing briefly in recognition. I lifted the shirt from her side and opened the shutters for light. The shot had torn the rib cage below her breast. She vas bleeding profusely. I reached for a pillow and strapped it to her chest with my belt to stop the flow. Her pulse was weak, but there was no indication of internal bleeding. I relaxed a little.

"I've killed him. . . may God forgive me," she whispered

"You did what you had to do, honey. Don't moralize for the son of a bitch."

"He was screaming my mother's name when he broke the door. I've never seen such hate!" An AK7 erupted from the vicinity of the pier. Kurt had turned his wrath on the *Walrus* on a late arriving crewman racing along the dock as the *Juanita* slipped her moorings and pointed to the open sea

The crew member fell headlong, quivered and lay still when a second burst raked his spine. The trio of marines had come awake and were sprawled on the *Walrus's* forward deck, rolling to shoulder a grenade launcher as the *Juanita* gathered knots. I watched anxiously from the window as Bower hurried from the wheelhouse to wave them down, exhaled when the speedy yacht drew from range. He was one cool number; he'd played the game to the hilt and now he'd wait his turn.

"Grit your teeth, baby. . . it's going to hurt!" Elisabeth smiled gamely as I gathered her in my arms and carried her across the room.

"My papers!" I bent to collect her things from the floor, stepping over the grinning corpse. Dan's Webley greeted us when I forced the door.

"She needs a doctor, you bastard. . . the truck?" His eyes darted from Elisabeth to the dead man lying at my feet.

"Klaus?"

"Who else?"

"You were warned not to bring her here, you insolent prig!" I gave him short shrift. Howard's truck was in motion with the Admiral at the wheel. "You heard me, boy!"

"Did you ever tell a woman what to do?"

"Please!" Elisabeth moaned, "I hurt."

Dan huffed behind us as I carried her down the stairs and kneed the screen, clucked his concern when we lifted Elisabeth to the truck bed and cushioned her with pillows from the lobby chairs. He was a doting old man, overcome with grief when he peeled back the blood-stained shirt to examine the wound.

"Her rib cage is shattered, Keithy. Fortunately the bullet was deflected, but she's lost immeasurable blood."

"There's a doctor at Grand Turk!"

He gripped my arm and shook his head. "We have plasma aboard the Hercules, son, and a right sharp medic! She'll need an immediate transfusion; we have no time to cast about." I wiped the perspiration from her brow; her lips were taut with pain and she was on the verge of shock, staring blindly at the turbulent sky.

"Morphine!" the Admiral bellowed.

I raced to the office and ripped an emergency kit from the wall, stumbled onto Green Eyes as I rounded the desk. He taggered to the door, watched silently as the Admiral broke the seal and applied a needle to Elisabeth's arm. She was unconscious when Dan tossed a key from his vest and shouted to the bewildered man.

"Board the *Walrus*, Constable . . and take the snifflin' brat along!" He pointed to the steward manacled to the railing. "We'll be needing a witness to make sense of this matter."

I returned Green Eye's .38 when he unshackled the kid, shouting from the head of the stairs when I heard the *Walrus'* engines roar. I doubt if Bower heard me but he was scanning the cliff with his binoculars when Seymour prodded the steward to the lower rise. I had a lasting impression of our saviors as I returned to the truck and keyed the ignition. . . of Sugar's strutting from the bar with the unwitting mob at his heels. . . of Rasta's gleaming teeth as he leapt high, twirling a tray with his fingers as only the natives can do.

I drove slowly to avoid the colossal puddles, down-shifting the turns, glancing back to check Elisabeth when we encountered a spat of rain. Dan spread his jacket over her midriff and crouched by her side, his massive jowels rippling with the motion, BB eyes focused on the road ahead. The Admiral was seated beside me twiddling his thumbs, his jaws jutting from the window as if he were commanding a dreadnaught from the bridge. We were a mile from the airport when we had an indication of further trouble. . . a blaring horn as a car barreled from the opposite direction and forced us onto the shoulder. A truck followed a moment later, swerving to the left to counter a head-on, the driver pointing desperately to his rear as the truck cornered the shoulder and continued full blast on the turn-pike.

The airport was in a turmoil when we screeched to a halt by the terminal building. The bar emptied, occupants in full flight. . . piling into their cars, scurrying for cover when a round of gunfire echoed from the ramp. I wheeled the pickup and glided to the far end of the lot, fanned the switch and asked the Admiral to take over. I palmed my revolver and spilled from the cab.

"Down, Goddamnit!" I shouted to Dan.

"Wolfgang?"

"Has to be!"

Dan loosened his Webley as I zigzagged for the terminal and circled the building from the rear. A shot shattered a tower window as I sprawled behind a line tug and scanned the ramp. Wolfgang was firing from the hip as he drew the ladder from the Widgeon's nacelle, pausing to aim as he kicked the chocks. The prop had been reset and he was ready to roll!

The Coast Guard Falcon apparently had pulled out before the fusillade erupted, but the DEA had overstayed. The Eagle was wing tip with the beleaguered Widgeon, tied down and unattended. I glanced wildly about looking for the C-130; located its high standing tail on the outbound taxi way, turbines whining, marines in battle dress peering from its yawning doors. The pilot had sensed trouble and taxied out of range. The marines were no help; they'd loaded their equipment aboard the Goose and had been caught empty-handed when the shit hit the fan.

The Goose? My heart flipped as I strained to bring her in view, but my view was obstructed by the abandoned fire truck and an overturned van. I considered the puny thing in my hand, the yardage to the Widgeon, as Wolfgang climbed aboard and slammed the door. . . reconsidered and retreated to the truck when he loosened a barrage from the cockpit window.

He had a start on an engine while I pointed a roundabout path to the waiting Hercules, winding number two when the Admiral handed me the shotgun and meshed the gears. Elisabeth had regained consciousness, but she was drowsy and unseeing, murmuring in German as she clung to Dan's hand. I had a quick word with the old man, nodded to the Admiral and bolted for customs as the truck humped a curb and disappeared.

The customs officer was huddled behind his desk, immobilized with terror. DEA pilots were cowering in the men's room, scrambling for the partitions when Wolfgang scattered another round. I shouted a reassuring word as I raced for the desk and slid to the floor by the trembling customs man. The window was long gone, the office littered with debris, but I had a frontal view of the Widgeon's spinning props as I upended the desk as a shield from Wolfgang's parting shots. The Goose was off to the right, seemingly intact. A magnesium flare fizzled short of her stubborn nose, bubbling the tarmac, spiraling smoke to the 30-knot gale. A man lay on his back by the overturned van, jelly oozing from his belly, a flare gun clutched in his lifeless hand.

"Dead man, Sim's mechanic!" the officer blurted. "He tryin' set fire to you airyplane when RAF fella take him down. Van belong Club Med. . . come bad time."

"Where's Sims?"

He pointed to the Widgeon. "Hidin' inside dat crazy ting, he one scared cat!" I thumbed him to the door and climbed to my knees.

The DEA peered from the John as I upturned the desk and levered it to the window. The bearded one dropped beside me as I aimed for the Widgeon's tires. "Back in your cage, Goddamnit!" He pointed to the revolver tucked in my belt.

"He's too far out, Keith. Let's go for the van and stroke him when he taxis by!" I studied him for a moment; he was right. . . the shot gun would only pepper the tires. I checked the safety and slid the revolver across the floor.

"Okay. . . aim for the cockpit and follow me through!" I opened the door as I crouched on my knees. It happened quickly!

Wolfgang blasted the throttles before the bearded one could fire. The Widgeon's tail rose from the ramp, but she refused to move. Wolfgang kicked rudder. . . the tail arced and a spume of gravel spun with the gale. I climbed to my feet with the shotgun in hand. Howard had pulled it off. Lashed a cable to the Widgeon's tail wheel and fastened it to the unyielding DC-3.

Wolfgang eased the throttles, looking down from the cockpit to check his wheels. When he fire-walled the Lycomings, the Widgeon lurched forward, the DC-3 wobbled as the cable tautened. . . then the Widgeon's tail wheel parted and the amphibian bolted onto the ramp, made a turn to the right, and smashed headlong into the Double Eagle. The gas tanks exploded a moment later. Sims tumbled from the cabin with his clothes afire. . . Wolfgang never made it. We stared helplessly at his blazing pyre as we rolled Sims from the inferno and attempted to smother his fire. He died before the medics could reach his side. . . a remorseful reminder of Iraq, of napalm and the stench of burning flesh. . . a walking nightmare for those of us who walked away.

Elisabeth lay aboard the C-130 with a long plastic tube embedded in her wrist. I made a soft promise while the medic applied a fresh compress and prepared her for the flight to Kindley Field (Bermuda). She was barely conscious, smiling from the pain that wracked her slender body, acknowledging with the ring as she raised it to my lips. That was her style, a rare combination of guts and a beautiful soul . . . a heritage from the beginning of time. She was clutching the net bag when I spoke briefly to the Admiral and dropped to the ground. Gone so quickly. . . I bowed my head and prayed.

The Hercules was aloft when we piled aboard the truck, winging to the north to avoid the storm, setting course for Bermuda before disappearing in the heavy cloud. A ray of sunlight appeared in the east as we detoured the carnage and came to a stop by my riddled Goose. I counted heads while Howard assessed the damage and drained the sumps. He was understandably quiet, avoiding my eyes when the marines settled in the cabin with their cases of grenades. . . shaking his head when the emergency crew retrieved their trucks and foamed the smouldering planes. The count came to five when the DEA climbed aboard and seated themselves on the floor; to six when Dan hoisted his hamper to the bulkhead, chewing a fresh cigar. Goose was designed for eight with minimal luggage, but Dan made two and we were nine when Howard returned from the telephone and fastened in.

"Wife put up plenty of flack, man. Say I come to bad association with all this shootin' she hear. . . ain't tell her 'bout that cable her nephew stretch from that old DC-3."

Seven

WE WERE SWEATING THE panel when we leveled off at 2500 feet in heavy clouds and looked back to see if our passengers were belted to the floor. I extended the wheels and dropped quarter flaps to soften the bumps, advanced the props to 2100, came back on the throttles. The overloaded lady was hard put to maintain a hundred knots but I was wary of the unstable air, afraid for her wings when we encountered the cyclonic squalls. We were on the edge of Hurricane Christina when we penetrated the line a half hour out. Lacking radar, we resorted to old tricks and avoided the cells by pointing 10 degrees from the spasmodic lightning. We returned to course when the glow receded and the downdrafts had us manhandling the wheel. I engaged the pilot heater when we entered an area of rain, retracted the gear and zeroed the flaps. . . set the quadrant to cruise speed when Howard agreed the worst of it was behind us. It would have been easier going at 500 feet, but I was afraid Kurt would sight the noisy Goose and realize Wolfgang had bought the park.

We dropped down when we reasoned the *Juanita* was in our lee, broke into the clear at 600 feet with the squall clawing our tail. I eased the throttles and leveled off; the eerie whistling ceased as Howard strained his harness to look back, increased when I edged a few knots. "Bullet holes. . . don't worry it, fella. They'll be whistling Dixie when we stroke the atoll."

We were on the feathered edge of Christina and flying tangent with her clockwise winds, barreling along over 20-foot swells with only a vague idea of where we were. The dark green sea was streaked with spume, the combers spilling horizontally as they caught the 40-knot gale. To the south the winds would be bending a hundred knots, to the north they'd dwindle to a spurious breeze. Hogsty Cay lay somewhere ahead in total darkness, the five o'clock sun screened by a massive envelope of cloud moving rapidly to the west.

"Storm carrying us like a piece of straw," Howard ventured as I studied my watch. "Needin' that beacon before we fetch up in Miami, man." When he reached to set up the homer at Hogsty Cay, I cautioned him to hold off.

"We can't risk it, fella. If Kurt monitors the signal, he come off the wall."

"They's too far back, Keith. . . ain't going to pick us up at 500 feet." I shook my head. The *Juanita* had long ears; if we activated the homer they'd wonder what they had. Would they be tracking us with radar, anticipating the Widgeon?

"That's it!"

"Say again to Howard."

"If they have us on radar they'll give us a fix."

"Gotcha, man!"

"Wolfgang's frequency?"

"He was workin' 120.9." I advanced the props while Howard traversed the VHF. The DEA pilots came forward when we shouldered the low hanging clouds, dropping to their knees and clinging to the bulkhead when the Goose groaned and rippled her wings.

"Have a heart, Slater!" the bearded one croaked. "Drop us at George Town if you're gonna play God!" He pointed to the rosy glow in the north. "We'll get Stone off your back if you'll take us home!"

"Shush, man!" Howard interrupted. He had a spate of German juiced with static. The *Juanita* was calling the Widgeon's numbers.

"Sound like they be 40 mile, Keith. Maybe you was right."

We leveled off at 1500 feet in moderate turbulence. Howard took over as I opened the window to the rumbling Pratt-Whitneys. When the *Juanita* repeated I held the microphone to the window and acknowledged in German. They responded immediately.

"What he say?" Howard whispered. I checked the compass and applied hard right rudder, nodded for Howard to level off when we rolled through 300 degrees.

"We're 20 off course. . . Hogsty's 290, but he's suggesting a 10 degree crab.

"Hold it. . . Kurt's on the horn. He wants to know what happened to the Yankee amphibian. Did it go as planned?" I delayed my response to search for words. When he repeated, I triggered the mike and mimicked Wolfgang's voice.

"Alles ging wie geschmiert, Kaeptn. Das amphibian wurde in Brand gesteckt, und der Pilot ist in Flammen aufgegangen." (Everything went smoothly, Captain. The seaplane was set afire, and the pilot consumed in flames.) Kurt was delighted.

"Grossartig! und was ist mit Dr. Klaus und der Juedin? Haben Sie Ihnen an Bord genommen wie befohlen?" (Fantastic! and what about Dr. Klaus and the Jewess? Did you take them aboard as ordered?)

Howard rolled back the trim when Dan lunged to the cockpit and cuffed the DEA aside. He was on to the dialogue, but his cheeks were puffed and he was clutching his fly.

"Don't overdo it, Keithy. Query the *Juanita's* position and fade, else he'll be wanting to speak with Klaus. Is there a toilet aboard this plane?" Dan added briskly. "My bladder is near to burst!" I pointed to the aft compartment; held the mike by the window to fuzz the transmission, clicked the button when the *Juanita* acknowledged. . . three hours, give or take.

We had Hogsty on the nose when we descended through the scud at 5:45, only a glimmer of light in the inky blackness, but a rewarding sight nevertheless. Tensions eased when we buzzed the lagoon with our bullet holes harmonizing high C. Andy had hung in! The high riding PBY was anchored dead center in the basin with her lights ablaze, the launch tied alongside her starboard blister. The strobes came alive as we passed overhead and made a long, shallow turn to the north. They'd maintained a watch from the tower and reacted immediately to the Goose, blinking the strobes to indicate it was safe to land.

I monitored the VHF while Howard set up a power approach to front the gale. I was mindful of the *Juanita's* radar, anticipated a call when they screened our descent. . . the call came before I could mute the volume; Kurt rattled the speaker with his staccato German.

"Conditions?" Were there indications of Slater's party. . . if so, we were to circle and advise. I hammered the mike and told him conditions were in the green. The reply was abrupt, concisely stated; we were to raise a flare at 20:00, a double flare when the *Juanita* responded with a light.

"Acknowledge!" he commanded in English. I clicked the mike in response. . . was my NATO German suspect?

A pounding gray line arced around the southeastern reach of the tiny island, long fingers of spume curled the dune rock and licked the rise. The lagoon's surface was marginal, tracered with salt, but the reef was absorbing the worst of the gale. I switched on the landing lights when Howard banked the Goose over the hill, eased the engines when we were angled to the strobes. We skimmed the basin and spread water from the keel, then the old bird porpoised and gurgled to a stop.

The strobes continued to flicker as Howard blasted the Pratt-Whitneys and pointed for the beach. Relieved of my head-set, I took over when he dipped into the forward hatch. The Navy team was hard at work, their torches blazing in the murky depths, moving about from where the torpedoes were grouped beneath the PBY's starboard wing. Downlights flooded the surface to facilitate the hoisting procedure A slender cable was rigged to the underpart of the wing, and we had a glimpse of Freddie's ingenuity as we thundered by.

An electric winch housed in the Catalina's spar had obviously seen use in the past. The cable was played to the recovery team; its usefulness extended to 40 feet. Andy was stationed in the blister with a control box in hand, shielding his eyes from the floodlamps while he waited a signal from below. Chug was kneeling by his side with a secondary line looped to the cable, nodding as we passed, tugging at the line when the cable tautened and shed water to the gale.

I traveled my window and looked back when the Goose grounded the beach, cut the Pratt-Whitneys when Howard rose from the hatch. A clutch of weedy disks broke surface, glinted momentarily in the glare and were drawn aboard the blister like a bale of pot in the not-too-distant past. The hook turned to the depths while the DEA muttered their asides, but my attention was given to the young lady in a wet suit and sparse bikini as she splashed through the shallows to catch Howard's line.

She greeted me with an icy stare when I dropped from the door to warp the Goose alongside the beach, dimpled briefly when Dan rolled his trousers to his pink knees and waded ashore with the marines. She had kind words for Howard, nodded politely to the DEA when we snared a pair of anchors and swung the amphibian to the gale. I braced myself when she noticed the gashes in the Goose's tail, but she contained herself to matters at hand; loosened her square-toothed smile when the gunnery sergeant stood by with Dan to question the routine they'd devised, when the divers disembarked from the PBY.

She'd paired with Chug to spell the divers at one-hour intervals, alternating with them to watch from the hill. . . "by that dreadful well". The torpedos were a problem, she added. They uncovered them one by one, then the navy team cut the casings with their torches, but when the skin was peeled away they were confronted with stainless steel shafts that had to be severed to free the discs. The discs were terribly heavy, and slippery with grime. It was grueling business to attach them to the cable, to wait while they were lofted to the PBY. All of this, plus inquisitive fish as they worked the bottom at 40 feet!

"How many have you done?" I questioned. She turned and responded to Dan.

"They were cutting the last of six when I heard that awful noise. I'd just returned to the hill when I realized it was the Goose!"

"You must be to a point of exhaustion, Ma'm," the sergeant commented. She shrugged and pointed to the inner reef, eyed me balefully as if I were Johnny-come-lately.

"I'm told there are six more. I can't speak for my brother, but after I see you to the tower, I want to go home."

I watched her carefully. She was close to tears, physically and emotionally spent. They'd recovered two-and-a-half tons of gold and the Catalina was loaded to the water line. The remaining torpedoes were located a thousand feet beyond the winch; it would be stupid to extend the Catalina's anchorage and float her back to the rocky shelf, to expose her to the worst of the gale. The alternative was to send the team ahead and load the launch by hand. But what then? Was it that important with the clock hanging 60 minutes? The old man nodded. . . it was extremely important to recover what we could. If word got out, the remaining bullion would be impounded or worse. . . savaged by the locals in a bloody free-for-all.

We weighed the pros and cons while the marines shouldered

their equipment and deployed to the tower, melting into blackness like bespectacled ghosts, night glasses taped to their sooted faces. They knew exactly what they were about; they had a topo map of the island. I was impressed, vastly relieved when I returned to Dan. They here hardened professionals, capable of containing the *Juanita* while we bent our backs to the gold. If I could persuade Andy into off-loading 500 gallons of gas, the PBY could accommodate another ton and a half. And the Goose? With the marines ashore, maybe another half ton. He winked when I defined the weights and balance of the diminutive Goose.

"I'll leave the logistics to your discretion, Keithy. Perhaps you can persuade your party to consider a healthy reward. . . fair enough? We must hasten, lad! I shall find my way to the hill to see what we have and return promptly at 7:45. May I suggest Howard stand by to assist me aboard your Goose? I dasn't soil my clothing if matters go as planned. God speed, we'll meet shortly in Florida, hey? And now, young lady, if you'll be so kind, would you point the path to your 'dreadful well'?"

Pamela refused to budge. Shivering from the cold, bone tired and emotionally drained. It was unfair to goad her to the hill. I relieved her of the flashlight and pointed the path for Dan; watched over my shoulder while we freed the raft from the sand. I had no intention of leaving her there, but I knew her stubborn ways. Her eyes widened when the DEA climbed aboard and spun the Johnson. She glanced hopefully to Howard, but Howard was wary and turned his back. She studied the lonely beach for a moment, would have left peacefully, I believe, if Dan hadn't jostled the flash when he bent to buss her check. It was a kindly gesture, well intended, but her eyes were drawn to his blood-stained suit.

"Oh my God!" She pointed to the blood from Elisabeth's wound and shrieked at the top of her lungs. "Something terrible's happened. . . don't deceive me!" Dan tried to explain, but she was on to hysteria. . . almost. "Was it Elisabeth?" she whispered. "Was she hurt?" I knew what was next. . . I motioned Dan aside, picked her up and tossed her into the raft. . . rolled aboard to grab her wrist when she retaliated with a mask.

We had words while we struggled, unpleasant words when she sunk her teeth in my arm and elbowed my groin. I let her go when the DEA cast off. . . hell's fire, she was a piece of work. Cowered in the bow, she thumbed her nose when I said she could sit it out in the PBY. She watched fretfully while Dan floundered away, knotted her brow when Howard gave us a shove and waded to the Goose. I reached for an ankle when she scrambled to her feet, but realized she was on to other matters when she pointed to the dock and shouted, "My suitcase! Please, don't forget my clothes!"

The crossing was tedious. . . a 30-knot gale will rattle your bones. Pamela paddled furiously from the bow when the force caught us broadside and flipped the raft on its heel. I marveled at her ability, gave her points. We lent our weight to cant the inflatable to the wind, shifted to the stern when the outboard spun air, sloughed our legs to dagger the drift when the gale turned abruptly from the south. It was 6:30 before we laid a line on the PBY. We held briefly by the stern while Pamela fluffed her hair. Conversation had been nil, reduced to shouts and grunts. . . until she climbed the stair, treading my fingers, muttering, "You insufferable jock!"

The storm made a westerly turn while we groped our way along the keel and tied alongside the launch. The clock-wise shift was advantageous; the hill would blunt the wind while we worked the bottom, but we'd be hard put to clear the rise with the cranky amphibians in the dead of night. We were momentarily sheltered by the PBY, by her enormous wing, but she was straining her anchors and wanting to fly. At the moment we could hack it midway from the lagoon, but if we loaded her full tilt she'd need it all. We'd gain a thousand feet if we drifted back with the gale, but the cables were insufficient and re-deploying the anchors would be dangerous. The alternative was to let her be, until we were aboard and ready to roll. With the engines turning we could tail the eastern shelf and we'd have it made.

Counter thoughts emerged from the bow, however. Andy's snow white head appeared in the forward well, florid of face when he loosened the starboard cable to front the gale. He was juiced. Offering a sloppy salute when he dropped from sight and closed the hatch. I laid it on to Chug when the old fellow traversed the cockpit window and wet a finger to the winds. Problems I'd had, the kid was brawny.

"Watch him, Chug!"

He nodded from the blister, pointed to Pam. "Don't worry it, man. . . be down in a minute." I stilled my anxiety and climbed aboard the launch.

The divers, coupling a fresh set of tanks, lifted their masks and offered a helping hand. Introductions were brief. A chief bosun's mate spearheaded the recovery operation. He was a stocky fellow, wide of shoulder, 50 perhaps. He'd flown from Norfolk the day before. His torch man was about my age, a lieutenant senior grade. He'd been loaned by AUTEC when Thompson commandeered the PBY. I spun about when a third man surfaced and blew his mask; an older man, judging from his gray. I suspected he was more than he seemed when he drew a net bag from the depths and deposited a corroded container on the floor. The object was weighty, but it wasn't gold.

"Homing device," he commented when I questioned the distraction. "Out-dates, of course, but I have reason to believe the missing prototype is amongst the trove."

" . . Missing prototype?"

"Space age technology for sanctuary, Major. The U-831 was bound for the Argentine. . . torpedo would be larger than the others," he added. His eyes narrowed when I pounded my fist.

"Did Thompson know this?"

"Of the prototype, yes."

". . . And Kurt had access to the file."

"Were you not advised to the facts of the matter?" I shook my head. Thompson's objectives were double edged. I gave him up and turned to the Chief.

"How many have you emptied?" He displayed six fingers.

"It's all aboard the PBY. The kid strung them out on the floor." I pointed to the strobe line, to where I'd flagged the remaining six. . . or was it five? Was I at the prototype when I jettisoned my tank?

"We have six to go. How long will it take?"

"Shit, man, we got it down pat! Them torpedoes are paper thin. When we cut aft of the warhead department, the shafts fall away and the disks slide off like donuts on a stick. I'm more worried for the Cat, Slater," he added. "She's low on her water line; two-and-a-half tons is all she'll take." I glanced at my watch; it was 6:45.

"Did Andy top the tanks at Great Inagua?"

"Every blessed gallon! She's carryin' 1600, minus a half hour burn. If he'll dump 600, we'll have it made!"

"I'll see what I can do."

"Good luck, old buddy. He's all yours!"

I nudged the raft to the blister to accommodate the kid, steadying it with my foot. He dropped from shoulder height, rebounded on his toes and fell flat on his face. We had a moment of silence, then the DEA recognized their prize foundering in the swill. His misfortune broke the ice; they restrained themselves when he crawled aboard and we got on to matters without a fuss. They'd already volunteered to crew the launch, to muscle the bullion while the divers worked below. Realizing the winch was useless for the moment, the distance too great to grapple from the wing, we agreed that Chug should stay with the PBY; he was acquainted with the procedure and it was important to quickly offload the launch. I made the point that the torpedoes lay in shallow water and the gold would be easier to handle, possible three disks at a time if they dangled a series of lines.

"There's 16 to a stick," the chief interjected. "They weigh 50 pounds each, give or take. . . call it 800 pounds, 'bout the heft of a warhead in World War II."

The capacity of the launch? "Close to a ton when we was haulin' grass," Chug started to say. I cut him short when the bearded one swiveled in his seat.

". . . All right! Two round trips to the PBY and one to the Goose, and make it light," I added. "She'll be carrying Dan and his boiled shirts." We synchronized our watches while the team checked their tanks. "We black out at 20:30 and turn the props at 20:45. . . and no stragglers! You'll have an hour and a half to grab what you can," I rasped to the older man.

"Yes, suh, Major Slater!" the DEA co-pilot asided. "Will you be circling with an F-15?" I ignored the remark; he'd find out in due time.

We were observed when they throttled the Briggs-Stratton and bent their heads to the gale. A flashing light from the tower indicated the marines were deployed and scanning the sea to the east. I waved to acknowledge while Chug maneuvered the raft to the stairs. It was to be our last communication; they would douse the strobes at 20:30 when Dan boarded the Goose. At precisely 21:00, they were to loosen a flare from the proximity of the lagoon and watch for the *Juanita's* response. Watch and wait. . . hopefully we'd be long gone by then. . . skimming the sea to the west with the hill on our heels to diffuse the yacht's radar until we were out of range. The fabric was loosely woven, however. . . God help us if Kurt was playing games. "Sorry we were late," I confided to the kid when he drew us in. "We had a ball up on Provo. . . Wolfgang bought the park."

"Figured as much. Sis said the Goose shot to hell. She's scared, Keith, out of her drawers. What happened, talk about it later?" I nodded, my thoughts were centered on the pilot in command.

"What's with Andy?"

"Drunk as a skunk, been wantin' to take off. He leveled a bottle while we was loadin' the gold. . . kept tellin' how he bombed the U-831 and all that crap. Jesus, he's at it again!" The starboard engines coughed, caught briefly as I vaulted the stairs. I side-stepped the ingots and raced to the cockpit, encountering Pamela's freckled back as the props clanked to a stop. She had an arm lock on Andy's neck, a hand on the overhead throttles. I pawed the master switch and slumped beside her.

"Good girl!" She flashed a smile.

"That's the nicest thing you've said all day!" Andy was not amused.

"Turn a me loose, you damn bitch!" I lost my temper and cuffed his jaw. He lolled against his harness strap, reaching feebly for the switch. I pried Pamela's arm away and jerked him upright in his chair.

"Are you out of your mind? We've five men out there. . . do we have to tie you down?" I laid it on the line; we weren't taking off until they were all aboard. He cringed when I said he was a lousy coward. His eyes were as red as an August moon; he reeked of booze, but his jaw was chiseled from granite when I added the punch line. . . we'd have to unload a ton-and-a-half of fuel!

"I'm calling the shots, Slater. We ain't gonna dump no gas!"

"Hell, man, we're not flying to Ottawa!"

"I've been flyin' Cats for 50 years. You tellin' me what to do?"

"Okay, I'll fly it out myself."

"Shit! You an' who else? Think you're a hot stick cause you fly a fuckin' Goose! Ain't none of us flyin' out if we wait another hour. . . look at that airspeed, she's gustin' 30 knots!" He reached for the switch. I grabbed his wrist.

"If you try that again I'll wipe you out!"

"He needs a drink," Chug interjected. "He's got the shakes."

Andy was quick to agree. "Been livin' with a bottle since they smoked our ass at Pearl. Keeps me straight, but someone stole my spare."

"There's a fifth in the Goose; will it get you through?"

He reckoned it would help. "It'll get us up coast, but I'll never make Georgia on a lousy fifth!" I cut him short, he hadn't been clued.

"Jacksonville. We're to land at Cecil, a pair of F-14's will vector us in." He brightened immediately and reached for his cap.

"Freddie said we might! Got me an old friend there. . . three star admiral if he ain't retired. Was flyin' co-pilot when we sank that cruddy sub." His eyes moistened when he pointed to the empty seat. "Were just a kid, fresh outa flight school an' wantin' Corsair's. Thing is, he couldn't shoot straight an' they sent him to Key West to pick his nose. Him with his brand new wings. . . flyin' with us black sheep while his buddies were hammerin' them Japs. Was our second time out. . . we wuz east of Caicos when we saw her shadow, trailin' oil like she been hit before. We made a run at five hunner feet an' dropped a pair ah. . ." The old fellow slumped against my shoulder, smiled serenely and rumbled a wheezy snore.

"My God, will he settle for a beer?" The kid shook his head.

"Sez it's worsin' water, make him sick! I'll go for it, Keith. When he wakes up he'll be off the wall."

"Can't spare you, kid. He'll have to wait until we quarter the Goose. Where's Pam?"

He spun on his toes, pointed astern. "She went for the raft!"

We high-stepped the ingots and scrambled aft, but she was already aboard when we reached the stairs. . . pleading when I skidded to the bottom and grabbed the line.

"Don't, Keith. . . let me go! It's in my suitcase. . . I hid it from Chug." She spun the outboard, and scampered forward while I tugged at the line. "I know what I'm doing, you idiot! I'm not as stupid as you think!"

"Let her go," the kid called down. "She's done it before."

I had a rudimentary lesson in seamanship when I payed off the line. She tied a lanyard to the Johnson's tiller and fastened it to the bow. The end result was likened to a bow string when she throttled the outboard and flattened herself to the gale, steering with her feet and countering the drift with her paddle. The westerly caught her when she rounded the starboard float, but she was totally in command when she disappeared in the rain. I was completely at a loss for words.

Our reluctant pilot was fast asleep when we returned to the cockpit. I studied the unfamiliar panel for survival insurance, ran the checklist and traversed the quadrant for feel while Chug transferred a half dozen ingots to the forward well. We calibrated what the old girl would take from the balance sheet, working our way aft . . . compartment-by-compartment moving the bullion forward until the Cat was hard on her nose.

It was 7:15 when we cleared the blister section and were ready for more. I started the auxiliary power unit to juice the batteries, climbed the pylon ladder while Chug took a breather. The dump valves were located directly overhead in a tiny compartment that linked the fuselage to the wing; the oblong pylon was utilized by the radio operator during the long anti-sub patrols in World War II. A small window on either side gave a measure of visual relief from the stifling confinement. The fuel tanks were contained within the wing, directly above the radio operator's perch. The tanks had a capacity of 22 hours at minimum cruise; fuel valves were arranged on the forward panel so he could transfer fuel from one tank to another for lateral stability and monitor the gauges for the cockpit crew. He could lighten the load in an emergency by opening the dump valves and dispersing high octane from the stern. The plumbing was ancient, but the gauges were matter-of-fact. She was loaded to the hilt!

The gauges confirmed 1500 gallons, roughly 18 hours with reserves. I calculated 600 gallons, at 6.7 pounds per gallon, and came up with a couple of tons we could safely displace. In wartime she'd carried depth bombs, blister guns and such, but she'd been stripped of all that. The compartment had been cleared of its heavy radios, the outsize equipment replaced by featherweight Collins' in the forward cockpit, the galley equipment removed to accommodate another bale of grass. If Andy hadn't topped off at Inagua we'd have it made; 800 gallons could take us to Jax with time out for lunch.

"Watcha got?" The kid called from below.

"Critical thoughts," I answered as I descended the ladder.

"I don't know how he got her in, but he'll need a rosary to get her out."

"We'd better dump before he wakes up and swallows his teeth."

"Not yet. The launch is dead astern and I don't think they'd like it."

The rain had abated when the launch drew alongside at 7:25. We had a brief glimpse of twilight while we man-handled the gold . . . an unearthly glow of reddish orange glazed the lagoon, bringing the tower in sharp relief with the blackness beyond. There was sufficient light to ease my mind. Pamela had made it ashore and was standing waist-deep with her luggage in the lee of the Goose. Then the cloudbank overcame and we were confined by the down lights while we winched the disks aboard. They'd hoisted the contents from a brace of torpedoes and were wanting a beer.

"Chief came up 'while back, said they were cuttin' number five," the bearded one shouted when Chug tossed them a Heineken from his cache. "Said to tell you they can't locate number six and the old man's shitting his pants."

"It hit a reef. . . it's out by the shelf!"

"Jesus, man! It's as black as a Grizzley's ass! Did you drop a flag?"

"I dropped a tank!"

"Bully for you. . . shall we toss him a shoe?"

I grabbed a mask and vaulted to the launch, calling back to Chug that I'd need his flippers. We were short for time, spinning our wheels, but luck was with us. . . the launch was equal to the gale, wide of beam. . . a shrimper's net boat before Freddie added it to his fleet. I ransacked the bow for an underwater flash, beamed their buoy when the Briggs-Stratton brought us alongside. The downwind trek was easy going, but the returns would be a bloody nightmare. . . and we had more to go.

They dropped their lines while I belted a weight and went over the side. I frogged the eerie depths, following the underwater floods to where the team had gathered the gold. The scene was reminiscent of Jules Verne's helmeted sailors harvesting the sea from Nautilus. Air bubbles rose from their masks, glistened and disappeared in the blackness above. Parrot fish ogled from the grass. . . schools of minows and a curious barracuda hovered nearby, drawn by the unaccustomed glare. An overweight grouper tagged alongside me as I frogged along the bottom. . . eyed the workings briefly, then darted to a stand of coral when the lieutenant raised his torch and extinguished its flare. They'd peeled the fifth submersible and exposed its gut . . . number 11 by total count. . . and were questing the whereabouts of number 12.

Hand signals sufficed; they realized I was short for air. The chief pointed to a light probing to the north, indicating the third man was at odds. I immediately beamed my flash to the east, pivoted to signal the wandering man and moved the beam to the shelf, repeating the procedure as I shot to the surface. The maneuver succeeded in turning him about. I had a giddy view of his flippers as I surfaced to oblige my lungs, following his glow as I clung to the launch. He terminated the strobe line and circled to the south. . . confused by the meandering shelf. . . 20 yards shy of the errant torpedo. I had no choice; I rolled on my back and shouted to the DEA..

"Toss me a line—I'm going back down!" There was no immediate reply. The bearded one was hoisting gold, the DEA co-pilot studying his watch.

"Ain't got . . . lessn' you take one of ourn!" I spat a residue of brine into the gale; they were dangling three.

"Make do with two!" I shouted back. He shrugged and tossed me a slack. "There's a Mae-West under the seat!" He handed it down. I tied the line to the vest and lowered my mask. "We'll be out by the strobes!"

He palmed a weak salute. "Anything else?" I mouthed the snorkel and went under. The acrimonious bastard. . . he'd grind his molars when I told him what I had in mind.

I followed the strobes to the east, flashing my torch to draw the older man's attention. When he responded, I beamed a correction to the north and surfaced for a bit of air. He was quick to follow, drew alongside me while I frogged the bottom to avoid the gale. We were on the shelf in a matter of seconds; the out-going tide caught us as we neared the channel, forcing us against the rocky face while I fruitlessly plied my light to where the tank should be. . . it had drifted to the bottom with the tide. I surfaced immediately to gauge our position from the strobes, and check our alignment with the PBY. We were yards to the north.

"It's off to the left!" I shouted when he emerged. "Watch for a tank. . . we've overshot!"

He rubbed his eyes to follow my glove. . . offered his mouth-piece, realizing we were pressed for time. We flipped and went under, alternating from his air while we searched against the tide. We located the missing torpedo at 7:45. . . a curl of purple from where I'd dished a mound of sand. My tank lay somewhat apart, partially silted, the straps dancing wildly with the tide.

The elated older man went immediately about his business, shearing the ruptured skin with a pair of snipers, pre-occupied with his prize until I pinched his arm. I mouthed a draught of air and frogged to the tank; tied my line to the straps and discharged the cartridges to the vest. The Mae West shot to the surface, tugging at the straps when it encountered the gale. I loosened the line a trifle, nudged the tank to see if it would hold and swam to the surface to scan the action.

The launch, low in the water, was heavily loaded. . . silhouetted by the down lights, and moving slowly to the PBY. They'd lifted their quota but would be pressed to transfer the gold and turn about in total darkness. The variable factor depended upon the *Juanita's* response to the flare. . . their offshore distance, the interim time until they lowered their boats, their means of approach when they probed for a landing. We allowed 30 minutes, a hazardous half-hour to pack up and scat. . . were we given to wishful thinking? More to the point, could Kurt have detected my voice and shuffled the deck?

I clung to the vest and signaled the launch, mindful of the quartering gale and the ridge, of the quieting sea so close by. The Catalina had swung on her starboard anchor, pivoting the stern on a direct line with the channel. . . offering a commanding view of her tail, of her firy exhaust when we turned the props; easy range for a raking AK7. Was 2100 a predictable ETA or loosely given to catch us offguard? Considering the weather, could they time their arrival precisely on the hour. . . vary it to an advantage? The *Juanita* had that capability. . . a computerized bridge, radar to center an outsized metallic object within a fraction of a yard!

The return signal was long coming, then a searching beam from the launch settled on the vest as I rose with the swell. They had my bearing. I filled my lungs. . . I'd lowered my mask when three short blips came from an unexpected source. . . a minute reddish glow midway from the Goose. I treaded water and cupped an ear . . . the unmistakable sound of an outboard motor permeated the roar of the cresting reef.

I flashed a response, angling the torch to reduce its glare. The answer was guarded, a quick blip as the raft neared the PBY. The strobes blinked off a moment later—I dove immediately. . . *Kurt had pulled the chain!*

The bottom was ablaze with floodlamps and the vivid blue of oxycetylene. The scuba team had arrived underfoot, cleared the debris and were torching the torpedo at length. . . peeling the skin from the aft compartment, ignoring the ingots spilling from the shaft as they cut forward to the nose. They were onto something, communicating with their hands. The older man was hovering with his camera, photographing the driving mechanism that hurled it across the reef, motioning me aside, then expressing indignation when I tugged at his belt. I crossed my arms and pointed to the surface, the floodlights pinioned in the sand. . . indicated ten minutes to allow for the launch. They grasped the situation at once.

The lieutenant extinguished his torch and circled the perimeter to douse the floods. The glow was reduced to headlamps and hand lights as they maneuvered in the dark like fireflies on a long summer night. The oldster lingered for a final exposure, traced the compartment with his glove as I quaffed his mask. He pointed to the partially-burned propellant cake and the graphite-vaned turbine. The torpedo was totally unlike the others, devoid of the heavy batteries that would link it to its origin. The simplified propellant had increased the warhead capacity doublefold, sufficient to devastate a super carrier with a single shot. The technology was 50 years ahead of its time. . . a monstrous weapon if copied and bandied about. Definitely not for Kurt!

He disconnected the homing device from the nose compartment while I collected the remaining artifacts from the flanneled chest. . . the chalice, the enameled plates and wires of rings, an imperial crown of rubies and diamonds. . . museum pieces from the Habsburg dynasty, priceless relics of the past. We added the lot to his net bag, tied it to my line and returned our attention to the gold. When the launch throbbed overhead we'd secured a baker's dozen and abandoned the remainder for another time. . . a like number, perhaps, but the compartment was cavernous and there may have been more. The oldster was disinterested. He'd recovered what he wanted, photographed the dive and knew exactly what he was about. He applied a detonator to the cake, reeled a fuse from his belt and signaled the lieutenant to light his torch. We rose immediately to the surface with our gaggle of lines. The lieutenant was last up.

A dull thud compressed my ears as the bag was hoisted from above. A blue glow illuminated the shelf when the propellant cake ignited. We had a tiny hand to help us as we rolled aboard with what we had . . . a bulging net bag, a half dozen ingots, a tauting line that held a few more. . . and a cautionary shout from Pam!

"Quick! The *Juanita's* offshore; the marines sighted them with their infra . . ."

"Red?"

"Yes!"

"Where?" She pointed to the east. It was totally black but I could distinguish the roar of the cresting reef. . . and Kurt's radar would be probing the lagoon, vectoring the tell-tale PBY! I called for a voice count to ascertain who we had. The co-pilot answered from the stern.

"Rodney here. . . Vince's watching the drunk!"

"Where's Chug?" The ingots sloshed aboard as he answered from the bow, thudded softly against the row at my feet.

"Andy went bananas, Keith. . . we hadda' tie him down."

"Did you feed him the fifth?"

"Roger, nursin' it like a baby. . . he'll come around. Figured I'd look after sis' when she kept askin' where you went."

"You're a lousy diver. . . I was afraid!" she said. I gripped her hand and shouted "Let's go!"

The co-pilot geared the engine and steered blindly for the PBY, cursing his displeasure when the gale pinged us with salt.

Pratt-Whitneys barked in the distance when we sighted a glow from the cockpit and swung the launch to the stairs. Yellow, then a wisp of blue, curled from the Goose's exhausts. Old Dan would be wading the shallows in his splendid white shoes. . . it was 8:35! I handed the rifle to the chief as he scrambled to the blister, warning him that an impetuous shot would draw immediate fire The older man was next; he climbed the stairs with his bag of tricks and disappeared. The lieutenant elected for the Goose when we reasoned it would be lightly loaded, but we had a nasty situation when I informed the DEA co-pilot he was to fly Howard's righthand seat.

"Crap off . . . ain't flyin' with no black!" He dropped the tiller and lunged for the stairs. I reached for his leg, but missed him in the dark. Chug blocked the stairs while I attempted to reason him out.

"Shape up, Goddamnit! We're IFR. . . he needs a hand." His response was negative, crudely put.

"Fuck you! Ain't flyin' with no nigger!"

"How dare you!" Pamela exploded.

He raised two fingers and cocked his wrist. "And fuck you, too, you little brat!" The answer was quick—a hairy arm, a thudding fist and he sprawled full length at her brother's feet . . . raised his head and collapsed on his face.

"Sorry, Keith!" I was stunned, but there was no time for amends. The pilot had brought it on himself, provoked a change of plan, and I was mostly to blame.

"Don't worry it, kid. . . can you handle it until he comes around?" He cast off without a word, called back when the lieutenant swung the launch to the gale.

". . . see you at Cecil. . . God bless!"

They were off and running when we levered the stairs and secured the latch. Pamela was upset, but she restrained herself. . . tagged behind me when I raced to the cockpit to confront our pilot. He was a very angry man. . . his hands tied with mechanic's tape and tethered to his harness with a six-inch strap. The bottle was cradled in his lap, reachable if he tilted his head. . . to that end he'd succeeded. The scotch was a third gone; residue drooled from his mouth when he fixed me with a livid stare.

"Turn-a-me loose! You got no right . . ."

"He's leveling off," the bearded one interrupted. "Had a tussle when the kid cut the lights. . . we had to tie him down!"

I let matters stand for the moment and climbed the pylon to open the valves. A gurgle responded from the tanks; a stream of 100 octane sloshed astern, gathered momentum as I traveled the valves full turn and dropped to the floor. Andy was beside himself when I popped the question.

"How long will it take to dump 600 gallons?"

"Ten minutes, you stupid shit. . . don't nobody light up!" I glanced at my watch; it was 8:41.

"What'll we need to clear the hill?" He raised the bottle, took a healthy swig and cleared his throat.

"Twenty-five-hundred. . . loaded like she is! Come on, fellas, don't put me down in front of that gal." I studied the dimly lit panel, cut the APU, ever mindful of its sparks. The gale was gusting 30 knots; the wind would bring the boat on her step, but we'd be short for run if she nosed a swell.

"We'll have to drift back."

"Been tellin' you that. . . ain't no way, less we sled the bill!"

I considered the odds—the *Juanita's* proximity, our exposure to her guns when the marines released the flare. "Okay! Give me five minutes and crank her up. When Howard's off our wing, ease back and go for broke!"

"Shut the valves. . . if that jockey's close he'll spark our ass! Mind them tanks!" I tucked the bottle in his lap, nodded to Pam, and climbed the pylon while she untied his hands. Andy had stroked one from the blue, copped a way out. . . a distraction of sorts while we maneuvered for reach.

Five-hundred gallons had drained from the tanks and we were on to six. . . two tons of volatile gas discharged to the gale. . . blanketing the lagoon with a lethal mist, racing for the channel with the out-going tide. The proximity of the Goose, one lousy spark? I called down to the chief when a flicker of blue reflected from the window.

"What do we have?"

"A Grumann on our starboard wing!" I pressed my face to the glass. Howard had drifted back to challenge the rise. . . steadying her with his throttles, fishtailing to hold her nose to the gale.

"Let him go!" The chief triggered his flash. I closed the valves and dropped to the companion way. Howard responded immediately and fire-walled the Pratt-Whitneys.

A muted roar reverberated the PBY, a spray of brine pinged the fuselage as the Goose rose with a swell and thundered to the west. . . cleaving a crest as she gathered knots and reached for the sky. . . then the telltale growl of engines aloft and the fading glow of her exhausts as she banked to the north and disappeared in the night.

"Go, man, go!" I wasn't sure who said it, but there was confirmation from the channel. . . a tracery of automatic gunfire and a spent slug rattling inside the PBY.

"Oh, my God!" I hurled Pamela to the floor and made my way to the cockpit. A second burst arced from the channel. . . fell short, but they had our vector.

"Cover yourself with a mattress, honey. . . heads down! For Christ's sake, don't shoot back," I shouted to the chief. Andy stroked the master switch and juiced the aux pumps, wheezed to his feet and turned the starboard prop. The engine caught and held; he turned number two and brought them up to quarter the gale, tra-versed his window to see what he had.

"God almighty. . . she hard on her nose, we' gotta drift back or clobber the hill!" He wiped his mouth and shouted in my ear. "Need a marker, Slater. . . can't see a fuckin' thing!" I tossed the bearded one a vest; he scrambled to the forward well and raised the hatch. . . tested the light and tied the vest to the starboard line. He was one cool number . . . he'd cottoned the action and would cast off when we signaled to let go.

"Ready?" The old fellow slouched in his seat and flexed the controls.

"Not yet! Someone's locked me rudder." I unlocked it with my foot. He gave it full swing and advanced the portside engine. "Gale's pullin' from the west, but reckon I'm ready if you'll latch the blister."

"Hold tight. . . I'll be back in a second!" A fiery tracer arced from the east. . . the Catalina shuddered; she'd taken a round through her tail. Andy blanched and gripped the wheel.

"See whatcha done, Slater?"

"Cross-fire!" the Chief shouted. "That ain't no AK-47, old buddy, they's poundin' us with a 20 from the yacht!" His rifle cracked as I scooped a flare from the rack and bolted aft. The response was immediate; muzzle flashes from the channel and a scream from Pam when she fielded a stray.

"Hold off, you're drawing fire!" I turned to the older man. "There's a kit in the galley. . . see if she's OK!"

"I'm all right, just take me home!"

"They're aiming for the tail," he snapped. "They want the Cat! Get on with it or they'll pick us off." It was precisely then that the marines released their flare, aiming to the north to reduce its glare.

The parachute drifted with the wind and brought the easterly reach to instant daylight. The *Juanita* lay at anchor beyond the reef, low down, completely blacked out. A diminutive pair of rafts were in the channel, firing at random. . . to the north a speeding launch was rounding the rise to the west. Kurt had planned his operation well, deployed his men in a pincer move, to contain the atoll!

The flare fizzled in the distance while we swung the blister full height, then we were shrouded again by the inky black. The marines, attempting to draw attention from the Cat, were on to the action but holding off until Kurt had men ashore. A grenade would suffice the speedboat but they were only three and the *Walrus* was wallowing miles behind; the frigate miles to the north. Kurt had unleashed his 20mm gun. Timing was critical. . . the rafts, heavily armed, would be difficult to dismember if they flanked the tower; if I hesitated any longer they'd have us by the balls.

"Okay. . . here we go!" The incendiary blossomed red as I hurled it astern. The result was instantaneous.

The 100 octane swooshed a path for a quarter of a mile, inundating the channel with a rolling fireball as it caught the outgoing tide. The lead raft was immediately incinerated. . . the crew flung skyward like broken dolls as the raft exploded and showered the second with burning debris. A secondary explosion rocked the lagoon when the concussion triggered grenades. Ammo went next, flaring the waters as they went over the side. We stood dumbfounded by the intensity of the last, watched helplessly as a tongue of fire shot from the channel and spread to the reefs, as if seeking survivors floundering in its wake.

And then the gale overcame and spun the residue to the east, extinguishing the flames in a veil of rain. Aside from a lick of fire here and there, a burning raft cast to the beach, everything went black. The merciful night had lowered its shroud on the decimated crew . . . on all but their agonized screams. . . sickening, when I realized what I had done, the rationale of Iraq. . . a bloody eye for a tooth. But there was more to contend with.

A rocket flashed from the tower, followed by another, by a double explosion and a rosy glow to the north. The marines had zeroed the launch, but unfortunately they'd drawn attention to themselves. The *Juanita's* 20mm barked and laced the tower, sparking rock as they raised its trajectory to level the upper walls. The response was quick; the marines had played it cool and deployed their 20mm on the ridge. Sharp-witted, battle-tested, they hammered the thin-skinned Benetti with continuous fire. . . silenced the gun, then dropped their sights to riddle its hull.

The yacht was listing from the stern when I latched the blister and scrambled to the cockpit. An S.O.S. blinked from the bridge when we traversed the windows to gauge the shelf. . . the captain had given it up, drawing his anchors to drive her aground! Vengeance, frustration, whatever. . . Kurt was incensed! An AK-47 opened up midship, raking the lagoon. . . it arced astern as he aimed for the Cat. The twosome dropped to the floor to barricade themselves with gold, a spent slug milking the blister brought a yelp from the chief. I reached for Pam and forced her to her knees, shouted to Vince when he raised the hatch.

"Cut the lines!" Two hundred feet of nylon shot from his hands and the Mae West emerged with its blinking light. Andy throttled the engines and focused his marker as we drifted rapidly astern.

"Take the rudder. . . ain't got no legs!" I straddled the controls, kicked right rudder to point the light, waiting until Vince secured the hatch.

The *Juanita* was aground and burning furiously from the stern, silhouetting the easterly reach as we continued to drift. Andy's face was ashen. . . his hands trembled as he reached for the quadrant, but his voice was steady when he shouted in my ear.

"Blister latched?"

"Hell, yes!"

"Oil?"

"Up!"

"Cowl flaps?" I brought them to trail.

"Go, man, we're hanging the shelf!" The rudder took a salvo

when he fire-walled the engines; we took a round in the cabin but we'd over-run the marker and were on the gauges when Kurt's tracers curled astern.

To this day I don't know how he pulled her off. Fifty years of reflexes ossified with booze. . . a sixth sense perhaps. . . the feel of her enormous wing as she gathered knots and strained to fly. Brotherhood, two aged relics welded as one. We belted a swell but he held her down, gauged the run with no reference to the panel. When he sensed he had it made, he reeled the tab, brought the wheel to his stomach. . . and the old boat obliged! I was in a cold sweat with the rudder locked on our bearing; followed him through until he found his legs and wheeled her to the north. We had a sprig of bush on our starboard float, but we'd cleared the ridge!

"God. . . damn!" The old fart grinned and collapsed in his seat.

"Take over, Slater. Drinks are on the house!" He turned to me then, there was a sparkle in his eye when he reached beneath his seat and produced his spare.

For sake of the record, it was 9:18.

Eight

THE GOOSE WAS CIRCLING 20 miles west of George Town when we picked up their running lights. The sky had cleared a bit; we had a high overcast and a spatter of rain, but Christina's fontal system lay a hundred miles behind. The PBY was hard put to maintain 90 knots with the load she carried.

Howard dropped a quarter flaps to draw alongside, throttling back as we continued on a northwesterly heading. We eased down to 500 feet and leveled off in loose formation. Andy had recovered sufficiently to build himself a sandwich; Pamela was asleep on his private mattress, twitching fitfully as she slept. The bearded one conned the controls while I communicated briefly with Howard on 121.9.

"Sure happy you made it, man . . . *Walrus* say they was one big explosion 'bout nine o'clock!"

"Any word from the frigate?"

"Roger! Dan were talkin' with the captain while back . . . say they was 20 mile out an' sendin' helicopter to pick what left. Whatcha all do, man. . . flame that gas?"

"Talk about it later. What's with the Coast Guard?"

"Man, they got us track. . . Falcon been conversin' with Miami an' axin' for help. They's short on fuel, Keith. . . callin' for an intercept at Andros town!"

"OK! Take her down to 300 and we'll play it by ear!" He clicked off. I set up the Bimini homer and took over the controls. Howard edged the Goose's wing under our starboard float and extinguished his lights, gauging his proximity by the Cat's exhaust. We'd fly as one to fox the radar watch at Andros. . . spin off at Freeport and take it from there. The bearded one was completely confused, wary of the close-flying Goose.

"Watch him, Slater! If he gets any closer we'll be swapping paint." I bent to study Andy's bag of tricks. With Howard tucked in we'd play it by ear.

The forward scanning radar was standard commercial and the GPS would be programmed for a Georgia lake, but the look behind warning device was strictly military, as were the pulse dampener, the chaff drop and his toggled flares. The old boat was slow, but the chaff would baffle a radar fix until she was miles apart—as would the magnesium flares if the Cat was tracked by infrared.

There was more. Freddie had exercised his ingenuity and provided an ultra high frequency transreceiver for covert communication. The UHF was coupled to a narrow metal box hidden beneath the seat. The military classification had been surreptitiously removed, but Vince was no fool.

"Shit! He's got a scrambler in tandem. Been wondering how he foxed us off Savannah last spring. It was black as a witch's ass. I swear to God we had his fix but ATC turned us east. . . said we were tracking a DC-3."

"It's his direct line to Freddie's van, old buddy. They pace him up coast and relay the action on high frequency. They can switch to VHF and simulate a ground station if he's out on a limb."

"Now you're telling me! What's the play, Slater? You're blowing my mind."

I laid it out the way it was. . . the international complications, the covert expediency for recovering the gold and drawing Kurt to the atoll. I described the bloody scene aboard the *Leopard*, explained the history of the brooch and the necessity for keeping Chug under wraps while I dealt with Paul . . . and later with Dan.

"The kid was a mess, emotionally shot. He was in no condition to be browbeaten, Vince, and he wasn't about to abandon Liz. Moreover, it was sundown and I was suspicious of the yacht, afraid they'd finish him off. To make a long story short, I helped him set sail and directed him to a friend. He buried the girl at dawn and scuttled the schooner off the North West light."

"My God! Wait'll Stone gets a load of this. . . he'll freak out. He's been counting on a bust since the *Leopard* left Barranquilla."

"Stone's not to know; he'll be briefed later on. Wax philosophic, man. Freddie's out of business for keeps. The State Department made a deal for his expertise. . . two years in the pen if he buttons his lip, 20 if he's greedy. There's an Air Force 135 waiting at Cecil to fly the bullion to Vienna. It's strictly hush hush. . . why do you think we're playing games with the Coast Guard and the DEA?"

"They were afraid of a leak. . . the State Department?"

"Right! The Navy loaned the hardware and the CIA rang Freddie's bell when we fingered the PBY. The equipment was at hand. . . the Cat, the van, communications, a derelict pilot who knew the ropes. Why not?"

"What's in it for him?"

"Two years probation. He was a problem at first. . . Had a bone to pick with the Navy, a blotch on his record from 1944."

"The sub? He told me all about it. . . figured he was nuts."

"I know, but he earned a Navy Cross in the South Pacific and was commended for bravery in Korea. . . a Silver Star for landing under fire. Never talks about that. I was long gone when they wrapped it up, but I understand they promised to review his record if there was evidence of the U-831." I pointed to the older man's overnighter cushioning Pamela's coppery hair; I'd read the identification strapped to its grasp. "They wouldn't have sent a captain from Navy Intelligence if they thought Andy was spreading flowers."

"Man, oh man! We've been tagging the bastard for the last six months and I end up in Noah's Ark." I checked my lovely Goose; the lit cock-pit indicated. Howard was studying his charts. . . Rodney had reconsidered and was flying the righthand seat. The sky had cleared; we had the moon overhead and the southern tip of Andros on our forward scan. It was two a.m.

We maintained 300 feet and chatted for a while, comparing notes. Vince had flown B-52's over 'Nam while hosing the MIG-21's. He'd taken his discharge in '78 when his wife insisted he stay at home. "And look at me now! Flying shitty props while my buddies are wearing leaves. And Rodney there. . . his Goddamned temper. They washed him out of flight school for bad rappin' a black CO. We're a bunch of misfits, Slater. . . trading punches with the old war horses strugglin' to make a buck. We grounded a Connie last spring," he added. "The pilot was an ex-Lieutenant Colonel with 400 missions in B-17's. I felt like a shit, but what could we do? He had forty bales of grass and was flying it all by himself."

The engines droned on; we had Andros on our wing at 2:35. Vince drowsed off and our passengers were sound asleep in the rear, our stalwart hero snoring peacefully with the decimated bottle clutched by his side. I'd switched tanks to balance our fuel, cycled the GPS for the bearing to Freeport, when the overhead speaker came alive and curled my toes.

". . Roger, Miami! We have him ten east of Congo Town. He's skinning the chop, but we're reading his pipes at 90 knots!" I turned down the volume; Pamela was awake and Andy on his knees.

"Fuckin' Falcon! Where the hell are we?" I flipped the scan to range the coast. Fresh Creek creviced the image from 30 miles.

Andy lunged to the cockpit. "Gimmie my seat!" I checked Howard's wing while he exchanged with Vince. "Angle for that line of rain, Slater! They got a radar dish at Andros with a hotline to Miami." I peered from the window; a shadowy mist loomed to the east. He had the eyes of an owl.

"Falcon's reading heat," the bearded one ventured. "You can't slip him in the rain, you bloody freak!"

"Mind your business, Fuzzy! I know what I'm doin'." I pointed for the rain, anticipating what he had in mind. "Black Bird on tap?" I checked Howard's wing.

"Yep!" Andy studied the scan, adjusted the sweep. The showers terminated over Nassau and the Berry Islands.

"Check Nassau for traffic . . . tell them we're an inbound DC-3." I set up the standby VHF and called into Nassau. They had an LTD charter on the approach and a 1011 taking off for Jamaica.

"Okay, I got it!" Andy shouted. He eased down to 100 feet, rolled the tab and leveled off. "Readin' heat, hey. . . wait'll they pick up that 1011!" The Falcon blasted our ears when we belted the showers.

" . . .Andros Radar, Falcon Two! We have a bandit ten east of Salvador Point, what do you read?"

The answer was long coming. "We have a fast-moving target at twelve plus twelve!"

"That's us!" the Falcon replied. Andros continued their sweep.

"We have an outbound from Nassau at 2000 feet. Falcon hit the spike."

We have a slow-moving target east of Andros Town. . . or did! We're requesting his altitude. . . do you have him on scope?"

"Negative! You're reading the mail boat; she's due at 1630."

"Shit!" Our number two receiver rattled. . . Nassau was pleading on 174.2.

"Look, fellas, we have a Delta reporting over his checkpoint, an outbound to Montego Bay and a DC-3 requesting traffic. We have no radar for IFR separation! Would you clear the air and let us talk?" I broke in to ease my conscience; the 1011 Captain was having fits.

"DC-3 turning west at 6000. . . advise the 1011 heavy we've cleared his climb. We'll file for Miami," I added. "Too many problems."

The 1011 captain was quick to agree. "Thank you, sir, we are climbing through eight. . . Hold it. We have a blinker over Andros! What the devil goes on?" The confused Coast Guard Falcon identified himself. . . Andy was delighted.

"Figured we'd lose him! Rain fizzed our heat and he locked what came along. That radar dish is set for the druggies flyn' coke outa Colombia," he added. "Got it angled too high if you skin the deck." He turned to Vince, remembering who he was. "Ain't never hauled no cocaine. . . got me self respect!"

Vince was fascinated, but Pamela was not amused. "You belong in jail!"

"Speak for your brother, ma'm. I'm callin' it quits if we make it to Jax. Got a church-lovin' wife to remind me of that."

The Falcon called in to Miami when we were over the Berry Islands; they'd tracked a lonely Aztec and given it up. "He has that old boat glued to the water, but we figure he's heading north. Scramble the 130 for an intercept over Grand Bahama . . we're returning to refuel."

I contacted Howard when we were 10 miles shy of High Rock, Grand Bahama.

"We'll split in 20 minutes. How is it going?" I inquired of Howard.

"Tired, man! Had to open the windows, the ole man smokin' a cigar."

"The kid?"

"Plenty help. . . working the channels when you freaked the Falcon."

"Rodney?"

Howard giggled, Rodney was a breeze. "Come find his surname were Blackman. . . ain't said a word since the old man set him straight."

We clicked off. The 130 was reporting over Bimini and Andy was in a sweat.

The Falcon was equipped for high altitude tracking, relying on their down scan and infrared to detect slow-moving targets penetrating the islands. Fast-moving targets were intercepted by the Coastal Defense, by F-16's. The druggies flew props, mostly by night, but their resources were multifold . . . Ocean drops, island drops, fuel caches and relay planes stashed amongst the islands to wait another night. To keep tabs, the Coast Guard maintained a 130 flying command post to monitor their goings and comings. . . an accounting board, so to speak, with covert communications to customs and the DEA.

"Man, they got the electronics to handle 20 birds at a time and a scan like them PC-3's." Andy pointed to the ruby red warning light. "Got our fix, Slater. . . altitude and knots. We'll give them the shits, but it's gonna be tough!" We were hammering High Rock when he cycled the UHF. A girl's voice responded immediately from Freddie's van.

"Gotcha, Santa. . . we read you loud and clear. Have an alert from Ft. Lauderdale; they've scrambled a pair of twins for an intercept at Walker's Cay!" He pressed his throat button, and advanced the throttles to climb.

"Okay, Rosie. . . advise when you have them over West End. What's your position?"

"North of Vero on I-95. . . we're in contact with Cecil on channel 12."

Vince was beside himself. "Jesus! That's Navy. . . you're freaking me out!"

Andy pointed to the GPS, leveled off at five hundred. "Set up Walker Cay, Slater. . . lost me glasses." Pamela grimaced and fixed them to his nose. He squinted at the heading and triggered the UHF. "Down-count five, Rosie. . . the 130's ridin' our ass!"

"Roger, Santa, we're counting now!" He turned to me, inclined his head toward Howard's wing.

"Tell Black Bird to split when I shoot the flares!" I contacted Howard on 121.9.

"Four minutes!"

"Read you, man!" He pulled off the wing to avoid the cannisters. Three minutes fled the clock. Andy pressed the pulse dampener at zero plus one!

A pulse was transmitted from the PBY to counter the 130's radar scan. The pulse was of short duration, but sufficient to erase our image until we'd gained a few extra miles. . . a defensive measure in wartime, sensing frequency changes automatically, counter pulsing to confuse the enemy's radar and delay a missile salvo from the ground or air. The device was included in Andy's bag of tricks, it's legality confined to the military. . . the 130 was off the wall.

"Goddamn. . . he pulsed us out!"

"Say again."

"He spiked us, Miami. . . we've got a screen full of snow."

Andy nodded and released the chaff. The cannisters tumbled from underwing and exploded midair. The chaff was immediately dispersed. . . as a glob at first, then the long tendrils of metal foil unwound and trailed for a mile behind us. The end result was total confusion. . . the 130's radar was hopelessly locked and the Cat had vanished with its sibling Goose. There remained, however, our tell-tale heat, the white hot of our exhausts.

"Pulse 'em, boy! That chaff ain't gonna last." I hammered the dampener, and Howard pulled ahead. Andy toggled the flares when the clock stroked zero.

The parachutes whipped behind us, unseen. . . the magnesium ignited and a brilliant glare brightened the Goose as she banked overhead to the west. We rolled tab and hit the deck, leveled off when we sapped the pines. The 130 responded a moment later; their infrared had homed the flares.

"Jesus Christ. . . I think he exploded!" The prop jobs were cautious; they'd tracked Andy before.

"Bull shit! He flogged you with a flare." There was a long silence while the 130 reconsidered.

" . . Could be. . . we have a target north of west Freeport. Hold tight. . . we'll work him on the computer!"

"Roger, Roger. . . we're turning west."

Andy grinned and savaged his bottle. "Ain't us!"

We were over the shallows and on to the open Atlantic when the 130 had a fix on Howard's bearing

"Target showing negative transresponder and ATC advise no inbound to Vero Beach. We have him bracketed 19. 2 miles north-west of Freeport at 90 knots."

"He'll have to file," Vince allowed. "He's on the ADIZ." I shrugged him off. . . Air Defense had tracked the action since we lifted off from Hogsty Cay.

Howard took his time, throttled back to simulate the PBY until we were over the horizon and off the scan. The moon was low in the south when he upped the Goose to normal cruise and filed for

Jacksonville International. ATC cleared him at once, acknowledged when he penetrated the ADIZ and stroked the coast at Cocoa Beach. The Coast Guard 130 was confused; they had his bearing, but they'd anticipated the Cat and backtracked to investigate Walker Cay. Stone's armada followed Howard up coast. . . we listened to their jabber until our VHF waned to a whisper. We were 100 miles east of Daytona at the time, lumbering along at 90 knots with Rosie monitoring the drama from I-95.

"Roger, Roger, we have you on high freq. . . the props are riding him hard; they scrambled a helicopter to wash him down."

"What's his position?"

"And who are you?"

"Slater! Santa's painting toys."

"Roger, Keith. . . he's south of Jax and complaining to ATC; said he's in-bound with a charter and has interference on his approach. . . the tower's hammering the DEA," she added. "Told them to circle east of Jax, but they've cleared the copter to the ramp."

"Thompson?"

"Waiting at customs. . . we've been talking on channel 10."

Vince gave it up. "Shit! Stone will send me to the boonies. . . wait'll he learns he's flogging a bogie!"

"Don't worry it, fella. He can sleep it off in a Holiday Inn." Howard filled us in later. He had smokies to his left and right when he taxied to the ramp. . . the sheriff's department, half-dozen deputies from the DEA and a dark blue sedan with Navy plates. The sedan drew alongside when he cut his engines; a badge was flashed when the deputies converged and they were quietly told to hold their water. "Fella wid the badge hustle Rodney 'n Chug to his car an' took off before they could see who they was. Man, that sheriff have some kind of fits! Kept hollern' with a bullhorn, but that car were followin' a siren-blowin' jeep."

The Goose was subjected to inspection, of course. . . a few slimy ingots customs overlooked. . . when Immigration examined Sir Daniel's impeccable credentials. The lieutenant was noncommittal; he displayed his orders and excused himself to phone his wife. Howard was clean; produced his passport with an outbound stamp from Providenciales. "They was axin' about you, man. Said the last I recollect, you was jawbonin' wid a pretty gal in a black bikini!"

There were questions to be answered, but he referred them to Dan, and the old fellow stressed his diplomatic immunity. In short, that was the end of it; he had business to attend and wished to be away. They'd all dispersed when Stone arrived with a reporter from the Miami Herald. Howard had filed for Cecil and was airborne when they arrived at the ramp.

Stone ordered the helicopter to fly him to Cecil, Rosie related. The Navy told them to buzz off. . . they required 24-hour notification with approval from the Base CO. "I've been around," she added. "Been to college and married a bum, but I've never heard words like that before. It's a shame, I understand he's a nice man, but he promised a bust and psyched himself out."

Pamela handed us coffee at five a. m. The stars had faded and we had a rosy glow in the east. Vince hit the mattress and I was monitoring the VOR for our turn into Jax. Andy was talkative and philosophic.

"Been tough, Slater. Takes a pile of money to keep this old boat in the air. She's slow and cranky . . . charters were sparse an' I was headin' for Brazil when Freddie came along. Ain't proud of myself for duckin' the law, but flyin's all I know. Like them World War II types flyin' Connies an' DC-6's for them potheads in the sticks. . .

ain't so much the buck that keeps us goin', it's the pound of them engines when we bust the coast, the knowin' we's the last of a past generation. God help us, we were flyin' biplanes before you jet pilots were born." He adjusted his glasses, squinted at the compass and corrected for the Jax VOR.

"Figured this was my last run when Freddie said we were to work with that government type. Had me old squadron insignia painted on old Betsy's tail when he said we might be landing at Cecil. . . figured I'd give them young bucks a turn, like coming back from a 50-year mission with a Nazi sub to tally the count. Base commander's an old buddy of mine. . . if he ain't retired. Betcha he's on deck when he hears this old Cat is wingin' the coast. The U-831 ain't no fairy story, Slater. . . seed it like yesterday. We had an oil slick when we dropped our bombs, but the CO was disbelievin'. . . me co-pilot was an academy type, but I was a crop duster an' he transferred me to the South Pacific."

"Keep your head up, Andy. . . grab yourself a shave and I'll see what I can do."

He sat quietly in his seat and stared at the blush on the horizon. Then he smiled and slipped from his harness, went aft to the head. Pamela came forward to the jump seat and leaned on my shoulder.

What in heaven's name did you say to that dear old man? He's crying like a baby. Do they intend to confiscate his PBY?" I squeezed her hand. The spinoff was worth every ounce piled in the hold.

"Proud tears, honey. . . vindication. . . It's taken long years to clear the record and mend a broken heart. His wartime co-pilot is top dog at Cecil. They were bad-rapped in 1944 but Andy's coming home."

I leaned on Rosie to request a favor when the Navy base had our lock. The diversion had run its course; the cool-headed gal would fold her antenna and join the countless vans cruising the endless highways. She'd make a super DJ, her sweet-sounding voice raising the top 10 for the 18-wheelers plying I-95.

"Gotcha, Keith! We have Cecil on the horn. . . tell Santa we love him and a big hug for Chug."

A pair of Navy F-14's straddled our wing when the early sun colored the slow moving sea. They circled overhead to pace our 90 knots, communicated with Jacksonville Control to help us through the ADIZ. They were belting the blue on after-burner, two tiny specks in the west, when Andy emerged from the head.

He'd scented himself with shaving lotion and gargled Listerine. Combed his mane and leveled his old Navy cap squarely upon his ears; a black tie had appeared from somewhere. His eyes were tinted with fatigue, but there was a certain glint, a sparkle of pride to his demeanor, when he lowered himself into his seat. I helped buckle him in.

The long-winged PBY was an awesome sight to the rednecks ogling from the boat dock bordering the St. John's River. The space age F-14's added grist, hanging full thrust with their gear extended to avoid a stall. Traffic came to a standstill along I-95 when we passed, sirens echoed from the Naval Air Station when we called in to the tower. The F-14's rolled skyward when he dropped its wheels and descended across the glistening morass. . . like a giant pelican returning from 50 long years at sea.

We braked midway down the active runway and followed a blinking jeep to the ramp. The sun was angling from seven o'clock, a bright cloudless day; the base personnel were out in force.

The old man peered from his window, jockeying the engines like the pro he was, until we came to a full stop abreast of the tower. A cheer went up when the PW's stilled; a braided admiral advanced from the line with his hat at proper angle. He saluted smartly and stood by with a wide grin on his ruddy face. Andy was close to tears. The admiral was long retired, of course, flown in from Norfolk early that morning.

I eyeballed the far side of the ramp when Andy unbuckled and rose from his seat. An Air Force 135 was parked beyond the tethered F-14's and PC-3's. A dark blue sedan and an armored truck were waiting nearby, but my attention was given to my Goose, to the massive man wearing a spotless white suit, to a tall Turks islander in crimson shorts and a sunburned kid in a borrowed shirt. There were others gathered by the sedan; Thompson in a rumpled jacket, the DEA pilot gesturing with his hands and the Austrian Consul General awaiting his gold. The Boeing 135 would be off within the hour, but it was the human element that touched our hearts.

A proud moment for the old fellow with golden wings fixed to his cap. He was a bit unsteady when he grasped the railing. We followed him down. . . four exhausted men and a freckled girl with an impish smile. He drew himself erect when the bosun piped him to the ramp; he belched ever so slightly, saluted the flag with his trembling hands. The yeomen cheered when the Admiral grinned and raced a few short steps to gather the gallant boozer to his side.

"They wouldn't believe us when we bombed that friggen sub," Andy muttered as they walked away. "Look at you now! All braid and stars. Hell, you was just a kid when I seen you last, fresh from Pensacola. . . it was your first ride in a PBY. . . and that bastard said we was intoxicated."

There is a rundown to the story that I'm hesitant to tell. Sixteen pieces of gold aboard the Goose were overlooked when the Catalina's cargo was transferred to the 135. I maintained a close lip when old Dan winked from the doorway as the stairs were drawn.

The Austrians would make up the difference from the spiraling rate of exchange. Knowing the old geezer as I do, I have reason to believe he'd planned it that way.

We split the spoils when we terminated our return to Fort Lauderdale. A check was forwarded to the master divers later in the month, another to the two gentlemen from the DEA. As for Andy, his indictment was quashed, his pension reinstated and I understand he bought himself a fixed-base operation at Spring Lake, Minnesota.

Chug and I were summoned to London in September when Kurt and his friends were indicted for piracy. I stayed on when Chug returned to register at Harvard.

I had a very personal matter to attend to. . . a long motor trip through the midlands of England while the leaves were still green on the trees. My companion was a tall, slender blonde with emerald green eyes and a golden soul. Highspirited and uncomplaining, she nevertheless was forced to walk lightly with a cane. Elisabeth has a lovely townhouse in London now. . . short blocks from the Austrian Embassy, deeded freehold in recognition of her service to the Republic. She also is a recipient of the OBE (Order of the British Empire), awarded in a private ceremony by Her Majesty, the Queen. A talented actress, you may have seen Elisabeth on British television. . . or more recently recognized her name on a sparkling marquee.

And Pamela? Those are difficult words to express. Sweet, elflike, dedicated, honest to the bone. . . there would be others more her age, better suited than me. She returned to Wood's Hole to complete her master's degree, then to Cairns, Australia to research a doctorate in Marine Biology.

I hear from them often. When vacations converge, we untie the spritely Goose and weekend the lower Bahamas. . . Chug with a desert rose to plant at Liz's grave on the tiny atoll. And now that the wreckage has been cleared by the Crown, we dive the lagoon near the cresting reef, sometimes recovering a forgotten item.

As for myself, flying is a spiritual thing, ingrained genetically in my soul, I think. Although my leg wound prevents high performance jets, I've taken lately to flying on occasion for NASA, with high altitude U-2's. . . environmental studies, researching volcanic airborne residue over Central America and recently the Aegean. But then, that is another story. Not of this time.

Lastly. . . a schooner with an undying desire to stay afloat. God gives soul to things alive; would he short an ancient ship with ribs of iron? One that seemed determined to return to the rugged shores from whence she came? To this ending I add these clippings from the *New York Times*.

Times wire service, Savannah, 18 October: William Lattimore, skipper of the trawler Betty B, reported a partially submerged schooner drifting north with the Gulf Stream 190 miles east of Cape Hatteras. The derelict, a large Halifax schooner, was heavily encrusted with marine growth and had been underwater for considerable time. Her masts and standing rigging were relatively intact, the Captain stated. Close inspection, hindered by heavy seas, was abandoned. The Coast Guard cutter Showalter was subsequently dispatched to the area, but no trace of the ghostly ship was found.

Times wire service, Boston, 22 November: The tanker Exxon Queen, inbound from Norway, reported a derelict under ragged sail 120 miles southwest of Halifax. A hurried inspection disclosed her decks were awash and she appeared to be sinking. Coast Guard spokesmen declined comment when asked if the mystery ship might be the *Leopard,* the latter vessel having disappeared with all its crew when tropical storm Christina ravaged the southern Bahamas in late July. There have been numerous sightings of a totally submerged hulk, unconfirmed reports of its rising slowly from the sea, midday, when the water temperature is variant.